A SWEET REVENGE

A DCI DANNY FLINT BOOK

TREVOR NEGUS

INKUBATOR
BOOKS

Published by Inkubator Books
www.inkubatorbooks.com

Copyright © 2022 by Trevor Negus

Trevor Negus has asserted his right to be identified as the author of this work.

ISBN (eBook): 978-1-915275-66-0
ISBN (Paperback): 978-1-915275-67-7

A SWEET REVENGE is a work of fiction. People, places, events, and situations are the product of the author's imagination. Any resemblance to actual persons, living or dead is entirely coincidental.

No part of this book may be reproduced, stored in any retrieval system, or transmitted by any means without the prior written permission of the publisher.

PROLOGUE

6.45pm, 13 December 1987
Silver Fern Care Home, Mansfield, Nottinghamshire

The late-night visitor stared unblinking at the old man lying in bed, listening to his every rasping breath. The frail, elderly man's chest hardly moved the bedclothes as he struggled to take precious oxygen into his disease-ravaged lungs.

As he fought his own personal battle for each breath, he barely registered that someone had come to see him. When the carer had introduced them, he never opened his eyes and just grunted. The visitor had smiled benignly towards the carer and sat down in the only armchair, positioned by the side of the old man's bed.

The carer had told the visitor that they wouldn't be able to stay long, due to the late hour, before quickly making her excuses and leaving the room. She had been surprised at both the hour of the visit and the fact that the old man had a visitor at all.

Fred Harper was like so many of the other residents at the care home, who never saw family or friends from one week to the next.

She had put the unexpected visit down to the time of year. As Christmas approached, it often stirred a pang of conscience in neglectful families, pushing them, with a certain reluctance, into making a visit to forgotten loved ones. She was just pleased that she'd been able to give Fred his medication before the visitor arrived, or it would have made the rest of her medication rounds late.

The old man's room was very small. It had a single window that was covered by dark brown curtains. They were ugly, but effective in keeping the cold air and the gloomy dark nights out. The room was dominated by the bed, in which the ailing man now spent his days. The only other furniture in the room was a wardrobe containing never-to-be-worn again suits, a chest of drawers containing underpants and vests to wear in bed, a single armchair now occupied by the visitor, and a bedside table, the top of which was covered in half-empty boxes of medication.

There were no family photographs or pictures in the room.

On the wall above the headboard was a large wooden crucifix, which had a set of ebony rosary beads hanging from it. There was a wall-mounted clock situated directly above the chest of drawers.

The clock ticked loudly, supplying an accompaniment to the man's rasping breaths. The overloud action of the clock effectively counted down the hours, minutes and seconds of the old man's life.

For a full twenty minutes, not a word was said between the two people in the room.

Stinging tears formed in the eyes of the visitor, and eventually they rolled slowly down both cheeks. They were quickly wiped away by a clean handkerchief.

There was a polite knock on the door. The same young carer half-opened the door and looked inside the room. With a sorrowful expression on her face, she said, 'I'm afraid you can only stay for another ten minutes, as we'll be closing the doors soon. I'm sorry.'

Without looking at the carer, the visitor replied softly, 'That's okay. He's almost asleep anyway. I'll be out in ten minutes.'

The carer closed the door behind her as she left.

The visitor stood up from the armchair and stepped across to the side of the bed, leaning forward until their heads were almost touching. A single sentence filled with hatred was then whispered into the old man's ear: 'Rot in hell, you vicious bastard.'

The visitor then placed a strong hand across the mouth and nose of the old man, preventing him from taking any further breaths.

Breathing was already a desperate struggle for him, and in less than a minute the chest stopped moving. There were no more feeble attempts to suck air in beyond the obstruction.

The man's eyes were now open and staring.

The hand was moved from the mouth and nose, down to the neck. Fingers deftly searched for a pulse.

There was none.

Fred Harper was dead.

The only sound in the room now was the ominous tick-tock of the wall clock. It was no longer accompanied by the ragged inhalations of the old man.

The visitor closed the old man's sightless eyes before

turning off the light, walking out of the room and closing the door.

The young carer was waiting behind the reception desk near the main entrance. She said cheerily, 'Are you off, then?'

The visitor replied, 'Yes. He's fast asleep now, and I know it's getting late. I'll come back and see him again in a few days' time, when it's a bit nearer Christmas. I've turned the light off and closed the door.'

'Thanks for doing that. I'll go and check on him later. Fred doesn't need any more medication until ten o'clock, so I'll let him sleep for now. See you soon.'

The carer felt smug that she had sussed out the reason for the unexpected visit and quickly added, 'Merry Christmas.'

Without looking back, the visitor replied, 'Yeah. Merry Christmas to you too.'

1

11.30pm, 10 January 1988
Osborne Grove, Sherwood, Nottingham

Manfred Bauer was getting ready for bed in his small two-bedroom flat.

The short, overweight man still found it strange that there was nobody shouting that the cell doors were about to be locked. Those shouts had always been quickly followed by that sudden rush of darkness as the cell lights were switched off by an invisible hand.

He had spent the last six of his sixty-two years in prison. Sentenced to ten years' imprisonment for a single moment of madness. There wasn't a night that passed when he didn't regret what he had done to those two ten-year-old girls.

Every night in the darkness, the nightmares were quick to come. They were always the same, terrifying images that haunted his soul.

The judge at his trial had been quick to point out that the

children at the East Glade Infants School in Leicester had all looked up to Mr Bauer, the friendly school caretaker, and for him to abuse that trust in the most vile and base way was beyond the pale.

Manfred Bauer had welcomed the jury's guilty verdict and fully understood the length of the custodial sentence. What he found harder to come to terms with was the fact that he had been released early.

He couldn't understand why he should be released. He genuinely believed he should still be incarcerated. He needed to be punished. That inner conflict meant he faced a daily struggle not to make the ultimate decision and take his own life.

He turned off and unplugged the small portable television, then flicked off the light switch in the living room. The flat was tiny, so it was literally two paces before he was in the claustrophobic bathroom, brushing what few teeth he had left. He splashed cold water on his face and reached for the grubby hand towel to dry off before stepping next door into the bedroom.

He removed his trousers and socks and got into bed, still wearing the vest and pants he had worn all day. The only light in the bedroom was provided by a scruffy table lamp that he had managed to pick up at a local flea market. It gave off a dim light, but he liked to leave it on. After all those years of pitch-black nights in prison, it was a little luxury he enjoyed. The feeble light did nothing to prevent the nightmares from returning every night, though.

Immediately after he had been sent down, unspeakable things happened to him in prison. Most of the scars from that time were mental, but some were physical and still very evident every time he looked in the mirror to shave. He could still feel the agonising sting of the home-made blade as it had sliced through the fatty flesh on his cheek during his first week in general prison population.

He had been moved onto the segregation block after that attack, where he was forced to spend his time with sex offenders and paedophiles. Animals who spent their days recounting stories of their twisted, lust-fuelled perversions. He didn't see himself as one of them. He had made one stupid misjudgement, a terrible error that he had paid a heavy price for.

Having spent most of his adult life in Leicester, Bauer wasn't used to Nottingham, the city he had been moved to upon his release.

This area of the inner city was rough and full of social deprivation. Gangs of youths loitered on every corner. Whenever he walked past them, he felt they were eyeing him up, assessing him. He felt sure they knew who he was, and what his history was. As a result of this dangerous feeling of intimidation, after just three months, he very rarely ventured outside the flat anymore.

He was pleased that his flat was on the first floor. It made him feel a little more secure, knowing that someone couldn't just smash a window and get inside.

As he slowly drifted off to sleep, he wondered how long it would be before the same images of the two young girls would appear. Their screams and agonised faces would eventually fill his head until he woke up dripping with sweat, panting for breath, feeling like he was about to die.

2

1.30am, 11 January 1988
Osborne Grove, Sherwood, Nottingham

The person watching from the shadows created by the white light of the streetlamps filtering through the mature lime and sycamore trees on Osborne Grove had been very patient.

The feeble light in the bedroom was still on. That wasn't unusual. It had remained on every time a watch had been kept on Bauer's first-floor flat.

It was now time to act.

Moving like a fleeting shadow, the figure moved into the tiny garden of the property and effortlessly climbed the drainpipe that led up to the bathroom window of Bauer's flat. The tiny transom window had been left open, as usual.

Dressed entirely in black, the lithe burglar slipped silently in through the open window. Once inside, they paused before removing a heavy claw hammer from the small daysack they were carrying.

The ghostlike figure then moved through the flat, following the rhythmic snoring sounds emanating from the nearby bedroom.

Gripping the vicious claw hammer, the intruder stood next to the bed and looked down at the sleeping figure, who was lying on his left side.

The claw hammer was raised high, and three blows were rained down in quick succession onto the right side of the man's head. There was a sickening crack as each heavy, deliberate blow landed flush against the man's skull, shattering the bone beneath.

The damage to the sleeping man's head was catastrophic. There was blood everywhere. The second two blows had caused blood to spatter onto the walls and ceiling. As well as the dark splashes everywhere, the blood that was now seeping from the man's head was rapidly soaking the dirty bedclothes.

The intruder reached into the daysack and retrieved an object, which was placed very carefully on top of the dead man's shattered skull.

With the mission completed, the killer left the flat as they had entered, climbing back out through the bathroom window and slipping silently down the drainpipe.

Once on the deserted street, the figure slipped effortlessly back into the shadows, disappearing into the night.

A real nightmare had visited Manfred Bauer tonight.

It would be his last.

3
―――

10.00am, 11 January 1988
Osborne Grove, Sherwood, Nottingham

DCI Danny Flint stood opposite the large, detached property on Osborne Grove, surveying the leafy street. It was like hundreds of other streets in the city of Nottingham. Tree-lined, and with large properties that had all seen better days. Most of the houses on the street were now subdivided into either flats or bedsits.

The difference between this street and the rest was that a vicious murder had been committed here overnight.

Danny walked across the street to DI Rob Buxton, who was already wearing a forensic suit and overshoes. Rob had been the first MCIU detective to respond to the call-out.

He said, 'Which flat is it?'

Rob pointed up and said, 'First floor. Can you see the open transom window at the top of the downpipe? That's the deceased's bathroom. It looks like it's also our killer's point of entry.'

Danny said quietly, 'A climber? Very unusual.'

'Indeed.'

'Who found the body?'

'The landlord. Today is rent day. This is one of those residencies where the landlord has a key for all his tenants' flats. It seems this guy doesn't accept no reply to knocking, especially on rent day. So he let himself in and found the body.'

'Lucky for us, I suppose. The body could have remained up there for weeks, without being discovered. Who's the landlord?'

Rob looked at his notebook. 'Landlord is Benny Fraser. It's definitely happened overnight, because Mr Fraser told me he spoke to the deceased yesterday, to remind him that this month's rent was due today.'

'Again, that's all good for us, it gives us a very short window when this has happened. Mr Fraser will need looking at closely, especially if he's owed rent.'

'He isn't. And today's rent is still in an envelope in the living room.'

'So not a burglary gone wrong, then?'

'It doesn't look like it. I don't know many burglars who would pass up an opportunity to take eighty quid in cash.'

'Me neither. Who's with the landlord now?'

'I've sent DC Singh back with Mr Fraser to his home address, to obtain his full statement. I've also got three detectives here, talking to the other tenants.'

'That's good. An early account from everyone is always the best way forward.'

There was a pause before Danny continued. 'Are there any other signs of a search? Is it possible he just missed the envelope?'

'There are no signs of a struggle and no sign of any type of search being carried out.'

'Okay. Let's go and have a look inside.'

Danny quickly put on a forensic suit and overshoes and followed Rob into the building. The two detectives were signed into the scene by a uniformed officer standing outside the front door.

The Scenes of Crime supervisor, Tim Donnelly, was waiting inside by the front door of the flat.

Danny said, 'What have we got so far, Tim?'

'It's still early days, but nothing much yet. I'm happy that the point of entry and exit is the transom window of the bathroom. It's quite a narrow window, so I would have expected to find fibres at that location. We've found nothing, which indicates the offender was wearing specialist clothing that doesn't shed.'

'Is that sort of clothing hard to obtain?'

'Not really. It can be picked up from most army surplus shops.'

'Prints?'

'None so far. We've found glove marks inside the flat and on the downpipe outside.'

'Not very encouraging. Any footmarks that could help us?'

Tim shook his head.

Danny said, 'Keep looking. Where's the deceased?'

Rob said, 'Bedroom, this way.'

Danny followed Rob and Tim into the small bedroom and saw the body of an overweight male still in bed. The bedsheets were down around his waist, and he was lying on his left side, facing away from the door. Danny could see there were massive injuries to the right side of the dead man's head and that blood loss had been extensive.

Danny pointed to the object that had been carefully placed onto the dead man's shattered head and said, 'What do you make of that?'

Rob said, 'I've never seen anything like it. I couldn't hazard a guess as to its meaning.'

Danny turned to his Scenes of Crime officer. 'Tim, have you ever seen the likes?'

Tim Donnelly said, 'I've been to many crime scenes where items have been left on or inside bodies to signify something. Though what the significance of a Mars bar could be is beyond me. Perhaps the killer just has a sick sense of humour?'

'Have we got photographs?'

Tim replied, 'I've got all the photographs we need. I'm just waiting for the pathologist to arrive. I want to run my thoughts by him as to exactly where I think the offender was standing when he did this. I think the blood splashes on the wall would indicate he was standing somewhere about here, at the side of the bed.'

A booming voice behind them said, 'That looks about right to me, Mr Donnelly.'

All three men turned to see the Home Office pathologist, Seamus Carter, standing in the doorway.

He said, 'Your man outside signed me in and told me you were all up here waiting.'

The two detectives stood to one side and allowed the burly pathologist into the small room.

His enormous frame strained against the forensic suit he was wearing as he bent over to examine the body. After a few minutes he said, 'Three distinct blows to the head. Delivered with some force as well. My guess is that any one of these blows could have proved fatal. Your killer was taking no chances here, guys.'

Danny said, 'Does it look like a frenzied attack to you?'

'I'd say the opposite, Danny. The spacing between the blows looks very deliberate. Then there's the careful placing of the chocolate bar. It looks very ordered and calculating to me. These blows were intended to kill this poor unfortunate, that's for sure. I'll be able to tell you more at the post-mortem later. Are the undertakers on their way?'

Rob said, 'They were requested half an hour ago, so they shouldn't be much longer.'

'Okay. Do we know who he is yet?'

'I've found paperwork in the living room that suggests his name is Manfred Bauer. The landlord has confirmed this. We have other lines of enquiry to follow up that will give us more of an idea exactly who he was, and whether he has any enemies.'

The pathologist stretched his back. As he straightened up, he grunted with the effort and said, 'Well, last night he certainly had at least one enemy, and now he doesn't have any.'

Danny said, 'Can you give us an estimated time of death?'

'Looking at the extensive rigor mortis that's already set in, my best guess would be the early hours of this morning, sometime between midnight and three o'clock.'

'Thanks. Where will you be doing the post-mortem?'

'Let's say City Hospital at three o'clock, shall we?'

'Okay. We'll see you there. I'll leave you here with Tim, to do what you've got to do. Rob, can you show me the rest of the flat?'

Rob nodded and said, 'This way, boss.'

Danny could now see for himself that there had been no search of the property by the intruder, and that the rent money was still in situ on the coffee table. The envelope it was in hadn't been touched.

Danny said quietly, 'What are these other lines of enquiry about Bauer?'

'The Police National Computer can tell us that Manfred Bauer was recently released from prison after serving six years of a ten-year sentence for indecent assault.'

'Ten years for an indecent assault, must have been a nasty case. They're all bad, but ten years for indecent assault is unusual.'

'I totally agree. I haven't had a chance to establish all the details of the offences yet.'

'The bottom line is this, sex offenders always have lots of enemies. That piece of information has opened a right can of worms for us. I want you to stay here and manage the scene with Tim. I'll get back to the office and start preparing things for a full briefing later, after the post-mortem has been completed. Let me have all the details on Bauer you've got so far. When I get back to the office, I'll get Fran to start researching him. I'll brief whatever staff there are in the office and get them out here, to give you a hand. Let's make an early start on the door-to-door enquiries for the immediate area, and task someone to start checking for any possible CCTV.'

Danny walked down the stairs and signed himself out of the scene. He then walked carefully around the perimeter of the building until he was at the base of the downpipe. He could see the grey fingerprint powder all over the downpipe as he looked up towards the transom window.

It would have been no easy feat for the killer to climb the downpipe and then manoeuvre their way in through the narrow transom window.

As was his habit, ideas and thoughts began swimming around the experienced detective's brain. He was trying to think like the person who had scaled the downpipe. Trying to imagine the preparation work carried out prior to the attack, and what the motivation was for the vicious killing.

He felt sure the murder would be linked to the dead man's previous crimes. The more they could find out about Manfred Bauer, the better their chances would be of catching his killer.

4

3.00pm, 11 January 1988
City Hospital Mortuary, Nottingham

Danny was the last to arrive in the examination room. The traffic from Mansfield into Nottingham had been horrendous, following a three-car pile-up at the Redhill roundabout.

He had dashed through the long corridors of the hospital to the mortuary and was slightly breathless when he burst in through the examination room doors.

Seamus Carter was standing on the far side of the stainless steel table, flanked by his assistant, Brigitte O'Hara, and Rob Buxton. All three were dressed in bottle-green scrubs. Also present in the mortuary, each with their own specific tasks, were two Scenes of Crime staff and DC Baxter, the exhibits officer. The pathologist grinned and said, 'Good of you to join us, Danny. I was about to start without you.'

Feeling a little disgruntled after his nightmare car journey, Danny replied tersely, 'I'm here now. Let's crack on.'

As he quickly donned the green, protective scrubs supplied by the mortuary technician, Danny looked over at the table and saw Seamus Carter begin his examination of the body of Manfred Bauer.

Bauer was a short man, but what he lacked in height, he made up for in girth. He was probably no more than five feet three inches tall, and Danny estimated that he must be close to eighteen stone.

Speaking into a Dictaphone as he began his visual examination, Seamus Carter confirmed verbally what Danny had been thinking.

Seamus spoke clearly in his pronounced Belfast accent: 'The body is that of a white male. Aged sixty-two years. Approximately five-feet-two to five-feet-four inches in height. Estimated weight, in excess of eighteen stone. The deceased was morbidly obese. There are infected ulcers on both legs, around the calves and knees. These were probably caused as a direct result of his excess weight and poor circulation. There are no other physical injuries around the torso that I can see.'

He paused and asked his assistant to turn the body. This was no easy task due to the weight of the cadaver. His assistant was aided by one of the Scenes of Crime staff in attendance.

Carter resumed speaking as he examined Bauer's back, 'There are no physical injuries on the back, but there is evidence of lividity on the left-hand side of the body. This is in keeping with the position the body was lying when discovered, indicating that he was killed where he was found.'

Bauer was then returned to his original position, on his back.

Carter then closely examined the deceased's head, paying

close attention to the three separate injuries on the right side of the skull.

Bauer had been completely bald in life, so the devastating injuries were plain to see. There were three distinct holes in the right side of Bauer's head. The area around each of the holes was depressed, where the bone underneath had been forced inwards by the weight of the blows.

Carter paused before describing each of the injuries. Finally, he said, 'Any one of these injuries would have been sufficient to cause death. I'm going to start the examination proper now. I will start with the head.'

Danny and Rob both stepped a little closer to the table, to observe the skilled pathologist as he began his examination.

After five minutes, the flesh covering the skull had been peeled back, exposing the bone underneath. The catastrophic injuries were now much clearer to see. Around each of the holes, the skull had been splintered, and fractures ran in every direction. There was a small disc of bone below each of the holes, which had been forced down into the victim's brain.

Carter then spoke directly to his assistant: 'Brigitte, I want you to get some close-up shots of these bone discs as I remove them from the brain, please. After I've taken them out, measure the diameter. It will give us some idea of the type of weapon used.'

The young assistant nodded and began taking photographs alongside the Scenes of Crime photographer.

After the third disc had been removed, Brigitte used a tape measure and announced, 'The diameters of the three discs are the same, twenty millimetres.'

Seamus Carter paused and turned to Danny. 'It's as I suspected. I think the most likely murder weapon is your common, or garden, claw hammer. The diameter of the discs punched out by the weapon is twenty millimetres. If memory serves me right from other cases I've worked on, I'm pretty certain that's the diameter of most claw-hammer heads.'

'Thanks, Seamus. Is there anything else you can tell us at this time?'

'These wounds are what killed him. I doubt he would have known anything about the attack. The first blow would have been enough to render him unconscious. The damage to the brain itself is extensive, and the blood loss would have been enormous.'

'Okay. How soon can you let me have your full report?'

'It's going to take me the best part of another hour to complete the full examination. If I find anything of significance, I'll contact you straight away. I'll be honest with you; I'm not expecting to find anything, either from the rest of the examination or toxicology. All things being equal, I should get my full written report to you in a couple of days' time, depending on how quickly the toxicology results come back to me. I know you're going to be busy preparing strategies for the investigation, and it's entirely your choice, of course, but there's really no need for you to stay. Your exhibits officer will be here for continuity of any samples taken.'

'Okay. We'll leave you to do your work. Phil and the Scenes of Crimes staff will remain here to assist.'

Danny turned to DC Phil Baxter and said, 'As soon as you've finished dealing with the exhibits here, get back to the MCIU offices as quick as you can. There will be a full debrief at seven o'clock this evening. I want you there with any updates.'

Phil Baxter replied, 'Yes, boss. No problem.'

As they walked back through the hospital corridors, Rob said, 'How did Fran get on researching Bauer and his previous crimes?'

'She was still hard at it when I left. We should have more

detail by the time of the briefing. Did the detectives turn up anything from the other tenants at Osborne Grove?'

'They were still interviewing them when I left. Jag contacted me just as I was leaving and told me that he'd obtained a full statement from the landlord. He also told me that he'd turned something up that could be interesting.'

'Will they be back for the scheduled briefing?'

'Yes. They all know to be back in time for that.'

As the two men reached their cars, Danny said, 'Any first impressions?'

'This has revenge written all over it.'

'I agree, but let's keep an open mind.'

Rob smiled. 'I always do.'

5

7.00pm, 11 January 1988
MCIU Offices, Mansfield Police Station

There was an expectant atmosphere in the briefing room of the Major Crime Investigation Unit offices. The room was filled with seasoned detectives waiting to hear the details of the latest murder case they would be tasked with investigating. It had been a relatively quiet few weeks, and the entire unit were keen to start working a new case.

The detectives who had been out to the scene on Osborne Grove were whispering in hushed tones to their colleagues who had been called in for the briefing.

Danny walked into the briefing room, followed by Rob Buxton and Tina Cartwright. The room instantly fell silent. Danny sat down between his two detective inspectors.

He said, 'Right. Let's make a start. Rob, what do we know about the deceased?'

Rob read from the notes he'd made in his enquiry log: 'Manfred Bauer was sixty-two years of age. Born in Hoffenheim, Germany. He moved to the UK at the end of the Second World War, when he was ten years old. His parents settled in Leicester, and Bauer had continued to live in the city until he was convicted of two counts of indecent assault six years ago. We're still trying to establish all the details of these offences. What we know so far is this, Bauer was a school caretaker who sexually abused two young schoolgirls. He was sentenced at Nottingham Crown Court to ten years' imprisonment and was taken to HMP Lincoln. He was released at the beginning of November last year.'

A voice at the back of the room said, 'That means he only served six years. How did he manage to get released so early?'

Rob said, 'We're still trying to establish the circumstances around his release, and how he came to be in a halfway hostel in Nottingham. I would prefer if you saved any other questions until after I've finished. Thanks.'

The voice said, 'Sorry, boss.'

Rob continued, 'We'll have completed all these enquiries by tomorrow morning, and I'll be in a better position to give you all the facts then.'

There was a short pause before he continued, 'We have established that Bauer has been living at Osborne Grove ever since he was released from prison. He occupied a small, one-bedroomed flat situated on the first floor. It was basic, typical of a halfway hostel. A full forensic examination of the flat has been carried out and a full search made. Tim, can you take it from there, please?'

Tim Donnelly, from the Scenes of Crime department, nodded and said, 'Forensically, we've found very little. We have numerous fingerprints inside the flat and have obtained elimination prints from the landlord and all the other residents. There are glove marks found at the point of entry. The offender has climbed a drainpipe at the side of the property and entered through a narrow transom window into the bathroom. To do this would take strength and suppleness. The transom window is only two feet wide by nine inches high, so it's fair to say our offender is very slim and very strong. There are also glove marks, in blood, at the same point around the bathroom window. This would suggest that the offender left in the same way he had entered, after committing the murder. To climb back out like this would be no easy feat.'

Danny said, 'Thanks. Did you find anything during the physical search of the flat?'

'Bauer had very little in the way of personal possessions. Toiletries were the bare minimum, and there was very little food in the flat. There was a bottle of vodka found that was still three-quarters full. So it doesn't look like he had a drink problem, or we would have found empty bottles. There was an envelope containing eighty pounds in plain view in the living room. This wasn't touched by the offender. There's very little other documentation. Details of his probation officer and an appointment card for the dole office. That's about it.'

DC Jagvir Singh said, 'Excuse me, boss. Can I ask something?'

Danny said, 'Go on, Jag.'

'Did you find any threatening letters?'

Tim Donnelly shook his head. 'No. There's nothing like that.'

Danny said, 'Why do you ask that?'

Jag said, 'I've spent most of the day with the landlord, Benny Fraser. He told me that Bauer had received a couple of threatening letters, and that he was very frightened. It's all in his statement, but I thought I should mention it now.'

'Thanks. Has Fraser seen these letters for himself?'

'Yes, boss. He couldn't remember very much detail about the content, other than that they threatened graphic physical violence, and were from some sort of vigilante group.'

'Could he remember the name of the group?'

'It was something to do with protecting innocents. The landlord just thought they were cranks who had found out about Bauer's past.'

'Was Fraser aware of Bauer's history?'

'Yes, he was. He didn't seem over concerned about the threats made in the letters. He thought they were idle threats made by gobshites. He had no concerns about the possibility of damage being caused to his property because of Bauer's presence.'

'Thanks, Jag. Come and see me with Fraser's statement after the briefing, please.'

He turned back to Tim Donnelly. 'Is there anything else from the scene?'

'Only the chocolate. The album of photographs taken at the scene will be available first thing tomorrow. You will all see that a Mars bar was placed carefully on the shattered skull of the victim. There was nothing else left to indicate the significance of this.'

Danny said to the gathered detectives, 'Make yourselves familiar with the photographs. I think the way the chocolate bar was positioned so carefully means this is definitely a signature from the killer. It's important we try to understand its meaning. If anyone has any ideas, come and see me after the briefing.'

He paused before continuing: 'Was there anything from the other tenants at Osborne Grove?'

DC Helen Bailey said, 'I've been interviewing the four other tenants with DC Blake. There's absolutely nothing.

None of them had much to do with Bauer. They all say he kept himself to himself and seldom ventured out of his room. There were no issues, that we can find, between him and any of the other men who live there.'

'Were any of them aware of his sex offender history?'

'Nobody said anything about that, and we haven't raised it with them yet.'

'Okay. That's an enquiry I want you both to focus on tomorrow morning. Go back and speak to them all again. We need to establish if any of them knew of his past. Also find out if he had said anything to anyone else about these threatening letters.'

Helen nodded and said, 'Will do.'

Danny turned to Rob and said, 'Who did you put on scoping for CCTV in the area?'

Rob said, 'DC Lorimar.'

Danny said, 'Glen, any joy with CCTV so far?'

'It's early days, boss. I've completed an initial sweep of the residential streets around Osborne Grove. That has drawn a blank. I need to start on the busier roads like Mansfield Road and Hucknall Road tomorrow morning. Up to now, I haven't found a single camera on any of the private houses in the area. I should have more luck on the main roads tomorrow.'

'Good. We've got a very specific window when the offence occurred, so you can afford to be quite precise, as and when you find any cameras. Check for any cab cameras on the late-night buses that may have been on the main roads, as well as the usual traffic cameras.'

'Will do.'

Danny spoke directly to DS Wills. 'Andy, I'd like you to master the house-to-house enquiries tomorrow morning. Try to get a section of the Special Operations Unit to assist. Come and see me after the briefing about the search parameters and the questionnaire. I don't want to create more problems by alerting the local community that sex offenders are being housed in their neighbourhood.'

Andy replied, 'Even though that community should have the right to be made aware. I think I'd want to know if that was happening where I lived, especially if I was a parent of young kids.'

'I hear what you're saying, and I do agree with you. However, we don't need that distraction while we're trying to investigate this murder, especially as there's already an inference that a vigilante group may be involved.'

There was a pause before Danny continued. 'Fran, I know you've been concentrating on researching Bauer. Are you making progress?'

DC Fran Jefferies said, 'I've been working on Bauer and his convictions history with Rachel. We're making some progress, but there's plenty more to look at.'

'Good. Are you both able to stay on for a few hours tonight, to try to move those enquiries along? We need to know everything we can about Bauer as quickly as we can. I also want to establish the details of Bauer's two victims. I want to know all about their family and friends. Were any threats made at Bauer's trial? These are emotive crimes, and feelings will have been running high in the community at that time. This could be a simple revenge attack for what happened to those two young girls.'

The two women both nodded. Fran said, 'Not a problem; we'll crack on with it.'

'Brilliant.'

Danny addressed the entire room and said, 'Are there any questions?'

DS Andy Wills said, 'Are you going to task someone with researching other burglaries in the area of Osborne Grove?'

Rob said, 'It doesn't look like a burglary that's gone wrong. It has all the hallmarks of a targeted attack.'

Danny was thoughtful for a moment, then said, 'It's a valid point, Andy. Let's cover all the bases. DC Williams, can you look at that tomorrow morning?'

Jeff Williams nodded. 'Will do.'

There were no other questions, so Danny said, 'Right. Except for the people I've asked to stay, finish up what you're doing and get off home. I want you all back here ready to go again at six o'clock tomorrow morning.'

The noise levels in the room suddenly erupted as detectives began talking amongst themselves about the new case and what they would be doing individually.

Danny shouted above the noise, 'DS Harris, can you see me in the office please?'

Danny walked back into his office, followed by DS Harris and DC Singh.

Danny said, 'Grab a seat. I want you two to run with this vigilante enquiry. Start researching whatever groups you can find out there. Start with Special Branch; they may have some intelligence on groups like this that usually exist under the radar. I want a full investigation carried out into Benny Fraser, but be discreet. This vigilante story could all be smoke and mirrors, and he's more involved in Bauer's death than he's letting on. Keep me posted.'

Lynn Harris said, 'Will do, sir.'

Jag Singh said, 'Here's a copy of the statement I took from Fraser today. It's very comprehensive, so if he's lying, we'll find out quick enough.'

'Good work, Jag. Like I say, I want regular updates from you both. This could be a crucial element of the enquiry.'

The two detectives left, closing the door behind them. Danny was now left alone with his thoughts. He already knew this was going to be an extremely difficult case to solve. Right now, he had zero forensics, zero witnesses and lots of suspects. He couldn't quite understand why, but he felt drawn towards the idea of a shadowy vigilante group taking the law into their own hands.

6

9.00am, 12 January 1988
MCIU Offices, Mansfield Police Station

Danny was deep in conversation with his two detective inspectors, Rob Buxton and Tina Cartwright. The discussions were to establish the best way to drive forward the enquiry into the violent death of Manfred Bauer.

Danny said, 'Rob, can you ask Fran and Rachel to join us, please?'

Rob opened the door and gestured for the two detectives to come into the office.

Danny asked Fran, 'Do you have a comprehensive antecedent history for Bauer now?'

Fran replied, 'We have all the available information, but it's hardly what I'd call comprehensive. Prior to his arrest for the indecent assault on the two schoolgirls, Bauer had no previous convictions.'

Danny was surprised. 'Really? Was it a case of "never been caught before"?'

'I don't think so. I've spoken at length with the detective who led the investigation into the indecent assaults. It seems that Bauer admitted the offences straight after his arrest and was genuinely remorseful. He had no understanding of what had happened and could give no explanation as to why he'd carried out the assaults.'

'What were the circumstances?'

'Bauer had befriended the girls over a period of six weeks. Apparently, they used to go and visit him in his little cubbyhole in the boiler room. They had previously made him cards and presents. In return, he had let them read comics and bought them sweets to eat whenever they visited him.'

'So what changed?'

'He couldn't give an explanation. For whatever reason, he suddenly saw the girls in a different light and began touching them. When they got frightened, he became aggressive and forced them to commit acts on him.'

'How did the girls get away from him?'

'After he had forced them both to masturbate him, he began crying. The girls ran away while he was upset. He made no attempt to stop them. The girls immediately ran home and told their parents, who alerted the police. Bauer was still in his cubbyhole when the police arrived to arrest him. He immediately confessed to what he'd done and was extremely remorseful, apologising to the girls and their families.'

Rob said, 'And I suppose it's all that bullshit contrition that got him released early.'

Fran said, 'That's what I said, but the investigating officer was adamant the remorse displayed by Bauer was genuine. The detective thought the offences were committed during a singular moment of madness from Bauer.'

'Did Bauer have any family?'

'No. He was single and lived alone after his parents died.'

Danny said, 'Were any threats made against Bauer at the time of the trial?'

'Nothing specific. There were the usual crowds outside the courtroom, baying for his blood, but nothing from a specific individual.'

'Not even from family members?'

'Not that the detective mentioned. It seems the parents were more interested in being supportive to their girls and helping to get them over the ordeal, rather than wasting their energy on Bauer.'

'Do we have all the details of the families?'

'Yes, boss.'

'That's great work. Well done.'

Danny was thoughtful for a minute; then he said, 'It's good that you've managed to obtain the investigating officer's take on these offences, but I want us to talk to the people who were involved. Tina, Rachel, I want you to go to Leicester and spend the next few days speaking to everyone who knew Bauer. Start at the school where he worked. Talk to his colleagues. Talk to any of Bauer's family, if he has any, and any friends you can find. Let's try to build up a true picture of this man, one who can suddenly flip from being a law-abiding citizen to sex offender. Something about that doesn't quite sit right. While you're in Leicester, speak to the families of the two victims. I don't need to impress on you both how sensitively these enquiries must be carried out. Take as much time as you need. If you need to stay overnight, that's fine; put it on expenses. I want a full debrief on your return. Fran, I'd like you to stay here and resume your office manager's duties. I'm sure I'll be calling on your expertise for research throughout this enquiry.'

As the three detectives left the office, Danny waited until

there was only Rob left in the office, then said, 'Rob, I want you to arrange for the two of us to go and see the governor at HMP Lincoln. I want to establish what sort of prisoner Bauer was, and whether any threats were made towards him prior to his release.'

'No problem. I'll make the arrangements as soon as possible, but it may take a day or two to get in.'

'I understand that, but make it as quick as you can, please. In the meantime, let's keep the enquiries that we've already started moving forward. Did Andy have any joy with the Special Operations Unit for the house-to-house?'

'He managed to get a full section for three days, so that should keep that moving along nicely. Have you thought about a press conference yet?'

'I'm going to hold off on that for a few days. Let's see what we can turn up first before we start alarming the public. As this looks like a targeted attack, I'm confident there's minimal risk to the wider community. Obviously, that could change if enquiries show something different. Crack on with that visit to the prison. The sooner we get that done, the better.'

7

11.30am, 12 January 1988
East Glade Infants School, Golding Street, Leicester

Mrs McGyver, the headmistress of the school, was in her late fifties. She had a round face with cheeks covered in tiny thread veins that gave her face a ruddy complexion. She had wire-framed, round glasses that perched on the end of her nose and a friendly smile. As the school secretary showed Tina and Rachel in, she gestured to the two seats in front of her desk. 'Please take a seat.'

As soon as the detectives were seated, she asked, 'Would you like anything to drink? Tea or coffee?'

Rachel shook her head, and Tina spoke for both when she said, 'No, thanks, we're fine. We've a lot of people to see today, so it's best if we just press on.'

A businesslike expression immediately replaced the

open, friendly smile. 'No problem, as you wish. My secretary said you wanted to talk to me about Manfred Bauer.'

'That's right. Mr Bauer was murdered in Nottingham two days ago. We're here to try to establish what kind of man Manfred Bauer was. Anything you can tell us about him could help us greatly.'

Mrs McGyver was thoughtful for a moment; then she said, 'It was all so horrible at the time. My overwhelming memory of the whole terrible affair was one of shock. I couldn't quite believe what Manny had done to those poor, sweet girls.'

Rachel said, 'I take it there were no early indicators that something like this could happen? No overt obsession with the young girls at the school?'

'Absolutely not. Just the opposite, in fact. Manny was lovely around all the children; they adored him. He had worked here for a long time. I did notice a slight change in him after both his parents died in quick succession. He became a little more insular, lonely perhaps. A bit unsure of himself. It was as though his confidence had deserted him.'

'Had there been any other complaints against him?'

'Not at all. The original police investigation covered all this. Why are you asking these things now?'

Tina said, 'Because we're investigating Mr Bauer's murder now. We have to look at things in a different way.'

Rachel said, 'After details of the assaults on the girls came out, did anybody make any threats towards Bauer?'

Mrs McGyver sat back in her chair and let out a deep sigh. She said, 'At the time, feelings around the school and among the pupils' parents were very tense. There was a very real, almost tangible, display of hatred towards Manny. Lots of threats were issued by disgusted parents. I'm not talking about the parents of the two girls here; I'm talking about the parents of other kids at the school. Manny went from being the affable school caretaker, who the parents all liked, to some sort of murderous monster. It was wrong what he did, totally wrong. But the reactions of some of those parents were akin to a lynch mob. Quite frankly, it was disgusting to witness.'

'Was there anybody in particular?'

'There were several. All were warned off by officers at the time, so I would think the local police will have their details if you want them.'

'You separated out the victims' families earlier, saying they didn't react like that. How did they react?'

Mrs McGyver stood up and walked to a filing cabinet. She took out a yellow box folder and sat back down. After a few seconds flicking through the photographs contained in the file, she held one out and said, 'This is the class photograph that shows Rebecca North and Jennifer Taylor.'

The headmistress pointed out the two girls.

'The two of them were such sweet, naïve, little girls. They were inseparable right through school. I believe they're still friends today. They were both ten years old at the time of the assaults. Rebecca's parents were completely disinterested in Bauer and the police investigation. All they cared about was making sure their daughter came through the whole traumatic ordeal as unscathed as possible. Little Rebecca had suffered horribly at the hands of Bauer, and they just tried to help her through it.'

'How is Rebecca now?'

'From what I hear, she's now a beautiful young lady of sixteen, preparing for sixth form at the grammar school. She has a very bright future ahead of her.'

'Sounds like she recovered from her ordeal very well.'

'I wouldn't know about that. The whole family tried to put it all behind them as quickly as possible. You aren't thinking of going to see them as well, are you?'

'We have to go and see them.'

'Well, don't expect any welcome mats. Do they even know that Bauer had been released from prison? After you phoned this morning, my secretary and I asked around the school, and nobody here knew he'd been released.'

'What about Jennifer Taylor's family?'

'They adopted a very similar attitude to the Norths. They too were very supportive of their little girl. Unlike the Norths, they didn't stay around here. They moved to Clifton in Nottingham, for a fresh start. I think their shared sense of adversity brought the parents of the two girls together. I believe they all remained friends after the Taylors moved.'

'So no threats from either family?'

'There is something I recall. Jennifer had an eighteen-year-old brother who was adamant back then that no matter how long it took, he would get revenge for the attack on his little sister. He'd recently joined the army when the assault happened. I think the police spoke to him a few times about the things he said and the threats he made.'

'Have you any idea why Bauer suddenly assaulted these two girls?'

'I've thought about that a lot. It was so out of character. The only thing I can come up with is that the death of his parents in some way affected his mental well-being.'

'Does he have any surviving family, or any friends who still live locally?'

'I don't think there's any family and definitely no friends around here. He's still very much an object of loathing. I don't see that changing just because he's now dead. There aren't many in this community who will shed any tears for Manfred Bauer.'

Tina said, 'Thank you for seeing us today. I'll leave you a card with the number for the incident room. Please call us if you think of anything else that you think could help us.'

The headmistress took the card. 'Of course. Can you find your own way out?'

As the two detectives were about to leave the office, Rachel said, 'Can you remember the name of Jennifer North's older brother?'

'Yes. Spencer was a pupil here. I think he joined an infantry regiment or the like. He was always a very bright and fit child. I'm sure the army life would have suited him.'

'Thanks again for your time, Mrs McGyver.'

8

1.30pm, 12 January 1988
32 Faversham Street, Leicester

Tina pressed the doorbell on the front door of the terraced house for a second time and stepped back. This time the door was opened straight away, by a man in his late fifties. He was unshaven, his clothes were scruffy and his hands dirty.

Tina said, 'I'm Detective Inspector Cartwright, and this is Detective Constable Moore. I'm looking for Rebecca North.'

The man looked at the identification cards being held by the detectives and said, 'I'm Terry North, Becky's dad. If this is anything to do with Bauer, you can just go. We're not interested. I got the letter saying he was going to be let out. Just leave us alone.'

Tina said, 'I understand you don't want to talk about the past, and the last thing we want to do is upset Rebecca or her family. The fact of the matter is that Manfred Bauer was murdered two days ago, and we have a duty to investigate his death.'

'Hallelujah! There is a God.'

Rachel said gently, 'Mr North, can we speak to you inside?'

'You're wasting your time. Rebecca isn't in, and she wouldn't want to talk about him anyway. I saw the looks on your faces when I said hallelujah. Did you really expect me to be anything but overjoyed that Bauer is dead? That man stole my daughter's innocence and almost ruined her life. Does it mean I had anything to do with his death? No, it doesn't. For me and my family, Bauer hasn't existed since the day he was sent down. It's the way our family has coped. So no, you can't come in. We're done here. I've got a garden to finish digging. Don't come back, or I'll have my solicitor onto you. We just want to be left alone.'

Rachel pressed on: 'Mr North, I know it's impossible for us to have any idea about how you're feeling. The last thing we want to do is to rake over old ground, causing more upset. I do have one question for you, though. Are you still in touch with the Taylor family?'

Terry North was thoughtful for a second, then said, 'Becky has stayed friends with Jenny. Why?'

'Because we will need to speak to Jenny and her family. We need to let them know that Bauer is dead.'

'So long as you're not going to start harassing them, I'll get their address.'

'We won't be harassing anybody. As we said earlier, we're duty-bound to investigate this man's death. I hope you understand that.'

'Wait here.'

North closed the door, leaving the detectives standing on the doorstep.

He returned after a few minutes with a piece of paper. He

said, 'Here's the address I have; it's probably the same one you've got in your records. I'll tell you now, I'm going to telephone them and tell them you're coming. I don't want them to get the same shock you gave me. Try to understand, I'm not anti-police. When this happened, the detectives who arrested Bauer were brilliant, but we just want to put it all behind us and move on as a family. The last six years have been very hard. Please don't come to the house again. You can call me and speak to me if you need anything else. I've put my phone number on the paper. I don't want you talking to Becky. She's done wonderfully well, getting over her ordeal, and I don't want her being set back. Can you understand that?'

Rachel took the paper and said, 'We understand. If we need to be in touch, it will be me who calls you. I promise you I won't speak to Rebecca.'

'Thank you. And thank you for telling me that Bauer's dead. Perhaps he would have been better off rotting in prison. Who knows?'

9

3.30pm, 12 January 1988
16 Summerwood Lane, Clifton, Nottingham

As Tina and Rachel walked down the path towards the neat semi-detached house, the front door opened. Standing in the doorway was a couple in their mid-forties.

In a strong Jamaican accent, the woman said, 'Are you the detectives who want to speak with us?'

Tina said, 'Mr and Mrs Taylor?'

The woman nodded. 'Jennifer isn't here. I've sent her to her friend's house. She doesn't need all this upset.'

'May we speak with you?'

The woman said, 'Come inside.'

The two detectives were shown into the sitting room and invited to take a seat. Mr Taylor remained standing behind his wife's armchair. He was stern faced and had his arms folded across his chest. His body language screamed *passive-aggressive.*

Tina said, 'Thank you for seeing us. Have you spoken to Mr North?'

Mrs Taylor replied, 'Terry phoned an hour ago and told us you had called. He told me that you were coming here. That's why I asked my husband to take Jenny to her friend's. I don't want you talking to her no more.'

'Did Mr North tell you that Manfred Bauer is dead?'

Mr Taylor growled, 'Yes, he did. And good riddance to bad rubbish.'

Mrs Taylor tutted and said, 'Hush now, husband. Please try to have the Lord's forgiveness in your heart.'

Mr Taylor shifted his weight from foot to foot and sucked air through his teeth.

Mrs Taylor ignored her angry husband and said, 'When this happened to our beautiful girl, it was our church that helped us through the tribulation. Our faith was strong, and the Lord gave us justice when that man was sent to prison.'

'Did you know Bauer had been released early?'

Finally allowing his arms to drop to his sides, Mr Taylor said, 'We got a letter. We couldn't believe it. The man got sentenced to ten years, and he was coming out after six. It was plain wrong. He should've served every minute of his penance.'

'Amen to that, my husband.'

Tina continued, 'I can see that you were upset by the decision the parole board came to. Did you know he was going to be living in Nottingham upon his release?'

Mrs Taylor said, 'What? Nottingham? Whereabouts?'

'So you didn't know where Bauer was living?'

'No, we didn't. We were told nothing about that. Jennifer is starting college at Carrington soon. What if she had bumped into him again?'

'Can you think of anyone who would want to harm Bauer?'

'I can think of lots of people, but none living under this roof. With the Lord's grace, we've come to forgive that man's evil actions. Vengeance has no place at the Lord's table.'

Rachel said, 'Does your son feel the same way?'

'Spencer is away with the army. At the time, he found it hard to come to terms with what had happened to his little sister. He felt it was his job to protect her, and that he had failed. He was angry for a long time, but the police cooled his ire. They told him the law would deal with Bauer.'

'Did Spencer know that Bauer had been released early?'

'I wrote to him and told him, but I haven't heard back.'

'You said he was away with the army. Is he overseas?'

'No, he's at Fulford Barracks in York.'

'What regiment is he in?'

'He's in military intelligence. He's a corporal now. He has three more years to do before he needs to sign on again. He loves his job.'

'Sounds like he's doing well.'

Mr Taylor said, 'Spencer was always a bright, athletic boy. The army has made him a strong, intelligent man.'

'Do you think Spencer could still be holding those same thoughts of revenge against Bauer?'

'Not at all. We've all moved on. I doubt he even thinks about the man anymore. It was all a bit raw for him back then; he was a hot-headed teenager. He's almost twenty-five now, a grown man with a responsible job.'

'Okay, thanks. We have to ask because of all the trouble back then.'

'No problem, Detective. Is that everything? Jenny will be coming home soon, and I don't want her upsetting.'

'That's everything, thanks.'

Mr Taylor showed the two detectives to the door. Tina

said, 'Thank you for speaking with us. I know it's not been easy reliving those dreadful events.'

Mrs Taylor said, 'You have a job to do. We understand.'

As they walked back to the car, Tina said, 'As soon as we get back, let's establish exactly where Spencer Taylor was on the night of the tenth. Hopefully, he was in his barracks.'

Rachel replied, 'I wonder why the detective we spoke to didn't mention the warnings Spencer had been given at the time?'

10

6.00pm, 12 January 1988
MCIU Offices, Mansfield Police Station

Tina and Rachel walked into the main briefing room at the MCIU offices just as Danny was starting the day's debrief.

Tina whispered to Rachel, 'Find a quiet office and make some phone calls to Fulford Barracks.'

'Will do.'

Tina then sat down as the debriefing started.

Danny said, 'Right, we're all here now. Let's start with the house-to-house. Andy, are you making progress?'

DS Wills said, 'It's been a little hampered by the early finish, but force policy dictates we can't do house-to-house enquiries during the hours of darkness. The Special Ops team have made good inroads so far and will be back tomorrow morning. The street parameters you wanted have now all been mastered, so the SOU sergeant can work through the area methodically.'

'That's good. Anything significant so far?'

'Not yet.'

'Okay. I'd like you to continue to oversee that.'

Andy nodded.

Danny searched the faces in the room until he saw DC Williams. 'Jeff, you were tasked with researching other burglary offences in the Osborne Grove area. What have you found?'

'I've gone back through the records for the last three months, working from the date Bauer was released. During that period, there have been thirty-five burglaries of dwellings within that subdivision. Only one of these involved a climber.'

'Details?'

'The living quarters of the New Inn pub, on Mansfield Road, were entered via a first-floor window and property stolen. The offence occurred during the early evening, while the landlord and landlady were downstairs working in the pub. The offender climbed up onto a flat roof at the rear of the pub and entered the living quarters by forcing a window. Jewellery and cash were stolen.'

'And the other offences?'

'Twenty-six were burglaries committed overnight. Entries have been by various methods, but in every one of these offences, property has always been stolen. No assaults were reported at any other offences.'

'What about the remaining eight?'

'They were all distraction-type offences committed against the elderly, by sneak-in opportunists.'

'Has the local intelligence officer established any patterns of offending?'

'No, sir.'

'Thanks, Jeff, that's good work.'

Danny paused, then said, 'Glen, how have you got on with the CCTV trawl today?'

'I've only managed to find one camera so far. The one I've found is located at a petrol station on Hucknall Road.'

'Have you viewed the footage?'

'Yes. The only thing of any interest is a pedal cyclist who was picked up by the camera as he rode in the direction of Osborne Grove at eleven o'clock, and then rode back along Hucknall Road at three o'clock in the morning.'

'Is the quality of the image any good?'

'Unfortunately not. It's poor. The street lighting is inadequate, so it makes the image very grainy. I've seized the tape, and we may be able to get it enhanced if you think it's relevant.'

'What's the general description of the cyclist?'

'It's hard to be accurate, but the rider looks to be around five feet six and very slim. They were dressed all in black, with a hooded top.'

'Male or female?'

'Couldn't say.'

'Okay. In the absence of anything else, make the arrangements to try to enhance the film. I want you back on it again tomorrow. I'm sure there will be other cameras at premises you haven't checked yet.'

'I still have a lot of Mansfield Road to work through. Hopefully, I'll have more luck tomorrow.'

Danny then addressed the entire team. 'I've received the full post-mortem report from the pathologist. It's on my desk and available to read; make yourselves familiar with the content. Likewise, the photograph album of the scene and the post-mortem. Talking of which, has everybody seen the photograph of the object left by the killer? Does anybody have any suggestions as to what that may mean?'

The room remained silent.

After a brief pause, Danny said, 'Helen and Sam, how did you get on revisiting the other tenants?'

DC Blake said, 'Helen's had to go home, boss. One of her kids has had an accident at school. Possible broken arm.'

Danny said, 'When was this?'

'About three o'clock this afternoon.'

'Did you manage to see all the other tenants before she had to go?'

'We did. Nobody had any idea of Bauer's past offending. A couple of them guessed that he'd been inside, but nobody knew what for.'

'Were any of them aware of the threatening letters we've heard about?'

'No, sir. They all said similar things about Bauer. That he was scared of his own shadow and rarely left his flat. He would often ask the other tenants to fetch him bread or milk from the shop so he didn't have to go out.'

'Have they all made statements?'

'Yes, sir.'

'Did any of them report any problems with the landlord, Benny Fraser?'

'No. They all said he was a good landlord. If you paid your rent on time, he was never a problem.'

'Good work, Sam. Do me a favour – find out how Helen's nipper is and come and let me know after the debrief.'

'Will do.'

Danny once again addressed the room: 'I've had no more updates from Scenes of Crime, so that's it for today. Tina, Lynn and Jag, come and see me after the briefing, please. I want everyone back here tomorrow morning at six o'clock. Thanks.'

Danny walked into his office, followed by Lynn and Jag. He said, 'Any progress on the letter writer?'

Lynn said, 'We spent the morning with Special Branch. There's a group known to them who call themselves the Guardians of Innocence. They have political ideals, calling for longer sentences for paedophiles. Branch believes they are a benign organisation. We can't say for certain that this is the group who sent the letters to Bauer. Their activities are more to do with political lobbying than targeting individuals.'

'Did you look deeper into Benny Fraser?'

Jag said, 'I've spent most of the afternoon researching him. He has a few convictions for deception and theft. Only one for violence. That was an assault occasioning actual bodily harm on his wife, following a domestic dispute.'

'Are there any logs of complaints from other tenants in his rented properties?'

'He has five houses of multi-occupancy dotted around the city. The only logged complaint I could find was one of sexual harassment against a female tenant. That incident was at one of the houses he owns in West Bridgford.'

'Detail?'

'I made further enquiries, and it seems it was a vexatious complaint. The female tenant in question owed five months of back rent. It was investigated thoroughly, but found to be a false allegation.'

'Good work, Jag. So, on the surface at least, it seems like Benny Fraser isn't a person capable of the levels of violence used in this murder?'

Jag nodded. 'I don't think he is, boss. He comes over as genuine, and he was very shocked at what he discovered.'

'Keep digging into this letter. Have a closer look at the Guardians of Innocence. Who is the financial backer for the group? Where are they based? What are their aims other than the political ones? If they have any, that is. It's not going to be an easy task, but those letters could be the key to this.'

As Lynn and Jag got up to leave, Tina walked into the office.

Danny said, 'Grab a seat and tell me how your day went. I'm a little surprised to see you back so soon.'

'After we visited the school, it was apparent that Bauer had no family or friends to give us an insight into him. That's the reason we're back so early. We've visited both families of the schoolgirl victims and informed them that Bauer was dead. The father of Rebecca North and the parents of Jennifer Taylor were all shocked to hear that Bauer had been murdered. Perhaps understandably, they were all quite happy that it had happened, though.'

'Any reason to think they may have been involved in Bauer's death?'

'None. Rachel's currently following up on one enquiry involving the older brother of Jennifer Taylor. At the time of the offences, Spencer Taylor was eighteen and had recently joined the army. Back then, he was extremely vocal about getting even with Bauer as and when he was released. Spencer was so outspoken that the investigating officers had occasion to speak with him on a dozen different occasions about various verbal threats he had made.'

'Why didn't the investigating officer in the case mention this when you spoke to him yesterday?'

'I don't know, sir. Maybe he thought the brother wasn't serious when he made the threats? I will be following that up and asking the question.'

'Do we know where Spencer Taylor is now?'

'According to the parents, he's at his army barracks in Fulford, York.'

There was a knock on the door, and Rachel stepped inside.

Tina said, 'Have you spoken to the army?'

Rachel nodded. 'According to the barracks at Fulford,

Corporal Spencer Taylor is currently on leave in Nottingham. He should be staying at his parents' house at Clifton.'

Danny said, 'When did his leave start?'

'He's been on leave since the ninth of January and is expected back at barracks by eight o'clock tomorrow morning.'

'That's very interesting. I want you two to travel up to York tomorrow morning. Go to Fulford Barracks and speak to Spencer Taylor's commanding officer. I want you to talk to Taylor as well, but don't push him at this stage. Try to ascertain what he knows about Bauer's release and get an account of his whereabouts over the last few days.'

'He knows that Bauer was released from prison early. His mother told us that she had written to her son to let him know. We also know that he hasn't been at his mother's address during this leave. They thought he had chosen to remain at the barracks.'

'So where has he been while he's been on leave?'

Rachel shrugged and said, 'Good question.'

'Go to York and establish exactly what Taylor knows, and where he's been while on leave. There must be a reason why he's told the army one thing and is doing something else. I'm no expert on army regulations, but I'm sure there's a good reason why they want to know where their personnel are when they're on leave.'

'Will do, sir.'

'This could be the breakthrough we need. It's the best lead we've got so far. I know it's all circumstantial, and there's nothing forensically that links him to the crime scene, but I want you to get to the bottom of his lies before you leave York. Understood?'

'Yes, boss.'

'I've got a visit to Lincoln prison booked for tomorrow morning, with Rob. I want to know what Bauer was like as a prisoner. Like I said, I know there's no physical evidence linking Spencer Taylor to our crime scene, so you'll need to tread carefully when you talk to him and his commanding officer. I want you to keep me updated on any developments.'

Tina nodded. 'I'll treat it as a general enquiry at this stage unless he says something really incriminating.'

'I'm sure you know what you're doing, Tina. Just don't get yourself boxed into a corner.'

11

9.00am, 13 January 1988
Fulford Barracks, Fulford, York

Rachel brought the CID car to a halt at the red-and-white barrier beside the guardhouse. As the armed soldier approached the vehicle, she wound the car window down.

Both Rachel and Tina held their warrant cards out for the soldier to inspect. Rachel said, 'I'm DC Moore, and this is DI Cartwright. We have an appointment to see Captain Fairbrother at nine thirty this morning. We're a little early.'

Allowing his rifle to hang on its sling, the soldier examined both warrant cards before glancing down at the clipboard he was holding. He flicked over one sheet of paper and said, 'No problem, Detective. As soon as the barrier's raised, park your vehicle in the lay-by at the side of the guardhouse, and we'll get your passes ready. It will only take a couple of minutes; then you can wait in the mess hall. You'll be able to get a tea or coffee there. Captain Fairbrother is busy until nine thirty, I'm afraid, so you'll have a bit of a wait. Pull in over there, please.'

The soldier pointed to the lay-by.

As the barrier was slowly raised, Rachel eased the car into the parking area. Both detectives got out and stepped inside the guardhouse.

The formalities were completed quickly, and they were issued passes to wear on lanyards around their necks. The sergeant issuing them said, 'Drive straight down the driveway to the main entrance. There's a visitors car park there. Make sure your car is locked, then walk in through the double doors. The mess hall is on the right-hand side. It will be empty, as breakfast finished an hour ago, but you'll still be able to get a brew. Please wait in there and don't wander off. Always wear your lanyards, or you will be challenged and removed from the base. Is that clear?'

Tina said, 'As crystal, Sergeant. Thank you.'

Ten minutes later the two detectives were sat in the empty mess hall, with two mugs of strong coffee on the table in front of them.

The only other people in the huge hall were two young soldiers, still in their catering whites, who were busily cleaning the surfaces of all the tables, ready for lunch.

Rachel took a mouthful of the lukewarm coffee, grimaced and said quietly, 'Bloody hell. I hope the food tastes better than the coffee.'

Tina said, 'That bad?'

Rachel pulled a face, confirming it.

Tina glanced at her watch. There was only another ten minutes to wait. She ignored her coffee and thought about the questions she would be asking Captain Fairbrother.

A soldier walked crisply into the mess hall and made his way straight towards the detectives. He snapped to attention as he stopped and said, 'Detective Inspector Cartwright and Detective Constable Moore?'

Tina nodded.

The young soldier said, 'Follow me, please. Captain Fairbrother will see you now.'

He immediately turned and started to walk away; the two detectives abandoned their mugs of coffee and quickly followed him. After a two-minute walk along corridors with highly polished wooden floors, the soldier stopped and rapped twice on a door. The knock was answered with a swift reply of, 'Enter.'

The soldier opened the door stepped inside, came to attention and saluted before saying, 'Detective Inspector Cartwright and Detective Constable Moore, sir.'

The voice said, 'Thank you. Show them both in, please.'

The soldier held the door open, and the two detectives walked inside. The soldier closed the door as he left.

Captain Fairbrother was a tall thin man in his late forties. He was dressed immaculately in the shirtsleeve order of his army uniform. He stood and said, 'Detectives, welcome to Fulford Barracks. I hope I didn't keep you waiting too long. I had matters that needed my attention prior to our appointment.'

Tina said, 'It's no problem; we were early. Traffic on the A1 was much lighter than we had anticipated.'

Fairbrother said, 'Please take a seat.'

As all three sat down, Fairbrother continued, 'You mentioned on the telephone last night that your enquiries this morning were concerning Corporal Spencer Taylor. Is he in any trouble at all?'

Tina said, 'We're at the very early stages of an enquiry that has a bearing on Corporal Taylor's family. At this stage, all we're trying to do is establish some facts. There's no way of knowing what involvement, if any, Corporal Taylor may have on the enquiry.'

'I see. Can I ask what the nature of the enquiry is that you're investigating, and how it may have a bearing on Corporal Taylor's family?'

'We're investigating the murder of a man who committed serious sexual offences against Corporal Taylor's younger sister. At the time the man was appearing in court for those crimes, Taylor made certain verbal threats towards him.'

'How long ago was this?'

'This all happened shortly after Spencer had joined the army. So just over six years ago.'

The captain was thoughtful for a minute, stroking his moustache with his index and middle finger as he did so.

Then he said, 'What makes you think Corporal Taylor may be involved in some half-arsed revenge attack on this man after all these years? The man is an exemplary soldier who has no disciplinary issues whatsoever. I find it hard to believe he would jeopardise his career over something that happened six years ago.'

Tina said, 'The threats he made at the time were numerous and very specific. They were verbal death threats. He swore that whenever the man was released from prison, he would be waiting for him and would see him dead.'

'I'm sure you hear those sorts of threats all the time, especially when you're investigating emotive cases such as this one obviously was. I do have some recollection of the events involving his younger sister's assault by that paedophile. There must be something else you're concerned about, other than the threats, or you wouldn't have travelled all this way.'

Rachel said, 'When I contacted the barracks last night to establish Corporal Taylor's whereabouts for the time of the murder, I was informed that he was on leave and was staying at his parents' home in Nottingham. We had already spoken to his parents. We knew that Spencer hasn't been anywhere near his parents' home during this recent annual leave. They didn't even know their son was on leave.'

The officer allowed a puzzled expression to cross his face and was thoughtful for a few seconds. 'I see. Have you established if Taylor knew this man had been released from prison?'

'Yes, we have. His mother told us she had informed him by letter. I'm trying to establish two things today. Firstly, I want to know where Corporal Taylor was during his leave; and secondly, why he told the army that he would be staying with his parents, when he clearly had no intention of doing so.'

'Right. Well, let's find out, shall we?'

Captain Fairbrother walked to the door of his office, opened it and shouted, 'Private Smith! Find Corporal Taylor and bring him here to see me. He's in the map room this morning.'

The soldier snapped to attention. 'Yes, sir.'

Fairbrother smiled as he walked back to his chair. 'I'm sure we can get to the bottom of this little mystery very quickly, Detectives.'

12

9.30am, 13 January 1988
HMP Lincoln, Greetwell Road, Lincoln

Rob Buxton parked the car in the small car park situated to the right of the huge gates that formed the main entrance to Lincoln prison. There was no need for them to drive into the confines of the prison itself. The governor's office could be accessed via the staff entrance situated to the left of the main gates.

The two detectives got out of the car and walked towards the smaller door. As they passed the large double gates of the main entrance, Rob said, 'It doesn't matter how many times I visit prisons, they always make my blood run cold.'

Danny laughed. 'It's a good job you're this side of the walls, then, isn't it?'

Rob didn't answer. He just shook his head slowly before ringing the doorbell for the staff entrance. The door was opened, and a burly prison officer stood in the entrance. This wooden outer door opened into a sterile area with a further metal door that led into the prison offices. The metal door would remain secure until the outer door was closed and locked.

The prison officer said, 'Can I help you?'

Danny and Rob produced their warrant cards. Danny said, 'DCI Flint and DI Buxton to see Governor McNeill. He should be expecting us.'

The officer locked the outer door and said, 'Yes, he is. This won't take a second.' He then ran a handheld metal detector over the detectives' clothing.

There were no indications from the detector, and the officer apologised, saying, 'Sorry about that, but there are no exceptions.'

Danny said, 'No problem.'

The metal door was then unlocked from within, and all three men stepped inside the prison proper. A young woman was waiting in the first office; she smiled and said, 'DI Buxton? We spoke on the telephone yesterday. I'm Linda Makin, the governor's secretary. I'll show you to his office. Follow me, please.'

After walking up a flight of stairs, Linda Makin stopped outside a heavy oak door. She knocked on the door, opened it and said, 'Governor, the two detectives I told you about are here.'

As she beckoned them into the office, she asked, 'Can I get you a tea or coffee?'

Danny and Rob thanked the secretary, but refused the offer of refreshments.

Governor George McNeill was now in his late fifties.

He had joined the prison service at twenty-four years of age after a brief, uninspiring career in the Royal Navy. He had risen steadily through the ranks until being promoted to the position of governor at HMP Lincoln four years ago. He had been in post ever since.

McNeill gestured for the detectives to take a seat and said, 'I understand you want information on Manfred Bauer. How can I help you?'

Danny said, 'Bauer was murdered at his home address in Nottingham two days ago. I'm trying to establish what Bauer was like as a serving prisoner? He served all his sentence at this prison a long time. He must have made some enemies during that time?'

'As you say, it was a long time, but not long enough in my opinion. I felt his release was probably two years too early. He had made good progress in coming to terms with what he had done, but he wasn't ready. Even Bauer thought he was being released too soon.'

With an incredulous look on his face, Rob said, 'Bauer told you that?'

'Yes. I spoke with him regularly after his release date came through. He really didn't think it was right that he should be let out of prison so quickly.'

'Is that normal?'

'It's extremely unusual, but Bauer was never what you would call a normal prisoner. He desperately wanted to be punished for his crimes.'

Danny said, 'How did he get on with the other inmates?'

'He was imprisoned here before I took the governor's job, but I read through his file this morning when I knew you were coming. It seems Bauer suffered the usual problems that most sex offenders experience when sent to prison.'

'What problems?'

'When he first arrived, he was allocated a cell on B Wing, within the general prison population. Word soon got out that Bauer had committed serious sexual offences against children. In that first month he was hospitalised after being beaten up on no fewer than three occasions. The last time he was assaulted, his face was slashed with a homemade blade. He required thirty-five stitches to repair the wound in his right cheek. After that attack, he accepted the inevitable and went on rule forty-three for his own protection.'

'So he was separated from the main prison population?'

'That's right. Bauer hated it, but at least the assaults stopped, and he was physically safe. He couldn't stand being locked up with the other sex offenders. He just withdrew into himself. My staff had to order him out of his cell every day. I saw him as an acute suicide risk throughout his time here. Surprisingly, his urges to kill himself grew stronger as his release date got nearer.'

'Why was that?'

'I think it was to do with his overwhelming need to be punished. Even when his face was slashed, he refused to name his assailant. He would only say that he had deserved it, for what he had done to those girls.'

Rob said, 'Maybe he had a point.'

'Maybe he did, Detective. But he was tried and imprisoned for his crimes. That should be enough punishment, not random physical violence dished out by other inmates.'

'Point taken. Did he ever receive any threats from outside the prison?'

'No. We monitor all mail into prisoners. Bauer never received any threatening letters, simply because he never received any letters.'

'All the time he was in prison, he never received a single letter?'

'Not one.'

Danny said, 'What measures did you put in place to help him adjust to being released?'

'Nothing here. Bauer was transferred to HMP Whatton for the last three months of his sentence. They have a specialist sex offender wing there, with staff trained to help prisoners get ready for life outside prison walls.'

'I see. I thought he had been released from this prison.'

'No. It's a scheme that's been in place for the last eighteen months. Any sex offenders due for release are sent to Whatton for the last three months of their sentences.'

Rob said, 'What's the thinking behind that?'

'During that period at Whatton, they are helped to get accommodation away from the areas they offended in. They are briefed properly about the importance of maintaining contact with the probation service. There are a lot of positive aspects that were neglected before. You should visit the specialist wing at Whatton. It will give you an insight into the measures that were put in place for Bauer, ready for his release back into the community.'

Danny said, 'We shall, Governor, and thank you for your time today. One last question. During your regular talks with Bauer, did he ever mention anybody who might want to harm him outside? Or did he ever give any indication that he was worried about his personal safety after he was released?'

'Never. To be honest, my only concern was whether he would survive his own hand.'

'You mean suicide?'

'Yes. I was convinced that shortly after his release, he would take his own life. Manfred Bauer was such a strange and complex man. He could never come to terms with what he'd done, and perhaps more importantly, why he had done it.'

'Thanks, your insight has been a massive help.'

'No problem, Chief Inspector. I'll ask Mrs Makin to take you back downstairs to the exit.'

13

10.00am, 13 January 1988
Fulford Barracks, Fulford, York

Tina Cartwright felt more than a little anxious as she waited for Corporal Spencer Taylor to arrive at the office of Captain Fairbrother. The last thing she wanted was to be forced into a situation where her options were limited. She had been instructed to take a cautionary approach, as the evidence linking Taylor to the crime scene was zero.

Tina could see by Captain Fairbrother's body language that he wanted a quick resolution to this mystery.

She said, 'Captain Fairbrother, would you mind if I questioned Corporal Taylor initially? Our enquiry is a very tentative one at this stage. All I'm really trying to establish is his whereabouts at the time of Bauer's death.'

'Of course. I'm intrigued as to where the corporal spent his leave myself, but I'm more than happy to leave the questioning in your capable hands. I would insist on being present, though.'

'That's not a problem. Thank you.'

There was a sharp rap on the office door, and Fairbrother barked, 'Enter!'

The door opened, and a tall, slim soldier in full uniform stepped smartly inside. He snapped to attention in front of Fairbrother's desk and saluted his commanding officer.

Fairbrother barked, 'At ease, Corporal.'

Taylor assumed the at-ease position and waited for the officer to speak.

With a wave of his hand, Captain Fairbrother indicated the two women in the room and said, 'Corporal, this is Detective Inspector Cartwright and Detective Constable Moore from the Nottingham CID. They would like to ask you some questions. You must co-operate fully. Understood?'

'Yes, sir.'

Corporal Spencer Taylor turned nervously to face the two detectives.

Tina Cartwright said, 'I want to ask you a few questions about Manfred Bauer.'

'What about Bauer?' The young soldier almost spat the name.

'Are you aware that Bauer has been released early from prison?'

'Yes. And I think it's disgusting.'

'At the time Bauer was convicted, you made several serious threats against him. Do you still feel the same way?'

'That was six years ago, Detective. In those days, I was a hot-headed teenager. I've grown up and matured since then.'

'How did you find out Bauer had been released?'

'My mother wrote to me and told me the news. I don't get it. You're a police officer; how can you even think about letting that monster out?'

'We have no say over when a person is released from prison, Spencer. Had you already booked your leave for the ninth to the twelfth before you found out Bauer had been released?'

'No. I booked it the day after I got my mother's letter.'

'On your leave pass you stated you were spending your time in Nottingham. Where did you stay?'

'At my parents' house, where I always stay.'

'Who can verify that?'

'Why do you need verification of where I stayed?'

'Your leave pass was from the ninth until yesterday, the twelfth of this month, correct? Manfred Bauer was murdered during the early hours of the eleventh.'

There was a look of genuine shock and disbelief on Taylor's face. There was a long pause; then he said quietly, 'And you think I killed him?'

'I know you didn't stay at your parents' house during your leave. So I must ask myself why you are lying.'

The young soldier's eyes darted to his commanding officer and then back to the detective.

He said, 'I didn't have anything to do with that pig's death. I was in Birmingham that night.'

'Who can verify that?'

Again, there was the furtive glance towards his commanding officer. Tina spotted it and said, 'There's obviously something you're worried about disclosing in front of your commanding officer. Let me impress on you the seriousness of your situation. Right now, you are a person of interest in a murder enquiry. If there's anything you can tell me that could change that situation, now's the time to say it.'

Taylor shifted uncomfortably, then said, in a voice little more than a whisper, 'I lied on my leave pass. I stayed in Birmingham for the duration of my leave. I never went to Nottingham.'

A clearly angry Captain Fairbrother spoke for the first time. 'So where did you spend your annual leave?'

'As I said, sir. I was in Birmingham. Sorry, sir.'

'You do know the standing orders relating to annual leave passes?'

'Yes, sir.'

'Are you aware of the reason why we need to know exactly where you are spending your leave?'

'Yes, sir.'

'Exactly where did you stay in Birmingham?'

For the first time, Spencer Taylor hesitated with his reply.

He looked down at his feet before saying, 'I was with my wife and baby, at her parents' house in Birmingham. I'm trying to get us accommodation away from there, but it's difficult.'

The officer was momentarily stunned. With a note of incredulity in his voice, he said, 'You were with your wife and child?'

'Yes, sir.'

'You didn't inform the regiment of your intention to get married, let alone that you'd gone ahead and done so, did you?'

'No, sir.'

'What's wrong with you, man? These are all flagrant breaches of army regulations. Why haven't you followed the correct standing orders?'

'It's a difficult situation, sir. I'm just trying to do the right thing. When Charmaine told me she was pregnant, I knew we had to get married.'

'That's all very commendable, but I'm still struggling to understand your reasons for breaching regulations. You could have done all of this by the book. You should have just come to me and told me the situation. It would have been a formality for me to grant your marriage. I could have then arranged for you to live in married quarters here on the base. Why all the deception?'

'It's Charmaine's father, sir. He has a long criminal record for dealing drugs. I wasn't sure the army would allow me to marry his daughter.'

Captain Fairbrother sat back in his chair.

He said, 'We will have some sorting out to do, but it's nothing we can't deal with, Corporal Taylor. The detectives need to know if you spent your entire leave in Birmingham?'

'Yes, sir. I was with Charmaine and my son, Alex, all the time. I never strayed from her father's house. I hardly ever see them as it is. So I wasn't going to waste any time going to see my own parents.'

'That's all going to change, Corporal. I'll arrange for you to be billeted in married quarters here as soon as we can. Then your wife and son can move in with you. There's going to be disciplinary issues for you to face because of the half-arsed way you've gone about things. Understood?'

'Yes, sir. Thank you, sir.'

'One last thing, I take it Charmaine has no criminal record?'

'No, sir. She hasn't.'

Tina interjected, 'I will need the full name of your wife's parents, as well as their address. We'll need to verify your alibi.'

'Her father's name is Brent Smikle, and her mother's name is Hyacinth. Their address is 23 Hamilton Court, Lozells, Birmingham.'

'Thank you. If everything checks out, you won't hear from us again.'

Corporal Taylor nodded.

Captain Fairbrother said, 'Good. That's all sorted, then. That will be all, Corporal. Dismissed.'

Corporal Taylor snapped to attention, saluted and walked smartly out of the office.

As soon as the door closed, Captain Fairbrother turned to the detectives and said, 'Well, Detectives, I think that solves your dilemma, but causes me a few more problems. Such is life, I suppose.'

Tina said, 'Those regulations he's breached. Are they serious?'

'The corporal will be dealt with in the correct way. All our regulations are there for a reason and must be adhered to. All our personnel know the consequences if they breach them. Corporal Taylor's a bloody good soldier and very good at his job. Nothing he's done is insurmountable. Can I ask you to let me know the outcome after you've checked his alibi?'

'Yes, of course. Thank you for your help today.'

Fairbrother stood up and walked to the door. He opened the door and shouted, 'Private Smith, escort the detectives back to their vehicle, please.'

14

5.00pm, 13 January 1988
MCIU Offices, Mansfield Police Station

The afternoon debrief had just finished, and Danny had returned to his office feeling more than a little frustrated. There had been no breakthroughs. No new CCTV had been found, and there was nothing evidentially from the hours and hours of painstaking house-to-house enquiries.

He had a planned meeting with Chief Superintendent Potter in the morning and had been hoping to have something positive to tell him.

The knock on his office door snapped him out of his melancholy mood.

He shouted, 'Come in.'

The door opened, and Tina Cartwright and Rachel Moore walked in.

Danny said, 'Give me some good news about Spencer Taylor.'

Tina said, 'It's nothing positive, I'm afraid. Spencer Taylor has a cast-iron alibi for the night of the murder. He was at an address in the Lozells area of Birmingham.'

'And you've checked this alibi out?'

'Yes, sir. The local CID have been to the address and spoken to all the occupants. They all confirmed, independently, that Spencer hadn't left the address. He spent the entire duration of his leave in the house with his wife and child. There's one other thing. Taylor doesn't drive, so he'd travelled to Birmingham from York by train.'

'So if needs be, we can check CCTV at the railway station for sightings?'

'If needs be, yes.'

'How was Taylor when you interviewed him at Fulford Barracks?'

'There's still a real sense of hatred towards Bauer, but there was also genuine shock and surprise that he was dead. I don't think he had anything to do with Bauer's murder, boss. He's had to admit to several court-martial offences to give us this alibi. It's not something he would have chosen to do. He's put himself in quite a lot of shit by telling us about Birmingham.'

'I hear what you're saying, but let's not discount him completely. Check the railway station CCTV tomorrow.'

'Will do, boss. Did we miss anything on the debrief?'

'Not a thing. We're fast running out of enquiries, and I've got to brief Potter in the morning.'

'Are you going to the press now?'

'The press has already reported on the murder, so there's no need to avoid public disquiet in the area. I'll be making a full press appeal asking for witnesses immediately after the briefing with Potter. You never know; it might just turn something up. God knows, we need something. Finish up what you've got to do and be back on duty tomorrow morning at eight. Thanks.'

As the door to his office closed, Danny sat back in his chair and rubbed his temples. This enquiry was rapidly losing impetus. He was running out of ideas to inject some much-needed momentum back into it.

He consoled himself with the fact that tomorrow was another day, and things could change quickly.

15

10.00am, 14 January 1988
Nottinghamshire Police Headquarters

It was the one part of his job that Danny hated. Updating the head of CID, Chief Superintendent Potter, on current enquiries being undertaken by the MCIU.

He knew it was necessary, but that didn't make it any less of a chore. It was bad enough when he had numerous ongoing enquiries into current murder cases. On occasions like this, when there was nothing positive to report, they were a nightmare.

He knew that Potter would be eager to criticize his team's efforts. It didn't matter to him the number of hours that had been worked, or the huge efforts every detective had made. All Potter would ever see were the negatives.

So it was proving today.

'Let me get this right, Chief Inspector. What you're telling me is that no meaningful progress has been made at all.'

'There have been no breakthroughs yet, sir.'

'Are you expecting any soon?'

'There's nothing forensically, and extensive house-to-house enquiries haven't turned anything up yet.'

'And you already said there's no CCTV? Even though this murder happened in one of the busiest areas of Nottingham?'

Danny shook his head. 'We've found nothing.'

He paused before continuing, 'I'm holding a press appeal immediately after this meeting, to try to generate any possible witnesses. The apathy from the general public so far has been very noticeable. Nobody is volunteering any information.'

'And we both know the reason for that, don't we?'

'I know what the man was sent down for. If that's what you're referring to, sir.'

As if to reinforce his point, Potter took out a local newspaper and said, 'Turn to the letters column on page thirty. Read the letter from a member of the public, titled "Scum on our streets", and then tell me what you make of it.'

Danny quickly read the letter in the newspaper. It was from an unnamed source. The writer, identifying himself as SA, expressed an overwhelming sense of relief and joy at the death of Manfred Bauer. The sentiments within the letter were both inflammatory and threatening. The writer extolled the virtues of the person who had taken it upon themselves to rid Nottingham's streets of yet another sexual predator.

Danny said, 'This is what I mean, sir. The general public appear to be totally against us on this enquiry. We're getting zero information coming into the incident room.'

'I suggest you make it a priority to track down this letter writer and establish what they were doing on the night of Bauer's murder.'

Danny sighed inwardly. Just what he needed, a lesson from Potter in how to run a murder enquiry. He folded the newspaper and said, 'I'll make it a top priority, sir. If there's nothing else, I need to speak with the press liaison officer before holding the press appeal.'

'Don't let me detain you any longer, Chief Inspector. Let me know when you've tracked down the person who penned that letter.'

Danny stood up and walked to the door. As he was leaving, he turned and said, 'Will do, sir.'

16

1.00pm, 14 January 1988
MCIU Offices, Mansfield Police Station

Danny was feeling fraught after the meeting with Potter and the ensuing press conference. As he walked in the office, he looked for Lynn Harris and Jagvir Singh. They were both busy at their desks. With no pleasantries, Danny said, 'Lynn, Jag, my office, now.'

Hearing the tone in Danny's voice, the two detectives dropped what they were doing and followed him into his office.

Danny said, 'There's a letter in this newspaper, written by some lunatic, about the Bauer murder. You two are looking at the vigilante side of things. I want you to track down the writer and interview them as soon as possible.'

Jag took the newspaper from Danny and said, 'I'll call the editor and see what details they have.'

'Good. Crack on.'

As Jag left the room, Danny turned to Lynn and said, 'Any further developments on the group you were looking at the last time we spoke?'

'You mean the Guardians of Innocence?'

'Yes. Anything?'

'Nothing more than what I've already told you. They are overtly political, focusing on putting pressure on government to increase sentences for sex offenders. There's very little available background information. I'm still trying to get to the bottom of the organisation. It's proving difficult to get the names of the people who are behind it. I'm also trying to establish who finances it and where they're based.'

Before Danny could say anything else, there was a polite knock on the door, and Jag walked back into the office.

He said, 'The editor was very helpful. She says the letter came from a regular contributor to their letters page. His name's Stanley Armitage. They have an address for him in Aslockton.'

'That's great work. I want both of you to treat this as a priority. Get straight out there and talk to this Stanley Armitage. I want this enquiry sorting out today. I want to know if I need to take this man seriously as a suspect, or if he's just some crank with too much time on his hands.'

17

3.00pm, 14 January 1988
6 Whitwell Road, Aslockton, Nottinghamshire

Jagvir Singh brought the CID car to a stop on Whitwell Road, in the village of Aslockton. The house he had parked outside was a red-brick, three-bedroom semi-detached property, probably built just after the Second World War. It was beautifully maintained, and the front garden was neat and tidy. As it was still winter, the carefully pruned roses were bare and not in bloom.

It was a smart street, where everybody took pride in the appearance of their property.

Lynn Harris said, 'This letter is disgusting. I'm surprised the paper even printed it. It glories in the death of Manfred Bauer and calls for all sex offenders to either stay in prison or face a similar fate upon their release. It's very close to being an incitement to violence.'

Jag nodded. 'I know what you mean. I couldn't believe it

when I first read it. The editor told me she had been in two minds whether to print it. She was so concerned that she ran it past their lawyer first. He was okay with it.'

'The part that's really disturbing is where Armitage talks about the hammer of justice coming down hard on Manfred Bauer. Do you think it's just a figure of speech, or a reference to the actual murder weapon?'

'There's only one way to find out. That's Armitage's house. Let's go and talk to him.'

As the two detectives got out of the car, Lynn said, 'Did you check if he has any previous convictions?'

'There's nothing on our systems for Stanley Armitage, and nothing coming back on this address.'

'Okay.'

As they walked towards the house, the front door was opened by an elderly man in his late sixties. He was short, which accentuated his heavy build that was borderline obese. His hair was grey and receding rapidly, and his thick-lensed spectacles perched precariously on the end of his nose.

The man folded his arms across his chest. 'Whatever it is you're selling, I don't want any.'

Lynn Harris produced her identification card from her pocket and said, 'We're from the CID. I'm looking for Mr Stanley Armitage.'

'Well, you've found him.'

There was no offer to step inside the house, so Lynn said calmly, 'We need to talk to you privately about a letter you sent to the *Bingham Gazette*. May we come in for a minute?'

There was a reluctance from Armitage. He hesitated for a few seconds before saying, 'You'd better come inside.'

The two detectives stepped inside the hallway, and Armitage closed the front door behind them. He then walked past them and said, 'Come through to the lounge.'

Once inside the lounge, he pointed at a settee and said, 'Take a seat.'

As he sat in the armchair opposite, he said, 'Is this to do with the letter I wrote about that shithouse Manfred Bauer?'

It was obvious to both detectives that Stanley Armitage was in no way physically capable of carrying out the murder personally. They also knew that he could still be involved in the organisation or planning of the offence. The questioning would need to be careful and thorough.

Jag took a copy of the letter from the folder he was carrying. 'First things first, Mr Armitage. Is this the letter you wrote to the *Bingham Gazette*?'

Armitage took the newspaper page and peered at it through his spectacles. As he read it, his lips moved as though silently mouthing the words.

After a full minute or so, he said, 'That's it, so what?'

Lynn said, 'Have you ever met Manfred Bauer?'

'Why would I know a monster like that?'

'You have some very strong opinions about a person you've never met.'

'What Bauer did is a matter of public record. It's not against the law to have an opinion, is it?'

'No, it isn't. When did you first become aware that Bauer was to be released?'

'I didn't.'

'Excuse me?'

'I didn't know Bauer had been released until I read about his death.'

Jag corrected him, saying, 'Until you read about his murder.'

Armitage nodded. 'Yes. His murder. That's when I wrote the letter. I was disgusted by the fact that he'd been let out so early from that shithole down the road. I saw what happened to him in Nottingham as a gruesome kind of karma.'

Lynn said, 'When you say "shithole", are you referring to HMP Whatton?'

'Of course I am. It's disgusting that we have to put up with that place being so close to this beautiful village. God only knows what other depraved monsters are locked up in there. I do know there's a specialist sex offenders wing in there. That's shocking, giving them creeps special conditions. All those bastards need is a length of hemp and a three-foot drop. They should all be strung up. I live here alone now; my kids have all grown up. But I feel for all the parents of young kids in the village. They must be worried sick, having that place on their doorstep.'

With his rant over, Armitage appeared out of breath and slightly red in the face.

Jag said, 'Are you okay?'

The old man snapped, 'Yes. I'm okay. I just feel very strongly about some things, that's all.'

Lynn said, 'Prior to reading about his murder, had you any idea where Bauer was living after his release?'

'It's like I said before: I didn't know he'd even been released until I read the paper. I could remember the case, though. Those poor young schoolgirls. I could remember the sentence he got at court, and I just felt outraged that he'd been let out so soon.'

Jag said, 'There are some very strong words in your letter. It borders on incitement to violence. Was that your intention when you wrote it?'

'Look, I'm not some kind of crazy vigilante. I admit, I did get carried away a little when I wrote it. They say you should never write a letter when you're emotional. I was raging at the time, and I think the letter reflects that.'

Lynn said bluntly, 'Are you in any way connected to the murder of Manfred Bauer?'

'Of course not. I'm just an old man disgusted at what our society is becoming, that's all.'

'Okay, Mr Armitage. Thanks for your time. Please try to think things through a little before writing another letter. There may be people out there who read your words and then act upon them.'

'I understand. I'm sorry you've had to come out here to talk to me.'

Just as they were about to stand up to leave, Jag said, 'Have you ever heard of a group calling themselves the Guardians of Innocence?'

The old man was thoughtful for a few seconds, then said, 'That does ring a bell. I went to a meeting held at the village hall in Bingham, when the sex offenders wing was first proposed for the prison at Whatton. I'm pretty sure that was something like Guardians.'

'How did you know about the meeting?'

'I received a letter. Well, it was more of a flyer stuffed through the letterbox. I've got it somewhere; just a minute.'

The old man stood up and left the room, returning after a minute or so clutching a leaflet.

He handed the leaflet to Jag and said, 'This is it.'

Jag read it quickly before passing it to Lynn. He said to Armitage, 'You said you went to the meeting?'

'I wasn't happy about what they were doing at the prison, so yes, I went.'

'How was it?'

'It was very well attended, but it was all a bit weird.'

'In what way?'

'The first part of the meeting was standard stuff. The main man stood up and made a speech, imploring all of us residents to engage with our local MPs and councillors, to try to get the new wing scrapped.'

'The main man?'

'The guy whose photo is on the flyer, Brannigan.'

Lynn said, 'Okay, so the first part of the meeting was standard. How did it then get weird?'

'As soon as Brannigan finished talking, he left in his flash motor. His henchmen stayed behind though. That's when things changed, and it all got a little nasty.'

'I don't understand, Mr Armitage.'

'After Brannigan left, most of the people from the village left as well. It was just a few of the younger hotheads who stayed behind. I stayed because I was curious. The thing is these henchmen were spouting a very different message to what Brannigan had said earlier. They wanted more direct action.'

'Direct action?'

'Their idea was for any sex offenders who had been released early to be given a good hiding as soon as they were let out. They said this would deter others applying for early release. I thought they were just bully boys. They sounded like something out of pre-war Nazi Germany. The concerning thing was that some of the young lads were really buying into their message. Their message was poisonous. Now they really are a bunch of vigilante cranks.'

'Who were these "henchmen"?'

'I've no idea. Musclemen who looked like bouncers, you know the type. There were a couple of women with them, though.'

'How many altogether?'

'About a dozen, I'd say.'

'And you're sure they were all part of Brannigan's organisation?'

'Definitely. They were all members of Guardians of Innocence. They have this badge on their jackets. It's the same as the emblem at the top of the flyer. That hammer and lightning bolt, or whatever it's supposed to be. Do you think they could have had something to do with what happened to Bauer?'

Jag said, 'It's very doubtful, Mr Armitage. Like you say, probably just a bunch of cranks. Do you mind if we keep this flyer?'

'Have it, son. It's no use to me.'

Lynn said, 'Thanks again for your time. Please have a think before writing any more letters to the paper.'

'Will do.'

As the front door closed behind them, Jag said, 'Any idea who this James Brannigan is?'

'None. But we're going to find out as soon as we get back to the office.'

18

6.30pm, 14 January 1988
MCIU Offices, Mansfield Police Station

Lynn Harris tapped politely on Danny's office door. The main office was now deserted. The other detectives had all left after the final debrief of the day. Lynn had remained, using the extra hours to research James Brannigan.

Danny was about to put his jacket on to go home, when he heard the knock. He shouted, 'Come in.'

He was surprised to see Lynn walk in.

He sat back down and said, 'You're working late tonight, Lynn. How did you and Jag get on with the letter writer?'

'That's what I want to talk to you about. We went to see Mr Armitage. He's just an old man venting his anger at having HMP Whatton on his doorstep. There's no way he's involved with the murder of Bauer.'

'Somehow, I didn't think he would be. You must have got

something from the meeting with Armitage, though, or you wouldn't still be here.'

She handed the Guardians of Innocence flyer to him and said, 'We recovered this from Armitage.'

Danny read the flyer and said, 'Guardians of Innocence? The group you and Jag were already aware of?'

'The same. I've spent all this afternoon researching James Brannigan. Mr Armitage described him as the "main man" at the meeting, and it's his photo on the flyer.'

'Okay. So who's James Brannigan?'

'Brannigan's a self-made millionaire. He's the owner and founder of a multinational plastics injection manufacturing company. Basically, any food or drink that's contained in plastic, you can almost guarantee the container or bottle will have been made by Polyplastech Ltd. The company are based in Northampton, but they have factories worldwide.'

'Why does such a successful businessman have an interest in what happens to convicted sex offenders?'

'I've just come off the phone to colleagues in Dorset. I've established that James Brannigan has one child, a daughter from his first marriage. She attended a residential private school in Dorset, from the age of seven. The girl was sexually abused by one of the teachers at that school, from the age of eight until she was ten. The schoolteacher was arrested and charged, but only after other children at the school also came forward and made complaints. It was only then that the horrific abuse suffered by Brannigan's daughter was discovered. The offender, Miles Harmon, received a sentence of nine years imprisonment. He was released eighteen months ago after serving less than three years of that sentence.

'The early release incensed Brannigan. From that moment, he has campaigned tirelessly to ensure that sex offenders serve their full sentences. Six months after Harmon was released, Brannigan set up the Guardians of Innocence.

The stated aims of this organisation are to put pressure on government to make changes to the early release scheme that currently exists.'

'That's good work, and all very interesting, but how does it help us? It sounds like the organisation he established is only interested in applying political pressure.'

'I agree, that's what it sounds like. From the outside looking in, that's what anybody would think.'

'I sense a "but" coming. What have you found?'

'When we spoke to Armitage, he told us about the meeting at Aslockton. After Brannigan had made his speech to residents, he left straight away. He left behind a group of men and women about a dozen strong, who were all members of the Guardians of Innocence.'

'Go on.'

'Members of this smaller group were giving a very different message to the younger elements who had attended the meeting. They were advocating positive action against any sex offenders released early from prison.'

'By positive action, do you mean violence?'

'Yes, sir. Their master plan, if you can call it that, is to harass and physically assault all sex offenders who are released from prison. They hope that by taking this action, it will discourage other similar offenders from seeking early release.'

'Do we know who this group of individuals are?'

'No, sir. Not yet. But as I said, they are part of Brannigan's organisation, so he will know who they are. No doubt they are being paid by him.'

Danny was thoughtful. It was still a massive leap from advocating assaults on sex offenders to being involved in the murder of one.

'Do we know where Miles Harmon is now?'

'I thought of that, boss. If Brannigan hated sex offenders

enough to harm them, then surely Harmon would be first on the list.'

'Did you manage to track him down?'

'Harmon's dead. It was cancer that killed him, not a vigilante group. He died within three months of his release.'

'I see.'

'He was released to an address on the Isle of Wight. He reported receiving several death threats to his probation officer immediately after his release.'

'Was there any investigation into these threats?'

'I've spoken to Hampshire police, and they investigated them, but couldn't identify a source. They stopped looking after Harmon was diagnosed with terminal cancer.'

'This is great work, Lynn. I want you to stick with it. At the earliest opportunity, get in touch with Brannigan and set up a meeting. We need to establish who this smaller group are, the ones who are actively promoting violence. We also need to establish how much of their activities are sanctioned by Brannigan. I want you and Jag to carry on researching James Brannigan tomorrow. Arrange that meeting as quick as you can. I'll see you in the morning.'

19

9.30am, 15 January 1988
HMP Whatton, Nottinghamshire

Stewart Tighe swept up the coins from the counter and placed them into his suit pocket.

Senior Prison Officer Parker said, 'Twenty-nine pence. You're not going to get very far on that, Tighe. Have you got transport arranged?'

The tall, skinny, thirty-five-year-old answered in his soft voice, 'Yes, boss. My parents are picking me up. I'm going to Carlton in Lindrick, to live with them on the family farm.'

'Back to mum and dad's, eh? I bet you're looking forward to that.'

The ironic tone in the officer's voice was completely lost on the apathetic Tighe. He just smiled benignly and said, 'I don't mind, really.'

The prison officer eyed up the sex offender. Stewart Tighe gave him the creeps.

There was something about Stewart Tighe that he just didn't trust. He always came over as being stupid – borderline imbecilic at times – but then he would flash a certain look, and the predator that he was could be seen. It was never there for long, but the experienced prison officer had worked around sex offenders long enough to recognise the extremely dangerous ones. He couldn't quite believe the parole board had made their decision to allow Tighe out so early. He had only served just over half of his twelve-year sentence.

With all the admin for the release completed, the officer said sharply, 'Sign here, Tighe. Let's get you out of here.'

Tighe signed where he was told to, and the prison officer pulled the keys dangling on the long chain from his pocket into his right hand. He unlocked the small metal door that formed part of the larger steel gates and said, 'Off you go then, Tighe. Behave yourself.'

The officer watched for a few moments as Tighe walked away. His mop of unruly, straw-coloured hair blew in the gentle breeze. It was a cold morning, and Tighe was dressed in a tight-fitting, navy blue business suit. He had the athletic build of a swimmer. Tall and thin, but with wide shoulders and a very narrow waist.

His physical appearance was unsurprising, as Stewart Tighe had been a swimmer all his life. He had earned his living as a swimming instructor and coach at the public baths in Worksop.

At least he had until the first boy had gone to his parents and told them exactly what had happened to him during the private one-on-one swimming lessons with Mr Tighe.

The police had acted quickly and arrested Tighe at his small bedsit in Worksop town centre. The detectives quickly traced other schoolboy victims of the swimming instructor's depravity. Six boys had eventually made identical complaints of rape against the swim instructor.

Tighe had been found guilty at Sheffield Crown Court and sentenced to twelve years imprisonment for the series of offences he had committed. That had been just over six years ago, when he was twenty-nine years of age. He had been surprised when the prison chaplain at HMP Leicester had informed him that he was to be released so quickly.

He had been surprised, but also overjoyed.

As the metal door clanged shut behind him, he shivered against the cold and clutched the brown paper bag containing his few belongings close to his chest as he looked around the car park.

There was no sign of his parents.

He was starting to feel an overwhelming sense of panic, when he saw the battered Land Rover Defender turn into the car park. The old vehicle was like a mechanical incarnation of his elderly parents. They were all on their last legs.

The vehicle came to a juddering stop beside him. The engine was faltering and spluttering as it noisily ticked over. His father slid the window back and barked at Stewart, 'Well, don't just stand there gawping, boy. Get in!'

In that instant, Tighe felt as though he had been transported back in time, to when he was an eight-year-old boy. His domineering father would always take him to the early morning training sessions at the pool. He only ever began swimming to please his father, but it had come to dominate his life. His father wouldn't allow a young Stewart to have any interest in girls, in case it affected his chances of swimming at the Olympics.

His father had been obsessed with the Olympic Games. He was desperately trying to live out his own dreams and aspirations vicariously through his only son.

Although an extremely talented swimmer, Stewart was never quite talented enough. He was never able to swim fast enough to make the national squad. As a result, he had always been a massive disappointment to his father.

Now as he walked around the Land Rover, he had his head down, staring at his feet. He opened the passenger door and saw his frail, downtrodden mother. She smiled weakly at him before sliding across the bench seat, allowing him to get in the vehicle.

He climbed in and slammed the door shut.

The old woman could barely stand to look at her son, the convicted sex offender. She loathed him for what he had done to those young boys. If it weren't for the fact that he had nowhere else to go, she would never have agreed to him living back at the farm.

As he got in the vehicle, Stewart said quietly, 'Hello, Mum.'

She stared straight ahead and said, 'Your room's all ready. It's liver and onions for tea tonight.'

He placed the brown bag on his lap and said in a whisper, 'My favourite.'

As the Land Rover was driven out of the car park, neither Stewart nor his elderly parents were aware that their every move was being closely watched.

20

4.30pm, 16 January 1988
MCIU Offices, Mansfield Police Station

Lynn Harris knocked on the door once and then walked into Danny's office. She knew he was alone and that he had an open-door policy for his staff.

As she closed the door behind her, Danny looked up. Seeing the look of concern on his young detective sergeant's face, he asked, 'Is there a problem?'

With a real sense of frustration in her voice she said, 'I've been trying to get through to James Brannigan all day.'

'And?'

'I finally managed to speak to his personal assistant, at the head offices of Polyplastech Ltd in Northampton. After all that, she informed me that James Brannigan flew to Boston this morning. He will be there, seeking new orders for his company, until the end of February. He's combining the business trip with a half-term holiday for his daughter.'

Danny was thoughtful. This was a significant blow to an already stalling enquiry. Right now, it was the only viable lead they had in the murder of Manfred Bauer.

He said, 'What date is Brannigan due back?'

'He's next in his office on the twenty-fourth of February.'

'Okay. It's a setback, but not the end of the world. Call his PA back and arrange for a meeting between Brannigan and myself for as near to the twenty-fourth as you can, please, Lynn.'

'I've done that. I thought that's what you'd say, so I made an appointment for you to see Brannigan in his office at ten o'clock on the twenty-fifth.'

For the first time since she had walked into the office, Danny smiled at his detective sergeant and said, 'That's what I love about this unit. Everybody knows exactly how I think.'

He chuckled before getting serious again. 'Well done. It's exactly what I would have wanted you to do. In the meantime, I want you and Jag to stay on the Guardians of Innocence enquiry. I want you to go back to Aslockton and speak to as many people who attended that meeting as you can find. Let's see if we can locate somebody who knows these bully boys who stayed behind after Brannigan had left. You never know, we might get lucky and establish who they are before we ask Brannigan.'

'Will do, boss. If it's okay with you, I'll also step up the financial investigation into Polyplastech Ltd. My old sergeant works on the Fraud Squad and knows his way around a financial investigation. Am I okay to liaise with him about the case?'

'Of course, it's a good call. I'm sure he'll know some shortcuts into obtaining the financial profile of such a huge company. Good work today, Lynn. Keep me informed how things progress, please.'

The young sergeant nodded as she closed the office door.

On his own in the office, Danny reflected on yet another setback. This enquiry was going nowhere fast. He had never worked a case with so little input or feedback from the general public. It was as though Manfred Bauer was the forgotten victim. He had been brutally murdered, and nobody seemed to care.

A note that had been left on his desk instantly reinforced that very thought. It was a note requesting him to contact Benny Fraser. The landlord wanted to know if it was okay for him to let the flat previously occupied by Bauer, as he was losing rent money.

As he picked up the telephone to call Fraser, Danny mentally resolved not to allow this enquiry to slide into the unsolved category for want of effort or tenacity, from either himself or his staff.

21

1.00am, 4 February 1988
Redgate Farm, Carlton in Lindrick, Nottinghamshire

It had been almost three weeks since Stewart Tighe had been released from HMP Whatton. It had been a gradual spiral down into depression since then. His father spoke to him like he was still a child, and it was obvious that his own mother loathed his very presence around the farmhouse.

He had refused to do any manual work around the farm, which had made an already tense situation worse. He was not allowed to move out of the farmhouse until his probation officer had confirmed it was okay to do so. He felt trapped and alone. It was ridiculous that a thirty-five-year-old man was still living with his parents.

His life now revolved around eating, sleeping and watching hours of inane television programmes, all day and all night.

He refused to move far from the main living room in the spacious farmhouse. His elderly parents occupied the snug at the back of the house anyway, and they seldom, if ever, came into the main lounge.

Stewart had brought his duvet cover down from the bedroom and now spent all day and all night on the soft, duck-down sofa. It was far more comfortable than the rickety single bed in his draughty old bedroom. He was well over six feet tall, and his feet stuck out the end of the bed.

As his depression took hold, he had also started drinking heavily. His father always had strong liquor in the house, and he had started helping himself from the plentiful supply of malt whiskies kept in the cellar.

It had reached the point already where, most nights, he would consume almost a full bottle.

He stared blankly at the television screen as the programme he was watching came to an end. It was another crap drama that had first been broadcast back in the seventies. He drained the last of the whiskey from his glass and crawled from the sofa across to the television. He switched it off and crawled back onto the sofa, feeling his way now the room was in darkness. He pulled the duvet cover around him and adjusted the pillows on the sofa.

22

1.00am, 4 February 1988
Redgate Farm, Carlton in Lindrick, Nottinghamshire

The shadowy figure had been standing in the darkness for hours, maintaining a position just two yards away from the main living room window of the remote farmhouse. As usual, the curtains had remained open, so the target could easily be seen inside the property.

He was in his usual position, lying motionless on the sofa, just staring at the flickering images emanating from the television screen. The different colours from the television gave different perspectives to the room as they constantly changed.

The television screen suddenly changed to a flat grey colour, signalling that tonight's broadcast had come to an end. The figure at the window remained perfectly still and continued to observe as the target crawled across the floor to switch the television off.

The target's routine was now becoming an identical

pattern. His actions throughout tonight were the same as every other night. The stalker always made mental notes of any windows that had been left insecure, where the other occupants of the house were, where guard dogs and alarms were located. It would take several more recces before the time would be right to take the next step.

Finally satisfied with the night's work, the figure dressed entirely in black had seen enough and slipped silently away from the farmhouse. It was only a matter of time before enough knowledge would be gained so that true justice could prevail.

As always, patience was the key.

23

3.00am, 7 February 1988
Mansfield, Nottinghamshire

Danny was doing everything he could to soothe his infant daughter. He was a light sleeper at the best of times, so when he heard Hayley start to cry, he was instantly awake.

He knew that Sue had been awake an hour or so earlier to give their daughter her feed, so he had taken his turn to go and check on her in the nursery.

Nothing he was trying was working.

It felt like his daughter was heavy in his arms, as though she were asleep. Her small head flopped forward onto his bare chest again, as though she were about to drop back to sleep.

No sooner had she done that than she would start crying again. This was a strange cry. One that he hadn't heard before. It was high-pitched and came out in gasps. He could hear that his daughter's breathing sounded unusually fast. She was almost panting.

He had already checked to see if she needed changing, but her nappy was clean.

He held her tiny hand as he tried to pacify her, his big hand completely enveloping her tiny one. Her hand felt ice cold. He checked her other hand; it was the same. He felt for her feet, and even through the babygrow, they both felt freezing cold. The room was warm, so there was no reason why her hands and feet should be so cold. Just as he was about to wake his wife, the door to the nursery opened, and a sleepy-looking Sue walked in.

Danny said, 'I can't soothe her tonight, sweetheart. She seems really listless, and her hands and feet are freezing.'

Just then the high-pitched crying started again. Sue took Hayley from Danny's arms and began rocking her gently; once again the baby's small head flopped forward, against her mother's chest.

Sue felt her daughter's hands and said, 'How long has she been making that noise as she cries?'

'It was that cry that woke me up; it sounds so different. That was about fifteen minutes ago. Why is it so high-pitched?'

Sue didn't reply. She just placed her ear against her daughter's chest, listening to her breathing. The baby's breaths came in sharp shallow bursts and were very fast.

She turned to Danny. 'Have you checked her?'

'What do you mean?'

'Have you checked her body for a rash?'

'When I got her out of the cot, I checked to see if she needed changing. I didn't see any rash. Why?'

Sue began frantically removing the babygrow and nappy being worn by her daughter. She quickly checked her naked daughter for any signs of mottling or a rash on her skin. There were none.

Sue said, 'We need to take her to the hospital now. I think she may have meningitis.'

A shocked Danny said, 'But there's no rash. It can't be that.'

'The rash comes much later, and it can be too late by then. We need to get her to the hospital now.'

Danny nodded, raced back into the bedroom and quickly got dressed. He took Hayley in his arms as Sue threw some clothes on.

As they walked downstairs with their daughter, Danny said, 'I'll get the car. It will be quicker if we take her ourselves rather than wait for an ambulance.'

Less than a minute later, Danny roared off the driveway. In the back of the car, he could hear Sue trying to soothe Hayley as once again the high-pitched crying started.

He stared straight ahead, unblinking. He gunned the powerful engine, racing through the deserted streets. He could see red traffic lights ahead at the junction. He slowed the car just enough for him to get the view into the junction before pressing his foot down hard on the accelerator. The car sped through the red lights. He was totally focussed. All he wanted to do was get his daughter to the hospital.

After a seven-minute high-speed drive that seemed as though it had taken half an hour, Danny braked hard and brought the car skidding to a halt directly outside the doors of the hospital. As the car came to a juddering halt, Sue had the back door open and was already getting out of the car with Hayley in her arms. She ran straight into the reception area and shouted, 'We need a doctor!'

The Casualty Department was quiet; the earlier surge of drunken louts had been and gone. A nurse she recognised came rushing over to them both and said, 'Dr Flint, what's wrong?'

Sue took a breath and said, 'It's my daughter, she's twelve months old, and I think she may have developed early-onset meningitis. I need the paediatric consultant to be paged immediately. Time is of the essence here.'

'Take a seat. I'll get straight on it.'

Danny and Sue both felt totally helpless. All they could do now was wait for the experts and pray that if it were the dreaded illness, they had spotted the symptoms early enough.

Danny totally trusted that his wife had made the right call. He silently thanked God that she was a medical professional and that she had recognised the signs so quickly.

He looked at his beautiful wife. Her face was drawn and pale. It was obvious from her expression that she was acutely aware of the enormity and seriousness of the situation.

He put his arm around her shoulders and said, 'Try not to worry, sweetheart. We're in the right place. Hayley's going to be okay.'

Sue didn't reply. She just stared down at Hayley's small face and continued to rock her back and forth ever so slightly, hushing her gently.

Danny said, 'I need to move the car from the emergency bay. I'll only be gone for a second.'

He ran outside and jumped in his car. He hastily abandoned it again, this time in the car park, and sprinted back to the Casualty Department. As he ran, he took deep breaths, filling his lungs with the frigid night air, trying to clear his head.

His brain couldn't yet process what he would do if anything happened to his precious child.

24

10.30am, 7 February 1988
King's Mill Hospital, Mansfield, Nottinghamshire

Danny had walked from the ward, through the long corridors back to the main entrance. There were three payphones in a row near the main doors. He had a pocketful of loose change that he'd obtained from the small shop near the entrance.

He stepped into the first booth and lifted the receiver, quickly dialling a number from memory. As the call was connected, Danny fed coins into the slot for the payphone.

The operator on the switchboard at police headquarters answered the call: 'Good morning, Nottinghamshire Police.'

Danny said, 'It's Detective Chief Inspector Flint. Can you put me through to Detective Chief Superintendent Potter, please?'

'Just a moment, sir.'

There was a pause and a loud click on the line.

Then a lisping voice said, 'Chief Superintendent Potter.'

'Sir, it's Danny Flint.'

Not expecting a call from the MCIU, Potter said, 'Is there a problem, Chief Inspector?'

'I had to take my baby daughter to the hospital last night. The paediatric consultant thinks she may have meningitis.'

As he said the actual name of the illness, Danny's voice faltered. He paused and swallowed hard.

Potter filled the gap: 'I'm very sorry to hear that, Danny. You'll need to take some time off, to be with your wife and daughter.'

Regaining his composure, Danny said, 'Thank you. The next forty-eight hours are going to be critical. The consultant assures me that even if the tests he's running confirm it's meningitis, he's satisfied that they've caught it early enough for it not to be a major issue. He's hopeful that Hayley will make a full recovery, and there shouldn't be further complications. Obviously, that's a best-case scenario, and it's still too early to say for definite one way or the other.'

'I understand that, but it all sounds quite positive. Take seven days off as of now, and if you need any more time after that, just let me know. Do you want me to contact your office and let your staff know what's happening?'

'Thanks, sir. I'll contact the office myself and speak to Detective Inspector Buxton. If he's going to temporarily oversee the Unit, I'll need to brief him properly.'

'As you wish, Danny. Take as much time as you need, and keep me posted how your daughter's doing. Take care.'

'Thank you and will do.'

Danny terminated the call and immediately dialled a second number. Once again, he fed coins into the payphone as the call was connected.

This time, Fran Jefferies answered the call. 'MCIU. How can I help you?'

Danny took a deep breath and said, 'Hello, Fran. Is Rob Buxton in the office yet?'

Recognising her boss's voice, Fran said cheerily, 'Good morning, sir. Yes, he's at his desk.'

'Can you get him and tell him to take this call, please.'

'Just a minute.'

There was a brief pause, and then Rob said, 'Morning, Danny. Where are you?'

'I'm at the hospital. We had to rush Hayley in last night. She's very sick; the doctor thinks it might be meningitis.'

'Bloody hell. Are you and Sue okay?'

'We're both scared to death, mate. It's a bloody nightmare, seeing your kid like that.'

'Is there anything I can do?'

'I've just spoken to Potter, and he's authorised me to take a week off while Hayley is being treated at the hospital. I need you to take charge of the Unit.'

'No problem. Take all the time you need. Don't worry about this place; it will be fine. You need to concentrate on being there for Sue and Hayley. Do you need anything at the hospital?'

'We're both going to be staying here for the duration, so I could do with a few things fetching from home. Can I see you near the main doors at eleven thirty? If I give you my house key, can you fetch some stuff from home for me?'

'No problem. There's nothing pressing here this morning. I'll see you there at eleven thirty. When will you know what's happening?'

'We'll find out later this morning if it's definitely meningitis or not.'

'Have the doctors given you any idea?'

'The consultant paediatrician who's treating Hayley seems to think it's almost certainly meningitis. But thanks to Sue recognising the early symptoms, if it is confirmed, it should be treatable with antibiotics. The next forty-eight hours are going to be critical.'

'At least that sounds positive, mate. I'll see you later this morning at the main entrance. Please give my love to Sue, and try not to worry. Kids are very resilient. I'm sure little Hayley will be fine.'

Danny could feel tears starting to sting his eyes as he thought of his tiny daughter now battling for her life.

He could barely speak as he said, 'I've got to get back up to the ward. I'll see you in an hour. Thanks, Rob.'

He put the telephone down and wiped his eyes with his fingers. He took a couple of deep breaths and began the long walk along the corridors, back to the wards.

25

5.30pm, 7 February 1988
MCIU Offices, Mansfield Police Station

Rob had finished the evening debrief. Nothing had been forthcoming. There were no new breakthroughs; the enquiry was stalling badly. At the end of the debrief, he said, 'Thanks, everyone. Finish up what you've got to do and be back here tomorrow morning at eight o clock.'

He made eye contact with Tina and said, 'Tina, can you ask Andy and Lynn to come and join us in Danny's office? I need to talk to you all before you go home.'

'Is it about Danny?'

Rob nodded. 'Let's do this in his office, not out here.'

After a few minutes, the four MCIU supervisors were all in Danny's office. Rob said, 'You've no doubt all noticed Danny hasn't been around today. Unfortunately, his daughter is seriously ill. She's in hospital with confirmed meningitis.'

There was a gasp from Tina. 'Oh no, the poor mite. Is she going to be okay?'

'I went to see Sue and Danny at the hospital earlier, just after the diagnosis had been confirmed. Hayley is being treated with antibiotics, and the paediatrician is hopeful she'll make a full recovery. It's a little too early to say for definite, as they will need to assess how she responds to the treatment and what progress she makes over the next forty-eight hours. Currently, all the signs are promising.'

Lynn Harris said, 'Thank God for that.'

Andy said, 'Is there anything any of us can do?'

Rob sat down in Danny's chair. 'The best thing we can all do is to ensure this office is run properly in Danny's absence. He asked me to take charge, but that's not how we do things here, is it? We work better as a team. Always have and always will.'

Tina nodded.

Rob continued, 'Danny's going to be off work for at least the next seven days, possibly longer, depending on how Hayley responds to treatment. I'd like to go over everything we've done so far in the Bauer enquiry. You all know it's grinding slowly to a halt. I can't help thinking there's got to be something we've missed.'

Andy said, 'I'm okay for time this evening, but if we're going to brainstorm this thing through, I'm getting a coffee before we start. Does anybody else want one?'

The gathered detectives all got a hot drink and then started to go over every enquiry that had been completed so far. They pored over witness statements and intelligence reports.

After two hours, they had worked through everything and come up with very little. Lynn was still hopeful that a breakthrough might be achieved from the further enquiries she was doing with Jag at Aslockton. Rob agreed and suggested extending those enquiries to other villages near to the prison at Whatton, to try to establish if there had been any other protest meetings held in the area.

Having gone through everything, the others had left, leaving Rob alone in the now-deserted MCIU office. Deep down, he knew there was only one way that fresh impetus would be injected into the Bauer enquiry. It was the one thing no seasoned detective ever allowed themselves to consider.

Rob's vast experience had shown him that sometimes an unsolved murder needed another murder to produce the evidence that would solve both crimes.

It was the unspoken scenario.

26

7.30am, 9 February 1988
Radford Road Police Station, Nottingham

Simon Pettigrew had been pacing the streets of Hyson Green since three o'clock that morning. His mind was in torment. The voices inside his head were giving him conflicting messages. Some were rejoicing in his actions, while others were scolding and accusatory. He was now sitting in a bus shelter, staring out at the deserted streets, slowly banging his head against the Perspex shelter in a slow rhythmic fashion. Trying to get the voices to stop.

Eventually, the back of his head became sore, and the banging slowed to a stop.

The thirty-four-year-old unemployed chef had a huge decision to make. He painfully levered his long, skinny frame off the bus shelter bench and stretched. It was time.

He walked along Radford Road towards the building he knew would give him relief from his torment.

Without pausing, he walked up the three stone steps and opened the door. He pressed the bell in reception, keeping his finger down on the button so the annoying buzzing sound was constant.

A gruff voice from within the main office shouted, 'Alright, alright! I've heard you; you can take your finger off the bloody bell.'

A door opened, and a police officer in uniform, with an angry expression on his face, stood behind the counter, appraising the person who had disturbed his report-writing time.

Simon Pettigrew knew he looked a mess. The black clothes he wore were dirty and dishevelled. His hands were covered in grime and stained with something unmentionable.

He looked directly into the eyes of the angry policeman and said, 'I'm here to hand myself in. I killed Manfred Bauer.'

27

9.00am, 9 February 1988
Radford Road Police Station, Nottingham

Rob Buxton and Glen Lorimar had been at the new police station on Radford Road for the last thirty minutes.

As soon as Rob had received the call from the control room about the man confessing to the murder of Bauer, he had contacted Glen, and the two of them had driven, at speed, to the city. The two detectives had made their way straight to the custody area of the police station to have a look at the suspect.

Simon Pettigrew was now sitting in one of the holding cells, wearing a forensic suit.

The two detectives then sought out the custody sergeant and PC Hibbert, the officer who had taken the first report from the suspect.

Rob said, 'What time was he arrested?'

PC Hibbert said, 'I arrested him on suspicion of murder at seven thirty. I've made a note in my notebook of the significant statement he made when he first walked in.'

'That's good. What did he say, exactly?'

'He said, "I'm here to hand myself in. I killed Manfred Bauer."'

Glen said, 'Has he signed your notebook?'

'No, he refused, but the request was made for him to sign my notebook in front of the custody sergeant. It now forms part of his custody record.'

'Good. It's not ideal, but it's often the case that, having made their confession, they don't want to subsequently sign anything. Has he signed for any of his rights?'

The custody sergeant said, 'The only signature I got from him was one declining legal advice. He doesn't want a solicitor informing. Apart from that, he hasn't signed a thing. I'm of the opinion that he needs to be assessed by a police surgeon before you interview him. There are definitely some mental health issues going on with this one.'

Rob said, 'That's your call, Sergeant. We're in no hurry. If that's what you think, then let's get a police surgeon travelling as soon as possible.'

'Already done, boss. I don't know if you noticed when you had a look at him in the holding cell, but Pettigrew has some strange staining on his hands that needs swabbing. I've put him in a dry cell so that if it is blood, he can't go stuffing his hands down the bog to wash it off.'

'I had noticed it; I suppose it could be caked-on blood that's been there a few days. A swab will soon confirm it. Has he said anything else since he was detained?'

'Not a word. He's just sitting in the holding cell, rocking back and forth. I've already had to go into his cell twice to tell him to stop banging his head on the wall.'

Rob then asked PC Hibbert, 'Have you done a PNC check on Pettigrew?'

'Yes, sir. Simon Pettigrew is recorded. He has previous convictions for assault and burglary.'

'Has he done any time?'

'Quite a bit. He was recently released from HMP Lincoln after serving four years for a dwelling house burglary, here in the city.'

Rob turned to Glen and said, 'Call Fran at the office and ask her to cross-reference Simon Pettigrew's prison record with Manfred Bauer's. It will be interesting to see if they had any contact while they were both in prison. I also want full antecedents for every burglary he's ever been convicted of. I want to establish if he's a climber or not.'

Glen walked behind the custody counter and picked up a phone.

Rob said, 'What's happened to Pettigrew's clothes?'

PC Hibbert said, 'I've seized them and bagged them all up separately. All the exhibit labels have been completed, and the clothes are now in the property store.'

'Good work. I'll need to submit those for forensic testing as soon as possible.'

He turned to the custody sergeant and said, 'We'll go and wait upstairs in the CID office. Can you contact me as soon as the police surgeon gets here?'

'Will do.'

Glen put the telephone down and said to Rob, 'Fran's looking at that. I've asked her to ring us in the CID office as soon as she gets any information.'

Rob nodded. 'Looks like we've got a bit of waiting to do upstairs.'

'I reckon it's bacon sandwich time, boss.'

'Sounds good to me, especially if you're buying.'

28

11.30am, 9 February 1988
Radford Road Police Station, Nottingham

Rob Buxton was becoming impatient.
Where is that bloody police surgeon?
He and Glen had utilised the time spent waiting to research the man now in custody on suspicion of murdering Manfred Bauer. Alarm bells were now starting to sound for the experienced detective inspector. What had at first seemed a promising development now looked anything but.

Two detectives from the MCIU had been despatched to search the bedsit in Carrington currently occupied by Pettigrew. Nothing incriminating had been found.

Telephone calls to his probation officer revealed that although Pettigrew had some mental health problems, he was under medication and had last been assessed two weeks ago by a community mental health team. They had found no reason why he should be detained under the mental health provisions. Unless something had drastically changed, he should be fit to interview.

Enquiries carried out by Fran had established that Simon Pettigrew had never been in contact with Manfred Bauer when they were both serving prisoners at HMP Lincoln. By the time Pettigrew had been sent to the prison, Bauer was already on the segregation unit for his own protection.

Although he had a string of convictions for burglary, all the offences he'd committed were similar. He was a skilled sneak-in burglar, targeting old-age pensioners. The reason for the lengthy custodial sentence last time was because he had committed a series of over twenty such offences. The two convictions he had for assault were both for actual bodily harm, committed when he was still a juvenile.

Rob and Glen were both aware that many similar confessions proved to be false. They were often just a cry for help from people who were ill or mentally unstable.

The telephone on the desk in front of him began ringing. Rob snatched it off the cradle and said, 'Detective Inspector Buxton.'

'It's the custody sergeant, sir. The police surgeon has just arrived. She apologises for the delay. Apparently, she's been stuck in traffic coming through the city.'

'Never mind; she's here now. Is she with Pettigrew yet?'

'Not yet. I thought you might want a word first.'

'Good man. I'm on my way.'

He replaced the telephone and said, 'Grab your jacket, Glen. The doc's here. Let's have a quick word with her before she assesses Pettigrew. I want to inform her that we may not have to interview him for very long to establish if he's the genuine article or not.'

29

12.10pm, 9 February 1988
Radford Road Police Station, Nottingham

Dr Sarah Tudor emerged from the examination suite, followed by Pettigrew and an escorting police officer.

The custody sergeant completed the necessary paperwork, updating the prisoner's custody record, and then said, 'Well, Doctor, what's the verdict? Is he fit for interview?'

'Yes, he is. He's obviously very troubled and does have issues, but his cognitive responses are fine. He's lucid and willing to cooperate with your enquiry.'

Rob said, 'I understand from his probation officer that he should be on some antipsychotic medication. Has he been taking it?'

'He did tell me about the medication he's on. He missed a couple of days last week and some more this week, which probably accounts for his strange behaviour today. He assures me that he has his medication with him and that he will continue to take it.'

The custody sergeant said, 'He does have tablets in his property. Do I need to consider calling the mental health assessment team?'

'I really don't think that's necessary. Go ahead with your interview. If it's going to be as easy to establish if he's telling the truth as you think it will be, I really don't see him coming to any harm.'

Rob said, 'Thanks.'

He turned to the custody sergeant and said, 'Can you book Pettigrew out to interview straightaway, please?'

The two detectives escorted Pettigrew to one of the interview rooms.

With the recording machine going, Glen introduced the persons in the room, and Pettigrew was again asked if he would like a solicitor present for his interview. He declined with a shake of his head. The experienced detective said, 'The tape can't show you shaking your head, Simon. Can you say verbally if you would like a solicitor present or not?'

'I don't need one. I just need to tell you what I've done.'

Glen cautioned Pettigrew, then said, 'Okay, Simon. We're listening. Exactly what is that you've done?'

'I've killed someone.'

'That's a very serious thing to admit. Who is it you've killed?'

'Manfred Bauer.'

'Who's Manfred Bauer?'

'That man who was killed in Sherwood.'

'Whereabouts in Sherwood?'

'Osborne Grove.'

'I see. And where on Osborne Grove did Bauer live?'

There was a brief pause as Pettigrew tried to understand the question. Then he blurted out, 'He had a flat in a big house. I don't remember the house number.'

'How do you know Bauer?'

'I'd rather not say.'

'Why not?'

There was silence, and Pettigrew looked away, disengaging from the detective. Glen decided not to push it. He didn't want to close Pettigrew down and stop him talking, so he deftly changed direction and said quietly, 'Tell me how you did it, Simon.'

'Did what?'

'How did you kill Bauer?'

'I smashed his head in.'

The cause of Bauer's death had been given as head injuries in all the local papers. It was common knowledge.

Glen said, 'Didn't it bother you, hitting Bauer in the face that many times?'

'No. He had it coming.'

'I've been to a lot of crime scenes, Simon. I've got to say this was one of the worst. How many times did you have to punch him to cause all those injuries to his face?'

'I lost count. This is his blood on my hands. The doctor has already wiped some of it off, but you can still see it. Look.'

He held out his hands for the detective to examine. Glen turned Pettigrew's hands over a few times and said, 'Yeah. I can see it. So you punched him in the face. Did you kick him as well?'

'I can't remember.'

'Where was he when you punched him the first time?'

'In his flat.'

'How come you were in his flat?'

'He asked me in for a drink.'

'Then what happened?'

'We started arguing, and I beat him up.'

'Well, you didn't just beat him up. You said you killed him. How did you know he was dead?'

'I checked his neck when he was on the floor. There was no pulse. He was dead alright.'

'What floor was he on?'

'The floor of the living room.'

'So you punched him in the face and beat him to death in the living room of his flat?'

'Yeah.'

'Then what did you do?'

'I walked out and left him there.'

'Weren't you worried that we'd find your fingerprints in the flat?'

'No.'

'Why not?'

'I was wearing gloves.'

'So how did you get all that blood on your hands if you were wearing gloves?'

The room was silent. It remained silent for a long time. Pettigrew just stared straight ahead, unblinking. Eventually, tears began to roll down his cheeks.

After a five-minute silence, Rob said gently, 'Why are you doing this, Simon?'

'What?'

'Why are you admitting to a crime, a very serious crime, that you haven't done?'

'What do you mean, that I haven't done?'

'I know for a fact that you haven't killed Manfred Bauer, Simon.'

'I could have, though.'

'How could you?'

'I get these urges to do something horrible. I hear voices

in my head, and sometimes they tell me to do terrible things.'

'But you didn't do *this* terrible thing, Simon. You didn't kill Manfred Bauer, did you?'

He slowly shook his head.

Rob said, 'Can you answer my question verbally?'

'No. I didn't kill him.'

'Can you tell me why you've come in here today and made all this up?'

'Because nobody's listening to me. I keep telling my probation officer that I need help. The tablets I'm on are making things worse, not better.'

'Well, before you leave here today, I'll arrange for the emergency mental health team to come to the police station and reassess you. Is that okay, Simon?'

He nodded and said, 'Would you? I just need some help.'

Rob glanced over at Glen, who switched off the tapes.

Rob said, 'Come on, Simon. Let's get you back to your cell. I'll get you a cup of tea and make the arrangements for you to be assessed.'

Fifteen minutes later the two detectives were back upstairs in the CID office.

Glen said, 'I've just spoken to the police surgeon. She's done a quick field test on the swabs taken from Pettigrew's hands. Whatever the staining is, it isn't human blood.'

'That's good. That was the only thing concerning me.'

'What a waste of a morning, boss.'

'I've got to say it was a lot easier to knock out than I thought it was going to be.'

'That's true. Thank God we never give all the details to the press. We'd be inundated with these nutters.'

'Don't be too hard on him, Glen. He's obviously got problems that need addressing. I wonder what the mental health team's verdict will be today.'

'I've no idea. It's a sobering thought that they could say he's fine and leave him to his own devices.'

'Let's get back to the office. I'll contact the custody suite later to find out what's happened to Pettigrew. Thankfully, he's not our problem anymore.'

30

8.00pm, 11 February 1988
Rainworth, Nottingham

Rob Buxton had just settled down for a relaxing evening in front of the television. He was sipping a cold beer and waiting for the film to start. It had been another busy, but unrewarding, day at work. He had taken the decision to deploy more staff to the area around the village of Aslockton in the hope of finding more witnesses to the meeting held by the shadowy Guardians of Innocence group.

Despite the best efforts of teams of dedicated detectives, they hadn't found a single witness.

He was about to take another sip of cold beer when the strident ringing of the telephone in the hallway interrupted his thoughts.

To prevent his wife racing from the kitchen to the hallway, he shouted, 'I'll get it!'

He knew that at this time of night, it was probably going to be work.

He picked up the receiver and said, 'Rob Buxton.'

'Rob, it's me, Danny.'

Rob's blood ran cold. He steeled himself to ask the question he was dreading getting the answer to.

He said quietly, 'How's Hayley?'

'That's why I'm calling so late. The doctors have just been in to see me and Sue. It's good news, mate; they've taken my baby girl off the critical list. She's not out of the woods yet, but things are moving in the right direction. It could still be a while before we can take her home. Until they've beaten the underlying infection, the doctor has to be concerned about her relapsing.'

Rob felt a huge wave of relief wash over him, but was still concerned. He paused for a moment, searching for the right response. Finally, he said, 'That's some good news, then. I'm so pleased for you both. How's Sue doing?'

'It's been extra tough on her. She couldn't feed Hayley; she was just too poorly and weak to latch onto the breast. It was so distressing for Sue; she told me she felt useless. When her daughter needed her the most, she couldn't even do the basics for her.'

'How's the little one been feeding, then?'

'The nurses have all been fantastic. They put in a nasogastric tube so they could feed her through that. It's been awful to see her lying there with all these tubes and lines stuck in her.'

Rob heard the break in Danny's voice as emotion got the better of him.

He said, 'Are you okay?'

'I am now, mate. This has really put things into perspective, though. We take so much for granted, never really understanding that everything could be snatched away in an instant.'

'Where are you now?'

'I'm just leaving the hospital. I need to go home and get a shower and some sleep. I haven't slept for about thirty-six hours. Sue's exhausted too, but she has managed to sleep a little at the hospital.'

'Don't try to drive in that state, Danny. I'm on my way. I can pick you up and take you home. Then you can call me in the morning when you're ready, and I'll take you back to the hospital.'

There was a real sense of relief in Danny's voice as he said, 'I'm not going to argue, mate. I can barely keep my eyes open.'

'I'll be there in ten to fifteen minutes. Just wait in the car park. I'm on my way.'

Rob put the phone down, suddenly thankful that he had only just started drinking his beer. He walked through to the kitchen and hugged his wife. 'That was Danny on the phone. His little one's out of danger. I'm going to pick him up from the hospital and drive him home. He sounds shattered.'

His wife squeezed him and said, 'Okay, sweetheart. Drive carefully and pass on all my love to Danny and Sue.'

Rob grabbed his jacket and his car keys and said, 'Will do. Won't be long.'

31

8.00am, 12 February 1988
King's Mill Hospital, Mansfield, Nottinghamshire

As Rob brought his car to a stop in the car park at King's Mill Hospital, he looked across at Danny in the passenger seat. He looked so different from the man he had picked up late last night from the same spot.

He had obviously slept well and had a shave and a shower. He looked back to normal. Like the Danny he knew from work, confident and in control. He was far removed from the dishevelled, scruffy man he had been last night.

Rob said, 'Are you okay?'

'Yeah. Thanks for picking me up last night. I would probably have wrapped my car around a lamppost if I'd tried to drive.'

'You did look dead on your feet.'

'I felt it. I don't think I've ever been so exhausted in my life.'

'I never asked last night because you looked so shattered, but what have the doctors said about Hayley?'

'What do you mean?'

'When can you bring her home? Is she going to be okay? Will she make a full recovery?'

'It's early days. What they said last night was that she has responded brilliantly well to the intravenous antibiotics so far. They were confident that she should be taken off the critical list. They expect her to improve gradually and to make a full recovery. They just don't know the speed of that recovery. It could take days or weeks for her to be well enough for us to bring her home.'

'Well, let's hope it's sooner rather than later.'

'They also told me privately that if Sue hadn't recognised the symptoms so quickly, it would have been a very different story. Meningitis is a killer; we've been so lucky.'

'She's bloody brilliant, that wife of yours.'

For the first time in three days, Danny laughed. 'You won't get an argument from me there, mate.'

'I'm just pleased it sounds like there won't be any long-term health issues for the little one. I know what that illness can do sometimes.'

'The doctors said that once she recovers fully, the only thing they will need to check later is her hearing. Apparently, it can cause deafness in babies of Hayley's age, so we'll have to wait for those tests to be done later. Fingers crossed she keeps responding well to the treatment, and that her hearing will be okay. Truth be told, Rob; I just want to get them both home.'

'I don't blame you. Now get inside and see how they're both doing. I'll talk to you later.'

'Thanks, Rob. I really appreciate you picking me up last night. I haven't asked you: is there any news from work?'

'Nothing that you need to concern yourself about. Everything's under control. Now go and be with your family.'

Danny got out of the car and said, 'Cheers. All being well, I'll be back in the office in a couple of days' time.'

'There's no rush, Danny.'

32

2.00am, 15 February 1988
Redgate Farm, Carlton in Lindrick, Nottinghamshire

The black-clad figure made their way through the bare muddy fields towards the remote farmhouse. It was the same route that had been used on every other occasion observations had been kept on the target, Stewart Tighe.

This time, the weight of the daysack was a constant reminder that tonight's mission would be different. Tonight, Stewart Tighe would pay in full for his crimes.

Approaching the farmhouse, the shadowy figure was disappointed to see the lounge light was still on. The back door was also wide open. Pausing at the stone wall that bordered the farmyard, the stalker squatted down and watched the back door. After five minutes, there was movement. The target emerged from the farmhouse, clutching an almost-empty bottle of whiskey in one hand and a cigarette in the other.

The tall, blonde man took a long swig of the fiery liquid. He then threw the empty bottle on the ground. It bounced and didn't smash. The skinny Tighe took a deep drag of the cigarette before coughing loudly.

Disturbed by the drunken man's cough, the farm dogs that were kept in the adjacent barn immediately began barking loudly.

Tighe slurred his words as he shouted, 'Shut the fuck up!'

The dogs continued to bark furiously.

He flicked the cigarette onto the floor and ground it out with the heel of his untied boots. He turned and staggered back inside the farmhouse, pulling the door behind him. He closed it, but didn't lock it.

The person who had been hiding by the wall now silently approached the lounge window and, from the dark shadows, watched as Tighe kicked off his boots and lay down on the settee. The television was already off. Tighe was so pitifully drunk he had left the back door to the farmhouse insecure.

The figure watching from the shadows allowed a cruel smile to form on their lips. This was going to be a simple task.

Slipping off the daysack, the stalker removed a package wrapped in blood-soaked newspaper and moved stealthily towards the barn and the now-agitated dogs. They would need to be silenced before the mission could continue.

Five minutes later, with the dogs now quiet, the stalker returned to the back door of the farmhouse. With a gentle shove, the heavy wooden door opened. Entering the farmhouse for the first time felt good. It was almost time for Tighe to pay in full for his crimes. From deep inside the farmhouse, the sound of Tighe snoring identified exactly where the target was.

The figure in black squatted down and once again opened

the daysack, removing a heavy claw hammer. Gripping the weapon tightly in a gloved hand, the stalker moved silently through the house. Creeping closer and closer until they were standing immediately behind the sleeping drunk.

Tighe was half lying down and half sitting up in what was obviously a drink-induced stupor.

There was no hesitation.

The figure raised the hammer in a high arc and brought the cold steel smashing down onto the mop of unruly blonde hair. The force of the first blow caused the hammer to almost wedge beneath the bone of the skull. The figure used both hands to wrestle the heavy tool from the man's head before smashing down two further blows on either side of the first. The three massive impacts on Tighe's head had effectively shattered the man's skull. The blonde hair was rapidly turning dark as thick, crimson-coloured blood oozed from the three wounds.

Taking a step back, the killer surveyed the damage, then placed the bloodstained claw hammer back inside the nylon daysack and removed a slim black object. The blood-soaked gloves left smears of Tighe's blood all over the object as it was carefully placed on top of his shattered skull.

With the mission completed, the killer immediately left the farmhouse and began the long walk back across the barren fields.

Back inside the building, a blood-soaked bubbly froth was escaping from Stewart Tighe's mouth. He opened his eyes and blinked once before slipping into an unconscious state from which he would never wake.

He was slowly dying on the settee in the lounge of his parents' farmhouse.

33

6.00am, 15 February 1988
Redgate Farm, Carlton in Lindrick, Nottinghamshire

A farmer all his working life, Eric Tighe was used to rising early. Even though he was now too old and infirm to work physically around the farm, he still directed all the activities undertaken by the labourers who worked for him, on a daily basis. Even if he'd wanted to, there was no way he could break the habits of a lifetime. It had been four thirty that morning when he had got out of bed and got dressed.

His wife, Mavis, slept next door in the spare room. They hadn't shared a bed for fifteen years, after his wife had complained about his loud snoring once too often.

As was his habit, he had gone downstairs to the kitchen and made himself a mug of very sweet tea to sip as he cooked sausages for his breakfast.

Every day started the same way for Eric Tighe. Sweet tea and fried pork sausages.

He finished his second mug of tea and walked through the farmhouse. He was surprised to see the back door wide open.

He walked to the open door and immediately saw the empty whiskey bottle on the floor and the discarded cigarette butt.

He cursed under his breath.

That useless, pervert son of his had been up all night drinking again. He wasn't going to stand for it any longer. He resolved to call his son's probation officer later that morning and tell him that the boy wasn't welcome to stay at the farm any longer. He was becoming a dangerous liability.

He knew his wife would also be happy to see her son leave the family home. She couldn't bring herself to forgive him for what he had done to those poor young boys.

The sooner he left, the better everyone would be.

He bent down and picked up the discarded Glenfiddich bottle. Still feeling enraged, he walked back inside the house. He knew his useless son would have passed out on the settee in the living room again. This morning, it was going to stop. He would wake him up and tell him to start making some arrangements to leave. He was in the twilight of his life; he didn't have to put up with any of this nonsense.

He banged the empty whisky bottle down hard on the sideboard, near the lounge door, and said loudly, 'Come on, you drunken piece of shit! Stir yourself!'

There was no movement from across the lounge. It was a dark unwelcoming room, with very little natural light. His son remained unmoving. He was either fast asleep or ignoring his father's voice.

Getting angrier by the second, Eric Tighe stomped across the room towards his son.

When he was just a few feet away from the settee, he stopped suddenly. His eyesight wasn't the best, but he had been around death and injury before. It was commonplace on a farm.

He could see that his only son was badly injured, probably dead.

He moved closer and could now clearly see the huge injuries to his head. His son's once blonde hair was now black, matted with dark, dried blood. His shoulders and the settee were also soaked in his blood.

Already knowing the outcome, the old farmer thrust his two middle fingers into his son's neck, feeling for a pulse from the carotid artery. There was nothing; the skin felt cold and clammy.

It merely confirmed what he had already known.

He looked down at the blood on his fingers, but felt no sense of loss. The love he had once felt for his only son had disappeared years ago. He now saw him as an embarrassing inconvenience. Just because Stewart was now dead, those feelings hadn't changed.

He walked back out of the room and into the hallway.

He picked up the handset of the dirty, cream-coloured telephone and dialled three nines.

When the operator asked which of the emergency services he required, Eric Tighe replied, 'Police, please. Somebody has killed my son, Stewart.'

34

8.00am, 15 February 1988
Redgate Farm, Carlton in Lindrick, Nottinghamshire

As the CID car came to a stop in the farmyard at Redgate Farm, Rob turned to Danny and said, 'Well, you certainly picked a good day to come back to work.'

'That's just what I was thinking. But Hayley's so much better now, and Sue can deal with anything medically she may need far better than I can. I couldn't justify staying off any longer.'

'I'm just glad she's still making progress, boss.'

'It's a nightmare. We've still got no date to get her home yet. The doctors are erring on the side of caution, I suppose. Even when we do get her home, she will need to have the hearing tests done later, but she seems fine.'

'It must still be a huge worry, boss.'

'I'm not going to lie, Rob. Until we get her home, there's no way I'll be able to relax.'

'Are you sure you should be back at work?'

'I'm sure. I need something to take my mind off what's happening.'

The two detectives got out of the car and walked towards a shivering uniformed constable, who was standing outside the back door with a clipboard. He was stamping his feet, trying to keep the cold frost at bay. Seamus Carter's Volvo was already parked in the yard next to the Scenes of Crime van and two other CID cars.

Their warm breath formed large white clouds in the frigid air as they both donned forensic suits and overshoes. Danny said, 'The circus got out here fast.'

Rob nodded. 'The first call came in just after six o'clock. I stayed in the office, waiting for you to arrive, while Tina and Rachel hotfooted it up here.'

'You should have come straight up here as well.'

'Nah, I knew you'd be in before seven.'

'Old habits, mate.'

The two senior detectives signed into the crime scene. Danny said to the young officer, 'Don't freeze to death out here. Step inside the back door and get warm. It's way too cold to stand out here for hours.'

'Thanks, sir.'

Danny and Rob then walked into the farmhouse. DC Rachel Moore was standing just inside the back door, talking to a Scenes of Crime photographer.

Danny said, 'Morning, Rachel. What have we got?'

'It looks identical to the Manfred Bauer scene.'

'What?'

'Massive head injuries and a Mars bar left on top of those injuries. Looks the same to me.'

'Bloody hell. This is miles away from Nottingham. What's

the connection to Bauer?'

'I don't know. I couldn't believe what I was seeing when I first arrived.'

'Where's the deceased?'

'This way.'

Rachel led the two detectives through the farmhouse and into the living room. Already in the room were the Home Office pathologist Seamus Carter, Detective Inspector Tina Cartwright, and Scenes of Crime team leader, Tim Donnelly.

Danny stepped forward to get a closer look at the body on the settee. The massive head injuries were instantly apparent, as was the chocolate bar.

Seamus Carter said, 'Good morning, Danny. How's your wee girl?'

'On the mend, thanks. This all looks scarily familiar.'

'Doesn't it just. I've made a rudimentary examination of the skull, and from what I can see, it looks like three distinct hammer blows again. It's difficult to be more precise because of the matted hair and that chocolate bar, but I think the post-mortem will confirm my suspicions.'

Danny became suddenly annoyed at the absurd sight of the Mars bar perching precariously on top of the dead man's shattered skull. He turned to Tim Donnelly and said sharply, 'Have you got all the photographs you need?'

Hearing the tone in Danny's voice, Tim replied, 'Yes, sir.'

'In that case, can you remove that bloody chocolate bar and get it bagged up.'

Tim moved straight in and lifted the candy bar from the shattered skull before placing it carefully into an exhibits bag.

Danny turned to the pathologist and said, 'Have you got somewhere in mind to carry out the post-mortem?'

'The mortuary at Bassetlaw Hospital in Worksop is probably the closest.'

'What time?'

The big pathologist glanced at his watch. 'Shall we say eleven thirty?'

'That's fine. Do you have an estimated time of death?'

'Sometime during the early hours of this morning is my best guess.'

Tina Cartwright said, 'The parents last saw him at nine thirty last night before they went to bed. He was in here then, watching the television.'

'Where are the parents?'

'In the kitchen, on the other side of the house.'

'And who's the deceased?'

Tina flicked open her notebook and said, 'Stewart Tighe. Parents are Eric and Mavis Tighe. They own the farm.'

Danny was thoughtful for a minute, then said, 'Why does the name Stewart Tighe ring a bell?'

Tina said, 'Probably because, like Manfred Bauer, Stewart Tighe was involved in a high-profile sex abuse scandal.'

'That's it. The swimming teacher who preyed on young boys.'

'The very same.'

'I thought he had years to serve in prison. Wasn't he given a very long sentence?'

'According to the PNC, he was convicted in '82 and was sentenced to serve twelve years.'

'So he's only served half his sentence. Exactly when did he get out?'

'His father told me that Stewart was released about a month ago.'

'Another high-profile sex offender. Well, there's the connection to Bauer. Call the office and ask Fran to start researching the Tighe case. By the time we get back, I want to know everything about Stewart Tighe and his victims. Tell her to find out who the original investigating officer was. I want them to meet me at the MCIU offices later this afternoon.'

Tina said, 'I'll go and make the call.'

Danny turned to Tim and said, 'Anything for us, forensically?'

'Nothing yet, but it's early days. There's no sign of any forced entry. From what the father was saying earlier, it could be that the back door was left insecure by the deceased before he fell asleep on the settee.'

'Okay, Tim. Keep looking.'

Danny turned to Rob and said, 'Let's go and talk to the parents. Rachel, can you show us the way to the kitchen, please?'

'This way.'

Danny turned to Seamus Carter and said, 'I'll see you at the hospital, at eleven thirty.'

'See you there.'

Danny nodded and then followed Rachel and Rob through to the kitchen.

Rachel said, 'Mr and Mrs Tighe, this is Detective Chief Inspector Flint and Detective Inspector Buxton. They're the detectives who will be investigating your son's death.'

The old farmer's weather-beaten face turned up toward Danny, and he said, 'I don't think it's going to be that much of a mystery, Detective. Our son did some terrible things, and I think someone has taken their revenge.'

Danny said, 'That's certainly one line of enquiry we'll be looking at. How long has your son been back home?'

'He was released from prison on the fifteenth of January, exactly one month ago.'

'Has he been living here ever since?'

'His probation officer made it clear that he was to live here. He only ever left the house once a week, to see his probation officer.'

'Where was that?'

'Somewhere in Sheffield. He had to go there instead of Worksop. He wasn't supposed to go into Worksop town centre at all because of what happened before at the swimming baths.'

'How's he been since he was released?'

With anger in his voice, Eric Tighe said, 'I'll tell you exactly how he's been, Detective. Fucking useless!'

For the first time, Mavis Tighe spoke. She quietly scolded her husband, saying, 'Eric Tighe, I won't have language like that used in this house.'

The old man grumbled under his breath at his wife before saying to Danny, 'All he's done is laze around the house every day. I swear the only time he ever moved off that settee was either to get something to eat or to have a shit!'

The old lady tutted again, 'Eric, please.'

He turned to his wife. 'But it's true, Mavis. He's a thirty-five-year-old man, and he never did a bloody thing. And then, at night, he would drink himself into a stupor while the television was blaring.'

He turned back to face Danny and continued, 'I'll be honest with you, Detective. I was going to ask him to leave today, before I found him like that.'

Rob said, 'Have you noticed anything strange around the farm since he's been back?'

'Yes. The dogs have been disturbed a few times at night. Suddenly barking for no apparent reason.'

'Where are the dogs kept?'

'During the cold winter months, I keep them in the barn at night, tied up. In fact, why aren't they barking? They should be by now. They'll want feeding.'

Danny turned to Rachel and said, 'Go and have a look in the barn, Rachel. See if the dogs are okay.'

Rob said, 'Was there anything else?'

Mavis Tighe said, 'He did receive a couple of funny letters.'

Rob asked, 'Funny letters?'

'Yes. They were weird. I think they were sent by some crank. They were full of vicious threats, because he'd been released from prison.'

'Do you have the letters?'

The old lady nodded. 'I stuffed them in the drawer of the bureau in the living room.'

Rob was conscious that the body of the woman's only son hadn't yet been removed from the living room, so he said, 'Can you show them to me later?'

She nodded.

Danny said, 'Who do you think killed your son?'

The old man shrugged. 'I don't know. There must be dozens of people out there who wanted him dead for what he'd done to those kids. I honestly couldn't tell you.'

Rachel came back into the kitchen and said, 'It looks like the dogs have been poisoned. They're still alive, but they're not in a good way. Do you have a number for the vet?'

Eric Tighe cursed loudly. 'I'll call him straight away, lass. Why do you think they've been poisoned?'

'Because there's chunks of half-chewed raw meat on the floor beside them.'

With genuine concern in his voice, the farmer said, 'Can I go to my dogs once I've called the vet?'

Danny nodded. 'Of course, Mr Tighe. We'll talk again later.'

As the old man stood up to leave the kitchen, Danny said, 'Does the Mars bar mean anything to you?'

'No. It doesn't. I thought it was strange the way it had been left on Stewart's head, but it doesn't mean anything to me.'

The old lady said, 'What are you talking about?'

'Whoever did it left a Mars bar on top of Stewart's head,' Tighe told his wife. 'Does that mean anything to you?'

With a puzzled expression on her face, the old lady shook her head.

Danny and Rob then walked back through the house to the living room. Danny said to Tina, 'What time are the undertakers coming?'

'Within the next ten minutes. They should have been here half an hour ago, but got lost, apparently.'

'Stay here with Rob. I want you to work the scene together. Obviously, there's no house-to-house be done. Ask Rachel to obtain full witness statements from both the parents before you leave today.'

He turned to Rob and said, 'As soon as the body's removed, get Mrs Tighe in here, and get those threatening letters recovered. I also want a full report from the attending vet. I want to know what type of poison was used on the dogs. I'm going back to the office to start organising the priority enquiries. I'll meet you at Bassetlaw Hospital later for the post-mortem.'

Rob said, 'Will do. I'll walk with you to the car.'

Outside the farmhouse, Rob said, 'What do you make of the old man?'

'Do you mean do I think he's a suspect?'

'Yeah. Seems to me he thought more of his bloody dogs than his own son.'

'I grant you, there doesn't appear to be any love lost between them. If it weren't for the similar head injuries, the Mars bar, and the fact that his son was a notorious sex offender, I would be looking a lot closer at him. There are too many similarities to the murder scene of Manfred Bauer. I'm even more convinced this is about getting payback against sex offenders. There may be something else that links Bauer and Tighe, but it isn't obvious to me.'

35

11.30am, 15 February 1988
Bassetlaw Hospital, Worksop, Nottinghamshire

Danny had met Rob outside, in the main car park. The two men had walked through the long hospital corridors to the mortuary together. Bassetlaw Hospital was a sprawling mass of single-story buildings and was spread over a large area. This was a mortuary neither detective was familiar with, so they followed the signs to pathology until they found it.

The mortuary examination room itself was very small and tight. There was only one stainless-steel examination table in the centre of the room. Like every other mortuary Danny had ever been in, this one had the same familiar chemical smell. He wrinkled his nose against the acrid odour as he donned the protective scrubs alongside Rob.

Seamus Carter and his assistant, Brigitte O'Hara, were already waiting in the room. As were two Scenes of Crime officers and DC Phil Baxter, who would be performing the role of exhibits officer.

The number of personnel in the small room made it feel even more claustrophobic.

Lying naked on the stainless steel table was the body of Stewart Tighe. His long, skinny frame only just fitted on the bench. His flesh was alabaster white under the bright lights. His head, covered in dark blood and matted blonde hair, was in sharp contrast to his white skin.

Seamus said, 'If we're all ready, I'll make a start.'

Danny nodded. 'Okay.'

The pathologist began the procedure with an external examination of the body, checking for any other injuries. He spoke his findings aloud into the handheld Dictaphone he preferred to use. With the assistance of one of the Scenes of Crime officers, Brigitte turned the body so the pathologist could examine the back.

No other external injuries were found.

The pathologist gave a brief summary of the age and general condition of Stewart Tighe before glancing across to Danny and saying, 'I'm going to start the examination proper by closely examining the injuries to the skull. Let's see if we can determine exactly what's happened beneath all that blood and matted hair, shall we?'

Using the grislier implements of his craft, Seamus peeled back the skin from the face and scalp, exposing the bone of the skull underneath. As the flesh was removed, it became obvious what had killed the man.

The Scenes of Crime officer took photographs at each stage of the process.

On the very crown of Tighe's skull, there were three distinct indentations. Fractures ran like spider's legs from the three round holes in the skull.

Seamus said, 'It's the power of three again, Danny. The

force needed to cause fractures like this was enormous. Whoever's doing this certainly knows how to kill.'

Danny said, 'Can you explain further?'

'The amount of force is excessive. One blow of this nature would be more than enough to kill anyone, but this offender always uses three. It isn't a random thing either. Look at how precisely spaced the blows were.'

'That was the same with Bauer.'

'Exactly my point, Danny.'

'Do you think it's a similar weapon?'

'Discs of bone have been pushed into the brain again. I'll extricate the discs as I remove the skullcap, and Brigitte can measure them. On first inspection, I'd say the weapon used looks similar. A general-purpose claw hammer or the like.'

The pathologist got to work again. This time, he used the electric autopsy saw, with the small metal disc cutter, to remove the very top of the skull. He handed the large bone fragment to Brigitte and started to remove the discs of bone that had become embedded in the grey brain matter.

He deftly used tweezers to prize the fragments away and handed them to Brigitte, who then placed them in an examination tray, where she measured them.

The young assistant said, 'Each disc is twenty millimetres in diameter.'

Danny said, 'The same as Bauer.'

Seamus said, 'You can see the massive trauma to the brain below each indentation. Numerous haemorrhages. The skull is almost filled with congealed blood.'

Danny took a step closer to see for himself the massive damage that had been caused to Tighe's brain by the hammer blows, before stepping back again.

Seamus continued his examination, which lasted another forty minutes. At the conclusion he looked directly at Danny. 'I would stake my reputation that this is the same killer.

There are so many similarities. The spacing of the blows, the force used, the weapon used … the list goes on.'

'It certainly seems that way. When can you let me have your full report?'

'I'll get it to you as quickly as I can – in any case, within the next two days.'

Danny nodded and started to remove his scrubs.

Seamus said, 'I hope little Hayley continues to improve and you get her home from the hospital soon. Please give her a big bear hug from me.'

'Thanks, Seamus, will do.'

Danny said to Phil Baxter, 'Do you need a hand to get all the exhibits back to the office?'

'No, thanks. I'm good, sir.'

'The briefing will be at five o'clock. Make sure you're there.'

'Will do, sir.'

Danny and Rob left the examination room and began the long walk back to the car park.

As they walked, Danny said, 'Did you recover the letters mentioned by Mavis Tighe?'

'Yes, boss. There were two.'

'Anything?'

'There's nothing to identify who typed them. The only thing is a stamp at the bottom of the letter, stating it's been sent by the Guardians of Innocence.'

'Content?'

'Both letters contain threats of physical violence that are both specific and graphic.'

'Where are the letters?'

'They're with Tim Donnelly. It's always better to keep the exhibits from a scene together.'

'Of course, you're right. But I want to see them for myself as soon as we get back to the office.'

'No problem.'

'Did Tim find anything else at the scene?'

'There's nothing startling to report forensically. Tim and his team have been working hard all day, but have so far drawn a blank.'

'I think we need to accept that whoever's responsible for slaughtering these men is incredibly aware of forensic evidence and evidence in general. That's two scenes now where there's been no fibres, no prints. Nothing.'

Rob nodded. 'It's such a remote location this time, as well. It makes me wonder where we're going to start. There's no house-to-house enquiries to be done, no CCTV, no witnesses.'

Danny muttered under his breath, 'It's a bloody nightmare.'

36

4.30pm, 15 February 1988
MCIU Offices, Mansfield Police Station

Danny was putting the finishing touches to a very short list of priority enquiries when there was a knock on the door.

The door opened, and an older man, wearing a smart charcoal grey suit, white shirt and grey tie, walked in. He was carrying two large box files under his arm.

He said, 'Hello, sir. I'm Detective Inspector Keith Milton. You asked to see me.'

The puzzled look on Danny's face must have been obvious, because Keith Milton continued, 'I'm the DI who investigated the sexual assaults committed by Stewart Tighe.'

Danny smiled and stood up. 'Of course. Thank you so much for driving over. I take it you've heard what's happened?'

'That Tighe has been found dead at the farm? Yes, sir. I'm aware of that.'

'Do you want a tea or coffee before we chat.'

'A coffee would be great, thanks. I've brought some of the paperwork from the sexual abuse case with me. Victim statements, that sort of thing.'

'That's great. Do you take sugar in coffee?'

'No, thanks.'

Danny walked into the main office and said to Fran Jefferies, 'Fran, can you make two mugs of coffee, white no sugar, please. I want to have a quick chat with DI Milton before the briefing, so I'm a bit pushed for time. Thanks.'

Fran smiled and said, 'No problem, boss. I'll bring them in.'

Danny walked back in his office, and as he sat down, he said, 'So tell me about Stewart Tighe?'

'I thought that would be your first question, sir. I've given my answer a lot of thought as I was driving over here.'

There was a momentary pause before Milton continued, 'Stewart Tighe is, or rather was, one of the most manipulative, dangerous, evil criminals I've ever had the misfortune to meet. That anybody in their right mind could consider this pervert was ready to be released back into the community astonishes me.'

Danny was a little shocked by the intensity in the voice of the detective inspector. 'I can see you still feel extremely strongly about this, Keith. Were the assaults on the young boys that extreme?'

'It wasn't about the level of the assaults, although they were all horrible and life-changing for the youngsters involved. I'm talking about the psyche of Tighe. He was malevolent. There was never an ounce of empathy displayed towards his victims. He was extremely cold and calculating in the way he manoeuvred the youngsters into positions where they would be vulnerable to his predation. A very dangerous individual, who would undoubtedly have committed further offences if this hadn't happened.'

'You sound totally convinced of that.'

'As sure as the sun will come up tomorrow morning, Tighe would have committed further offences against children. It's just what he does. I'm still convinced that I only managed to scratch the surface of his offending.'

'I understand you identified six victims?'

'They were the six lads who were brave enough to speak out. I'm convinced there were many, many more.'

'And all young boys?'

Keith Milton nodded.

There was a polite knock on the door, and Fran walked in carrying two mugs of coffee.

She placed them on the desk, and Danny said, 'Thanks, Fran.'

As Fran left, Keith Milton picked up his mug and said, 'Thank you.'

He took a sip of the piping hot drink and said, 'Can I be blunt, sir?'

Danny thought the older detective had been blunt already, but he said, 'Please do. I want to hear what you think; that's why I asked you here.'

'What I think is this. A large part of me is glad that Stewart Tighe's dead. I know the way he died is wrong, and I would never make my personal views on this known to the public. I also know that whoever did this has prevented a hell of a lot of suffering and ruination of young lives in the future.'

'Strong views, Keith.'

'They're my own private thoughts on the matter.'

'Those boys were all aged about ten when this happened, I believe.'

'The youngest was nine. The others were all eleven.'

'So most of them are young adults now. Have you kept in touch with them and their families?'

'I'm still in charge of the CID at Worksop Police Station, so I've continued to offer the boys and the families my support over the last six years. I think you're about to ask me if any of the teenagers or any of their close families are capable of killing Tighe?'

'Well, are they?'

Milton shrugged. 'I would very much doubt it, but who knows what goes on inside people's heads?'

'You obviously maintained a very good rapport with the families of the victims during your enquiry. Did you use a detective solely dedicated to them throughout your investigation?'

'Yes, I did. I asked DC Sara Lacey to take on that very difficult role, which she performed admirably.'

'Is Sara still on your team?'

'Yes, but she's a detective sergeant now.'

'My detectives will spend a lot of time talking with the victims and their families during the enquiry into Tighe's murder. Obviously, I want to cause as little distress to those families as possible. I think it would assist me greatly if you would agree to DS Lacey being temporarily seconded to the MCIU.'

'As long as it's only a temporary secondment, and she's only here while the enquiries into the families are being undertaken, I have no problem with that at all; I think it's a good idea. It will save the MCIU time, and if there's anything to find within the families, Sara will find it. She's an outstanding detective.'

'That's great. I look forward to meeting her. How soon could she start?'

'I'll call her as soon as I leave here. Off the top of my head, I don't think her workload right now is too onerous. Let me speak to her first, and I'll call you this evening with a start date.'

'That's great. Thanks, Keith. Are you okay to leave the paperwork you brought with me? I'm going to be briefing the team very shortly, and I'd like to familiarise myself with the case before I speak to Detective Sergeant Lacey.'

'No problem, sir. You can keep the paperwork for as long as you like.'

Keith Milton stood and was about to walk out the door when he turned and said, 'One last thing: man to man, detective to detective.'

'Go on.'

'When you catch the person or persons who did this, pin a medal on them from me. Cheers.'

37

5.30pm, 15 February 1988
MCIU Offices, Mansfield Police Station

'Quiet, everyone. Let's make a start, please.'
Danny waited for the assembled detectives to fall silent and then began the debrief into the murder of Stewart Tighe.

He said, 'Tina, could you give us all a brief outline of the victim and the location, please?'

Tina said, 'The victim is Stewart Tighe. His name will probably be familiar to most of you. Tighe was convicted in 1982 for the sexual assaults of six young boys, all under the age of twelve. At the time of the offences, Tighe was the coach of a swimming club based at Worksop Municipal Baths.'

She paused, waiting for the detectives to finish making notes, before she continued. 'Tighe was found dead this morning in the lounge of his parents farm, at Carlton in Lindrick near Worksop. Redgate Farm is extremely isolated and is accessed via a single dirt-track road at the bottom of Water Lane. The nearest adopted road is the A60. There are no other properties within a mile and a half of the farm. It is surrounded by farmland. Redgate Farm is an arable farm. Two crops are grown every year, potatoes and sugar beet, for the nearby factory in Newark.'

Danny said, 'Thanks. Can you explain to everyone who hasn't been to the scene why we think his death is linked to Manfred Bauer?'

'Apart from the fact that both men were high-profile sex offenders, there are a number of similarities. The main one being, as at the Manfred Bauer scene, that a bar of chocolate was again placed carefully on top of the wounds that killed Tighe. It was a Mars bar, the same as before.'

She paused to allow that information to be noted and then continued, 'The farm had three Alsatian guard dogs, which were kept in the barn overnight because of the very low temperatures. These dogs had been drugged with raw meat that had been coated in poison.'

'Thanks, Tina. Any news on the dogs?'

'The vet is hopeful that they'll all survive. He's going to run some tests on the pieces of meat that were recovered near the dogs and let us know what type of poison was used.'

'Follow that up, please. It could be that the offender used a poison that's not widely available.'

'Will do, sir.'

Danny said to Rob, 'Would you update everyone on the cause of death, please?'

Rob said, 'The injuries to Stewart Tighe are almost identical to those suffered by Manfred Bauer. Three heavy blows, with what is believed to be a claw hammer, to the top of the head. Measurements have been taken during the post-mortem, and these show that the weapon used had a twenty-millimetre diameter, the same as the one used on Bauer.

There were no other injuries to the deceased. No defence wounds or evidence that he fought his attacker. From the position in which the body was found, it's more than likely that Tighe was killed while he was asleep on the settee.'

'Thanks, Rob. Anything else from the post-mortem?'

'A full album of photographs was obtained, so everyone should make themselves familiar with the injuries sustained.'

Danny turned to Tim Donnelly and said, 'When will the photographs be ready?'

'There will be a full album of photographs from the scene, as well as the post-mortem, available first thing tomorrow morning. There will also be a video of both the scene and the post-mortem to view.'

'Was anything found at the scene that will help us forensically?'

'There was no forced entry. Access was gained via an unlocked rear door. We've recovered no fibre evidence, and although there are numerous fingerprints recovered, I fully expect them to belong to the deceased and his parents. We've obtained full sets of elimination prints and will be checking all the prints found against them.'

'Why are you so convinced you haven't found the offender's prints?'

'Because whoever is carrying out these attacks is extremely forensically aware. I just can't imagine them making such a fundamental error at the scene.'

'So nothing forensically?'

'No, sir.'

'Will you be running tests on the Mars bar and the letters recovered?'

'Yes, sir. The Mars bar wrapper and the letters will all be subjected to a ninhydrin test for fingerprints.'

'Can that enquiry be fast-tracked, please?'

'Yes, sir.'

Danny turned to Lynn Harris. 'Lynn, I want you and Jag to see me after the briefing so we can go over the letters that were sent to Tighe. They will undoubtably form part of your enquiries into the Guardians of Innocence.'

Lynn nodded and whispered something to Jagvir Singh, who was sitting beside her.

Danny said, 'Okay. It will be clear to all of you that the similarities between the Bauer murder and this murder are so jarringly obvious that we've got to consider the two offences to be the work of the same person. The two murders will now be linked, and all future enquiries will come under the umbrella of Operation Hermes.'

He paused before continuing: 'Because of the remote location of Redgate Farm, there will be no house-to-house enquiries as such. What I do need is for two detectives to visit each of the properties that surround the farm and make general enquiries about anything unusual that has been seen or that has happened over the last two months. DC Singleton and DC Blake, I want you to undertake that role, please. If you liaise with DI Cartwright after the briefing, she has a list of the properties to be visited. I want full lists of everyone who resides at those properties, including any itinerant labourers.'

The two detectives nodded.

Danny then turned to DC Jefferies and said, 'Fran, I'd like you to research Tighe's prison record. We already know everything about his offending, but I'd like some information on his life in prison. Where he was incarcerated, what his record was like? Whether or not he was under rule forty-three or in the general prison population. When you've ascertained where he was, I want you and Rachel to visit the prison. Don't do the digging over the phone. We always learn more from face-to-face meetings, and any paper records will also be on hand, to be examined properly that way as well.'

Fran said, 'Will do, sir.'

Danny continued, 'I'm expecting Detective Sergeant Sara Lacey to be joining us from Worksop CID for the duration of the Operation Hermes enquiry. Sara was the dedicated family liaison officer for the victims of Tighe's crimes six years ago.'

Danny looked directly at DC Helen Bailey and said, 'Helen, I'd like you to work alongside DS Lacey and carry out all the enquiries into the victims of Tighe and their families. As well as the victims, that enquiry will also include talking to the staff of the swimming club where Tighe was a coach. It's a massive undertaking, but it's possible that any one of the people you speak to could be our killer. They all have motive, and from my understanding, they're all still living reasonably local to the murder scene.'

Helen said, 'Do you know when DS Lacey will be starting?'

'I'll know for definite later this evening, but I'm hoping she can start tomorrow. Come and see me afterwards. I have a file containing the original witness statements. You'll need to photocopy them all.'

'Will do, boss.'

'Okay, everyone. That's it for tonight. Back on duty at six thirty tomorrow morning.'

Danny turned to Tina and Rob. 'Let's sit and go over the details for the press conference.'

Rob looked at his watch and said, 'Danny, why don't you get off to the hospital? Tina and I can easily sort out the details for the press conference. I'll sit down with Lynn and Jag and go over the letters, and Tina can sort out things with Nigel and Sam about the neighbouring properties. I'm not planning on going home anytime soon, so I'll still be in the office if DI Milton calls back about Sara Lacey. Just go and spend some time with Sue and Hayley.'

Danny was shocked that since coming to work that morning and being confronted with another murder enquiry, he had not once looked at his watch. He had no idea of the time, or how long he'd been at work. He also realised that the only time he'd thought about Hayley was when Seamus Carter had mentioned her earlier.

He was suddenly consumed by an irrational guilt and felt an overwhelming desire to be with his baby girl.

He said, 'Thanks, I will. I'll see you both tomorrow morning, bright and breezy.'

'No problem. Everything will be sorted here, don't worry.'

38

1.00am, 16 February 1988
King's Mill Hospital, Mansfield, Nottinghamshire

The light in the children's ward was subdued. Danny was sitting beside his daughter's cot, just watching her tiny chest rise and fall. She looked so small and vulnerable. Her bottom lip quivered a little as she breathed in.

Danny had heard her cry once, about an hour ago. He had been half asleep in the chair next to the cot. His brain must have been set to respond to his daughter, because within seconds he was wide awake. Hayley had woken up hungry and had begun to cry. Danny almost smiled when he heard it. It was normal, healthy crying, not the reedy, high-pitched wail she'd had when she was dangerously ill.

Sue had expressed milk earlier, and Danny now used that to feed his daughter. After feeding her, he had gently patted her back until she had got rid of any wind. He had then checked her nappy to see if she needed changing, before gently rocking her in his arms until she drifted off to sleep.

Now, as he stared into the cot at one of the two most precious things in his life, he could feel himself becoming emotional at the thought of almost losing her.

He felt tears run down his cheeks and into his stubble.

He put his hand through the bars of the cot and, using his index finger, gently stroked her tiny hand.

He heard soft footsteps approaching and turned to see Sue standing there. In the half-light of the ward, she looked tired. She whispered, 'Does she need feeding?'

'I've just fed her. You were asleep, so I didn't wake you. She's dropped back off now.'

'You should go home and try to get some rest, sweetheart. You've got to be at work in five hours.'

Danny stood up and embraced his wife. Now that he had got closer, Sue could see his red-rimmed eyes. She brushed away his tears and said, 'Are you okay?'

Danny squeezed her tightly and whispered, 'We almost lost her.'

'But we didn't. She's on the mend now and will continue to get better. You must try not to worry about her.'

Danny kissed his wife and whispered, 'I'll always be worried about her.'

Sue took his hand and said, 'Come on, let's get a coffee before you go home. Hayley's fast asleep now.'

In the relatives room, Sue made two small coffees and said softly, 'I never had the chance to ask you when you got here last night – how was work?'

'Busy. There was another murder the night before I started back. Rob was waiting for me when I walked in the office. I never even took my coat off; we went straight to the scene.'

'Where?'

'At a place called Carlton in Lindrick, up near Worksop. It's miles from Nottingham, but it's definitely linked to the Bauer murder.'

'You haven't told me much about Bauer. If it's so far from Nottingham, how can the two be linked?'

'There's lots of reasons. Let's not talk about my work. Have the doctors said any more about when Hayley might be allowed home?'

Sue shook her head. 'They want her to finish this current round of intravenous antibiotics first. I think they will make a decision then.'

Danny pulled his wife in close and held her tightly in his strong arms.

Sue didn't say anything; she just let her head rest on Danny's chest, listening to his steady heartbeat.

She pulled away, kissed him and said, 'Go home and get some rest. I'm going back on the ward. I'll see you tomorrow. Stop worrying; she's going to be fine.'

39

6.00am, 16 February 1988
MCIU Offices, Mansfield Police Station

Danny walked into the MCIU offices and wasn't surprised to see Rob already there. He said, 'Am I alright to take my coat off today?'

Rob smiled and said, 'Yeah, you can take your coat off. It was a quiet night. How were Hayley and Sue?'

'No change. Sue is managing to rest while Hayley is asleep, but she looks shattered.'

'Do you want a coffee?'

'That would be great. Have you been home at all?'

Rob nodded. 'I left here just before ten o'clock last night. DI Milton didn't phone back until nine thirty. It's good news, though: DS Lacey will be starting with us at eight o'clock today.'

'That's good news. I think she's going to be invaluable dealing with the families of Tighe's victims.'

'More than you know. Keith Milton told me last night that he'd spoken to a couple of the victims' parents about Tighe. Apparently, none of them were aware that he'd been released early. I've made a few preliminary calls with the prison service this morning, and it seems that because of an oversight by their admin department, none of the victims' families were notified.'

Danny picked up the mug of hot coffee made by Rob. He took a sip and said, 'That's disgusting. It's bad enough that he's been released early, but for them not to inform the victims just rubs salt in the wound. As soon as Sara Lacey arrives this morning, I want her and Helen out visiting the parents of the victims. I think we're going to need to pour a lot of oil on some very troubled waters.'

'There could be a bright side to them not being notified.'

'Go on.'

'If none of the families knew Tighe had been let out, doesn't that rule them out as suspects in our enquiry?'

'It should, but we'll need to be certain that they hadn't found out another way. Any one of them could have seen Tighe or heard gossip from a third party that he was out. It would be very convenient for them to cry foul about not being notified if they had found out from somebody else that Tighe had been released. They could then have taken their revenge, killed Tighe and claimed not to have even known he was out. No, we'll need to treat this situation very carefully. I want to see DS Lacey and DC Bailey as soon as they arrive. This enquiry still must be handled correctly.'

'Okay, boss.'

'Did you sit down with Lynn and Jag and talk through the letters that were recovered from the scene?'

'Yes. Lynn is well on top of that enquiry. She and Jag are covering a lot of ground. They're a little stuck until Brannigan returns from his trip to the States.'

'When is he back?'

'On the twenty-fifth. It's in your diary, boss.'

'Of course it is. Have you got a few minutes now? It was so full-on yesterday, I never got the chance to ask how things had progressed while I was off.'

'I'll be honest, the Bauer enquiry has all but come to a standstill. I went over everything with Tina, and it doesn't matter what we tried, it's grinding to a halt. The big problem is we're getting bugger-all information coming in from the public. Until Brannigan returns, we can't push the Guardians of Innocence enquiry any further forward. I put extra staff out into the villages around Whatton to see if we could locate another witness from the one meeting we know about. That achieved nothing except a lot of wasted man-hours. We did have a crank walk into Radford Road nick and confess to Bauer's murder, though.'

'And?'

'Simon Pettigrew has serious mental health issues. I interviewed him with Glen. We quickly ruled out his confession. He could give no detail other than what he'd read about the case in the papers.'

'Are you satisfied he's not involved at all?'

'More than satisfied. He's not connected to the death of Bauer. I also arranged for him to be examined by the on-call mental health team before we released him. As a direct result of their examination, Pettigrew was sectioned under the Mental Health Act. He's currently in Mapperley Hospital. He's not well at all.'

'Anything else?'

'No, boss.'

As Danny walked into his office, he turned and said, 'Thanks for talking me into going early last night, Rob. I needed that. I think it was a release from all the worry I'd had, to just throw myself back into work and blank my mind off to everything else. Thanks for giving me back some focus, mate.'

'You're welcome. I'll let you know when Sara Lacey arrives.'

40

2.00pm, 16 February 1988
HMP Leicester, Welford Road, Leicester

Fran Jefferies had spent all morning researching the prison records of Stewart Tighe. There were very few details; only scant information was available. Now, as per Danny's instruction, she had travelled to HMP Leicester with Rachel Moore, to delve a little deeper into the records by speaking to prison staff face to face.

The governor of the prison was away on holiday, so Fran had arranged to speak to the junior governor, Linda Berry.

Rachel stopped the car outside the imposing façade of Leicester Prison. The twin stone turrets, either side of the large gates, and the stone battlements topping the walls had been designed by William Parsons in 1828, to give the prison the look of a medieval castle.

The main car park was to the immediate left of the gates.

Rachel drove the car slowly up to the barrier, which was controlled by a prison officer.

He approached the car as Rachel wound down the driver's window. She said, 'DC Moore and DC Jefferies from the Major Crime Unit in Nottingham. We're here to see the junior governor, Linda Berry. She's expecting us.'

The prison officer scanned his clipboard and said, 'Park your car in the visitors bay, please.'

Having parked the car, the two detectives walked back to the barrier and showed their identification cards to the prison officer, who said, 'This way, please.'

Ten minutes later, they had been taken into the offices of the prison and were standing outside the office of the junior governor.

The door opened, and they were greeted by a middle-aged woman, wearing a dark business suit and wire-framed glasses. Her round face was framed by shoulder-length, greying hair.

She gave an open, friendly smile and said, 'Detectives, I'm Linda Berry. I spoke to one of you earlier. I understand you want to talk about a recent release, Stewart Tighe.'

Fran said, 'I'm DC Jefferies. It was me you spoke with earlier. This is DC Moore. We're currently investigating the murder of Stewart Tighe. I was able to look at some of the prison records that were available, but they are very brief and offer scant detail. It would help us enormously if we could get some personal insight into Tighe.'

'What sort of thing are you looking for? The prisoner's conduct would have been monitored and documented daily.'

'It would be the behaviours that weren't documented per se. How he interacted with other prisoners, staff, that sort of thing.'

Rachel added, 'Was he ever the subject of violence or

threats while he was a prisoner here? We could find no written record of any assaults committed against him.'

'I've served at this prison for the last eight years. I can remember Tighe when he was first sent here after his conviction. He was an extremely arrogant individual. Back then, he commanded an imposing, physical figure. He was well over six feet tall, very fit and strong. As you would expect from a swimming coach.'

'He didn't scare easily, then?'

'On the contrary. Tighe was terrified about being placed in general prison population. He went straight on to rule forty-three.'

'Segregation?'

'Yes. He had been on the segregation unit for the entire duration of his remand in custody as he awaited trial. This was ordered by the then-governor, for Tighe's own safety. His was quite a high-profile case. After his trial, when he had been found guilty and sentenced, he elected to go straight back onto the segregation unit.'

Fran said, 'How did he interact with the other prisoners? The other sex offenders?'

'He was very cocksure of himself. He ruled the roost amongst that lot.'

'Was he ever violent towards the other prisoners?'

'Physically, no. But he knew how to apply mental pressure on somebody. He was extremely manipulative and controlling. Look, I need to tell you something, but this would be between you and me, and not for the public record, okay?'

'Okay.'

'I was amazed when we got the order to prepare transfer papers to HMP Whatton, ready for Tighe's early release. I couldn't believe that the parole board had deemed him fit for early release. In my opinion, Tighe remained a serious and real threat to other children.'

Rachel said, 'Don't the prison service have any input into these hearings?'

'We do. But we must evidence everything we say. Tighe was too clever, too cunning, to ever do anything that would jeopardise his release.'

'You mentioned transfer papers. Wasn't Tighe released from here?'

'No. Like all sex offenders who have been given early release, he was sent to a specialist unit at HMP Whatton. This is done to help prepare them for integration back into society.'

'So when was Tighe transferred?'

The junior governor looked on her computer records, then said, 'He was transferred on the fifteenth of October, last year. Three months before he was due to be released.'

'Any problems?'

'None that are listed on here. He was released on the fifteenth of January, on schedule. God knows why, but he was.'

Fran said, 'Did Tighe ever receive any threatening letters while he was a prisoner here?'

'As is standard across the prison service, all mail is intercepted, both in and out. There's no record of any threatening letters. The only person who regularly corresponded with Tighe was a young woman from the swimming team he used to coach. She wrote for the first few years he was here; then slowly the letters dried up and eventually stopped.'

'Do you have her details?'

'Just a minute.'

Once again, she flicked through old records on her computer screen. 'Here it is. The woman's name was Elaine Potter. She's described on here as being a significant relationship.'

'What exactly does that mean?'

' "Significant relationship" covers the entire spectrum. It can relate to husband and wife, boyfriend and girlfriend, or casual lovers.'

'Did Tighe write back regularly?'

'He carried on writing to her for six months after her letters stopped.'

'Is her address listed on your records?'

'Yes. It's shown on here as being number twelve, Pickwick Terrace, Manton, Worksop. The last letter was sent in '85, so it might not be a current address.'

Rachel said, 'That's great, thanks. Is there anything else you think we should know about Tighe?'

'Nothing I haven't already said. I've already given you my opinion on the decision to release him. It should never have happened. Stewart Tighe was still a very dangerous individual.'

'Thanks for taking the time to speak with us today. It's been extremely useful.'

When the two detectives were back in the car park, outside the prison walls, Rachel said, 'What do you make of Tighe's prison pen pal, Elaine Potter?'

'I think we need to talk to DS Lacey and see if Potter figured in the original investigation into Tighe. We also need to let the boss know that Tighe was released from HMP Whatton and not here. That's something else he had in common with Manfred Bauer.'

41

4.00pm, 16 February 1988
23 Barnard Street, Gateford, Worksop, Nottinghamshire

DS Sara Lacey had arrived at the Major Crime Investigation Unit offices at seven thirty that morning, ready to start work at eight o'clock. It was one of her many quirks. She couldn't abide poor timekeeping and was always early for every shift and every appointment.

Now in her late thirties, Sara had recently passed her promotion board to the inspector rank. A dedicated detective for most of her service, she wasn't relishing the prospect of being back in uniform. But the monetary rewards on promotion meant she wasn't able to turn it down when it was offered.

There was a time when she had harboured ambitions to work on the MCIU permanently. She had applied twice, but been unsuccessful on each occasion. It was partly this rejection that had spurred her on to take her promotion exams. She had been promoted to the rank of sergeant eighteen months ago, remaining on the CID at Worksop. She had immediately sat her inspector's promotion exams. She passed the exam easily and had now passed her board, so it was only a matter of time before she achieved the next rank. Although she still felt a little disappointed never to have been given the opportunity to work on MCIU, she felt satisfied with the way her career had developed.

She still wanted to make a good impression on the MCIU, though, so had chosen her favourite navy blue, pinstripe suit and a cream blouse to wear for her first day. It was the suit she normally reserved for giving evidence at the Crown Court.

Danny Flint had briefed her and the detective she was working with, Helen Bailey, on the enquiries he wanted completing. It was what she had been expecting after speaking with DI Milton the night before.

She was to revisit all the immediate families of Tighe's victims. It would be down to her to establish if any of them could fall into the category of suspect for the murder.

The original enquiry into the child abuse committed by the swimming coach had been one of the most sickening and traumatic cases she had ever been involved with. Her role had been to maintain a close liaison with each of the six young boys who had been Tighe's victims. She had to ensure that the families of those children were constantly updated and apprised as to how the enquiry was developing.

She had been there, alongside the parents, as each of the boys had been medically examined by the police surgeon and a specialist paediatrician. A painful and traumatic experience that was necessary to establish the extent of the abuse perpetrated on the victims by Tighe.

It had been an emotional time for everyone, and there had been a lot of overt rage within most of the families. She knew there were several men within those family units who, if given the chance, would exact a horrible revenge on Tighe.

It was now her job to establish if they had.

Four of the six families had been seen throughout the day, and after long interviews with the family members, Sara was happy to rule them out of the murder enquiry. The main thing the two detectives had been faced with throughout the day was the sense of outrage from the families that they hadn't been notified by the prison authorities or the probation service that Stewart Tighe had been released. That outrage had increased further when Sara had informed them that Tighe had been residing at his parents' address, in nearby Carlton in Lindrick, ever since his release.

Sara had been satisfied that the outrage and surprise were genuine. None of the family members they had interviewed thus far had any inkling that Tighe had been released from prison early.

As the CID car came to a stop on Barnard Street, Sara glanced at her watch. It was almost four o'clock. The debrief was scheduled to start at five thirty. They would have time to speak with the next victim and his immediate family before driving back to Mansfield.

Helen Bailey switched off the car engine and said, 'Which one of the boys lives here?'

Sara replied, 'Timothy Carr. At nine years old, he was the youngest boy abused by Tighe. It probably affected him the worst. What that bastard did to Tim was disgusting. The abuse he suffered was also perpetrated over the longest period of time. Timothy was being abused regularly by Tighe over a period of six months. He was too terrified to speak out, and it was only after he started experiencing medical issues with his bowel that doctors discovered the extent of the abuse he had suffered. He was the last victim to be added to the original enquiry.'

'Poor little lad. Have you kept in touch with him?'

'More than the others. He's much stronger now. His parents arranged and paid for private specialist counselling for their son. That decision has paid dividends. Timothy is doing very well at school and is expected to achieve good enough grades to go to university.'

'That's good. His parents deserve massive credit for that.'

'I'd better warn you now, Helen. We won't get a warm welcome from Mr Carr.'

'How do you mean?'

'Dave Carr has worked on the coal face at Manton Colliery all his life. He's as hard as nails. During the first enquiry, when details of the abuse first emerged, we really had to grip Dave Carr. I genuinely thought he was going to try to kill Tighe for what he had done to his only son.'

'Did he make any death threats?'

'None. But that's the thing with Dave: He would just do it without making a fuss about it. I know he's got it in him. If they haven't been informed about Tighe's release, like the other families, I expect the roof to come off. Be ready for fireworks, and just let me do the talking. Okay?'

Suddenly, Helen felt really pleased she had the experienced detective working alongside her. She said, 'I'll follow your lead, Sarge.'

'Why don't we dispense with the sarge bit. Just call me Sara, okay.'

'Fine by me.'

'Come on then; let's go and have a chat with Dave Carr.'

The two detectives got out of the car and made their way down the path to the front door of the neat semi-detached house.

After two attempts at ringing the doorbell, the door was opened by a mountain of a man who had a face like thunder. That face had several dark blue scars, caused by coal dust getting into open cuts. It was a tattoo worn with pride by a lot of miners.

He glared down at the diminutive Sara Lacey and growled, 'There's no need to ask why you're here.'

'I take it you've heard, then?'

'Yes. I've bloody heard. A taxi driver told me last week that he'd taken Stewart Tighe in his cab to Sheffield. He also told me that he had picked him up at his parents' bloody farm.'

'What day last week, exactly?'

'It was the thirteenth. I remember the date, because I thought how bloody typical it was to hear something about that monster on the thirteenth.'

There was a pause; then Dave seemed to lose some of the rage. He said quietly, 'I suppose you'd better come inside.'

Sara said, 'Are your wife and Tim at home?'

'Liz is in the kitchen, and Tim's in his room.'

As they walked into the house, Dave said, 'I've been trying to find out ever since if it was true and that the bastard was out. Your visit tonight confirms it was true.'

As they walked into the lounge, Sara said, 'Where were you on the night of the fifteenth?'

'That's an easy one, lass. I was at my second home, a thousand feet underground. I've just finished a week of night shifts. Why?'

'And that can be verified, can it? You didn't throw any sickies during the week?'

'I never throw a sick day. I was at work all week. Now for the second time, why do you want to know?'

'What you heard was right. Stewart Tighe was released early from prison. He was let out on the fifteenth of January.

He was found dead on the morning of the fifteenth of February.'

'And you think I could have done it?'

'I never said that.'

'I'll tell you straight, Detective. If I'd been presented with the opportunity, I would gladly have choked the life out of that bastard and not batted an eyelid. I didn't kill him, more's the pity.'

With a cast-iron alibi, Sara was satisfied that Dave was not personally involved in the death of the paedophile, but she still had some tentative digging to do.

Before she could ask anything else, a middle-aged woman with a pretty face walked into the lounge. There were just the first hints of grey in the woman's blonde hair, and what were once fine lines around the eyes were becoming more pronounced.

Sara said, 'Hello, Liz.'

The woman said in a low voice, which contained real venom, 'I've been listening at the door. You've got some nerve coming here accusing my husband of God knows what when you haven't even got the decency to let us know that monster was back living on our doorstep.'

'I wasn't accusing anyone of anything. It was a mistake by the prison authorities not to have informed you. That shouldn't have happened.'

'What shouldn't have happened is that bastard being let out of prison.'

'I can't argue with that, Liz. You both know my feelings on Stewart Tighe.'

The room was filled with a heavy silence.

Sara broke the sombre mood. 'How's Timothy doing?'

Liz replied, 'He's fine. We haven't told him about the rumour, as he's got important exams coming up.'

'So he doesn't know that Tighe had been released?'

'No, he doesn't. And I want it to stay that way, just for now. I don't want his head filled with bad memories because of that piece of shit.'

'When did Dave tell you?'

'Last night, when we were in bed. It's the first chance we've had to talk, as he's been on nights.'

Sara turned to Dave and said, 'Who's the taxi driver who told you about Tighe?'

'It's my cousin, Geoff. Why?'

'I'll want to talk to him, that's why.'

'He won't have had anything to do with this. Our Geoff's as soft as grease.'

'I'm not saying he's had anything to do with what's happened, but I need to find out who else he's told. We both know how much bad feeling there was at the time this all happened. There are a lot of people in this community who would be glad to see the back of Tighe.'

Liz said, 'And rightly so.'

'I'll need your cousin's full name and address, Dave.'

'Okay, but you're wasting your time. His name's Geoff Barnes. He lives at six Redgate Close, Manton.'

'Thanks. I'm not going to disturb Timothy. I hope he does well in his exams. I'll come back in a day or so to get full statements from both of you so we can discount you from our enquiries.'

Dave Carr nodded. 'No problem. I'm off work for the next three days.'

Liz walked the detectives to the front door.

She opened the door and said quietly, 'You know how it is, Sara. Don't expect anybody around here to be sorry that monster's dead.'

Sara turned and said, 'Take care, Liz. Keep doing the best for your boy; he's the most important person in all this.'

Liz nodded and closed the door.

Helen said, 'Do you believe them?'

'Yeah. Dave wouldn't lie about being at the pit; it's too easy to check. Come on, we've still got time to see Geoff Barnes before we need to get back for the debrief.'

42

5.30pm, 16 February 1988
MCIU Offices, Mansfield Police Station

Danny quickly glanced around the room at the assembled detectives. The room had fallen silent as soon as he had walked from his office into the main briefing room.

He said, 'Let's make a start. I know it's been another long day, and we're all ready for home. Rachel, Fran, I'll start with you. How did you get on at Leicester prison?'

Rachel said, 'The main thing we learned was that Stewart Tighe was released from HMP Whatton, the same as Manfred Bauer. He was released after undergoing the same resettlement course on the sex offender wing there.'

'Fran, I need you back in the office tomorrow. Rachel, I'd like you to go to HMP Whatton with DS Wills first thing tomorrow morning and make some enquiries into this resettlement course. I want to know who runs it, what it entails –

anything you can find out, basically. It's something we now know that both our victims had in common, so let's see if it takes us anywhere.'

Danny cursed inwardly; he had already been informed about the courses held at the sex offender wing at HMP Whatton by the governor of Lincoln prison when he had interviewed him about Bauer. He just hadn't followed up on the suggested enquiry, by the governor, to visit the sex offender wing at HMP Whatton.

He wondered what else he hadn't pursued fully because of his young daughter's predicament. Quickly banishing those thoughts, he said, 'Was there anything else you learned about Tighe?'

'Only the clear perception from staff within the prison service that Tighe remained an extremely dangerous offender. It seems that the decision to release Tighe early came as a huge shock to the prison service.'

'Had there been any threats received by Tighe?'

'No. There is one thing we discovered that requires further investigation. Apparently, he had regular correspondence with a woman who was a member of the coaching staff at the same swimming club as Tighe. The prison described theirs as a "significant relationship".'

'How regular is "regular correspondence"?'

'Letters back and forth every week for the first three years of his sentence. He continued writing to her for another six months after her letters stopped.'

'Do you have her details?'

Rachel flicked through her notes. 'Her name's Elaine Potter. She lived at number twelve, Pickwick Terrace, Manton, Worksop, back then.'

'That's good work, you two.'

Danny immediately turned to DS Sara Lacey. 'Does that name mean anything to you, Sara?'

'Not specifically. I spoke to quite a few of the members of the swimming club and their coaching staff. That name doesn't ring any bells with me.'

'I'd like you and Helen to follow that up first thing tomorrow morning. I want you to visit the address we have for Elaine Potter. Talk to her and find out what they corresponded about. You already have the enquiry to revisit the swimming club allocated to you, so just tag it onto that, please.'

Sara made a note and said, 'Will do, sir.'

'Have you made any progress with the families of the victims?'

'Yes, sir. We've seen five out of the six families.'

'Anything?'

'So far there was only the Carr family who had any idea that Tighe had been released early.'

'Are they possibles?'

'Of all the victims' relatives involved, I would have said that the person most likely to have any involvement in what happened to Tighe would have been Timothy Carr's father, Dave.'

There was a pause before Sara added, 'However, Dave Carr has a watertight alibi. At the time of the murder, he was underground at Manton Colliery, working a night shift.'

'Has this been verified?'

'Yes, sir. I contacted the colliery manager before this debrief. He confirmed that Carr was at work all week.'

'But you said the Carr family were aware that Tighe had been released?'

'Dave Carr's cousin, who's a taxi driver in Worksop, had told Carr that he thought he had picked up Stewart Tighe in his cab on the thirteenth.'

'Have you spoken to this taxi driver?'

'Yes, sir. Geoff Barnes wasn't one hundred percent sure it

was Tighe, but he had mentioned it to his cousin the day after he had taken him as a fare. He said that Carr hadn't believed him.'

'Has Barnes mentioned it to anybody other than his cousin?'

'No. After Dave didn't believe it, he didn't tell anybody else of his suspicions.'

'Do we know where Barnes took Tighe in his cab?'

'To the Probation Service offices in Sheffield. He remembers it because it was such a big fare.'

'So nothing from the families of the victims to be overly concerned about?'

'We still have the family of Greg Townroe to see tomorrow, but nothing so far.'

'That's good work, both of you. Sara, I want you to make Elaine Potter your first call tomorrow morning, please.'

'Will do, sir.'

Danny then turned to DS Lynn Harris and DC Singh. 'Lynn, Jag, have you anything new to report on your enquiry about the threatening letters?'

Lynn said, 'No, sir, but Jag has done some interesting research on serious assaults that you might think is relevant.'

'Go on, Jag.'

'I decided to research all serious assaults over the last twelve months in the county. I found that there has been a massive increase in cases of physical violence against men with previous convictions for indecency.'

'How massive?'

'There have been over twenty cases of serious physical violence being used against men with indecency records. An increase of over sixty percent on the previous twelve months.'

'Has anybody been convicted for any of these crimes?'

'No, sir.'

'So, as well as the three murders, we also have a sharp

increase in physical violence being used against previously convicted sex offenders.'

'Yes, sir.'

'That's good work, Jag. Come and see me after the briefing with the details of the cases you've found, please.'

'Will do, boss.'

Danny then painstakingly went through the remaining staff, gathering information on their respective enquiries, making notes as he listened to their progress.

At the conclusion of the debrief, he said, 'That's another good day's work, everyone. There's still a lot more to do. Back here for six thirty tomorrow morning, please.'

He turned to Sara Lacey and said, 'Sara, I'm conscious that you and Helen are going to have a lot of statements to obtain over the next few days. Come and see me after the briefing with a list of all the people we need to obtain witness statements from, so I can delegate other officers to take some of that load.'

Sara said, 'Will do, sir. Thanks.'

Danny walked back to his office, grabbed his coat and walked straight out. He suddenly felt an overwhelming urge to be with his family, and he could be at the hospital within fifteen minutes.

43

7.30am, 17 February 1988
MCIU Offices, Mansfield Police Station

DC Fran Jefferies was feeling irritated. She had been given yet another research task, which meant another day in the office. Yet she knew it was an important role and one that had proved vital in many of the successful enquiries undertaken by the MCIU.

She had been part of the MCIU since its inception and was well regarded for her meticulous approach to mundane research. It was both a blessing and a curse. It meant she was extremely well thought of by the DCI and both the detective inspectors, but it also meant for much of the time, she was stuck in the office.

She intended to talk to Danny about her predicament, today.

The telephone on her desk began to ring, and thoughts of any future conversation with her DCI evaporated.

She picked up the phone and said, 'MCIU. DC Jefferies.'

There was a brief pause on the line as the call was put through. Then a man with a low, gravelly voice said, 'Is that the incident room for that bloke who was murdered at Redgate Farm?'

'Yes, sir. Can I help you?'

'It might be nothing, but the other blokes at the farm said I should report it, so that's what I'm doing.'

'Okay, sir. What exactly is it that you want to report?'

'Like I said, it might be nothing, but I saw a car parked up in a lay-by near the fields belonging to Redgate Farm. It was there three or four times last month.'

'How far away from Redgate Farm is this lay-by?'

'By road, probably about a mile, but straight over the fields it's probably half that distance.'

'What time of day did you see this car?'

'It was always late at night. I used to pass it when I was driving back from the pub.'

He laughed before continuing, 'I only ever drink shandy, Officer. Honest.'

Fran chuckled at the man's feeble joke before saying, 'And you said you've seen it more than once?'

'Yeah. It was there four or five times, at least. I thought it was shaggers.'

'Sorry?'

'Shaggers! People having sex in their cars.'

'Oh, right. Did you ever see anybody with the car?'

'Never, but the windows always looked a little steamed up, if you get my drift.'

'Do you know what sort of car it was?'

'I'm not great at cars, but I reckon it was one of them new Sierras. Either black or dark blue.'

'That's great. What I'm going to do is get an officer to

come and see you, to talk to you a bit more. What did you say your name was, again?'

'It's Bill. Bill Tandy.'

'And where can we find you, Bill?'

'I'm always either working somewhere on the farm, or having a swift pint at the Green Dragon pub.'

'Which farm is that?'

'I work at Petticoat Hill Farm. It's about five miles from Redgate Farm.'

Fran finished scribbling the details down onto her notepad and said, 'Thanks for the call, Mr Tandy. We'll be in touch.'

Fran put the phone down, grabbed her notepad and walked over to Danny's office. She knocked politely, then walked in.

She said, 'Sir, I've got a lead on a possible vehicle sighting from a farm labourer.'

Danny said, 'Go on.'

Fran outlined the details of the call she had just received.

Danny listened carefully and then said, 'Contact either Nigel or Sam on the radio and pass that information on to them. They're currently visiting all the neighbouring farms in the area.'

'Thanks, sir. Will do.

Fran hesitated at the door. Danny said, 'Was there something else?'

Fran turned and said, 'Yes, sir. There is something on my mind that I'd like to talk to you about, if you've got five minutes.'

44

8.30am, 17 February 1988
12 Pickwick Terrace, Manton, Worksop

Just as the two detectives approached the front door of the house, it was opened by a young woman. She was startled to see the two women on the garden path, but regaining her composure quickly, she said, 'Can I help you?'

Sara Lacey held out her identification card and said, 'I'm Detective Sergeant Lacey, and this is DC Bailey. We want to talk to Elaine Potter.'

The look of shock reappeared on the woman's face. She spluttered, 'That's me. What do you want to talk to me about? Is everything okay?'

Sara said, 'We need to ask you a few questions about Stewart Tighe. Can we step inside?'

'I have to be at work for nine thirty. Can't this wait?'

'I'm sorry, it can't. It shouldn't take long, though. Where do you work? We can always give you a lift if it would help?'

'I work at a shop in the town centre. If you could give me a lift, that would be a massive help. It's not Elaine Potter anymore. I'm married. My surname's Jones now.'

'Isn't this your parents' house?'

'It was. When dad retired from the pit, my parents moved to their little bungalow at Mablethorpe. My dad rents this house to me and my husband now.'

'Can we step inside?'

'Yes, of course.'

Elaine Jones unlocked the door, and the three women stepped inside. Sara said, 'Is your husband home?'

'Kev works away. He's on the North Sea rigs.'

'That must be tough. How long have you been married?'

'Just over two years. You said this was about Stewart Tighe. Has something happened to him in prison?'

'When was the last time you spoke to Stewart?'

'Just before he was arrested. Why?'

'Have you been in touch with him since?'

'We used to write to each other when he got sent to prison.'

'Were you friends?'

Elaine coloured up a little and said, 'It was a bit more than that. Stewart was my first serious boyfriend. He was quite a bit older than me. When we first met, I had just turned eighteen, and he was twenty-seven.'

'How long were you seeing each other?'

'For the eighteen months prior to his arrest.'

'Was it serious?'

'We had talked about me moving into his bedsit, in town.'

'Why didn't you?'

'My parents never liked Stewart. Going out with him

caused all sorts of problems between me and my parents. My dad never trusted him from the start.'

'Were you and Stewart intimate?'

Elaine looked down at the floor and nodded.

Sara paused and then continued softly: 'I'm sorry to be asking all these awkward questions about a part of your past that you might want to forget, but there are things you need to know.'

Elaine looked up and stared into the detective's eyes.

Sara could see tears starting to well in the young woman's eyes.

As gently as she could, she said, 'Stewart Tighe was released from prison in January. He was living at his parents' farm in Carlton in Lindrick. Three nights ago, he was attacked at the farm and killed. We are investigating his murder.'

Sara saw the colour drain from the woman's face.

'That can't be right. He still had six years to do.'

'I'm sorry, Elaine.'

There was a long pause as Sara allowed Elaine to regain her composure. Then she said, 'I need to understand why you continued to write to Stewart after he was sent to prison?'

'Because I refused to believe any of it. At the time, I thought all those boys were lying, and that Stewart was innocent.'

'You worked alongside him at the swimming club. Had there been any signs of what was happening between him and the boys?'

'He always paid the younger lads a lot of attention. I just thought he was a brilliant coach. He would constantly encourage them to do better. He'd stay behind long after everyone else had gone home, to train the youngsters.'

'When did you realise he wasn't the innocent man you thought he was?'

'When I met Kev, I suppose.'

'What happened?'

'We had been dating for a few months. I didn't think it was serious at the time. Kev is a lovely guy and very good looking, but I thought we were just having fun.'

'Okay, so what happened to change that?'

'Kev found out about the letters I was writing to Stewart, and he went crazy.'

'I can understand he would be upset, but why did he feel so strongly about it?'

'One of the boys Stewart had interfered with was the youngest son of one of Kev's cousins.'

'What was the boy's name?'

'Greg Townroe?'

'How did you resolve things with Kev?'

'I realised how much I liked him, I suppose. What I thought hadn't been serious was. I made things up with Kev and promised to stop writing letters to Stewart.'

'We understand that even after you stopped writing to him, Stewart Tighe maintained contact with you for quite a while. What happened to all the letters he sent to you?'

'I always showed them to Kev. Then we would sit and burn them on the fire together. He made me see how Stewart had taken advantage of me when I was just an impressionable young woman. Kev helped me see the monster behind the man. That's why I love him.'

Helen Bailey said, 'You told us earlier that your husband was working away on the rigs. Where exactly?'

'He's out in the North Sea somewhere. I can tell you the name of the rig he's on, but not where it is.'

'What's the name of it?'

'He always calls it Piper Delta Four.'

'How long has he been away?'

'He had to get the helicopter from Aberdeen on the tenth of February. He left here the day before on the ninth.'

'When's he due back?'

'Not until the tenth of June.'

'Which oil company does he work for?'

'Shell. Why are you asking me all these questions about Kev?'

Sara interjected, saying, 'I told you earlier that Stewart was murdered. We are investigating his murder. One of your husband's young relatives was badly assaulted by this man, and then he later discovered that his new girlfriend had been in a relationship with the same man. I think that would give him good reason to have strong feelings against Stewart Tighe.'

'But I've just told you he's away, working.'

'That's the reason we're asking you all these questions, so it will be easy for us to confirm what you're saying is true, and that your husband had nothing to do with Stewart Tighe's death.'

'I didn't even know Stewart was out of prison. If he was going to let anybody know he was out, it would have been me, surely?'

Sara shrugged. 'I can't answer that. I think we're done for now. Do you still want that lift to work?'

Elaine nodded. 'Yes, please. I daren't be late; I haven't been there long. It's Wainwright's Boutique, on the High Street.'

Helen said, 'Try not to worry, Mrs Jones. I'm sure your husband had nothing to do with any of this. I'll call you again tonight to put your mind at rest, after we've completed our enquiries, okay?'

'Thanks. Bloody Stewart Tighe, he's still causing me grief.'

45

9.00am, 17 February 1988
HMP Whatton, Nottinghamshire

It was the day Wilf Kelham had thought would never arrive. He had always assumed that he would die in prison, but today, he was going to be released.

He walked along the metal landing of the sex offenders wing at HMP Whatton with his head down, following the prison officer known by all the inmates as 'Handy Harry'. He had avoided making any sort of eye contact with the burly prison officer when he had opened the cell door earlier. He knew this prison officer was a nasty bastard at the best of times. In the morning, he could be pure evil.

When he had been ordered out of the cell, Wilf had just gathered up his scant belongings and followed the prison officer along the landing without saying a word.

Wilf Kelham had served twelve years of an eighteen-year sentence. He had been sixty-two years old when he was convicted at Lincoln Crown Court for the abduction and rape of two nine-year-old girls. The girls had been building sandcastles on a beach at the holiday resort of Chapel St Leonards in Lincolnshire.

As he walked along the prison corridors, his mind drifted back to the events that had led to him being locked up for so long.

At the time of the offences, he'd been working in a slot machine arcade and living in a dirty, scruffy caravan near one of the main holiday camps.

On one of his days off, he'd seen the two young girls playing on their own on the beach not far from his dilapidated caravan. He had enticed the girls away from the beach, telling them that his dog had just had puppies.

Once they were inside the caravan, he had locked the door and raped both girls before taking them back to the beach. He had left them at the far end of the beach, almost a mile away from where he had taken them.

Nobody in the holiday resort had realised that there was a predator living amongst them until it was too late. Luckily for the police, a witness had seen the scruffy old man walking away from the beach, holding the two young girls by the hand.

The witness had been able to provide a very good description. A sketch was made by a police artist. Wilf Kelham had been quickly identified to the police as a suspect from this sketch. He was arrested at his caravan, and detectives had been able to find forensic evidence linking him to the crimes committed against the two nine-year-old girls.

He had been in no position to deny the charges and had pleaded guilty at court. He had served every day of his sentence on the sex offenders wing at HMP Whatton. He had felt comfortable among men of a similar disposition to himself. It had come as a massive shock when he had first been told he was to be released. He had grown used to his life in prison. He was warm. Had clean clothes and a hot meal three times a day. All that was about to be taken away, and he was feeling extremely nervous about what the day would bring.

A sudden barked order from 'Handy Harry' snapped Wilf Kelham back to the present: 'Stand here, Kelham!'

A softer voice then said, 'Thank you, Mr Parker. I can take it from here.'

Kelham was relieved to see the prison welfare officer, Joanna Preston.

As soon as the overbearing Senior Officer Parker had left the office, she said, 'Are you okay, Wilf?'

Happy to see a friendly, smiling face, he replied, 'Yes, miss. Have you sorted me out somewhere to live?'

She beamed a smile and said, 'Don't you worry. Everything's been sorted out. You'll be staying at a halfway hostel in Newark. Your probation officer will be there to meet you this morning. She will go through everything with you. Your benefits have all been sorted out, so you'll have your own money to spend. There will be some rules that you'll have to abide by while you're living at the hostel. The probation officer will go through all those with you. Any questions so far?'

'How am I going to get to Newark?'

'Sorry, Wilf. I should have said. I'm going to drive you over there myself to make sure you arrive okay. I'll be there to introduce you to Sally Greaves, your probation officer.'

'Thanks, miss. You've been so kind to me.'

'There's no need for thanks. It's my job to get you ready to live outside these four walls again. Have you got all your medication?'

Kelham had suffered an almost catastrophic heart attack six months earlier. It had nearly claimed the sex offender's life. But for the emergency CPR performed by prison staff on the wing, he would have certainly died. It was one of the deciding factors in the decision to release him early from prison. The parole board had concluded that he was now too old and too infirm to pose any continued threat to children.

He rattled the small brown bottle of pills, which he always clutched in his right hand, and said, 'Right here, as always.'

'Excellent. Let's get all the paperwork sorted out, and then I'll take you to Newark.'

46

10.00am, 17 February 1988
HMP Whatton, Nottinghamshire

Rachel and Andy had been made very welcome by the governor's secretary at HMP Whatton. When they had first been shown into the main office by a prison officer, the secretary had explained how the governor, Wilson Redmayne, was dealing with some urgent business within the prison. She had assured the two detectives that he wouldn't be long and had brought them two hot coffees.

They had now been waiting for twenty minutes. Just as Andy was about to enquire with the secretary what had happened to the governor, a very tall and very large black man came bustling along the corridor. He wore a smart grey suit and an open-neck white shirt. He looked to be in his mid-forties, but it was hard to gauge, because his head was completely shaved.

He smiled as he approached the two detectives. Andy

could now see that the man was perspiring quite heavily and was slightly out of breath.

He extended a massive hand and said, 'Wilson Redmayne. Please forgive me for keeping you waiting, Detectives. We had a small crisis on B Wing that needed addressing urgently.'

Andy shook the governor's hand. 'I'm DS Wills, and this is DC Moore. No problem; we haven't been waiting long. Is everything sorted now?'

Wilson also shook hands with Rachel as he said, 'Yes, thank you. I just need to get my breath back. B Wing is on the very far side of the prison, and I've virtually jogged back here.'

He half sat and half collapsed into the captain's chair that was positioned behind his impressive walnut desk.

Regaining his composure, Wilson said, 'Now then, Detectives. How can I help you today?'

Andy said, 'We're interested in the pre-release scheme that's being piloted for the sex offenders held here.'

'It's not just for prisoners here. We have sex offenders transferred in from other prisons three months ahead of their release date.'

Rachel said, 'Why was the scheme set up here?'

'The programme is very much my baby. I studied a similar one that has been running in Sweden for the last ten years. Their results are quite outstanding. Only twenty percent of sex offenders released under their system go on to reoffend. If we could achieve anywhere close to that figure, it would be huge. Right now, the numbers of sex offenders released here who go on to reoffend is running close to sixty percent.'

Rachel was shocked at the number. 'I never realised it was so high.'

'In the past, these men have served their time and then

been kicked back out into society, with no support or backup. It then becomes the easiest thing in the world for them to slip back into their old predatory ways. I'm convinced that the scheme I've established here will not only help the prisoners and stop them reoffending, but it will also be a massive help to society in general. I don't need to tell you what devastation is caused by the offences these men commit.'

Andy could see that Wilson was passionate about his subject, and said, 'How long has the scheme been in place at Whatton?'

'We started the scheme in July last year, and so far, there have been fifteen offenders who have benefitted from the programme. We had intended starting earlier, but I struggled to convince the person I wanted to run the scheme to take the job. At first, I had to run it myself, but that wasn't ideal.'

'If it's "your baby" as you said, why didn't you want to run the scheme yourself?'

'Unfortunately, I couldn't. The role of governor at any prison is a very demanding one. You've seen a small glimpse of what it can be like this morning. There's always something that needs my urgent attention. No, the scheme deserved to have somebody dedicated to overseeing just that.'

'So who's in charge of the scheme now?'

'Since the middle of December last year, it's been run full-time by our senior welfare officer, Joanna Preston. Technically, she's employed by the probation service, but she falls under my remit now. She has an office just along the corridor from me here at the prison. We're in constant liaison and see each other most days. The entire set-up works very well.'

Rachel said, 'Can we speak with Ms Preston this morning?'

'I'm afraid not. You've just missed her. She's helping to rehouse an offender at Newark today, and then I believe she's on leave for a few days. I agree, though, it would be useful for you to speak with Joanna.'

Andy said, 'You mentioned earlier how it had been difficult for you to convince Ms Preston to take the role. Do you know why that was?'

'It's no secret, Detective. At first, she didn't like the idea of working exclusively with sex offenders. For the previous two years, she had been the welfare officer on B Wing, working with the general prison population. She had done such a fantastic job that I knew she would be right for the programme. She just took some persuading to see that for herself, that's all. And now she's doing a brilliant job.'

'When did she agree to take the job?'

'In December last year. I had allowed the scheme to start in July, so it was a massive relief to me when she finally agreed to take the job.'

'Can you find out when we can speak with Ms Preston, please?'

'Yes, of course.'

Wilson pressed a button on his telephone and said, 'Sylvia, could you find out the details of Joanna Preston's annual leave? I believe she starts it today.' He turned to the detectives and said, 'Sylvia won't be a minute. Is there anything else I can help you with?'

Rachel said, 'I understand that Manfred Bauer and Stewart Tighe were both released under this scheme.'

Wilson glanced across at his desktop computer and typed furiously on the keyboard.

'Yes. Bauer was transferred in from Lincoln, and Tighe from Leicester. Bauer was one of the first men on the scheme. Of the fifteen men who have benefited so far, why the interest in those two?'

'Shortly after their release, both these men were murdered at the addresses they had been released to.'

Wilson looked troubled. 'This is one of the other problems that our offenders always have to confront. All the hatred directed at them often manifests itself in extreme violence.'

Andy said, 'I can't go into details, but the two murders do appear to be linked in several ways. Did these men associate with each other while they were both serving prisoners here?'

'You need to speak to the senior warder on the sex offenders wing. He would know the answer to that question. I'll arrange for you to see him after this meeting.'

Once again, he pressed the button on his telephone and said, 'Sylvia, sorry to keep disturbing you, but I need you to arrange for Senior Officer Parker to meet my guests in reception as soon as he can, please. Do you have those annual leave details for Joanna?'

Wilson began scribbling on his notepad before replacing the handset.

He said, 'Joanna's on annual leave from today. She's not back at work until the twenty-fifth of this month. She's booked a week away in the Lake District. She's a very outdoorsy kind of woman.'

Rachel said, 'Me too. I love walking. The lakes will be beautiful this time of year. Can we make an appointment to see her on the first day that she's back at work? It would be useful for us if we can ascertain exactly what the scheme provides.'

'Yes, of course. I agree, you do need to speak with her. I'll arrange it for eleven o'clock on the twenty-fifth. There's a myriad of little things that she helps to put in place that help to break the cycle of reoffending. Things like helping them to get accommodation away from the areas they originally offended in is just one example. Briefing them properly about the importance of maintaining contact with the probation service. There are so many positive aspects that were always neglected in the past.'

'Thank you. Eleven o'clock would be fine.'

'If there's nothing else, I'll walk you to reception to meet Senior Officer Parker.'

Andy said, 'Thanks for your time, Governor Redmayne. We look forward to speaking with Ms Preston.'

Five minutes later, Andy and Rachel were waiting in a side office at the prison reception area.

The door opened, and a very smart-looking officer, in full uniform, said, 'You wanted to see me? I'm Senior Officer Parker.'

Andy made the introductions and said, 'We're interested in two inmates who were both transferred in to undertake the pre-release scheme.'

'Names?'

'Manfred Bauer and Stewart Tighe.'

'Yes. I remember them both. Very different characters. One full of remorse, constantly blaming himself for what had happened. That was Bauer. The other one, Tighe, was a scheming, manipulative evil bastard who should never have been allowed to set foot outside these walls. What's your interest in those two?'

'Did they associate with each other here?'

'Not possible. Bauer was released from here in October last year before Tighe even arrived.'

The prison officer paused before continuing. 'How the ice maiden and the parole board thought Tighe was fit for release, I'll never know. Evil sod.'

Rachel said, 'Sorry. The ice maiden?'

'I do apologise. That's my pet name for Joanna Preston. She's a bit like the ice maiden. Very aloof from the staff. Walks around in a world of her own most of the time.

Anyway, is there anything else you need to know about Bauer and Tighe?'

Andy said, 'No, thanks. That was all.'

'Good. I'm sorry to rush, but I need to get back on the wing. The cons are in a very strange mood. We've already had one incident today; I don't want there to be another.'

Neither detective inquired what that incident might have been. Andy said flatly, 'Can you escort us out of the prison, please?'

'Of course. This way, Detectives.'

47

10.00am, 17 February 1988
Nottinghamshire Police Headquarters

It had been just over a month since Danny had made the onerous trip to headquarters to brief Chief Superintendent Potter.

This morning's meeting was going no better than that one had. Danny was in the unenviable position of having very little progress to report on.

Potter leaned back in his chair, removed his spectacles and rubbed the area on the bridge of his nose where they sat. Danny thought his line manager looked exhausted.

Eventually, Potter said, 'It's not looking good, is it?'

'No, sir. The house-to-house enquiry has been completed for the Bauer murder. I even extended the perimeters to cover some of the Sherwood area as well as Carrington. All to no avail.'

'Any CCTV?'

'We have grainy images of a figure on a pushbike in the area at the relevant time, but the quality is too poor to use.'

'I think you should put it out in today's press release anyway. If nothing else, someone might recognise that person as themselves, and we can then rule them out altogether.'

Danny nodded. 'Will do, sir. I think it smacks of desperation, though.'

'But that's exactly what we are. We're desperate. We have a murder that looks destined to remain unsolved, and another that is already floundering. Did you ever track down the letter writer from the newspaper?'

'Yes, sir. He was just an old man, angry at the prison in Whatton, venting his rage in the newspaper. There was one thing we gained from that enquiry, though. It strengthened a line of enquiry that we were already tentatively looking at.'

'Which is?'

'A businessman has founded a group that protest the early release of sex offenders. It appears that some of his followers are quite zealous and advocate the use of physical violence. We're looking closely at the Guardians of Innocence and its founder, James Brannigan. The problem we have is that Brannigan is out of the country until the twenty-fifth of this month.'

'Will he be seen then?'

'Already arranged, sir. In the meantime, I have two detectives digging into the finance and membership of the group.'

'At least that's something, I suppose. Keep me informed how the meeting with Brannigan goes.'

'Will do.'

'Right. What's happening with the Stewart Tighe enquiry?'

Danny outlined how little forensic evidence they had found at the scene, and that, because of the remote location, how few enquiries could be carried out in the area of the murder.

Potter listened intently and then said, 'I understand you have seconded a detective sergeant onto your team from Worksop CID, to assist with enquiries into Tighe's original victims and their families. Any use?'

'DS Lacey has been a great help, sir. She was the family liaison on the original enquiry into the sexual assaults committed by Tighe. She has a very good rapport with the families. She is following what could be a positive lead this morning, into an associate of one victim's family.'

'That sounds positive. Anything else?'

'We're following up on a vehicle sighting that came in yesterday. That will also form part of the press appeal later today.'

Potter looked thoughtful.

After a lengthy pause, he said, 'I know you dislike these meetings, Danny, and that to you, I must always appear to be negative. I want you to understand that I'm asking you the questions that I get asked in the senior command briefings. I do understand that you're dealing with a high level of public apathy in both cases. I suppose what I'm trying to say is this: Stick at it.'

Danny was shocked. It was a side of Potter he'd never seen before, and he wondered just how much pressure he was getting from above.

He said, 'Thank you, sir. I'll make sure my team keep pushing for that breakthrough.'

Potter half-smiled and nodded.

Danny knew the meeting was over, so he stood up and walked to the door. As he reached for the handle, he heard Potter say, 'Forgive me, Danny. I never asked how your daughter was doing?'

Danny turned. 'She's recovering very well, but she's still in the hospital at the moment.'

'It's good to hear she's recovering well. I've got two boys myself. I know children can be such a worry at times. If you need any more time off, just let me know.'

'Will do, and thank you, sir.'

Danny stepped outside the office.

For once, he felt quite uplifted. This was a new side to Adrian Potter. Maybe there was hope moving forward after all.

48

6.30pm, 17 February 1988
MCIU Offices, Mansfield Police Station

The evening debrief had just finished, and Danny walked back into his office, followed by Tina and Rob. He slumped down in his chair. It had been another long day, and he was ready for home.

He told Rob, 'It was good work by Nigel and Sam today. The statement they obtained from Bill Tandy about the vehicle sighting is first class. That vehicle could be our first real breakthrough. I want you to grip this enquiry, Rob, and make sure we explore every possible chance to identify the vehicle and subsequently the driver. If we find the car, we could find our killer.'

'Will do, boss.'

'What did both of you make of the enquiry carried out by Andy and Rachel at HMP Whatton?'

Tina said, 'I think it's vital we talk to the welfare officer who runs the early release scheme as soon as we can. We need to find out exactly who knew what about the arrangements made for the release of Bauer and Tighe.'

'My thoughts exactly. It's too much of a coincidence that both our dead men were part of the early release project. You know me, I've never liked coincidences.'

Rob said, 'If the murders are connected to this early release scheme, then there's another big issue that needs addressing. If there have been fifteen men released on this scheme, what made Bauer and Tighe stand out from the rest? Who were those other offenders? Where are they now?'

'That's a very good point. For all we know, there could be other victims already out there.'

Danny scribbled in his enquiry log before turning to Tina and saying, 'Ask Andy to contact Governor Redmayne first thing in the morning. I want him to obtain a comprehensive list of all the other sex offenders released under his project. I want to know their names, addresses, details of their probation officers, the works.'

'Will do.'

'There's one other bit of business that I need to tell you about. I'm going to change the office manager. Fran Jefferies is to be given an outside investigative role. I'm going to task Jeff Williams with the role of office manager. From now on, this role will be a six-month commitment. It's unfair for talented detectives to be constantly stuck in the office. I think overall this will be a good thing for the MCIU. Do either of you have any thoughts?'

Tina said, 'Fran's a quality detective. Her research skills will be sorely missed. Did she approach you, boss?'

'Yes, she did. She felt undervalued. I stressed to her the importance of the work she currently does, but she's like the rest of us. We all want to be out there, dealing with the public and catching criminals.'

Rob said, 'As far as I'm concerned, I think it's a great idea. Whoever takes on the role should have the same research skills that Fran has. It will be good for others to utilise those skills occasionally. I'm all for it. I'd have Fran Jefferies on my team any day.'

'That's great. I'll speak to Jeff tomorrow, because right now, I think it's home time, and I need to get to the hospital.'

49

7.00am, 24 February 1988
Mill Lane, Newark, Nottinghamshire

Wilf Kelham cut a scruffy shambolic figure as he shuffled slowly along the path at the side of the river. It was a cold morning, and there was a low mist swirling along the top of the river as it flowed slowly by.

There wasn't a soul about. He sometimes passed joggers and dog walkers on his early morning stroll, but today he had seen nobody.

It had been a week since his release from HMP Whatton. Life in the halfway hostel on nearby Coopers Yard wasn't too bad. It was very crowded and busy, but his room was clean and tidy, and most of the other people living there were okay. There wasn't the undercurrent of constant danger that there had been inside prison. The staff who ran the hostel were friendly and helpful.

On the first day, after he had been dropped off by Ms Preston and introduced to his probation officer, he had settled into his room and then gone for a stroll outside.

He had wanted to be alone, to feel the cold winter sun on his face and to breathe fresh air. To his joy, he had discovered that the River Trent ran past the bottom of Mill Lane. He had always been fascinated by water.

Ever since that first moment of discovery, Wilf had spent hours every day walking along the riverbank.

His favourite walk of the day was the early morning one, when everywhere was so quiet and peaceful. He had got into the habit of rising every day at six o'clock and leaving the hostel early. Whatever the weather, he would then spend an hour walking along the riverbank towards the castle. Once at the castle, he would pause and rest a little before turning round and walking back to Coopers Yard, ready for breakfast.

Today had been no different.

At six o'clock on the dot, he had got up and glanced out the window of his room. It wasn't raining, but it looked cold, so he had wrapped up warm. He had made his way downstairs and out into the cold morning air. It was just starting to get light, but it would be another hour before the sun rose properly.

He had breathed in deeply, feeling the frigid air scorch his lungs. When he exhaled, his breath came out as a cloud of white vapour.

Having taken an hour to reach the castle, he had leaned against the metal railing with his back to the river and looked up at the magnificent stone ruin.

He took a moment to fully get his breath back before setting off on the return journey. As usual, he would take his time going back. He took pleasure from the many waterbirds and other wildlife that were active on the riverbank.

As the watery sun peeped over the horizon for the first

time, Wilf started the long walk back to Coopers Yard. He could almost taste the cornflakes he would be having for breakfast. The walk along the river always made him hungry.

For the first time in years, Wilf Kelham felt happy and content with life.

50

7.00am, 24 February 1988
Mill Lane, Newark, Nottinghamshire

By always staying forty yards back, it had been an easy task to follow the old man along the riverbank, undetected. He never looked back. He just shuffled slowly along, looking straight ahead. On the odd occasion he did stop momentarily; he would turn slowly and stare at the river as it flowed slowly by.

Today had been no different to all the other days the old man had been observed. He had followed the same identical routine. Out from the hostel just after six o'clock, followed by the lonely walk from the hostel to the castle. Then the brief rest before the walk back along the riverbank.

The person observing the old man had been relieved to discover this pattern of behaviour. It would have been impossible to carry out the mission inside the busy halfway hostel, but the man's regular walk along the secluded riverbank path provided the perfect opportunity.

Having finalised a plan, the figure allowed the old man to finish his walk.

The next time their paths crossed on the riverbank, it would be different.

It was almost time for Wilf Kelham to face the ultimate justice for his crimes against children.

51

6.30pm, 24 February 1988
MCIU Offices, Mansfield Police Station

Danny sat in his office with Rob and Tina. The mood was despondent. It was almost as though a black cloud hung over the entire MCIU department. The last viable enquiry into the Stewart Tighe murder had drawn a blank. There had been no further sightings of the dark car described by the farm labourer Bill Tandy. Rob had put teams of detectives out in strategic positions along the country lanes near to where the vehicle had been sighted in the hope it would return.

Nothing had been seen.

Checks on traffic cameras on the main roads that led to the country lanes had also drawn a blank.

Rob looked downcast. 'I know it's not what you wanted to hear, boss.'

'It's not your fault. If we can't find the car, we can't find it. I don't want it to be totally discounted, though. Until we speak to the person who had parked in that lay-by near Redgate Farm, we have to treat it as though it was parked by our suspect.'

'All those man-hours parked up on that lane, and not one sighting.'

'That could be a positive. That could mean that it was never a courting couple in the first place. Keep looking.'

'That goes without saying, boss.'

Tina said, 'On a brighter note, James Brannigan returns tomorrow. Are you still going to see him with Lynn?'

Danny nodded. 'Yes. I sat down with Lynn earlier today to go over our strategy when we talk to him.'

'Do you think it will take us anywhere?'

'I'm hoping at the very least it will open up more lines of enquiry. Whether or not we're on the right path is a different matter. Right now, it's all we have.'

Rob said, 'Don't forget, Andy and Rachel have an appointment to see that welfare officer at the prison tomorrow, as well. That could give us some useful insights.'

'True enough. Let's see where we are tomorrow night; it could all have changed by then. I'll see you in the morning.'

52

10.00am, 25 February 1988
HMP Whatton, Nottinghamshire

Governor Redmayne's secretary had shown Andy Wills and Rachel Moore to the office occupied by the prison welfare officer, Joanna Preston.

Although a very high position within the prison, the welfare officer role was nothing to do with the prison service. Although Joanna Preston was directly answerable to the governor of the prison, technically she was a civilian, employed by the probation service.

It had been Wilson Redmayne who had headhunted Preston to be the lead on his early release scheme. At the time, she had been the education officer, again employed by the probation service, on B Wing of the prison.

The new role was a substantial promotion, as well as a huge increase in both salary and responsibility.

Her office reflected that high position. It was almost as big and spacious as the governor's.

The secretary knocked politely on the door and waited for the invitation to enter the room. When it came, she opened the door and said, 'Joanna, the two detectives I mentioned this morning are here.'

Joanna Preston stood to receive her guests and said, 'Thanks. Show them in, please.'

Andy and Rachel walked in and introduced themselves. They were a little surprised to see that the welfare officer was so young. Joanna Preston only appeared to be in her late twenties. She was quite tall, probably an inch or so taller than Rachel, and extremely slim. She looked very fit. She was dressed immaculately, in a dark grey business suit. Her shoulder-length dark hair was tied back in a tight ponytail.

She walked from behind her desk and greeted the detectives with a warm smile and a handshake. The smile was welcoming, but there was a fire and intensity in her green eyes.

She said, 'Would you like a drink?'

The two detectives declined the offer, so Joanna said, 'Please take a seat. How can I help you?'

Andy Wills said, 'We came to see Governor Redmayne last week and spoke to him about the early release scheme he introduced to the prison. He advised us that we should really speak to you, as you administer and effectively run the scheme. We're here to find out a bit more about how it works.'

'I spoke to Wilson when I arrived this morning. He explained to me that two of the men released under the scheme have since been murdered. I was shocked, to say the least. I strive to put each man into a safe environment. I'm fully aware of the hostility these men face daily. I know it's a constant threat.'

'As you appreciate that threat so keenly, what steps do you take to house the men safely?'

'It's an extremely long process. The first thing I endeavour to do is to house the men away from where the committed their previous offenses. This alone is sometimes not an easy task, depending on the individuals' resources and support.'

'Can you give me an example?'

'Would you mind if we stick to the two men you are interested in? I still have a duty of confidentiality towards the other men released under the programme.'

'That's entirely up to you, but I'd better tell you now that I want the full details of the other men released and their current locations, before we leave today.'

Joanna Preston's mood suddenly changed. She snapped angrily, 'That's totally out of the question. These men have all served their sentences and are now entitled to a fresh start. Those details are strictly confidential.'

'Ms Preston, we're dealing with two murder enquiries. One of the things that links those crimes is the fact that both men were released from this prison under your scheme. We cannot discount this link. It also means that every prisoner released in this way could be in real danger. Any subsequent enquiries to check on the locations and welfare of the released men would be discreetly done. We would ensure that the detectives would do nothing to expose the men or jeopardise their welfare.'

Joanna was thoughtful and then said, 'I'll need to clear this with Wilson first. I wasn't expecting any of this.'

Rachel said, 'Speak to the governor, but it's the right course of action to check on these men. They could be in danger. All we're interested in is their welfare.'

Joanna considered that. 'That welfare check could be easily achieved with telephone calls to their individual probation officers.'

Andy said, 'Let's sort this issue out at the end of our conversation. You can speak with the governor, and I'll talk to the senior investigating officer. I'm sure we'll come to an agreement.'

'Very well.'

Andy took a moment for everyone in the room to relax a little. Then to break some of the tension, he said, 'Tell me about the steps you took before housing Manfred Bauer and Stewart Tighe?'

'Those two cases illustrate perfectly the differing challenges. Manfred Bauer had no support network at all. His only contact on the outside world would be his probation officer. I needed to find somewhere away from where he'd committed his crime, so Leicester and the surrounding towns were all out of the question. The accommodation had to be comfortable, but at the same time, used to housing men released from prison. I made sure the location was within walking distance of the office of his probation officer so he didn't feel totally isolated.'

Rachel said, 'Although Osborne Grove is quite a nice street, the surrounding area is quite rough. When we spoke to his fellow residents, we established that Bauer was too terrified to leave the flat. Were you aware of that?'

'I wasn't aware, but then again, unless his probation officer contacted me specifically, there's no way I would know. My role ends when the prisoner is housed and placed under the care of their individual probation officer. It then becomes that officer's job to keep a check on the released man's welfare. There's no way I could do follow-up welfare checks on every man. My role has to have a definitive end point.'

'I suppose so. How did Stewart Tighe differ from Bauer?'

'There was a good family support network in place for Stewart. His parents were willing to accommodate him within their home. This meant he had daily contact with other people, which is always a good thing.'

'You mentioned that one of the main criteria was to house these men a good distance away from where they had committed their crimes. Carlton in Lindrick is not far from Worksop. How did you decide that it would be okay for Stewart Tighe to reside there?'

'I took the time to go and inspect the farm his parents own. Although it's only five miles from Worksop town centre, I felt that its remote location helped it to be a suitable residence. Prior to his release, it was stressed to Stewart that under no circumstances was he ever to travel into Worksop town centre. His probation officer was based in Sheffield, so there was never any need for him to go anywhere near the centre of Worksop.'

Andy said, 'How vital is the role of the probation officer in the success of this scheme?'

'It's crucial. All I do is try to prepare the men for release while they are here. That includes education in the changes to our society. Some of these men have been in prison for years. They need to be aware of those changes to better adapt to them.'

'What else do you do?'

'I sort out their finances. What benefits they can claim. I try to ensure that they are financially stable before they are released.'

'Employment?'

'Part of the probation officer's role would be to find the men suitable employment.'

'Is it part of your role to notify the victims and their families about the imminent release of these men?'

'Definitely not. That's down to the prison service and the parole board. That job is not part of my remit.'

Rachel said, 'None of Stewart Tighe's victims had been notified of his release.'

Joanna looked shocked. 'That's awful. You need to raise that with Governor Redmayne. That should never happen. I know you might not think it, but one of our main concerns during this process is for the victims of these men.'

'I'm sorry, but how does early release reflect that concern?'

'Whether or not these men are released is not our decision. It's made by the parole board. All this scheme does is to try to ensure there's less chance of the offender committing similar crimes in the future. That's the sole measure of success. I believe it will only ever work if we show care and compassion to the previous victims, as well as the men we are releasing.'

There was a long pause.

Joanna broke the silence and said, 'I think it's time we dealt with the elephant in the room. I'll go and see the governor and ask him to join us. Feel free to use the telephone to contact your office. I'll be straight with you; I'll be pushing for the welfare checks to be carried out by the probation officers and not your detectives. Having the police suddenly turn up in their lives could cause these men all kinds of issues.'

She stood up and left the room.

Andy picked up the telephone on the desk and dialled the number for Danny's office. As he dialled, he said to Rachel, 'What do you think?'

'I think she has a point. If all we're interested in is their welfare, we can't really argue against what she's suggesting as an alternative.'

Andy nodded. Then he spoke into the phone: 'Boss, it's Andy. We're getting some resistance to obtaining details of the other offenders.'

There was a brief pause; then Andy continued: 'The welfare officer is concerned that police officers checking up on these men in their new locations could compromise their safety. She's suggested that the men's probation officers carry out any routine welfare checks to establish that the men are all safe and well.'

There was a longer pause before Andy said, 'I'll put that to her and the governor and see if the probation officers will ask that question. Okay. No problem. Cheers, boss.'

Having only heard half of the conversation, Rachel looked puzzled.

Andy said, 'I forgot Rob's in charge today, as the boss is in Northampton this morning. He's suggested a compromise. He's happy for the probation officers to do the checks provided they ascertain if any of the men have received any threatening letters or other threats.'

Just at that moment, Joanna Preston and Wilson Redmayne walked back into her office.

The governor said, 'I'm sorry, Detectives, but I'm with Ms Preston on this one. I'm not willing to disclose that information without a judge's order.'

Andy said, 'I've spoken to Detective Inspector Buxton, and he's suggested a compromise.'

Joanna said, 'Which is?'

'He's happy for the welfare checks to be carried out by the men's own probation officers provided the men are all asked if they've received any threatening letters or other threats against their well-being, in their new locations. Is that a viable option for you?'

Joanna turned to the governor and nodded.

Redmayne said, 'That's agreed, then. We'll arrange for the probation officers to carry out those checks and ask those questions on your behalf.'

Joanna said, 'I'll speak to all the officers today and get the checks done within the next twenty-four hours. Obviously, if there have been any threats, as you describe, I'll contact you immediately.'

'If any threats are discovered, that will obviously necessitate further discussion between you, the governor, and Chief Inspector Flint. I'm sure we would insist on full access to that man before something drastic happens and we have another murder victim on our hands.'

Redmayne smiled and said, 'Let's cross that bridge when we come to it. If you're finished, Detectives, I'll walk you to reception.'

Andy turned to Joanna and said, 'It was nice talking to you. Thanks for all your insights and help.'

'No problem, Detective. I'll crack on and start making those calls.'

As the two detectives followed Governor Redmayne through the corridors of the prison, Andy said to him, 'I can see why you wanted Joanna Preston to run the scheme. She's as smart as a whip, very motivated and tough.'

'My thoughts exactly. It's her military background, I suppose. She has an inner strength I admire, and her organisational skills are second to none.'

As they reached reception and the exit, the governor said, 'Have a good day, Detectives. I'll make sure Joanna contacts you with the results of all the welfare checks. I'll ask her to provide either positive or negative feedback on the question of threats.'

'Thank you, Governor. I'll pass on what you've said to Detective Chief Inspector Flint. He may want to speak to you personally at some stage.'

'No problem. We're all on the same side. Anything we can do to help, we'll do. I hope you understand that, right?'

'Of course. Thanks again.'

53

10.00am, 25 February 1988
Polyplastech Ltd, Northampton

The drive down the M1 motorway, from Nottingham to Northampton, had been uneventful. Danny and Lynn had spent the entire journey discussing what they already knew about the businessman James Brannigan.

The vast Polyplastech Ltd factory site was five minutes from the motorway. It had been built on thirty acres of pristine countryside, much to the chagrin of local environmental groups. It was, however, one of the main employers in the surrounding area and a massive boost to the local economy.

The entire site was hidden; it couldn't be seen from any public road. This masterpiece of planning had been achieved by a mixture of hard landscaping and strategic tree planting.

Danny had driven from the main road onto the long winding driveway that led to the factory site.

As he drove into the visitors car park outside the main

office block, Lynn said, 'This is one of fourteen Polyplastech factories that are spread across the world. Brannigan also owns luxury houses in over a dozen countries. The property he calls home is an Elizabethan manor house standing on ten acres of land just outside Oxford, in the picturesque village of Steeple Claydon.'

'So he's mega-rich and decides to live in the UK. Does that make him a patriot, or somebody with a distinct lack of imagination?'

'I don't think anybody would ever describe James Brannigan as lacking in imagination. He built this business empire up from a single factory unit in Bicester to the worldwide conglomerate it is today.'

Danny smiled. 'You sound very impressed with Mr Brannigan, Lynn.'

'I just think it takes a special, freethinking, and driven person to build something like that.'

'I agree. All that drive and ambition can come with a heavy price, though. Have you asked yourself why his daughter was at a boarding school when the abuse happened? Why his wife divorced him shortly afterwards? Why he's currently separated from his second wife?'

'I can see you've been doing your research, boss.'

As he parked the car in one of the visitors' bays, Danny said, 'Let's see if we can get answers to some of those questions from the man himself.'

Fifteen minutes later the two detectives were sitting on a leather sofa inside the spacious office of James Brannigan.

The businessman's personal assistant had remained with them after explaining that her boss was currently in another office, on an urgent private telephone call to Australia. She had assured them that the call wouldn't take long, and he would join them shortly.

After an awkward five-minute silence, the door to the

office opened, and James Brannigan walked in. He was still recognisable as the man whose photograph adorned the Guardians of Innocence flyer, but he looked very different today. Gone was the staid businessman in the dark business suit on the meeting flyer.

Brannigan was in his early forties. He was a tall, slim man with an even tan and smartly cut, short blonde hair. Beneath the fringe were bright, piercing blue eyes and a white smile.

Today, he was dressed in loose-fitting linen trousers that were a dark beige colour and a white muslin shirt that was open at the neck.

He looked like an advert for an exotic beach holiday, not one of the UK's most successful businessmen.

The surprise at his appearance must have registered on Danny's and Lynn's faces because Brannigan said, 'Detectives, forgive me for the delay, but the call was urgent. Don't worry, I don't dress for work like this every day. It's just that we didn't fly back until late last night. It was gone midnight by the time we arrived home. I'm feeling a little jet-lagged and grabbed the first thing I could lay my hands on this morning. So this is the Florida look.'

He sat down in another leather settee directly opposite Danny and Lynn and said, 'I understand you've driven down from Nottingham this morning to see me. What is it I can help you with?'

Danny was conscious that Brannigan's assistant was still hovering in the room. 'Some of what we want to discuss is personal.'

Immediately understanding the detective's inference, Brannigan said, 'I would prefer that Alex stays.'

It was said in a way that wasn't open for debate. For the first time Danny got a glimpse of the hard-nosed businessman.

Danny said, 'Very well. I want to ask you some questions

about a group calling themselves the Guardians of Innocence.'

'Yes.'

'My understanding is that you established this group four years ago.'

'It's almost five years now.'

'What was your motivation?'

'The reasons are all very well documented. I have one daughter, Tiffany. My beautiful girl was physically abused by a paedophile masquerading as a teacher at her school. The police did a brilliant job caring for my daughter and prosecuting the offender. The court who tried the offender also did a great job. The offender, Miles Harmon, received a sentence of nine years' imprisonment from the judge. Then it all went wrong.'

'In what way?'

'This monster had been sentenced to nine years, not long enough for my liking, but still nine years. Then I was informed that the bloody parole board had decided to release Harmon early. This excuse of a human being only did three years in prison for effectively ruining my beautiful girl's life.'

'How did you feel about Harmon at the time?'

There was a lengthy pause before Brannigan answered the question with one of his own. 'Do you have children, Detective?'

'I have a young daughter.'

'Then you will recognise and understand the feelings I'm about to express.'

Again, there was a momentary pause before he continued, 'If somebody had put me in a room alone with Harmon at that moment in time, I would have happily torn him to pieces with my bare hands.'

Danny didn't respond immediately, deliberately allowing some of the emotion to dissipate; then he asked quietly, 'That awful abuse of your daughter, did it affect you as a family in other ways?'

Brannigan locked eyes with Danny and said, 'Very astute, Detective. I can see you've been doing some background work on me.'

'Did it?'

'It cost me my first marriage. It had been my wife's idea to ship Tiffany off to that bloody pretentious boarding school. I was perfectly happy for her to be educated locally, but no, my wife had insisted that a private school education would be best for Tiffany. I knew then it was a selfish decision, and one my wife had made on the grounds of what was best for her and not my daughter. Like an idiot, I went along with the decision to support my wife.'

'And that decision weighed heavily?'

'Of course it did. Unknowingly, I had agreed to send my daughter to a place where she would be systematically abused over a long period of time. How would that make you feel?'

Danny remained silent. Eventually, Brannigan continued, 'It drove an irreversible wedge between us. I was glad when she filed for divorce. It was very expensive, but I was relieved that I would never have to see the selfish cow again.'

Changing tack, Danny asked, 'How is Tiffany now?'

Brannigan smiled and said, 'My daughter is wonderful. She is a happy and blooming teenager now. I've paid for the best therapy and counselling money can buy. It seems to be working for her. She has managed to move on from that dreadful ordeal.'

'Have you?'

'I'm sorry?'

'Have you moved on? Or is there still a part of you that would like to tear Harmon, or people like Harmon, to pieces with your bare hands?'

'Detective, I can assure you that my inner rage has subsided. I no longer feel that way. That doesn't mean to say I will ever stop striving for change. These monsters who harm our children, our innocents, should be caged for life. They need to be placed where they can do no more harm, and remain there, not be released back onto our streets.'

'And that's why you established the Guardians of Innocence?'

'I'm a man with influence. Money can't buy everything, but it can buy you a lot of bloody influence. I spend a small fortune every year lobbying the government to get a change in the law. My local MP totally agrees with my sentiments. He's currently preparing a private members bill to put before the house. If successful, this bill will effectively ban convicted sex offenders from applying for early release. That's the sole aim of the organisation.'

'Apart from lobbying government, what else does your organisation do?'

'The membership of the organisation is growing. I attend meetings up and down the country and speak to as many people as I can. The message is being spread far and wide. The aim is to have a large enough membership of the organisation to be able to apply pressure on every individual member of parliament. That's the only viable way we can achieve this change.'

'You've described what you want to achieve personally, and how you want to achieve it. Do any of your members have different ideas how to best press home that desired change?'

'I don't understand.'

'Is violence against convicted sex offenders ever discussed at your meetings?'

'Never. That would be illegal. My lawyers go through

everything I ever say at these meetings to ensure there are no issues like that.'

'Again, that's you personally. Do you have any idea what else is being discussed at your meetings after you've spoken?'

'I'm a very busy man. I usually attend the meetings, make a speech and then leave.'

'I have spoken to a witness who attended one of your meetings in Nottinghamshire. He has told me how groups of hard men, who were part of your organisation, stayed behind after you had made your speech, solely to incite younger members of the audience to seek out paedophiles and carry out violent retribution. Would you have any idea who these men are?'

'Where was the meeting you're referring to?'

'It was a meeting organised by your organisation to protest the sex offenders wing at HMP Whatton. Do you recall that meeting?'

Brannigan was thoughtful. 'Yes, I do. It was very well attended. There were lots of our members in attendance.'

'After you had delivered your speech, did you stay in the hall to answer questions?'

'Not on that occasion. If I remember rightly, and Alex will be able to confirm this, I had to be in Krakow, Poland, the next day. I left straight after the meeting.'

'Who were these hard men, these members of your organisation who were in the audience? The witness described them to us as being your security.'

'I don't have security. I have a driver, that's it. I'm a businessman, not Prince Charles.'

'So you have no idea who these men who were inciting violence at that meeting were?'

'No, I don't. I can try to find out for you, Detective. There may be some way I can find out who was there. The problem is, these are all open meetings. Anybody can turn up.'

There was a pause. Then Brannigan said, 'Can I ask you a question? Why all the sudden interest in a political group. I established almost five years ago?'

'Over the last year there's been a significant rise in violent crime against sex offenders in Nottinghamshire. That's my interest. I'm trying to establish if that rise in violence stems from your group.'

'My aims and intentions for the Guardians of Innocence have always been the same. I want change through political pressure, not physical violence.'

'Do you think it's possible there are elements within your organisation who believe in using totally different methods to achieve that change?'

'It's possible. I'm certainly not aware of any such splinter movements within the organisation. I've attended countless meetings, up and down the country, and have never witnessed anybody inciting violence in the way you've described. There are people who come who hold very strong views on what is a very emotional subject. Personally, I've never witnessed a lynch mob or anything like it.'

Danny turned to Lynn. 'Is there anything you want to ask?'

Lynn said, 'Are there many female members in your organisation?'

'There are always women at the meetings I attend. I have no idea on numbers, though. I can ask Alex to prepare a breakdown of the membership if that would help.'

'That would be great, thanks. I also understand that you provide financial help to a lot of small firms and businesses nationally. Would it be possible for us to have a list of all the businesses you've assisted that are based in Nottinghamshire?'

Brannigan looked puzzled. 'Can I ask why you think that would help?'

'Sometimes people get a misguided sense of loyalty towards somebody who has helped them. They can go above and beyond in trying to say thank you, if you get my drift.'

It was a skilfully vague reply that left Brannigan thinking. Eventually, he said, 'I don't think that will cause us an issue.'

He turned to his assistant and said, 'Alex, can you sort those two matters out as quickly as you can, please.'

He turned back to the detectives and said, 'If there's nothing else, I do have urgent matters that need addressing. It's always the same whenever I've spent any time away from the office.'

Danny said, 'That's all for now, Mr Brannigan. Thank you for your time and for being so open about what are obviously very personal matters.'

'I'm always happy to help the police. As far as I'm concerned, you have a thankless task. You don't appear to be supported by some members of the public, and you're definitely not supported by politicians and the judiciary. I wish you luck.'

The two men shook hands. Danny said, 'I hope Tiffany continues to recover fully from her ordeal.'

'And I hope that's a pain you never have to experience with your own child, Detective. Alex will sort out that information you requested, and then show you the way out.'

54

1.00pm, 25 February 1988
Steeple Claydon, Buckinghamshire

James Brannigan didn't often drive himself, so when he got the chance, he tried to enjoy the experience. He kept a fleet of luxury cars at his house in Steeple Claydon. As it had been a beautifully crisp morning, without a cloud in the sky, he had decided on driving his Aston Martin Vantage convertible. The burgundy red sports car had a cream leather interior and walnut dash. It had been built two years ago, to his own personal specifications.

When he had left the factory just outside Northampton, it was still a beautiful day. He'd retrieved a fur-lined leather flying jacket from the boot of the car and had taken the top down.

The drive through the winding country lanes with the roof down had been exhilarating. The cold air biting into his face had felt refreshing and helped him think clearly. He was happy how the meeting with the detectives had gone. He had controlled his inner rage at why they should be questioning his ideals, and concentrated on giving nothing away.

Only once had he been rattled.

That had been by the female detective, who had nonchalantly thrown in the request for business information. He had agreed to the request, as he did not want to appear obstructive in any way. A refusal could have appeared churlish.

It was a mistake.

He needed to make a telephone call to avert any damage to his plans.

He slowed the powerful car down as he drove into the picturesque village of Steeple Claydon. His house was located half a mile beyond the far end of the village.

As he drove slowly through the narrow streets, he saw what he had been looking for. In the distance, next to the village pub, stood the quintessentially English red telephone box.

He gently applied the brakes, and the car came to a stop directly outside the public phone box. He flipped open the glove compartment on the walnut dash, where he always threw his loose change. He grabbed a handful of coins and got out of the car. Both the street and the phone box were deserted.

Unlike many public telephone boxes in the UK, this one was in pristine condition. It was clean, fresh and in good working order. He picked up the handset and dialled a number from memory. As soon as the call was connected and the pips sounded, Brannigan fed the payphone several coins.

A voice on the other end of the phone said, 'Stealthsafe Security.'

Brannigan said, 'Davy?'

'This is Davy Johnson. Who's asking?'

'James Brannigan. Are you alone?'

'I'm sorry, Mr Brannigan, I didn't recognise your voice. Yes, I'm alone. What's up?'

Brannigan explained about the visit by the Nottingham detectives. Then he said, 'They were asking a lot of questions about the Guardians and how the group may be connected to an increase in violence against paedophiles. Has something happened while I've been away?'

'Things are progressing. We're moving the agenda forward as planned.'

'I don't want you getting ahead of yourself, Davy. Things must only be done when the time is right. You must wait for me to sanction any direct action.'

'I know that, Mr Brannigan. It's getting harder and harder to contain some of our people, though.'

'You must keep them under control, especially now the police are starting to sniff around. We've managed to stay under the radar this long. We need to keep it that way.'

The pips on the phone sounded again. Brannigan thrust in more coins and said, 'The police will probably be in touch with your company about me. I had to give them a list of all the companies I give financial backing to in Nottinghamshire.'

An incredulous Davy Johnson said, 'You had to?'

'Alright, I didn't have to, but I did. It was a mistake. It's easily remedied, though. When the police contact Stealthsafe, get your sister to deal with them. She doesn't know anything about the Guardians of Innocence stuff. She can talk to them about the security work your company's involved in and what financial backing I've given you. You must stress to her that it's important not to let them start digging too deep into other things. Do you think she can do it?'

'Our Barbra? Of course she can do it. She hates coppers. It's a shame you gave them that connection in the first place, but I'll sort it.'

'See that you do, Davy. It's almost time for us to take that direct action.'

Brannigan put the phone back on its cradle, terminating the call. He scooped up the unused coins from the returns tray in the phone box and walked back outside to the car.

He smiled at the throaty roar of the V8 engine before accelerating out of the village towards home.

Behind the smile, there was something niggling at the back of his mind. It was the throwaway comment made by Davy about it becoming harder and harder to keep certain people under control. Maybe he had taken his eye off the ball, spending so long in America. He knew he would need to tighten things up, or events could easily spiral out of his control.

Up until now, Davy Johnson had always managed to keep a lid on the violence. There had always been the risk of certain violent elements within the group taking control. He hoped he wasn't too late.

55

7.30am, 26 February 1988
MCIU Offices, Mansfield Police Station

Danny was sitting in his office with Rob, Tina, Lynn and Andy.

He opened his notepad and said, 'Thanks for coming in early, I wanted to have a quick meeting before everyone else arrives at eight o'clock. We need to discuss how the two enquiries are progressing, and debrief the two meetings we had with James Brannigan and the welfare officer at HMP Whatton. Andy, can we start with you at HMP Whatton? What was the welfare officer like?'

'Joanna Preston? She was much younger than I'd expected. Ex-military, very organised and intelligent. I can see why the prison governor wanted her to run the early release scheme. She's a tough cookie as well. She was very happy to stand her ground about disclosing the details of the other men released under the programme.'

'So I understand. Rob called me last night and told me about the compromise he'd had to make with her. I haven't got a problem with that, but make sure you chase her up on that information today. I want to know from those probation officers, as soon as possible, that the other early release candidates are all fit and well. I don't want Ms Preston to be under the impression she can drag her heels.'

'Will do.'

'Anything else that stands out about her?'

'A prison officer we spoke to referred to her as the ice maiden. She does come across as someone who's resolute, and I can imagine she doesn't suffer fools gladly, but she was willing to engage and talk to us. I don't know if that's a fair assessment, as it's based entirely on that single meeting. It was just a first impression I got.'

'I want you and Rachel to dig a little deeper into her background. Joanna Preston's someone who was fully aware of all the details relating to the release and rehousing of both Bauer and Tighe. I want you to be discreet when you're conducting those enquiries. I want to maintain a good working relationship with HMP Whatton, and Governor Redmayne in particular. It sounds like it got a bit fractious yesterday.'

'It never got that bad, boss. There were differences of opinion, but everything was resolved very cordially. I understand, though. Discretion required.'

'Any other viable lines of enquiry that stemmed from that meeting?'

'Nothing from the meeting, but you've just made me think of something that maybe myself and Rachel could explore a bit deeper.'

'Go on?'

'You mentioned that Joanna Preston had all the details of

both men's release packages. It just made me think: There may be other individuals, within the prison service and the probation service, who also had access to that information. Maybe we should start looking into that possibility.'

'Good point. Can I leave that enquiry with you and Rachel?'

'No problem.'

'Right. Let's go through the meeting that Lynn and I had with James Brannigan. It went pretty much as we had expected it would. Brannigan maintained that the Guardians of Innocence organisation is only interested in achieving its aims through non-violent methods. We already know there are some people within that organisation who think very differently. Thanks to Lynn's very astute question, placed at the perfect time, we've managed to obtain a list of all the small businesses that Polyplastech Ltd have assisted financially over the last few years. I was a little surprised when Brannigan agreed to give us that information without a struggle, but by that time he was bending over backwards to show us how cooperative he was being.'

Rob said, 'How will that list help our enquiry?'

'I'm hoping that somewhere within that group of companies, there will be a group of like-minded individuals who maybe have a different agenda to James Brannigan. I'm looking for companies that have a high uptake of membership within the Guardians. Businesses that have a workforce that could be useful to Brannigan.'

Lynn added, 'My first thoughts were companies that provide security at concerts, nightclubs, sporting events, that sort of thing. Our witness thought the thugs at the meeting in Whatton were employed as security for Brannigan. This is something he categorically denied, but maybe security is their day job.'

Danny said, 'It's quite a lengthy list to work through. Rob, I want you and Tina to provide two detectives from each side of the MCIU to assist Lynn and Jag in working through these companies. Let's start talking to people. I want you to get out there, rattle a few trees and see what drops out.'

The two detective inspectors both nodded. Tina said, 'No problem with staff from my side. The enquiries into Manfred Bauer have all been completed.'

Rob said, 'And all the enquiries left to do on the Stewart Tighe case should be completed within the next day or so.'

Danny said, 'I'm always loath to put all my eggs in one basket, but it seems like we don't have much option right now. Let's start working through this list and see if we can turn something up.'

That was the signal for the end of the meeting. As the others left the room, Tina remained behind and said, 'Have you got a minute, boss?'

'Close the door, Tina. What's on your mind?'

'I've been thinking about the Mars bars left at both scenes.'

'Do you have a theory?'

'No, I don't. We've spent hours in the office, brainstorming ideas, and have still come up with nothing. It suddenly dawned on me last night that there's one person we know who may have seen something like this before.'

'Go on.'

'I know I initially didn't get on with the woman, but Professor Whittle was a massive help to us when we were investigating the Stephen Meadows and Mike Grant cases last summer. It occurred to me that she may have seen cases like this, either here or in the States. Where unusual, bizarre objects have been deliberately left at murder scenes.'

Danny wrote the name *SHARON WHITTLE* in block capitals in his notepad. He said, 'That's a good idea. I'll give her a call and have a chat. Hopefully, she won't be halfway across the world, investigating somebody else's mess. Good thinking, Tina. Thanks.'

56

6.30am, 27 February 1988
Mill Lane, Newark, Nottinghamshire

The weather was foul. It was bitterly cold, and sleety showers had been falling thick and fast all morning. During a brief break in the showers, the figure hiding in the dark recesses overlooking the hostel at Coopers Yard had seen the front door open.

It had been precisely six o'clock when Wilf Kelham had emerged from the hostel. He was dressed for the cold damp weather, wearing a long army surplus khaki greatcoat, thick woollen scarf and hat. The old man didn't own a pair of gloves, so both his hands were thrust deep into the pockets of his coat.

The odd position of his arms had made his already slovenly, shuffling gait even slower.

Although cold and wet, the inclement weather had suited

the black-clad figure now paying close attention to the old man. Nobody in their right mind would venture out onto the riverbank during conditions like this.

Using the darkness at the river's edge, the figure began following the old man. The exact location for the planned attack had been identified on one of the previous recces. As the old man approached the predetermined spot on the riverbank path, the stalker moved in closer to Kelham.

As the old man shuffled along, head bowed against the cold wind and spitting rain, he had no idea of the malevolent force approaching him from behind.

At precisely the moment Wilf Kelham reached the desired spot, his attacker struck. The old man was pushed violently from behind, landing face down in an area of short grass. Three concussive blows were delivered to the back of his head in rapid fashion. The first blow from the claw hammer was delivered with such force that the head of the hammer penetrated deep inside the old man's skull. The claws of the hammer snagged on the woollen hat, and as the attacker's arm came back to deliver the second blow, they flicked the old man's hat from his head. It landed ten yards away on the path.

The first blow had been more than enough to kill the target, but this killer had a certain style and followed up the attack, delivering two more huge blows with deadly relish.

Each of the two subsequent blows made a sickeningly loud crack as the steel head of the hammer smashed through Kelham's skull, driving deep into his brain.

In the distance, the killer could hear the sound of training shoes splashing along the wet pathway at the side of the river. It was the sound of an early morning jogger using the riverbank path, and they were getting closer.

The killer stuffed the bloodstained claw hammer under

their jacket before placing the special object on top of Wilf Kelham's smashed skull. The attacker smiled grimly before sprinting off towards Mill Lane.

Another mission had been successfully accomplished.

57

7.45am, 27 February 1988
Mill Lane, Newark, Nottinghamshire

Danny had been about to leave his house, to make the short drive into work, when the telephone had rung. Thinking it could be the hospital, he had snatched up the receiver in a cold panic, only to be informed by the control room that a body had been found at the side of the River Trent, at Mill Lane in Newark. Early indications were that it was murder. The circumstances at the scene made it appear to be part of the Operation Hermes series.

By the time Danny arrived at Mill Lane in Newark, Rob Buxton and Andy Wills were already there, and had started to take charge of the scene.

Just as Danny got out of his car, it started to rain again. He walked down Mill Lane towards Rob. It was bitterly cold, and he pulled the collar of his raincoat up to try to thwart the icy wind.

'Morning, Rob. Where's the body?'

'It's on the side of the path, next to the river. I've got uniform cops at each end of the path now to prevent anybody else using it. Scenes of Crime are on their way. I've asked them to bring a tent to cover the body. In the meantime, we've done what we can with a sheet of tarpaulin that was in the boot of one of the panda cars first on scene.'

'Control room said it could be part of Hermes. Does it look like it to you?'

'Death has been caused by blunt trauma to the head, and there's a Mars bar in situ again. So, yeah, it does look identical to Bauer and Tighe.'

'Except this one is outside. Show me the body.'

The two detectives made their way from Mill Lane onto the path at the side of the river. There was a line of police tape that Rob had already put out leading along the side of the footpath.

'Keep to the right of the tape, boss. There are still footmarks on the left of it at the moment. The problem is, they're going to be washed away soon, with all this bloody rain.'

'We need to commandeer some buckets or bowls from somewhere and cover as many of the footmarks as we can. Scenes of Crime may be able to do something with them when they get here. They should be able to get photographs of them, at least.'

Andy was standing beside the tarpaulin that covered the deceased. He was trying to ensure nothing around the scene was disturbed any more than was necessary.

Rob said, 'Andy, get some buckets and the like from somewhere and cover as many of the footmarks on the path as you can. Tell one of the uniform lads up at Mill Lane to give you a hand.'

Andy nodded and made his way back along the path.

Danny squatted at the side of the body and carefully raised the tarpaulin sheet at the head end. The deceased was an elderly white male. The wounds to the back of his head were both devastating and obvious.

Danny lowered the sheet again. 'Any idea who he is?'

'We know exactly who he is. His name is Wilf Kelham. There was a piece of paper in his coat pocket with his name and room number on. He's one of the residents of the halfway hostel on Coopers Yard, just off Mill Lane.'

'As soon as we get some more people here, I want them to start talking to the staff and other residents at Coopers Yard. Let's see what we can find out about Wilf Kelham.'

'Will do. I've done a basic Police National Computer name check. There's a Wilf Kelham shown who's about the right age, with a string of previous convictions.'

'All sex offences?'

Rob nodded. 'The most recent conviction was for two counts of rape, committed on two very young children.'

'Okay. Let's firm all that up as soon as possible and get our staff into Coopers Yard. We need them to be in there asking questions about Kelham. Have you requested a Home Office pathologist?'

'I told the control room to call out the next on-call pathologist as soon as I saw the body.'

'Hopefully, it will be Seamus Carter, as he's dealt with the other two bodies.'

'I did request that, if possible. But the control room haven't confirmed who's travelling yet.'

'Do we have an ETA?'

'Should be here within the next fifteen minutes. Scenes of Crime should be arriving anytime now as well.'

'Good work, Rob. Who found him?'

'A young woman running along the footpath. She saw

what she thought was a pile of old clothes. It was still quite dark at that time. She carried on running at first, but then noticed a woollen hat a little further on. She thought something wasn't right, so went back to look at the clothes again and saw it was a body.'

'Where is she now?'

'I asked one of the uniform lads to drive her home. She was soaking wet and freezing cold. She was dressed for running, not standing around in this weather.'

'Please tell me she lives locally.'

'She lives at Balderton, just down the road. She's a serious runner who runs along this footpath two or three times a week, depending on her shifts.'

'What's her name?'

'Rosie Moss.'

'Okay. As we've got everything squared away here, we need to go and see her. I want to talk to her personally.'

'I told her to stay at home this morning, as we would want to see her later.'

Andy walked back along the path to where they were standing and said, 'I've covered as many footmarks as I can. Scenes of Crime have just arrived and are awaiting your instructions, boss.'

'Thanks, Andy. Have any more of our staff arrived yet?'

'DI Cartwright, Glen, Simon, Phil and Fran have all just pulled up.'

Danny turned to Rob and said, 'Manage the scene with Tina. Get the identification confirmed as soon as possible, and make a start on talking to the people at Coopers Yard. Ask for more staff to come to the scene if you need them. I'll take Fran with me and talk to the woman who found the body. We need to get a good first account from her while the events are fresh in her mind. What's her address?'

Rob retrieved his notebook from his coat pocket and said, 'It's 63 Fairholme Close, Balderton. Do you know where that is?'

'I'll get directions from the uniform lads. I'll be back here as soon as I've spoken to Rosie Moss.'

58

8.30am, 27 February 1988
63 Fairholme Close, Balderton, Newark, Nottinghamshire

Danny had obtained directions from one of the local uniform constables, briefed Fran Jefferies on what they knew so far, and then drove to Fairholme Close at Balderton.

After a ten-minute drive, Danny parked the car outside number 63. It was an unremarkable but smart-looking semi-detached house on a nice street.

The two detectives walked down the path to the front door, and Fran rang the doorbell. Almost immediately, the door was opened by a large woman in her fifties, wearing a housecoat.

Fran said, 'Good morning. We're from the CID. We'd like to speak to Rosie Moss. Is she here?'

'Rosie's my daughter. She's told me what happened;

dreadful business. Please come inside out of the rain. Let me take those wet coats. Can I get you both a cup of tea?'

As Danny removed his soaking wet overcoat, he said, 'A cup of tea would be lovely, thank you.'

Mrs Moss directed the detectives into the main lounge and said, 'I'll give our Rosie a shout and put the kettle on. Please make yourselves comfortable.'

Carrying the wet coats, the woman stepped back into the hallway and shouted up the stairs, 'Rosie, love! The police are here to see you.'

A couple of minutes later, the door to the lounge opened, and a tall, slim young woman, dressed in a grey sweatshirt top and white tracksuit bottoms, walked in. Her long, dark hair was still quite wet, but it had been pulled back off her face and tied in a ponytail. Her face appeared red and flushed.

She said, 'Sorry. I'd just got out of the shower when you got here. I was trying to warm up after the run this morning.'

Fran said, 'No problem, Rosie. My name's Detective Constable Jefferies, and this is Detective Chief Inspector Flint. We're from the Major Crime Investigation Unit. Obviously, it's important that we talk to you as soon as possible, but I also understand that you've witnessed something traumatic. Are you okay talking to us right now?'

Rosie Moss half smiled and said, 'It was horrible, but I'm used to seeing bad wounds and injuries. I've been a nurse at the Casualty Department in Newark Hospital for the last three years.'

Danny said, 'So you must have realised quickly that those injuries you saw couldn't have been caused by a fall?'

'As soon as I saw the massive wounds on that poor man's head, I kind of knew he was dead. And yes, it was obvious to me that he hadn't got them tripping over.'

'I'd like you to take your time and tell me what you remember.'

There was a pause. Just as Rosie was about to speak, the door opened, and her mother walked in, carrying a tray of hot drinks.

She placed the tray down on the coffee table and said, 'Here we are, three mugs of tea. I've made you one as well, Rosie love, and put three sugars in it.'

'Thanks, Mum.'

The older woman could sense she had interrupted something.

She backed out of the room, saying, 'I'll leave you to it, then. If you need anything, I'll be in the kitchen.'

As soon as the door closed, Fran said, 'Your mum's lovely.'

'Yeah, she's a proper fusspot.'

Danny said, 'You were about to tell us what you saw this morning?'

Rosie picked up her mug of tea, feeling the warmth on the palms of her hands.

She took a breath and said, 'I was about half an hour into my run and was on the stretch that takes me along the path at the side of the river. It was still very early, so it was quite dark on that stretch.'

'Doesn't it bother you running in the dark?'

'It wasn't pitch black; I could see where I was going. At that time of day, before the sun comes up, it can still be quite gloomy, especially on rainy days. It's a run I do often, so I know the route very well. I run every other day, and I do this route at least twice a week.'

'I thought you must be a serious runner, to go out in these conditions.'

'I'm a member of the Newark Harriers. I have a cross-country race coming up in March, so my training schedule is quite hectic. I work out every day and run between ten and fifteen miles every other day before I start work.'

Danny smiled. 'That's a huge commitment.'

'It is, but I enjoy it.'

'I'd like to get back to this morning's run. What was the first thing you saw that looked strange?'

'I saw what I thought was a pile of old clothes that somebody had dumped by the river. They were just at the side of the path, so I carried on running. It was when I saw the hat that I thought something wasn't right.'

'What hat?'

'About ten yards further on from the pile of clothes, I saw a woollen hat on the path. It made me stop and turn back.'

'Any reason why?'

'I don't really know. It just looked so out of place there. Anyway, whatever the reason, I stopped and turned back towards the pile of clothes. Once I stopped, that's when I heard it.'

'Heard what?'

'I heard footsteps around the bend in the path. Because it was so wet, I could hear someone running away. I could hear their training shoes on the wet path.'

'You said "running". How could you tell they were running?'

'I'm used to that sound. I listen to the sound made by my own trainers to gauge my pace as I'm running. This person was moving quickly. There was something else as well.'

'Go on.'

'It was a person who does a lot of running.'

'I'm guessing that you know this because of your involvement in the sport?'

'This might sound weird, but when I see, or hear, people running, I can instantly tell if they're any good. It's to do with the footfall. The person I heard running away was an athlete, pure and simple. The footsteps I heard were light and balanced. I'm guessing that if it hadn't been so wet underfoot, I wouldn't have heard a thing.'

Fran said, 'Did you see anybody?'

'No. Like I said, the river curves there, so the path bends out of sight.'

Danny said, 'When you returned to what you thought was the pile of old clothes, what did you do?'

'As I got closer and bent down, I could see that the main garment was an old army coat. The collar had risen, so I pulled it back away from the old man's head. That's when I saw the massive wounds.'

'Did you touch the man?'

'My first thought was that he was dead. I did touch him, because I checked for a pulse in his neck. There was nothing. That's when I decided to call the police.'

'How did you do that?'

'I knew there was a public telephone box halfway up Mill Lane, so I sprinted to the phone box and dialled three nines.'

'Then what?'

'I was told the police were on their way. Whoever it was I spoke to told me to wait by the telephone box. I stayed inside the phone box because it was raining hard by then, and that's when I saw the car.'

'What car?'

'There was a dark-coloured car that drove out from one of the side roads off Mill Lane. It drove slowly past the phone box, up towards the main Farndon Road.'

'Did you see who was driving?'

'Not really. The windows in the phone box are very small, and they were wet from the rain. I could just make out a figure dressed in black sitting in the driver's seat.'

'Do you know the name of the road the car came out of?'

Rosie was thoughtful for a second or two. Then she said, 'Yes. The car came out of Blake Terrace. I know it was that road, because I'm always glad to see the sign for Blake Terrace as I run up Mill Lane. It means I'm almost halfway up the hill. I use street signs as time checks on my run. I always clock the sign, then look at my watch. It gives me an indication of how I'm doing, pace-wise.'

'Do you know what make the car was?'

'I'm sorry, I don't. I'm rubbish at car makes. I haven't got a clue. All I can tell you is that it was a dark-coloured four-door. It was either black or a very dark blue and looked fairly new.'

'Is there anything else you can remember?'

'Yes, there is something else that's just occurred to me. I think I'd seen the old man earlier this week. I was out on another early morning run, and I'm sure I passed an old man near the castle. I'm sure he was wearing one of those long army coats as well. It's possible it was the same chap.'

'Have you seen anybody else hanging around on that footpath near the river over the last few weeks?'

'Not anyone who looked suspicious. I'm always seeing other runners or folks walking dogs, but that's it.'

'How are you for time, Rosie? Do you have to be at work today?'

'My shift should start at ten o'clock this morning. Why?'

'Because I'd like you to make a written statement to my colleague while all this is fresh in your mind. If I clear it with your boss, are you okay to make the statement now?'

'If you can clear it, of course.'

'Who's your supervisor at work? If you were ringing in sick, who would you need to get a message to?'

Rosie smiled and said, 'That would be Sister Bould. Good luck; she can be a bit fierce.'

Danny winked. 'So can I. We'll see what she says.'

He stood up and walked from the lounge into the hallway. He tapped on the kitchen door and said, 'Mrs Moss, do you mind if I use your phone? I need to call the hospital and speak to Rosie's boss.'

'Of course. The phone's in the hall. If you look in the book at the side of the phone, the number where Rosie works is under N for Newark Hospital. Is everything okay?'

'Thanks. Don't worry, everything's fine.'

Danny made the call and spoke to Sister Bould, who was actually very friendly and happy to help the police. Danny assured her that Rosie would be at work by midday.

He walked back into the lounge and told Rosie everything was sorted, and that she didn't have to be at work until noon.

He turned to Fran and said, 'There's statement paper in my car. I'm going to leave you here to obtain a detailed statement from Rosie. Take your time and obtain as much detail as you can. I need to get back to the scene. I'll make sure someone is here to pick you up at eleven thirty; that should give you plenty of time. If Rosie needs a lift to work, make sure we sort that out for her as well.'

Fran said, 'I'll nip out to the car and get the statement paper.'

Danny turned to Rosie and said, 'Thanks very much, Rosie. You've been a great help. I just need to get my coat back from your mum.'

Rosie said, 'I'll grab it for you.'

As soon as Danny had got his coat and Fran had got the statement paper from the car, he left Fairholme Close.

As he drove back to Mill Lane, his head was spinning.

There was a lot to organise.

He now needed a team to carry out house-to-house enquiries along the length of Mill Lane and the roads that ran off it, especially Blake Terrace. There would be the post-mortem to attend. Interviews with all the staff and residents of Coopers Yard to organise. Research into the background and offences committed by Wilf Kelham.

It was going to be another very long day.

59

8.00pm, 27 February 1988
MCIU Offices, Mansfield Police Station

Danny had just finished debriefing the day's events with the staff of the MCIU, Scenes of Crime and the Special Operations Unit. It was now time to sit down with his two detective inspectors and fine-tune the enquiries that would need doing tomorrow.

The formal identification of Wilf Kelham had been undertaken while his body was still in situ at the side of the river. Geoff Hargreaves, the manager of the halfway hostel, had confirmed the identity of the dead man to Rob Buxton.

Hargreaves had informed the detective that Kelham had only been a resident at the hostel since the seventeenth of February, having been recently released from HMP Whatton.

The post-mortem of Kelham had thrown up no real surprises. Fortunately, it had been Seamus Carter who had attended the scene and who had carried out the subsequent post-mortem. The cause of death had been the three distinct hammer blows to the head. The post-mortem had revealed clumps of woollen fibres deep within the brain tissue. Samples had been taken, to see if these fibres were a match for the woollen hat that had been found near the body. The hat had also been recovered by the Scenes of Crime department. There had been fragments of bone, blood and other tissue found on it. Samples of these fragments had also been sent to the laboratory for forensic analysis.

The rain had caused too much damage to the footmarks on the footpath where the body had been discovered. Despite Andy Wills's best efforts to cover them, they were of no use.

Danny knew that, once again, forensically they didn't have much.

He turned to Rob and said, 'You're managing the house-to-house enquiries. How far into it are we?'

'Obviously, it's still early, boss. We've had to pull out of the area tonight much sooner than I would have liked. As you know, we can't carry out door-to-door enquiries when it gets dark.'

Danny nodded. 'I understand. Are Special Ops available to help us for a few more days?'

'As this murder has been designated part of the series under the remit of Operation Hermes, we have the overtime budget to pay for their services. We have two sections of Special Ops, who should be on rest days, working overtime on this enquiry for the next two days.'

'That's great, but I want them hard at it. If we've only got them for two days, I want Mill Lane and all the surrounding streets completed.'

'You don't have to worry about staff from Special Ops. Their lads are always highly motivated. They're coming on duty tomorrow at seven o'clock. I'll be here to brief them. All the streets have been mastered, so it's just a matter of knocking on doors and talking to the residents.'

'Make sure your briefing stresses for them to be on the lookout for any private CCTV systems the residents may have. This enquiry could be vital, Rob. The description of the car seen by Rosie Moss isn't a million miles away from the description of the car seen parked near to Redgate Farm before Tighe was murdered. Let's see if the Special Ops teams can find another witness who saw the car in the days leading up to this attack. We know that Kelham was only at Coopers Yard for ten days prior to his death, and we know that his habit was to take this early morning walk along the river. There's a very good chance his killer has been watching him and studying his routine, biding their time. If that was the case, then the car may well have been in the area prior to the day of the murder.'

'I'm on it, boss.'

'I also want you to task Andy and Rachel to revisit HMP Whatton and talk to Joanna Preston again. If Kelham was only released from the prison ten days ago, I want to know what her involvement in his release was and who the probation officer is who was looking after Kelham's welfare.'

Rob made a note. 'Will do.'

Danny turned to Tina. 'How are we getting on with the enquiries at Coopers Yard?'

'All the staff working at the hostel have been seen and statemented. There are still three more residents to be seen. It's already been arranged for those three to be seen and interviewed first thing tomorrow morning.'

'Anything startling so far?'

'Nothing. What is apparent is that Kelham was very much a creature of habit. It seems that everyone at the hostel knew about his early morning strolls along the river.'

'Have we got statements from the residents we've seen so far?'

'Yes, boss.'

'As soon as the last three are seen, I want you to delegate somebody to start researching those residents. I want to know if anybody living there had history with Kelham. I know everything is pointing towards this being part of the series, but you never know. Let's keep an open mind.'

'Nobody at the hostel would have known about the Mars bar left at the other scenes, boss.'

'That's very true. I still want the other residents researched though. Talking of research, I want you to talk to DC Williams first thing tomorrow and roust him up. I delegated him the simple task of researching Wilf Kelham. I wanted him to establish all the details of his previous offending. In particular, the rape case he last got sent down for. I've got to say, I was very disappointed in his efforts today. Make sure you see him in the morning and give him a not-so-gentle kick up the arse. If he doesn't produce results tomorrow, he'll be feeling my wrath.'

Tina said, 'Will do. This was always going to be the problem with changing officers from their usual roles.'

Danny could feel his anger rising. 'I'm not accepting that, Tina. Everyone on this unit is here because they're talented detectives who know how to work unprompted and unsupervised. Jeff Williams is no different. I won't tolerate him sulking like an errant schoolboy because he's been given a different role to perform. Speak to him tomorrow, and get him back on track, or I will. And I can guarantee he won't like what I have to say.'

'Yes, sir.'

'I'll see you both here at seven o'clock in the morning. The murder of Wilf Kelham has given us another chance to identify this serial killer. Let's make sure we make the most of that opportunity and prevent any more deaths.'

The two detective inspectors left the office, and Danny began writing notes into his enquiry log. As he wrote, he saw the name *SHARON WHITTLE* written in block capitals.

He glanced at his watch, then reached inside his desk drawer and retrieved his diary. He found Professor Whittle's personal contact details and dialled the number.

The call was answered on the fourth ring. 'Hello. Sharon Whittle.'

Danny said, 'Professor, it's Chief Inspector Flint. My apologies for calling so late. Are you okay to talk?'

'Danny, what a nice surprise. Yes, it's fine. Is everything okay? Do you have more work for me?'

'I just need to pick your brains about something that has us all puzzled. I have the same strange object being left at multiple murder scenes, and nobody has any idea what it means.'

'I tell you what, Danny. Instead of doing this over the telephone, why don't you fax all the details to my office, and I'll give it my full attention tomorrow. I'll be in the office at seven o'clock. I'd only planned on catching up with all my boring paperwork tomorrow. Is that okay with you?'

'That would be great. Can you remind me of the fax number for your office? I'll get all the details sent tonight so they're waiting for you first thing in the morning.'

Sharon gave Danny the fax number and said, 'I've worked on a few cases in the States where killers have left the most bizarre objects at scenes. There's always a hidden meaning. I'll talk to you tomorrow when I've read the details of your cases and carried out some research. I'll call either late tomorrow afternoon or tomorrow evening. Will that be soon enough?'

'That would be great, Sharon. Thank you.'

Danny hung up and immediately began drafting out the report he would fax to Professor Whittle. He glanced at his watch again, let out a long sigh and once more picked up the phone.

He needed to call the hospital and let Sue know it was going to be yet another late finish.

60

6.00am, 28 February 1988
Mansfield, Nottinghamshire

As Danny walked down the stairs of the four-bedroom detached house, he was greeted by the delicious aroma of grilled bacon.

He walked into the kitchen and saw his wife with her back to the door, busily buttering two slices of toast.

Last night had been the first night Sue had spent at home since Hayley had been admitted to hospital. She had finally been convinced that her daughter was well enough to be left in the care of the nurses on the children's ward, and had returned home for a much-needed full night's sleep.

He tiptoed across the kitchen, placed his hands on her hips and kissed the back of her neck.

Sue jumped a little at the pleasant surprise. Danny said, 'I didn't hear you get up.'

'I was awake when you got in the shower. I want to get

back to the hospital to be with Hayley, but I thought I'd cook my man some breakfast before he disappears for another day.'

'I'm sorry. I know it was another long day yesterday, and you're probably not interested right now, but we had another murder that's identical to the other two I'm already investigating. We're getting nowhere fast on either of those, and I'm hoping this one isn't going to be the same.'

Sue could hear the tension in her husband's voice.

She sounded upbeat as she said, 'This is nearly ready. Take your jacket off and sit at the table. The bacon's cooked, and your eggs are nearly poached. Coffee's already on the table.'

Danny nodded, slipped off his suit jacket and poured himself a cup of coffee from the two-person cafetiere.

Less than a minute later, Sue placed the plate of bacon and eggs in front of Danny. The sight of the delicious food reminded Danny just how ravenously hungry he was, and he began to devour the breakfast. As he tucked in, Sue poured herself a coffee and said, 'There's something important that we need to talk about, as well.'

He swallowed a mouthful of egg and said, 'It's not Hayley, is it? She's okay, isn't she?'

'Hayley's fine. This is about me, I'm due to start work soon. My maternity leave has run its course, and I'm due to go back to the hospital. The hospital administrators have been very understanding about what's happening with Hayley right now. They have extended my maternity leave until Hayley is well enough to return home.'

Danny placed his knife and fork on the now empty plate and said, 'How do you feel about that?'

'You know how much I adore taking care of our beautiful daughter, but I'm desperate to get back to work as well. I hadn't realised just how much until Hayley became ill. Being back in the hospital, helping our daughter recover, has rekindled my love of medicine. I will want to go back to work, sweetheart.'

Danny was worried, and his face must have betrayed those feelings, because Sue continued, 'There's really no need to worry about Hayley. She's making a wonderful recovery and continues to go from strength to strength.'

'I know she is. I just thought another few months with her mum looking after her, when she does finally come home, would have been ideal. But if your mind's made up, we'd better get in touch with the child minder we had organised and let her know what the situation is.'

Sue smiled, stood up and handed Danny his jacket. 'We'll discuss it more tonight when you get to the hospital. Thank you, sweetheart.'

Danny took one last sip of coffee, kissed his wife and said, 'I understand that medicine is your calling, and that being a doctor is much more than a job. I would never deny you that. Let's just make sure we do the best for our daughter that we can, okay?'

Sue nodded and grabbed her coat. 'Of course, sweetheart. Can you drop me off at the hospital on your way in to work, please?'

61

11.00am, 28 February 1988
HMP Whatton, Nottinghamshire

Andy Wills and Rachel Moore had discussed what they were going to ask the prison welfare officer at HMP Whatton during the long drive from Mansfield to the prison.

Andy had wanted to concentrate on exactly what had been put in place by Joanna Preston, as well as who else would know about the details of when and where Wilf Kelham was being released.

Rachel, on the other hand, had wanted to concentrate solely on Preston herself. She had found the welfare officer slightly odd during their last interview. She also recalled a throwaway comment made by a prison warder, who had described her as 'the ice maiden'. Rachel felt that Preston's display of emotion, when she had been informed that Bauer and Tighe had been murdered, had been very false and affected.

The two detectives had settled on a strategy where Andy would conduct the questioning of Joanna Preston while Rachel observed the body language and emotion displayed by the welfare officer during the interview.

After the detectives had been escorted to Preston's office inside the prison, they had found the welfare officer waiting at her office door to greet them.

She said, 'Come in, please. I take it you're here to collect the information you requested last time, from the released inmates' probation officers?'

Andy waited for the door of the office to be closed before shaking his head and saying bluntly, 'No. The reason we're here to talk to you again so soon is because Wilf Kelham, the prisoner released most recently under your scheme, was found dead at Newark yesterday morning. He'd been murdered not far from the hostel you housed him in.'

Joanna Preston sat down heavily and remained open-mouthed. It was a long time before she spoke. A little too long, Rachel noted.

Eventually, she spluttered, 'How?'

Andy replied, 'He died from head injuries he sustained after being attacked on the river path at the bottom of Mill Lane at Newark.'

Preston said flatly, 'That's terrible.'

'Who else knew the details of Kelham's release?'

'What do you mean?'

'Well, I understand that you arrange everything; that's your role. What I want to know is, who else would have access to that information? In a nutshell, who knew where Kelham was being released to?'

'Within the prison?'

'To start with, yes, within the prison.'

'Everything is prepared by me and then signed off by the governor.'

'Are you telling me that just you and the governor knew the details?'

'No. Of course not. There's a hell of a lot of paperwork to be completed during the release of any prisoner. This scheme is no different. The paperwork generated would have all the details of when and where Kelham was being released. It would also show where he was going to be living after his release. His new address would be clearly marked on that documentation.'

'Who would have sight of that documentation?'

'Any prison officers on duty during the release procedure at the gate, as well as the admin staff preparing the documents.'

'Can you supply their names?'

Joanna Preston laughed. 'I could, but it won't do you any good.'

Andy frowned and said, 'I'm finding it hard to understand your frivolous attitude, Ms Preston. A man has died. It's no laughing matter.'

Preston's mood changed instantly. She went from amiable to aggressive in a split second.

She snarled, 'Nobody's laughing at the man's death, Detective. I laughed at your complete lack of understanding of the prison system. Gossip is rife within any prison. When one of the only freedoms men have is to tittle-tattle over minutiae, you can't stop it. In this place, what one person knows, be it prison officer or inmate, will be public knowledge within hours. I can almost guarantee that on the day he was released, almost every person in this prison would have known where Wilf Kelham had been rehoused. It's just the way of any prison institution.'

Andy was shocked by the venom in the welfare officer's

comments. He said, 'So all those safeguards you told us about when we first spoke to you don't really count for much?'

Andy could clearly see the suppressed anger beneath the surface as Preston replied, 'I do my very best to ensure that the men released under the scheme are housed in a safe environment. I cannot be held responsible for what happens to them every hour of every day after their release.'

She'd spoken in a matter-of-fact tone.

The coldness and lack of empathy was again noted by an observing Rachel Moore. The welfare officer truly was an ice maiden.

Andy said, 'Who was Wilf Kelham's probation officer?'

'Sally Greaves. She's an experienced probation officer who works from the Sheffield office.'

'Didn't Stewart Tighe's probation officer also work from the Sheffield office?'

'I believe so, but that isn't too surprising. Under the probation services latest reorganisation, a lot of Nottinghamshire, parts of Lincolnshire and Yorkshire all fall under that office.'

'Thanks for that. You mentioned earlier that you now have the results of the enquiries we asked the probation officers to carry out?'

'Yes. All the details have been collated and are in this folder. You can take it with you if you like. What I can tell you is that there are no reports of any threatening letters or any verbal threats being made to the other prisoners who were released. They are all fit and well and still living in the original accommodation provided for them.'

'Thanks. We'll take the folder for our enquiry records. Are there other releases planned for the not-too-distant future?'

'No. We're in a quiet period now. Kelham was the last man scheduled to be released for quite a while. I'm genuinely sorry about what happened to the old man. Is there anything else I can help you with today?'

Once again, Rachel made a mental note of the false show of compassion, immediately followed by a statement devoid of any emotion whatsoever.

Andy replied, 'No, that's it. Thanks for the prompt action obtaining the probation officers' reports.'

62

3.00pm, 28 February 1988
MCIU Offices, Mansfield Police Station

Danny responded to the polite knock on his door, saying, 'Come in and grab a seat, Lynn. How are you and Jag getting on with the businesses being helped by Polyplastech Limited? Is it looking promising?'

Lynn Harris sat down and said, 'We're making reasonable progress, but ever since the murder of Wilf Kelham, there's only been the two of us working through the list. There's a lot of companies to get through. The reason I've come to see you now is to update you on a company we're going to have a close look at tomorrow. It sounds really promising.'

'Go on?'

'It's a company called Stealthsafe Security Ltd. They've been helped massively by funds from Polyplastech. They don't appear to do any security work for Polyplastech. The amount seems to be an awful lot of money for philanthropic reasons alone.'

'How much are we talking about?'

'It was over two hundred thousand pounds in the last financial year.'

'That does seem a lot.'

'I tasked the Fraud Squad to do a full breakdown of the accounts for Stealthsafe. I wanted to try to establish what all that money is being spent on. The Fraud Squad have assured me that the transfer of funds between companies is legal. Any company can make a cash donation to another company provided it's not done in a way to avoid paying tax.'

'Have you been to Stealthsafe yet?'

'Not yet. I've phoned the company today and made an appointment to see the finance director, Barbra Johnson, tomorrow afternoon.'

'That's good. Where are they based?'

'In Nottingham. Their offices are at Colwick Park.'

'Okay. Well, let me know how it goes tomorrow. See if you can establish if there are any links between Stealthsafe and the Guardians of Innocence rallies and meetings. It could be our witness has been right all along, and there was security at the meeting.'

'Will do, boss.'

Lynn had just closed the door to the office when the telephone started to ring.

Danny snatched up the phone. 'DCI Flint.'

'Hi, Danny. Is now a good time?'

Danny immediately recognised the voice of Professor Sharon Whittle.

'Now's a perfect time, Sharon. Have you managed to find anything that could help me?'

'I read your report. I have to say it's a new one for me. I've been to a lot of murder scenes where strange objects have been left by the killer. I can't say I've ever seen chocolate left at a scene before. It's never until the murderer is identified that the relevance of an object such as this is fully understood. Have you got any suspects?'

'I'm looking at the possibility of a vigilante group being involved. A bunch of like-minded people wanting to strike back at paedophiles.'

'I can't see this chocolate bar having any relevance to a group. Do you know who runs the group you're looking at? Because I think this object is much more likely to be meaningful to an individual. The placing of the bar of chocolate actually on the dead person makes me think that brand of chocolate bar means something very personal to the killer.'

'I do know who the organiser of the vigilante group is.'

'Well, research the background of that person. I take it you've already started looking at them closely. Have you established the reason why this person would want to establish such a group, anyway?'

'We have. The man's daughter was sexually abused over a lengthy period before the offender was caught and jailed.'

'Research the offences against the girl. Go into them with a fine-tooth comb. See if there's mention anywhere of this chocolate bar being used during or after the assaults. Sometimes, paedophiles will control their victims with threats; others placate their victims with bribes. For some, it's a mixture of the two.'

'Thanks, Sharon.'

'You should also do that with your three dead men. Reinvestigate the reports of their previous crimes and see if there's any mention of Mars bars within the paperwork.'

'Okay.'

'There's something else, Danny. You need to establish as many common denominators as possible that link your three victims, not just the fact that they are all sex offenders. These men haven't been selected at random. There will be a reason why the killer has chosen them. Concentrate on all those common factors and you may even be able to predict the next attack. Look at things such as the crimes they committed, who they were committed against, where they were going to live upon release, who they would be living with, the type of housing. Somebody within your enquiry will have all that information to hand. That's where you need to look.'

'Okay. Will do. From what I sent by fax, is there any single thing glaringly obvious to you?'

'The one thing that stands out like a beacon, for me, is HMP Whatton. I'm sure you will have already started making enquiries there.'

'Yes, we have. Why does it stand out for you?'

'Because of the way some of the victims were transferred in before their release. It seems to me like that transfer brought them into contact with somebody who has a real axe to grind against paedophiles. Try as I might, I can't find a reason why those men were targeted. Out of all the men released on the scheme, why those three? That's still a mystery to me; there doesn't seem to be any pattern that's obvious. Maybe you could look at all future releases from HMP Whatton? I don't know how big a task that would be for you.'

'I'll look into it. Thanks for taking the time to study this for me.'

'Anytime. Do me a favour and keep me informed of any developments. I'm intrigued by the killer's use of the chocolate bar. I'd love to know what the relevance of it is.'

'Will do, and thanks again.'

Danny put the phone down and walked into the main office. He saw Andy and Rachel working at their desks. He said, 'Have you two got a minute? I want to know how you got on at Whatton earlier.'

The two detectives followed Danny back into his office, where Danny said, 'Well?'

Andy said, 'We spoke with Joanna Preston again. It didn't really take us very far. I swear that woman has an answer for everything. When she knew the shit had hit the fan again, she was eager to distance herself from the release scheme.'

'What do you mean?'

'Well, she was very quick to point out that all responsibility for the men's welfare is transferred from her to the probation officers once they are released. It's very convenient for her. She just houses them, then immediately washes her hands of them at that stage.'

Rachel said, 'I found the woman quite strange during our first meeting. So today, while Andy questioned her, I took a back seat specifically to observe her manner and body language. It was quite enlightening.'

'Go on, Rachel. I'm listening.'

'It's almost as if she's acting out a part. She says all the right things at the right times. She exaggerates her feelings when she thinks she needs to show sympathy. It's all just way too much; it's over the top. She's quite a complicated woman. Her mood changed dramatically today at one point when Andy was questioning her. She suddenly flipped and went from being helpful and amiable to extremely aggressive in a split second. Then, just as quickly, she flipped back again.'

Danny was thoughtful. He was listening to Rachel, but hearing the voice of Professor Whittle at the same time.

After a few moments, he said, 'Rachel, I want you to follow your detective's intuition. Have a close look at Joanna Preston. She's one person who we can say for certain knew everything there was to know about our three dead men. I want you to be discreet, but I want you to thoroughly investigate her background. I want you to go deeper than we have already. I want to know what she did prior to joining the probation service. And her record within that service, working alongside the prison service. Research her family, and let's see if there's anything there that we should know about.'

As the two detectives stood up to leave, Danny said, 'Are there any other men due for release under the scheme?'

'Joanna Preston said that Wilf Kelham was the last for a while.'

'But she didn't say, specifically, when other men are due for release?'

'No. She didn't.'

'Okay. I'll phone the governor and ascertain when other prisoners are due for early release.'

Andy said, 'Have you got something in mind, boss?'

'I'm considering placing all the men released under this scheme in the future under twenty-four-hour surveillance. It will be a massive undertaking, so I need to think it all through first. Good work today. Let me know what you find out about Joanna Preston.'

Danny was thoughtful for a few minutes; then he picked up the telephone and dialled the number for HMP Whatton.

He got through to the switchboard and said, 'I'd like to speak to Governor Redmayne, please.'

After a few seconds, a voice said, 'Wilson Redmayne.'

'Governor Redmayne. I'm Detective Chief Inspector Flint. I'm investigating the murders of the three men released from your prison under the early release scheme. I was hoping to meet you away from the prison, to discuss something about that programme. I don't want our meeting, and what we discuss, to become common knowledge at the prison.'

There was a long period of silence. Then Governor Redmayne said, 'This all sounds very mysterious, Chief Inspector. What is it you want to talk to me about?'

'I'd rather not discuss the details over the phone, as it's a delicate matter. Is there somewhere we could meet in person?'

'It's my day off tomorrow. I always play golf on my day off. I could meet you at ten o'clock tomorrow morning at Wollaton Park golf club. My tee is booked for eleven o'clock. Will an hour be long enough to discuss whatever it is you want to speak about?'

'More than enough. I'll see you at the golf club at ten o'clock.'

'Just come to the clubhouse. I'll meet you there, and we'll have a chat over a coffee.'

'Thanks.'

Danny put the phone down. He hated all the drama, all the cloak and dagger. But he also knew that if what he was starting to think was possible, he needed to be very careful how he proceeded.

63

7.00pm, 28 February 1988
Steeple Claydon, Buckinghamshire

James Brannigan was enjoying a single malt and listening to an Elton John CD. He never got much time to just sit and relax, so he was enjoying the moment.

His peace was shattered by the ringing of the telephone.

He pressed pause on the CD player and picked up the phone. With a tone of annoyance in his voice, he said, 'Brannigan.'

'Mr Brannigan, it's me, Davy Johnson.'

'What do you want?'

'I just wanted to let you know that the police are coming to the office tomorrow.'

'The CID?'

'Yeah. They've made an appointment to see my sister tomorrow afternoon.'

'Have you briefed her properly?'

'Yeah, she knows what to say and what not to say.'

Brannigan thought for a moment. This was getting a little too close for comfort. He couldn't afford any mistakes now.

After a brief pause, he said, 'Davy, I think you and your lovely wife need a holiday. Get a flight to Alicante in the morning and get yourselves booked into a hotel. I think you both need some winter sun.'

'But the business is extremely busy at the minute. I can't afford to spend time away from work.'

'Don't worry about whether you can afford it. I'll pick up any slack financially. I want you and your wife off the grid. I don't want either of you being questioned by those detectives. Barbra will be able to stonewall them better than you and your wife, because she knows fuck all. If you're not around to question, I can't see them digging too deep. It makes sense for you to stay out of the way for a while.'

'I'll ask Cheryl and see what she thinks.'

Brannigan was losing his patience. He snapped, 'This isn't a bloody debate! Get two flights booked tonight and get yourselves over to Spain. I want you out of the way until this all blows over. Understood?'

'Okay, okay. I wish you'd stop worrying. There's nothing that can be traced back to my firm, so there's nothing that can be traced back to you.'

'And that's the way I want to keep it. Book those flights. Call me tomorrow when you've landed in Alicante.'

'Okay, Mr Brannigan. It'll have to be five star all the way if I'm going to persuade Cheryl.'

'Whatever, Davy. I don't care what it costs, just get it booked.'

Brannigan put the phone down.

For the first time since he had started his crusade, he started to doubt the wisdom of his actions.

He poured himself another single malt and flicked the CD onto play.

64

10.00am, 1 March 1988
Wollaton Park Golf Club, Wollaton, Nottingham

Danny walked into the clubhouse at Wollaton Park golf club and looked around the spacious lounge. It wasn't very busy. A few of the members were standing at the bar, ordering bacon cobs and coffee prior to playing their rounds of golf.

At the far end of the lounge, Danny saw a black man sitting alone.

As he approached, he could see there was a full cafetiere of coffee and two empty cups on the table in front of the man. As Danny got closer to the table, the man stood up and said, 'Mr Flint?'

Danny nodded. 'Mr Redmayne, thanks for seeing me, and apologies for all this cloak-and-dagger stuff. I think when you've heard what I have to say, you'll understand why I wanted to meet you somewhere away from the prison.'

Redmayne poured two cups of coffee and added milk before saying, 'I was intrigued by your telephone call, Chief Inspector. What is it you need to talk about?'

'Call me Danny. As you're aware, I'm investigating the murders of three men who were all released from your prison under the new early release scheme. This is in no way a slight against the way you run your prison, but I cannot afford to ignore the distinct possibility that there's a direct link between the staff at your prison and the deaths of those three men.'

With a note of incredulity in his voice, Wilson Redmayne said, 'You think one of my prison officers was involved in the murders?'

Danny shrugged. 'I don't know. What I do know is that all three men were released from your prison, and all were subsequently murdered. There's strong evidence to suggest that these are not random killings, and the men were targeted. It's imperative that I establish who would have had the relevant knowledge of these men. Who would know all the details of their previous crimes? Where were they going to live? Who were they going to be living with? The types of properties they would be living at? It's essential that I know who would have access to all that.'

'Do you have somebody in mind who would have access to all that information?'

'This is my problem, Governor. I can't say with any certainty who knows what in your establishment. It could be one single person, or it could be several who have access to all that information. It's impossible for me to know. The only thing I can say for certain is that all the victims were released from your prison.'

'I understand your dilemma, but why did you need to see me today?'

'I need to change the direction of my focus, and to do that,

I'm going to need your help. Instead of looking for the killer, I need to focus on the next possible victim. If the pattern remains the same, the next victim will also be released under your new scheme.'

Curtis stroked his chin thoughtfully. 'So you need to know who's about to be released, but you can't afford for every Tom, Dick and Harry at the prison to know that you want this information.'

Danny was pleased that the governor had understood so quickly and said, 'That's it in a nutshell. If everyone's aware that we're watching the men who have been released, it will defeat the object.'

A very worried Redmayne replied, 'Don't you have concerns that you are treating these men like the proverbial tethered goat, used as bait for the man-eating tiger?'

'Do you see any alternative? If we do nothing, the killer will still be out there, possibly stalking his next victim. At least if we're watching that potential victim, we stand a chance of preventing another death and, hopefully, catching the killer.'

There was a pause before Redmayne said, 'Yes. You're right. What do you need from me?'

'I'll need at least a week's notice of any scheduled releases from the prison. Could you do that?'

'That won't be a problem. I'm in daily contact with Joanna, who organises all the arrangements for the men's release. I'll know in plenty of time who's being released and when. I'll make sure I also know the details of the addresses they're going to be released to.'

'For this to work, it's imperative that nobody knows what we're planning.'

'Even Joanna?'

Danny thought to himself, especially Joanna, but just nodded and said, 'It's the only way this will work.'

'Okay.'

'Are there any scheduled releases coming up soon that you're aware of?'

'I'll have to check, but I think there are two men due for release next week.'

'Can you remember the dates?'

'I think the release date for both is the ninth of March. As soon as I confirm that, I'll call you with the details.'

'Thank you.'

Danny handed over a business card and said, 'The number for the direct line into my office is on that card. I've also written my home phone number on the back. I want you to call me anytime, day or night, if there are any changes that I need to know about. As you can imagine, organising a surveillance on this scale isn't going to be easy, especially if two men are going to be released on the same day.'

'I'm back at work tomorrow, Danny. I'll confirm the details as soon as I can and call you.'

'I know I don't need to stress this, but please be discreet how you obtain that information. If anybody suspects something is different, it could jeopardise the whole operation.'

'I understand. I realise why you wanted to see me here now.'

'I hope I haven't put you off your golf.'

The governor chuckled and said, 'Don't worry about that. My golf is a lost cause already. I'll call you tomorrow.'

Danny shook hands with the governor and walked out of the clubhouse.

As he walked back to the car, Danny realised he would now need to brief Adrian Potter about his plan, as the cost of such a surveillance would be astronomical.

Danny prayed that Potter would forget the pounds and pence for once and sanction the plan.

65

12.30pm, 1 March 1988
Nottinghamshire Police Headquarters

Danny leaned back in the chair.
He was in Adrian Potter's office, sitting directly opposite the diminutive detective chief superintendent. He had just finished outlining his plan to place prisoners released under the new scheme from HMP Whatton under twenty-four-hour surveillance. Danny had gone to great lengths to explain the reasons why he felt this was the only way to protect the released men and to stand any chance of identifying the killer.

Potter was silent for a long time; then he said, 'Why the sudden change of direction? I thought you were keen on this vigilante group, Guardians of something. I thought you believed that someone within that group was responsible.'

'The Guardians of Innocence is the name of the group

you're referring to. We're still investigating them as one possible line of enquiry.'

'But now you want me to authorise you to carry out round-the-clock surveillance on two men as well?'

'It's the only thing we can do. We have no idea who is targeting these men. I do know that the information being used by the killer must be obtained from documents generated by that early release scheme. My problem is that, potentially, there are several people who could have access to that information. Watching the released men, who will be under certain restrictions anyway, is by far the cheaper option.'

'Cheaper! Have you any idea how much a surveillance operation like this will cost?'

'No, sir. But I do know how much it will cost to investigate more murders if we don't catch this person.'

'You're that sure this killer will continue to target these men?'

'I don't want to do nothing, and take that risk. Do you?'

Again, Potter was silent for a long time.

Finally, he said, 'Very well, Chief Inspector. You can run your operation for one calendar month, then we will reassess it. Good luck.'

Danny stood and said, 'Thank you, sir.'

As he walked from Potter's office, his mind was racing. Having gained permission to carry out the operation, all he had to do now was organise it.

He made straight for the offices of the Special Operations Unit. He needed to speak with Chief Inspector Chambers, to establish if any of his staff could assist in the month-long operation.

66

5.00pm, 1 March 1988
MCIU Offices, Mansfield Police Station

As soon as Danny had returned from headquarters, he had called Rob and Tina into his office to discuss the surveillance operation.

Chief Inspector Chambers had placed C Section of the Special Operations Unit at Danny's disposal for one month. Danny had worked with C Section on several previous operations. He had arranged to meet with Sergeant Turner as soon as details of the men due for release were provided by Governor Redmayne.

Until those details were known, the planning for the operation couldn't start in earnest.

Rob said, 'The manpower available for such an undertaking is a bit deficient. We can probably provide a team of two to watch the men during daylight hours, and a team of four during the hours of darkness, when an attack is more likely.'

'That doesn't sound ideal. Are you sure that's all we can manage?'

'Right now, Lynn and Jag are still working on the Guardians of Innocence enquiry. They've a hell of a lot of work to do, and are already working alone. Jeff is working as the full-time office manager, and Helen is still working with DS Lacey, trying to complete the family enquiries for the Tighe murder. If you include us three, that leaves us nine members of staff, plus whatever SOU can offer, to watch two men around the clock.'

'It's actually less than that. I want Andy and Rachel to continue working the enquiry they're currently on, for now. If that doesn't bear fruit, then they'll be able to drop into the observations teams later. The same goes for Helen and Sara. As soon as they finish their enquiries with the families, they can drop into the observations teams as well. For now, we'll have to make do with seven detectives and eleven men from Special Ops.'

'Okay, boss. As soon as we know the details of the addresses the men are being released to, I'll be able to organise things better. When are you expecting to hear from the governor?'

'Tomorrow morning.'

Tina said, 'I'll check with Sara and Helen to see how much more work they have to do.'

Danny said, 'Thanks. We'll reconvene tomorrow, once we've got all the details. I'll make sure Sergeant Turner is here as well, to assist with the planning. The Special Ops guys are doing this all the time.'

No sooner had Tina and Rob left the office than there was a knock on the door. The door opened, and DC Jeff Williams walked in.

He said, 'I've completed the research into the offences committed by Wilf Kelham. I'm sorry for the delay, but I was waiting to hear back from the police in Inverness.'

Danny said, 'Grab a seat. What have you managed to find out?'

'The two young girls attacked and raped by Kelham were cousins. They were both nine years old and on holiday at the time. The two families used to meet every year at the seaside, to catch up. One family lived in London, and the other north of the border, in Glasgow. The problem I've had has been trying to trace the family who lived in London. It turns out they emigrated to Australia six years ago and are now living in Perth.'

'Okay. What about the girl whose family lived in Glasgow?'

'I've had to circulate their details with all the Scottish forces, because the address shown on the file no longer exists. The house they lived in at the time of the attack was demolished five years ago. I've finally managed to trace the family to Inverness. The police in Inverness have just faxed through the address there.'

'That's good work, Jeff. How many family members are there?'

'The girl had a mother, father and two older brothers. From what I can gather from the police in Inverness, listed at the house now are just the girl, the mother and the two brothers. I've checked records, and the father passed away two years ago.'

'Do we know if the family have been informed about Kelham's release?'

'I checked with the probation service, and they sent a letter to the demolished property. I can't be certain, but I don't think the family were ever made aware of Kelham's early release.'

Danny considered that. Usually, he would send two detectives from the MCIU to interview the remaining family members, but he was acutely conscious of the lack of staff for his observations operation.

After some deliberation, he said, 'Jeff, I want you to contact the CID in Inverness and ask them to visit the family. I want them to ascertain if they were aware that Kelham had been released early. I want them to obtain details of each family member's whereabouts on the dates between Kelham's release and his death. If they can all be accounted for, I'm happy to leave the enquiry there. Stress to the detectives in Inverness that if they have any concerns whatsoever, they are to contact us, and I'll send a team from here to investigate further.'

'Will do, boss.'

As the detective stood to leave the office, Danny said, 'Is everything okay?'

Jeff turned and said, 'I'm fine, boss. I wasn't too enamoured about being tied down to the office, but to be honest I've quite enjoyed getting stuck into trying to find these families. It's different, but I'll get used to it.'

'Good man. When you've drafted out the fax request, let me see it before you send it.'

'Will do.'

As the door closed, Danny scribbled the names of Sara and Helen onto the list of officers available to be deployed on the observations.

9.30am, 2 March 1988
MCIU Offices, Mansfield Police Station

Danny was getting himself a coffee in the main office when the telephone in his own office began to ring. He raced inside, closed the door and snatched up the telephone. 'DCI Flint.'

'Chief Inspector, it's Wilson Redmayne. I have the details of the two men who are being released on the ninth of this month.'

Danny sat down and grabbed a pen and notepad. 'Okay, fire away.'

'The first man is Jason Mellors. He's fifty-five now. He was sentenced to twelve years imprisonment, in '82. He's served half his sentence.'

'Do you have any details of the conviction? There may be a pattern we haven't spotted, one that involves a particular type of sexual offence.'

'Rape of a fourteen-year-old boy.'

'Right. Where's he going to be living?'

'He's been allocated a housing association flat in Cotgrave. It's located on the first floor of a house at number 22 Rectory Road, Cotgrave.'

'Got that. Who's the second man?'

'Andrew Vickery.'

'Offence?'

'He was sentenced to nine years in '84, for a string of indecent assaults committed on schoolgirls who attended the school near his home on the Bestwood estate. He's also served just under half his sentence.'

'And the address?'

'The local council have provided him a ground-floor flat, in Kirkby in Ashfield. It's located on the Coxmoor estate at number 16 Warwick Close.'

'Do you have any up-to-date photographs of Mellors and Vickery?'

'Only the same ones that will be on your police records. We always keep the photograph taken at the point of charge for our records.'

'Okay, thanks. I'll get the photographs from our records. Do you have any specific information on either man that I should know about?'

'What do you mean?'

'I suppose what I'm asking is, which one of the two do you think is most likely to become a victim?'

'The man who was subject to the most press coverage at the time of his arrest was Andrew Vickery. He was dubbed "the Beast of Bestwood" by the tabloid press. His offences were a string of particularly nasty assaults.'

'I don't want you to think this is a criticism of you or your scheme, Governor, but if the assaults were so bad, how can this man be considered for release so early?'

'It's a fair question, Danny. All I can say is that sometimes people do change. Andrew Vickery is nothing like the troubled young man he was when he first came to HMP Whatton. He's far more mature now. He was only nineteen when he committed these offences. He's educated himself and worked hard within the system. He's changed enough for the parole board to recommend his release. This scheme just facilitates that decision.'

'I take it Joanna Preston has made all the arrangements for both men's forthcoming release?'

'Yes. That's all part and parcel of her role.'

'Do you have details of the probation officers for each man?'

'Sorry, I don't. They haven't been allocated yet. I'll send their names through as soon as I know them.'

'Thanks. I take it nobody knows you've pulled these files?'

'Nobody is aware of my interest. I photocopied the files myself first thing this morning. The original files are still where I found them in Joanna's office.'

'That's great. I'm relying on you, Governor.'

'No problem. I'll be careful when I look again for the probation officers. Are you still none the wiser about who may be targeting these men?'

'I'm afraid so. That's why we're having to be so careful about who knows what we're planning.'

'I get that.'

'One last thing. Do you know if any other releases are planned for the near future?'

'After Mellors and Vickery, there are no further releases scheduled until the end of June. From what I could see this morning, the next series of releases will all be to locations outside Nottinghamshire. Two are being released to addresses in Lincolnshire, and one other to an address in Staffordshire.'

'I didn't realise they could be released anywhere.'

'We have sex offenders sent to HMP Whatton from all over the UK. It's just a coincidence that the most recent ones were all released to addresses in Nottinghamshire.'

'Thanks for your prompt call this morning, Governor. Hopefully, one of these two men will have stirred the interest of our killer.'

'When I hear you speak like that, Chief Inspector, I still think of that tethered goat, waiting for the tiger. I'm also acutely aware that this is probably the only realistic chance we have of catching that proverbial tiger.'

'I think so. Don't forget, though, secrecy is the key.'

'Understood. I'll be in touch again in a couple of days.'

'If anything changes, you must call me immediately. I don't mind if you call me at work or at home, and don't worry about the time.'

'Will do.'

Danny put the telephone down. It was time to start planning the next phase of Operation Hermes.

68

11.30am, 2 March 1988
MCIU Offices, Mansfield Police Station

Danny handed the photographs of Jason Mellors and Andrew Vickery to his two detective inspectors and Sergeant Graham Turner from the Special Operations Unit.

He said, 'These are the two men due to be released from HMP Whatton on the ninth. Their names are Jason Mellors and Andrew Vickery. Attached to the photograph is a brief summary of their antecedent history, and the addresses they are being released to.'

As he handed the SOU sergeant his copy of the photographs, Danny said, 'Thanks for getting here so promptly, Graham. I know we've only got a week to prepare for their release, but in that time, I want you to find suitable premises to keep observations on their respective flats. I've a feeling that's going to be no easy task.'

The tough sergeant replied, 'I've got good contacts with all the council housing departments. If there's any empty flats or houses in the two areas, I'll find them.'

'The flat to be occupied by Mellors is being provided by the East Midlands Housing Association. Do you have any contacts with them?'

Turner nodded. 'A few. I'll get straight on it, and hopefully I'll be able to find suitable locations. If all else fails, we do have observations vehicles. Various vans that we can disguise. These are never ideal for a long job. Premises will be the preferred option, if I can find them.'

'Agreed. I also want you to liaise with Tina, to establish a working rota. I want the teams carrying out the obs to work twelve-hour shifts, with an hour overlap for each change. I know that's a long time to maintain obs, but we need to keep the changeovers down to a minimum. That way we stand less chance of being compromised. I've already checked the locations of both addresses. They're both in the middle of estates occupied by a high volume of repeat offenders. Criminal elements are always on the lookout for any police operations in their neighbourhoods. It's vital that we keep this one under wraps for as long as we can. Ideally, wherever possible, I would like one detective and one SOU man on duty at all times.'

Tina said, 'That won't always be possible, but we'll do our best to find a workable solution.'

Danny turned to Rob and said, 'I want you to concentrate more on the logistics of the operation. As the staff are going to be working twelve-hour shifts, they'll need food and drink to be provided. They'll also require specialist equipment, night-vision goggles, etc.'

Rob said, 'I'll get onto the Catering Department today and see what they suggest. It will probably be a packed meal of some kind.'

Graham turned to Rob and said, 'Let me have a list of your requirements for equipment, boss. I'll be able to help get that squared away for you.'

'Thanks.'

Danny said, 'You all know what's required. We'll meet again here at ten o'clock on the sixth to put the final touches in place. Graham, can you let me know as soon as you get suitable premises, please. I don't want to be scratching around for obs vehicles at the last minute.'

'Will do, boss. I don't think getting observation posts will be too much of an issue. The issue will be how good the view of the target premises is from those observation posts. I won't know that until I get out on the ground.'

Danny nodded. 'In the meantime, I'll be speaking to the divisional commanders for each area. I want to make sure that the uniform sergeants and inspectors are all aware of the observations on their areas. I want them to know exactly how to respond should we call them for assistance. Right, we all know what we've got to do, so let's get cracking. I want everything in place by the sixth.'

69

3.00pm, 2 March 1988
Stealthsafe Securities Limited, Colwick Park, Nottingham

Barbra Johnson was in her early forties. A glamorous peroxide blonde, she played up the image of the archetypal 'dumb blonde'.

She was far from it.

Barbra was an extremely astute businesswoman, with qualifications for accountancy and bookkeeping. She had worked for her brother's company for the last five years. She knew everything about the business and about her brother's other sideline involving the Guardians of Innocence. She had never let on to her brother, or his wife Cheryl, that she was aware of the activities of this shadowy group. Or that she knew what role some of the company's employees played within that group.

Barbra missed very little; she was always listening in on other people's conversations. In truth, she was a lonely middle-aged woman with a boring life that revolved around number-crunching accounts. To compensate for her dull existence, she liked to live her life vicariously, listening to the exciting exploits of other people.

She liked nothing better than to listen to the men in the staff canteen as they told each other stories of violent encounters they had been involved in. The stories recounted were generally about beating senseless certain types of men, ones that were loathed by most members of society.

The security staff never noticed Barbra listening intently to their wild tales.

After she had informed her brother that the police were coming to ask questions, she hadn't been surprised when he'd phoned back an hour later, asking her to deal with the police. He told her he'd booked a last-minute deal for him and his wife, as they needed a break. He would be on holiday in Spain for the next few weeks.

Dealing with the police didn't faze Barbra. She would answer all their questions in a suitably vague way until they got bored of asking them. There was no documentary evidence that could connect Stealthsafe Limited to the Guardians of Innocence organisation. She had seen to that.

After hearing what some of the employees had been doing on behalf of that organisation, she had made sure there were no links to the company. The only thing she couldn't hide was the link to Polyplastech Limited and its owner – also the founder of the Guardians of Innocence, James Brannigan.

She had seen the detectives arrive and met them at the main entrance before they had the chance to speak to any of the employees.

She had painted on an ingenuous smile and said, 'Good afternoon. I'm Barbra Johnson. I think you're here to see me?'

The female detective said, 'Mrs Johnson, thanks for seeing us so quickly. My name's Detective Sergeant Harris, and this is Detective Constable Singh. Is there somewhere we can talk?'

Barbra said, 'We can use my office. Follow me.'

As they walked through the premises, Lynn Harris said, 'I understand you're the finance director. Is the company director here as well? We may need to speak to him.'

'I'm sorry. My brother's in Spain on holiday right now. I'm sure I'll be able to answer any questions you have.'

Barbra showed the two detectives into her office and said, 'Can I get you a drink?'

Lynn said, 'No, thanks; we've not long had one. The main questions I have are financial ones, so you're probably the best person to ask. I'm interested in the funding you received from the corporate giant Polyplastech. Can I ask how you managed to achieve such a high level of funding? From my enquiries, I understand it was in the region of over two hundred thousand pounds during the last financial year.'

Barbra was a little surprised that the detectives had been so thorough already. They must have had specialist help to establish that information from the company's registered accounts. She didn't allow her expression to betray her surprise.

She smiled and said, 'It really isn't any secret; we were just extremely fortunate. I read an article stating how Polyplastech Limited were keen to offer financial help to smaller businesses that may work for them in the future. That financial help was by the way of either start-up loans or rescue packages. At that time, this company had quite a high toxic debt that we just couldn't shift. On the spur of the moment, I wrote a letter to the accounts department at Polyplastech, enquiring about a financial rescue package. I made the request on the understanding that we would be able to offer a preferential rate to Polyplastech for any security work they required at any of their UK-based factory sites in the future. Part of the services we provide are night-time security patrols around business premises. It really was just a speculative punt on my part. I was as surprised as anyone when they wrote back and offered to wipe the debts and provide capital for investment into new equipment and transport.'

'That was extremely fortunate. How did your brother take the news?'

'Obviously, he was overjoyed. In truth, the business was only a few months away from being wound up. As a company, we just couldn't cope with the interest on those debts. Once that was wiped from the books, we've done very well. Profits are rising, and business is generally good.'

Jag Singh said, 'You mentioned that the finance package from Polyplastech was provided on the understanding that at some stage you would provide staff for security at their factory sites. Have you got any contracts for that type of work in place with them yet?'

'Not yet. But I'm sure it's only a matter of time. This company will really take off when that happens.'

'Has Stealthsafe carried out any uncontracted work for either Polyplastech or for James Brannigan personally?'

'We don't do uncontracted work. Why would we do any work for James Brannigan personally? I don't understand your question.'

'Mr Brannigan is the founder of an organisation called Guardians of Innocence. Has Stealthsafe ever provided any security staff at meetings held by that organisation? Or have they ever carried out any other work on their behalf?'

Barbra put on a blank expression. 'Guards of what?'

'Guardians of Innocence?'

'Never heard of them. Who are they?'

'Is your brother a member of that organisation?'

'If he is, he's never mentioned it to me. Are they like the Freemasons or something?'

Lynn said, 'Was the finance you received from Polyplastech paid to this company for services already rendered by some of your employees?'

Barbra knew exactly which services the detective was referring to, but she said, 'We haven't done any work for Polyplastech yet. I've just told you we're still waiting for our first contract.'

'How well does your brother know James Brannigan?'

'As far as I'm aware, he's only ever spoken to him once. That was to thank him for bailing the company out, just after we got the financial rescue package.'

'Have you ever spoken to James Brannigan?'

'No. All my dealings were made through the accounts department at Polyplastech. I wouldn't know James Brannigan if he were standing in front of me. Is there anything else you need to know? Would you like access to examine the company's books? I can arrange that for you.'

'That won't be necessary, thank you. When is your brother back from Spain?'

'He only flew out yesterday. He got a cracking late deal. Too good to turn down. Knowing our Davy, right now, he'll be on the booze in some sleazy bar in Benidorm.'

'When will he be available for us to interview?'

'He's gone for three weeks. He needed a break; he was exhausted. It will do him and Cheryl the power of good.'

'Okay. Thanks for your time today, Mrs Johnson. We may have to speak again.'

'No problem. If there's anything else you need, you have my number.'

As she spoke, she fluttered her long eyelashes at Jag, who just looked away.

Annoyed at the detective's lack of interest in her flirting, Barbra huffed, 'Can you see yourselves out? I've got a stack of work to do.'

Lynn said, 'Of course, no problem. Thanks again.'

As they made their way back through the premises, the two detectives walked by the staff canteen. One of the employees saw them as they walked by the door. He shouted, 'Can I help you?' before dashing out to confront them in the corridor.

The burly security guard said, 'What are you two doing back here?'

Jag took his police identification from his jacket pocket and said, 'There's no problem, mate. We're from the CID, here to see Mrs Johnson.'

'Oh, okay.'

'Yeah, she was just telling us that a lot of you guys do work for the Guardians of Innocence. How about you?'

'I'm still new here, so I haven't yet. Most of the lads who have been here a while have done jobs for them.'

'What sort of jobs?'

'Security stuff, the usual.'

'Thanks, Colin.'

'My name's not Colin.'

'Sorry, I thought that's what you said. What's your name?'

'Steve Bainbridge. Why do you want to know my name?'

Jag could see that the security man was becoming wary, so as they walked away, he said cheerily, 'Thanks, Steve. Be seeing you.'

As they got back in their car, Lynn said, 'You crafty sod.'

Jag laughed. 'I don't know what you mean, Sarge.'

'I'm sure you don't. I think we need to look a little closer at Stealthsafe Security Limited. The lovely Barbra Johnson was obviously lying through her teeth.'

70

5.00pm, 2 March 1988
MCIU Offices, Mansfield Police Station

Danny was hard at work preparing the operational order for the planned observations that he hoped would snare a killer. When he heard the knock on his office door, he didn't look up from his paperwork. He just shouted, 'Come in.'

Andy Wills said, 'Sorry to disturb you, boss. Rachel and I have an update for you on Joanna Preston.'

'Sorry, I just wanted to finish that section of the op order. Both of you grab a seat. What have you found?'

Rachel said, 'I started by researching her work life prior to joining the probation service. Joanna was ex-army. She joined the Women's Royal Auxiliary Corps straight from school, just after her sixteenth birthday. She joined on the junior soldier scheme and looked set to make the army her career. She served for five years and was based in Guildford, Surrey. She left at the age of twenty-one.'

'Have you spoken to the army?'

'Yes, sir. Preston had an exemplary record as a soldier. The army were very sorry to lose her. Her record states that she was brilliant in the field, very fit and very strong. I spoke with her commanding officer, who believes Preston only left the army because she couldn't be considered for combat roles.'

'Did she do anything else between the army and the probation service?'

'Not that I can find. She may have done some casual work somewhere, but there's no record. There's a gap of three months. The next recorded employment is with the probation service. Specifically, working within the prison system. She started her first job in July 1983 when she was posted to HMP Nottingham. Her home address is in Bingham, so she requested a transfer to HMP Whatton in July 1985. She initially worked as the welfare officer on B Wing, but in December of '87 she transferred onto the specialist Sex Offenders Wing at the prison, specifically to run the early release scheme that was being piloted.'

'Are there any issues with her record in the probation service?'

'None that I can find. If anything, it's the opposite. Wherever she goes, she does a great job. Governor Redmayne actively headhunted her for the role running the early release scheme.'

'What about her home life?'

Andy said, 'As I said, her home address is at Bingham. I've done a drive-by of the property; it's a standard new build, three-bedroom semi, on a nice modern estate. Nothing out of the ordinary. She obviously lives well within her means. She isn't married and lives alone.'

'Vehicle?'

'Dark-coloured Ford Sierra.'

'What about family?'

'We've only just started to research her family. Her army records showed that her next of kin was her stepfather, Frederick Harper. She also has two sisters. Apart from those three, we can't find any other relatives.'

'No mother still on the scene?'

Rachel said, 'From the scant information we've found so far, it seems that her mother died six months before Joanna joined the Army.'

'Anything interesting about the family?'

'There is something I found that's strange. I haven't had time to establish all the details yet. I've only got half the story.'

Danny was intrigued. 'Go on.'

'Both the sisters are younger than Joanna, and both made allegations of being sexually assaulted by the stepfather.'

Danny was thoughtful; then he said, 'You said allegations.'

'Yes, sir. I found a brief note of the allegations on the school records of the two girls. But then I couldn't find any record of Frederick Harper ever being charged by the police with any sexual offences.'

'So the two girls made the allegations and were either not believed, or there was insufficient evidence to charge. You need to get to the bottom of that. Do you have addresses for the stepfather and the sisters?'

'The only address we have so far is from Joanna's army record. Obviously, we'll start there, but it's unlikely they're all still living there. I think we'll need to do a lot more digging.'

'Yes, you do. Specifically, you need to establish what the exact nature of the allegations of sexual abuse were against the stepfather. Why would a woman with that sort of history in her family want to spend her life working with sex offenders? We need to know if there was any substance whatsoever to those allegations. Locate the stepfather and the two sisters as soon as you can. You need to speak with them and establish the truth. You'll need to tread very carefully when you speak to the family. It will be difficult, because the two sisters will be wanting to know why you're asking questions after all this time. I want both of you to follow this enquiry through. Keep digging and come and see me again when you've established the truth of these allegations.'

71

7.30pm, 2 March 1988
MCIU Offices, Mansfield Police Station

Danny had completed as much as he could do on the operational order, and was putting his jacket on to go home when he heard voices in the previously empty main office.

He walked out of his office and saw Lynn Harris and Jag Singh still sitting at their desks, hard at work.

'It's been a long day for you two,' he said. Then, 'How did you get on at Stealthsafe Security?'

Lynn said, 'It was inconclusive. I definitely think there could be something there, though.'

'Why inconclusive?'

'The only management available to talk to us was the finance director, Barbra Johnson, and she was extremely vague.'

'Where was the director of the company?'

'The company director is Barbra's brother, Davy Johnson. He owns the company. He's currently on holiday in Spain and won't be coming back for another three weeks.'

'I see. What did the finance director have to say, then?'

'I questioned her about the finance deal the company has with Polyplastech Ltd. She gave us chapter and verse on that, but denied any knowledge of the Guardians of Innocence. She claimed she'd never heard of them. She's never met James Brannigan and has only ever dealt with the accounts department at Polyplastech Ltd.'

'What were the staff like?'

'We only saw a few. They looked very unsavoury. Typical unlicensed bouncers, if you ask me.'

'Did you speak to any of them?'

'In conversation, Jag managed to get one of them to slip out that staff there were doing jobs for the Guardians of Innocence. Jobs that he described as "the usual stuff".'

Danny said to Jag, 'And this was after Barbra Johnson had denied all knowledge about that group?'

'Yes, boss. She was obviously lying through her teeth. There's something going on there for sure. God only knows what work those thugs are doing for the Guardians.'

Danny was deep in thought for a few minutes before coming to a decision.

He said, 'I want you to forget about the list of other companies for now and concentrate solely on Stealthsafe Securities. Lynn, I want you to concentrate on the finance side of things. Jag, I want you to go back to the company and obtain a list of all their employees. Do all the relevant police records checks on their staff. If they're as unsavoury as you suggest, the results should make for interesting reading. I also want you to reinvestigate all the unsolved serious assaults on known sex offenders that you found earlier. Let's see if you can tie some of the thugs working at Stealthsafe to those assaults. If you can find that link, it could lead us to the murders.' He paused. 'Good work today.'

Lynn said, 'That's a lot of work for two detectives, boss. We would get results much faster if we had more staff.'

'I'm sorry, Lynn. There's no available staff to help you. Everyone else will be committed, working on the planned observations. Just work through things methodically. There's as much as overtime as you want. I'm relying on you both to do as much as you can.'

'Okay, boss.'

As he walked out of the office, Danny said, 'Keep me informed of any progress.'

Jag nodded. 'Will do, sir.'

72

9.00pm, 2 March 1988
Mansfield, Nottinghamshire

Danny swirled the ice cubes in his glass of single malt and stared at the television set in the lounge. The nine o'clock news was about to start. It had been another long day.

Sue walked in and flopped down onto the settee next to him. She looked shattered.

Danny said, 'Can I get you a drink?'

'No, thanks. All I want is a nice cuddle.'

Danny took a sip of his drink before reaching forward and putting the glass on the coffee table. He slipped his arm around his wife's shoulders and said, 'Have the doctors said when Hayley might be allowed home?'

Snuggling into Danny's side, Sue said, 'Not yet. I don't see why they are being so cautious; she looks fine now. I just want her home with us.'

There was a pause before Danny said, 'Do you still want to go back to work as soon as she comes home?'

Sue sat up and looked into Danny's eyes. 'Yes, I do. Why are you asking me this now? I've already spoken to the child minder; everything's in place. Why are you asking me again?'

'It's work. I'm setting up a twenty-four-hour surveillance on two men, with very little staff. My shifts after the ninth of this month are going to entail long hours and at varied times of the day. I won't be able to guarantee being home on time. How's that going to work with the child minder?'

Sue let out an exasperated sigh. 'Bloody hell, Danny! How long is this surveillance job likely to last?'

'At least a month. Maybe even longer.'

There was another long pause before Sue said, 'Look, as and when I do go back to work, my first couple of weeks will be spent on reintegration to the wards and other administration tasks. So, initially, we'll manage. I'll ask Vanessa if she can cover the period that allows me to work from nine o'clock in the morning until five o'clock at night. Basic office hours. It's probably a couple of hours longer than she would look after other children, but if we both speak to her and explain the situation, she may agree. After that initial two-week period, I'll be expected to be back on the shift pattern, and I won't be allowed to work basic nine-to-five shifts. At that stage, we'll have to reassess the situation.'

'This was always going to be the problem, sweetheart. We both have jobs where there are no set hours. If the child minder can't give us some degree of flexibility, we either find one who can, or abandon the idea of you going back to work so soon.'

Danny could see by the look on her face that Sue was livid.

After taking a few deep breaths, she said, 'I'll make an

appointment for us both to go and see Vanessa so we can discuss all our options. Let's not make any decisions yet.'

'Agreed. I might get lucky and only have to run the surveillance for a couple of days.'

'However long the observations run for, our situation will still need clarification. You'll never give up your work, and I have no intention of abandoning my career, either. That means we owe it to our daughter to find the best possible solution for all three of us.'

Danny held his wife tightly and said, 'I'm sure there's an answer to be found if we look hard enough.'

73

10.00am, 6 March 1988
MCIU Offices, Mansfield Police Station

Graham Turner was the last to arrive for the meeting with Danny, Rob and Tina.

Danny said, 'Grab a seat, Graham. I want to get started. First things first, how are you doing with observation posts on the two addresses?'

'Both are now in place. The one that caused more difficulty was the flat at Rectory Road in Cotgrave.'

'What was the problem?'

'I couldn't get premises anywhere that gave a view of the rear of the house. But then when I did the night recce, I found there was no access to the back of the property other than through the front garden, so it didn't matter. Anybody wanting to gain access via the rear windows would have to approach the premises from the front.'

'Good work. So we've got an observation post sorted for Jason Mellors?'

'Yes, sir. His flat is at number 22. We've got the first-floor flat at number 25. It's virtually opposite the target premises.'

'Is there any issue about how long we've got it for?'

'The housing association are happy for us to have it for as long as we need it. I told them we needed it to carry out observations against drug dealing in the area.'

'Will the handover of staff cause any issues?'

'It shouldn't if people are careful and stick to the planned exit and entrance strategies.'

'That's great. What about the Kirkby in Ashfield address for Andrew Vickery?'

'That was much easier. Number 16 Warwick Close is on the ground floor, at the end of a block of flats. I was able to acquire the flat that's on the first floor of the next block. In effect, officers in there will have an elevated view of the front, side and rear of number sixteen. There's also an unlit alleyway that runs between the two blocks.'

'Do you foresee any problems with the changeovers if it's that close?'

'Not really. Again, it's just a matter of people taking care when they swap over. When I did the night recce on the Coxmoor estate, I did flag up one thing that could cause us a problem.'

'Go on.'

'The Coxmoor estate is dog rough. It's low-level housing, crisscrossed with unlit alleyways. It would be very easy to miss somebody approaching the target premises. Whoever's observing that flat will always have to be on high alert. The street lighting's crap all over the estate. It's a burglar's paradise.'

'Did you have any problems with the local council, obtaining the flat for obs?'

'None at all. One of the housing officers at Ashfield Council is ex-job. We can have the empty flat for as long as we need it. It's a bit of a dump, but who cares? It gives a great view of the target premises.'

'Thanks. That's good work.'

Danny was just about to ask Rob if he'd managed to acquire all the equipment they would need, when there was a knock on his office door.

He shouted, 'Come in!'

Jeff Williams walked in and said, 'Sorry to disturb your meeting, sir. You asked me to bring you this information as soon as I got it. It's about the enquiries in Scotland relating to Wilf Kelham.'

'Yes, Jeff. What's the outcome?'

'The CID in Inverness have now interviewed all the victim's family. They're satisfied that none of the family were aware that Wilf Kelham had been released from prison. They hadn't been contacted by any agency to let them know.'

'That's great, thanks.'

As soon as Jeff closed the door, Danny turned to his two inspectors and said, 'So DS Lacey and DC Bailey will also now be available for the observations rota. That means the final numbers will be nine detectives, including us three, plus eleven Special Ops officers. Do you think you can provide a rota that will adequately cover both addresses for one month, on a twenty-four-hour surveillance, with just twenty staff?'

Tina nodded. 'The addition of Sara and Helen will be a massive help. I think we'll always have cover, but I don't know if we'll always be able to have what you wanted. It might not be possible to always mix the detectives and the SOU staff, and we may not always have four officers on nights, as you wanted.'

'Don't worry about mixing the teams, but try wherever possible to have two inside the premises and two outside as a fast-response team on the night shift. Daytime cover will have to be just the two inside the obs point. Is that manageable?'

'Shouldn't be a problem.'

Graham asked, 'Boss, did you manage to brief the uniform staff who work in the two areas?'

'I've briefed the inspectors and the sergeants, and they're going to remind their staff on every night shift what's happening, and how to respond to any backup calls.'

'That's good. I think having that backup in place could be vital. Especially on the Coxmoor estate. That place is like a warren.'

'All in hand, Graham. How are we set for the equipment required?'

Rob said, 'We've got everything we need, including plain vehicles for the handover of staff. I've arranged for packed meals every day for the staff working the twelve-hour shifts. It won't be anything startling, but I'm sure it will fill a hole.'

'Have you established what communications channel we're going to use?'

Tina said, 'We'll run the obs on the back-to-back channel so it doesn't interfere with divisional radio traffic. But the obs teams will also have a radio tuned into the divisional frequency, to request backup if required.'

'Good. I think we're all set, then.'

Graham said, 'We just need to run through the handovers at both observation posts before the operation is due to start.'

'Can you organise that?'

'No problem.'

'Tina, can you bring me the rota as soon as you've prepared it, please.'

'Will do.'

'That's it, then. Thanks, everyone.'

74

**5.00pm, 6 March 1988
MCIU Offices, Mansfield Police Station**

Danny was on his way out of the office to go home. It was the first day in a month that he had finished work on time.

As he walked out of the door, he passed Andy and Rachel in the corridor. Andy said, 'We were just on our way to see you, boss.'

'Why? Is there a problem?'

'No problem. We just wanted to give you an update.'

Danny leaned against the wall wearily and said, 'Go on.'

Rachel said, 'We've finally located an up-to-date address for one of Joanna Preston's sisters.'

'Which one?'

'The younger one, Theresa Harper.'

'Is it local?'

'Yes, she lives here in Mansfield.'

'That's great. Go and speak to her first thing tomorrow morning. Ask her general questions about the historical abuse and see what she offers up. Try to make her think you're looking at reinvestigating the stepfather. You can't afford to let her think that you're interested in anything else.'

'Understood.'

'I've kept you both out of the planned observations, so just follow this enquiry and see where it takes you. We could be miles off the mark, but I need you to either implicate Joanna Preston, or rule her out as a suspect once and for all.'

75

7.00pm, 6 March 1988
Steeple Claydon, Buckinghamshire

James Brannigan was sitting alone in his smoking room. When he had renovated the house, he had paid extra to have the high vents, which were needed to allow the air to circulate properly, installed in the thick stone walls.

His only vice was a taste for classic Cuban cigars. The smoking room he had created was his own private space. It was where he always went to think things through, to make the right business decisions. All his biggest deals had been formulated in this small room.

Today, he had another problem to resolve, another decision that needed to be made.

He unlocked the humidor made from Spanish cedar wood and selected one of his favourite cigars. The Partagas Serie D cigar was one of the oldest Cuban cigars, dating back over one hundred years. It was a robust size and had a delicious woody finish that Brannigan adored.

He prepared the cigar and lit it, savouring that first mouthful of smoke as it made his taste buds come alive. He leaned back in the tan-coloured buffalo leather armchair and allowed his head to rest further back on the soft leather until he stared up at the ceiling.

As he savoured the delicious smoke, and the room slowly filled with its heady aroma, his mind started to work through his current problem.

When he had established the Guardians of Innocence movement, he had been full of pent-up rage and frustration. He had desperately wanted to exact revenge for what had happened to his daughter. He had initially toyed with the idea of paying somebody to kill Miles Harmon, the man responsible for sexually abusing his daughter. He had quickly discounted the idea, as he knew any such plan would be traced back to him.

After learning of Harmon's early release and his subsequent death from cancer, he had felt cheated. It was under those circumstances, with all those feelings racing through him, that he had first met Davy Johnson.

Johnson had suffered at the hands of abusers as a youngster, when he was in the care of the local authority. The two men had met at a charity fundraiser and got talking. They were both businessmen, albeit in different leagues, and both had a deep-seated hatred of paedophiles.

After several subsequent private meetings, the idea of the Guardians of Innocence had been born in this very room. It had later been decided by the two men that Brannigan would use all his influence and money to try to achieve a change in the law, while Johnson would use the staff of his security firm to take a more hands-on approach. It would be down to Johnson to mete out their own brand of justice whenever they discovered where a paedophile was living, and when Brannigan felt the timing was right.

He took another long pull on the cigar and allowed the smoke to rise slowly from his mouth. His mind turned to the problems he was facing right now.

He had been surprised when he had learned of the brutal murders of the three paedophiles. That kind of action hadn't been sanctioned; it was way too early. He had given explicit instructions to Johnson that his staff were only to administer beatings. It was far too soon to take that ultimate step.

Johnson had, of course, denied that his men had anything to do with the killings, but Brannigan didn't believe him. Either Johnson had deliberately gone directly against his orders, or some of his staff were now out of control.

Either way, it was a dangerous situation that needed addressing urgently.

He had been shocked at the depth of the police investigation into the murders and how quickly they had suspected there was a link between the murdered men and the Guardians of Innocence. The recent visits to his own and Johnson's business premises by the police had confirmed his worst fears. The police were actively seeking a link that would tie Johnson, and subsequently himself, to the vicious series of assaults, even, possibly, the murders.

He closed his eyes and allowed the solution to this problem to filter into his brain.

His first thought was that he needed to establish distance between himself and Johnson. He allowed his mind to formulate the strategy that would achieve this.

The first thing he needed to do was call his MP and tell him to drop the private members bill. The MP already knew there was no appetite within either chamber for a change in the law. It had only been the large cash payment into the offshore account that had persuaded his grasping MP to pursue it in the first place.

Secondly, he would call Detective Chief Inspector Flint and personally inform him that he had decided to shut down the Guardians of Innocence movement. He would explain to him that the last thing he had ever wanted was to inadvertently cause a backlash against men released from prison. He would stress to the detective that had never been his intention.

Finally, he would talk to Johnson and tell him to back off and to control his thugs. If he agreed and distanced himself properly, Brannigan would see to it that Polyplastech would continue funding any shortfall in Johnson's security business.

Once things had settled down again, and the police had stopped prying and making enquiries, he would then discuss the way forward with Johnson.

His plan to hide the activities of his organisation in plain sight had been a dismal failure.

He needed to take his movement underground. It would be as though the Guardians of Innocence had never existed. He would then ensure that, in the future, Johnson only used a few handpicked, trusted individuals. Only these men would be used to carry out the physical retributions against the monsters who continued to walk freely in towns and cities, posing a threat wherever they went.

76

9.00am, 7 March 1988
Harrop White Road, Ladybrook, Mansfield,
Nottinghamshire

The rain that had been falling heavily all morning was starting to ease. Rachel switched off the windscreen wipers and drove the car steadily through the streets of the Ladybrook estate.

Andy stifled a belch in the passenger seat and said, 'Excuse me.'

Rachel said, 'Charming.'

'I knew I shouldn't have had that sausage and tomato sandwich this morning. I love them, but they don't love me.'

'Very healthy, I'm sure. This is Harrop White Road. Can you see number sixty-three?'

Rachel slowed the car to a crawl, allowing other traffic to pass, until Andy said, 'Here it is, the one with the red door.'

Rachel parked the car, and the two detectives looked at

the semi-detached house. There were no curtains in any of the windows, and the garden looked neglected.

Andy said, 'This doesn't look very promising. Looks empty to me.'

The two detectives got out of the car, opened the small wooden gate and walked down the path to the front door.

Andy used the letterbox to knock loudly. It made an echoing noise that was the telltale sound of an empty property. He lifted the letterbox and peered into the hallway. There were no carpets, and a mountain of junk mail and unopened letters.

Rachel had moved across the front of the house and looked through the front window into what would have been the lounge. There wasn't a stick of furniture to be seen. Using the car key, she rapped loudly on one of the windowpanes, the sharp sound once again reverberating through the house.

There was a wooden gate at the side of the house, which was half open. Andy opened it fully and walked to the back of the property. The back garden was in a worse state than the front. Nobody had tended this garden for a long time. He looked through the kitchen and the dining room windows and saw the same story. The house was empty.

He walked back around to the front of the property and said, 'There's nobody here, Rach.'

As they made their way back up the garden path, a voice said, 'Nobody lives there now. Can I help you?'

Rachel turned and saw an elderly woman standing at the front door of the neighbouring property. The detectives walked back down the path and across to the bordering fence so they could talk to the woman.

Rachel took out her identification and said, 'I'm DC Moore, and this is DS Wills. We're from the CID. We're trying to find Theresa Harper. Do you know where she's gone?'

The old lady squinted at the identification and then said, 'Hopefully to a better place.'

'Excuse me?'

'I'm sorry, duck. Theresa killed herself at the beginning of December last year.'

'Do you know if she had any family?'

'I know she had two sisters. One of them works at a prison somewhere; I don't know where, though. The last I heard, the other sister was poorly.'

'What about her parents?'

'Her mum died years ago, but I think her stepfather's still alive.'

'Do you know where her stepfather is now?'

'I did hear that he was living in some care home. He'd gone a bit funny, duck. Couldn't look after himself anymore, if you know what I mean.'

'Which care home?'

'I know it's over at Mansfield Woodhouse. I can't remember what it's called, though. I think it's "Silver" something or other.'

'Okay, thanks. You mentioned a sister who was poorly. Any idea where she lives?'

'Yeah. Theresa was close to her. I used to see her a lot; she only lives a couple of streets away on the estate. I've got her address somewhere. Do you want it, duck?'

'Yes, please. That would be a massive help.'

As the old lady turned to go back inside her house, she mumbled, 'Won't be a minute.'

After five minutes, she returned clutching an old envelope.

She said, 'I've written it down for you. Her name's Maggie, and she lives at 16 Milford Crescent. It's not far from here, on the other side of the estate.'

'Thanks.'

Andy said, 'Any idea why Theresa took her own life?'

'I haven't got the foggiest. She was such a pretty little thing; I could never understand why she couldn't find herself a nice fella to settle down with. Must have been lonely rattling round in that big house.'

'I suppose so. Thanks for your help.'

'No problem, duck.'

As they got back in the car, Andy said, 'What's all this "duck" talk?'

Rachel laughed. 'Don't tell me you've never been called "duck" before. How long have you worked around here?'

'Nope, can't say I have. Come on, let's go and talk to Maggie.'

77

10.00am, 7 March 1988
Steeple Claydon, Buckinghamshire

James Brannigan picked up the telephone in his office and dialled a number from memory. The telephone was picked up on the third ring. A woman's voice said, 'Good morning. You've reached the office of William Maytoft, MP. How can I help you?'

'Good morning, it's James Brannigan. I need to talk to Bill urgently. Can you put me through, please?'

The secretary knew exactly who James Brannigan was. She placed the call on hold and pressed the intercom to speak to her boss. 'Sir, I've got James Brannigan on the phone. He says he needs to speak with you and that it's urgent.'

Maytoft didn't want to upset one of his main backers, so he said, 'Okay, Stella. Put him straight through.'

After a few seconds' delay, the call was put through. Brannigan said, 'Good morning, Bill.'

'Hello, James. What can I do for you?'

'I've been giving certain matters a lot of thought. I've decided that I no longer wish you to proceed with the private members bill. I want you to withdraw it.'

There was silence.

Brannigan knew that William Maytoft would be trying to process what he'd just told him.

After a long delay, the politician said, 'Can I ask why, precisely?'

'I just don't think it will do any good. Nobody's bothered really, are they?'

'But it's not that simple. I can't just withdraw the bill at this late stage. It will make me look ridiculous.'

'Oh, I'm sure you can. Later today, I'll be forwarding the same amount of money to the same offshore account as I did before. By the time that money lands in your account, I want your private members bill withdrawn. Is that understood?'

There was another pause; then the career politician said in a smarmy voice, 'If you're sure that's what you want, then who am I to argue?'

'Good. I'll transfer the money. Make sure you get cracking and drop the bill, today.'

'Will do, James. If you ever need my assistance with anything else, you know where to find me.'

Brannigan terminated the call.

78

10.00am, 7 March 1988
16 Milford Crescent, Ladybrook, Mansfield,
Nottinghamshire

Unlike the Harrop White Road address, 16 Milford Crescent was obviously lived in. It was a neat, semi-detached house that looked clean and tidy outside.

Despite persistent knocking on the front door and the windows, there was no reply.

Andy said, 'I'll get some paper from the car and leave her a note.'

He walked back up the garden path and sat in the car. He quickly wrote a note requesting that Maggie Harper contact the MCIU office as soon as possible. He wrote the office number on the paper, then walked to the front door and posted the note.

Rachel said, 'Bloody hell. This enquiry is really doing my

head in. Talk about as one door closes, another shuts! We're getting nowhere fast today.'

Andy nodded. 'I know what you mean. Let's have a drive over to the nick at Mansfield Woodhouse and see if we can trace a care home called "Silver something or other".'

The two detectives walked back to the car and had one last look back at the house. Nothing stirred, no curtains twitched, so they got in and drove away.

79

11.30am, 7 March 1988
MCIU Offices, Mansfield Police Station

Danny was in his office putting the finishing touches to the operational order that would cover the planned observations at Kirkby in Ashfield and Cotgrave.

The strident ring of the telephone disturbed his thought process. He snatched the receiver from the cradle. 'DCI Flint.'

'Chief Inspector Flint, it's James Brannigan. I was hoping we could have a chat. Is now a good time?'

Danny was intrigued. He put his pen down and said, 'Now's as good a time as any. What's the problem?'

'I think, inadvertently, I may have been the problem.'

'I don't understand.'

'When I established the Guardians of Innocence, the last thing I ever intended was to cause a problem for the police, and it seems that's what I may have done. After your visit, I took a long hard look at what I was doing. I could see how some ignorant louts might feel my organisation was giving a green light for vigilante-style retribution against convicted sex offenders.'

'And it took my visit to your business premises for you to realise that, did it?'

'Yes, Chief Inspector, it did. I've always thought that the organisation was about bringing pressure to bear on elected politicians who could change the law. Your visit opened my eyes to the fact that this was a romantic notion and probably very naïve on my part.'

'I see. So why the phone call today?'

'Over the last few days, I've had long conversations with my daughter. She stressed to me that all she wants is to move on from the whole sordid event. She told me that the movement I created is preventing her from doing that. I was upset to hear her say that she felt I'd become preoccupied with the organisation rather than being a father to her.'

'That must have been distressing for you.'

'It was extremely disconcerting. I was amazed at how level-headed and mature my teenage daughter has become. I felt I owed it to her to listen to what she had to say, and to do something about her fears.'

'Is there something about your organisation you wanted to talk to me about specifically?'

'No. Not at all. The reason I've called is to inform you that I'm disbanding the Guardians of Innocence with immediate effect. I cannot allow misguided fools to take actions, which could be illegal, in the name of the organisation. I'm not saying that's what's happened, of course, but after your visit, I could see there was a possibility of something like that happening in the future. That, combined with my daughter's wishes, brought me to this decision. It has always been a rather time-consuming passion that took me away from my business for far too long.'

'What about the politics of the movement? Hadn't you lobbied your MP to take out a private members bill?'

'Yes, I had. I've already had a conversation this morning with my MP, William Maytoft. I've asked him if he could withdraw his private members bill. He assures me that he can, and it will be taken out of parliamentary business from today.'

'Why would you do that?'

'I've always been a realist. I knew there was never much chance of his private bill ever getting passed through the house. There's just no appetite for a change in the law amongst our politicians. Most of them are doing all they can to lessen prison populations, not increase them. I didn't want to waste everybody's time.'

'You really have had a massive change of heart, Mr Brannigan.'

'I was in a bad place when I established the organisation. I was angry at what had happened to my daughter, and then when they let Miles Harmon out early, I was enraged and felt I had to do something. I can see now, looking back, that I probably overreacted. Anyway, it's all in the past now. As of today, the Guardians of Innocence will no longer exist.'

'Okay. Well, thanks for letting me know.'

'No problem, Chief Inspector. Good luck with your investigations into the deaths of those men.'

The call was terminated by Brannigan, and Danny slowly put the telephone down. His mind was racing at what he'd just heard.

After a few minutes of deep thought, he stepped into the main office and saw Lynn Harris and Jagvir Singh working at their desks.

He said, 'Lynn, Jag, I need to speak to you in my office.'

As the two detectives walked into his office, Danny said, 'Grab a seat. I've just had a very interesting telephone call from James Brannigan. He called me to tell me that he's disbanding the Guardians of Innocence. As from today, that organisation will no longer exist.'

Lynn tutted. 'How very convenient,' she said.

'My thoughts exactly. I don't know what you did at Stealthsafe Securities when you visited, but it's really rattled his cage. How are the enquiries into their staff coming along?'

'We've been promised the full list of employees by four o'clock this afternoon.'

'It's been three days since you requested that information. They're taking their time, aren't they?'

Jag said, 'I've been chasing them every day. I had to threaten them with a court order just to get them to make the commitment to provide it by four o'clock today.'

'As soon as you have the list, get cracking. I wasn't sure before, but now I'm convinced that these bloody so-called Guardians are behind the increase in violence towards sex offenders. There will be a link between the staff at Stealthsafe and the assaults. It's going to be down to you two to find it. If you don't receive the list at four o'clock, come and see me.'

'Will do, boss.'

As the door closed, Danny was left alone with his thoughts. *Is it possible that James Brannigan is really behind the deaths of those three men and countless other serious assaults?*

It was totally contradictory to the theory put forward by Professor Whittle, who was convinced the killer would be undertaking a very personal mission of revenge.

He wondered if those two drives could ever overlap.

Brannigan had very personal reasons to act against known sex offenders, and he had the resources and power to find other people to carry out that revenge on his behalf.

For the first time since the murders began, Danny felt he was getting closer to the answer.

80

11.30am, 7 March 1988
Silver Fern Care Home, Mansfield Woodhouse,
Nottinghamshire

It hadn't taken Andy and Rachel long to establish that the only care home in the Mansfield Woodhouse area that had the word "Silver" in its name was the Silver Fern care home, on Debdale Lane.

The care worker on reception greeted the two detectives with a warm smile when they first walked in. That initial smile changed to a businesslike expression after they had identified themselves as police officers.

With a cautious tone in her voice, she asked, 'How can I help you?'

Rachel said, 'We'd like to talk with one of your residents, Mr Frederick Harper.'

'I'm sorry, Mr Harper's dead. He passed away in December last year, just before Christmas.'

'Do you know the exact date he died?'

The care worker stood up and walked over to a large filing cabinet, where she quickly retrieved a Manila folder. She flicked through the paperwork and said, 'Here we are. Mr Harper died on the thirteenth of December. I can remember the night he died, because something weird happened.'

'In what way weird?'

'I used to nurse the old man a lot, and he never had any visitors. Honestly, months would go by, and nobody ever came to see him. Then, on the night before he died, one of his daughters showed up to visit him. I just put it down to the fact that it was nearly Christmas. Relatives often call in to see their loved ones just before the holidays. I think it's to ease their own consciences as much as anything.'

Andy said, 'Can you remember which of his daughters came to see him?'

'I think it was the eldest. I'm not a hundred percent sure, because I'd only ever seen one of the daughters before.'

'Can you remember her name?'

The young woman concentrated hard for a few moments, then said, 'I'm sorry, I can't. I think it was Jane or June, something like that.'

'Don't worry, it might come to you later. How did Mr Harper die?'

'He just passed away in his sleep that night. He'd been extremely poorly for a long time. The poor man could barely draw breath towards the end. It was a combination of COPD and pneumoconiosis that killed him. He'd worked down the mine all his life, and he loved smoking his fags. He was also suffering with severe dementia.'

'What time was he found?'

'I was on duty that night. I took his ten o'clock medications in to him, and he had passed away.'

'Were you the last person to see him alive?'

'No, that would have been his daughter. She left at seven o'clock, as we had to close the doors. She told me the old man was asleep when she left.'

'How did she seem to you?'

'She was okay. She said she was going to pop back and see him again, a bit nearer Christmas. She even wished me Merry Christmas as she left.'

'Thanks. Anything else you can remember about the daughter that night?'

'Yeah. She was dressed all in black, like she'd been to a funeral or something.'

'Thanks. Can you give me your name, please? We may have to talk to you again.'

'My name's Mandy, Mandy Godber. I'm not in any trouble, am I?'

'No, you're not in any trouble. We just need to know who we've been speaking to, that's all. Don't worry, everything's fine.'

81

4.00pm, 7 March 1988
MCIU Offices, Mansfield Police Station

Danny saw Andy and Rachel walk back into the main office. He opened his door and said, 'How did you get on today, speaking to Joanna Preston's sister?'

The two detectives walked over, and Rachel said, 'If you've got five minutes, we can update you now. It's a bit of a long story, but there's been an interesting development.'

Danny sat down and said, 'Close the door behind you.'

Andy closed the door, and the two detectives sat down.

Rachel said, 'We went to the address we had for the younger sister, Theresa Harper. The property was empty and had been for some time. A neighbour informed us that Tina had taken her own life in December. The same neighbour gave us an address for the other sister, Maggie Harper, and a clue where the stepfather might have been.'

'A clue?'

'The neighbour knew the old man was in a care home at Mansfield Woodhouse, but she couldn't remember the name of it. All she knew was that the name had the word "Silver" in it.'

Andy said, 'We drove to Mansfield Woodhouse police station, made some enquiries and found there's a nursing home called Silver Fern.'

'And how was the old man when you spoke to him?'

'We couldn't speak to him. He passed away just before Christmas.'

Rachel said, 'But that's where we found something interesting.'

'Go on.'

'We spoke to one of the carers at Silver Fern, a young girl called Mandy Godber. Mandy was working the night Frederick Harper died. She told us that the old man's eldest daughter had visited him on that evening. The daughter was the last person to see the old man alive.'

'Did she say how the old man died?'

'Natural causes. Harper was suffering from chronic COPD and pneumoconiosis. Mandy told us that she had never known that particular daughter to visit before that evening. She also told us that the woman was dressed all in black, like she had come from a funeral.'

There was a brief pause while Danny made notes and absorbed what he was being told. Then Andy said, 'We've made further enquiries and found that the funeral for Theresa Harper was held at Mansfield Crematorium on the thirteenth of December. That's the same day the old man passed away. The funeral was held at two o'clock. Frederick Harper was visited by a woman we believe to be Joanna Preston between six o'clock and seven o'clock, and the old man was later found dead by Mandy Godber at ten o'clock.'

Danny was thoughtful. 'So why go and visit your stepfather on the same day you bury your sister, when you've never visited him before?'

'That's what we were thinking, boss.'

'I want you to make enquiries with the coroner and find out everything you can about the death of Frederick Harper. Have another look at the suicide of Theresa Harper. Find out which detective initially dealt with it and speak to them. I want to know if any suicide note was left. How she took her life, the works. Start again from scratch. I want you to keep on this. We could be on the right lines here.'

Andy said, 'Will do, boss.'

'You said you've got an address for the other sister as well?'

Rachel said, 'She lives on the Ladybrook estate. We visited the address, but nobody was home. We left a note for her to contact us here as soon as possible.'

'Okay. Hopefully, she'll be in touch sooner rather than later. The sister could hold the key to all this. That's good work today.'

Andy said, 'Should we speak to Joanna Preston yet?'

Danny shook his head. 'Not yet. There's nowhere near enough evidence to move on her yet. All we have are our suspicions; it's not enough. We need to find some hard evidence before we speak to her. The observations are all in place, ready for when the next two prisoners are released, so we have some leeway to try to find that evidence. Keep at it, both of you.'

82

6.00am, 9 March 1988
Warwick Close, Kirkby in Ashfield, Nottinghamshire

DC Phil Baxter was the first name on the rota to man the observation post at Warwick Close in Kirkby in Ashfield. He was working alongside PC Matt Jarvis of the Special Operations Unit. The two men had been driven onto the Coxmoor estate in a plain Ford Escort van and dropped off in an alleyway two streets away from the target premises at 16 Warwick Close.

The two men had worked together on several operations before and were comfortable with each other, each man knowing the capabilities of the other.

They had quickly made their way through the dark, rain-soaked streets to the rear of the flat they were using as an observation post.

Phil Baxter had used the key provided to gain access into the run-down first-floor flat.

As they walked in, he wrinkled his nose and whispered, 'Jesus, what's that fucking smell?'

Matt placed the heavy bag containing all the equipment they would need on the bare uncarpeted floorboards and replied, 'It's damp. This place hasn't been lived in for a long time.'

He moved to one of the two windows that overlooked the target premises, and looked through the dirty net curtain.

'This is the best view, Phil. I'll set the gear up here.'

'There's no rush. Vickery isn't being released until nine o'clock this morning.'

'It's better if I get set up now while it's still dark outside. We'll need to keep movement down to a minimum in here, as we're so close.'

Phil nodded. 'Okay, mate. I've got a couple of flasks with hot water in my bag. Do you want a Maxpax coffee?'

'Sound, no sugar in mine.'

Within ten minutes the binoculars, camera and night-vision glasses had all been set up, and a photograph of Andrew Vickery had been pinned to the wall. It was placed there as a constant reminder of who they were observing and, in effect, who they were protecting.

Phil picked up one of the three radios the men had with them and said, 'OP One to control, report signal strength. Over.'

The radio was on its lowest volume setting, but in the still of the empty flat, the reply, when it came, still sounded loud. 'This is control to OP One. Your signal strength is good. Receiving you loud and clear. Over.'

'To control, you're the same. Can you confirm the channel for Kirkby section officers, please?'

'Channel twenty-nine. Over.'

'Received. I'll check comms on the hour. Over.'

'Received. Control out.'

There was nothing for the two men to do now except wait in the cold, damp flat. It was still raining hard outside, and the wind was lashing the rain against the glass. Phil looked around the flat that was to be his base for the next twelve hours. The only furniture in the room were the two fold-away chairs they had brought with them. The chairs and all the other equipment they had brought with them would remain here for the duration of the operation. It would just be batteries, films and refreshments that would be brought in from now on. It would make the handovers much simpler if large amounts of equipment weren't being carried in and out every time.

The only crumb of comfort was that the toilet still worked. Otherwise, they would have had to use a bucket as a makeshift latrine.

Matt took a sip of the boiling hot coffee, then stood up and checked the route out of the observation post. This needed to be familiar to both men, in case they needed to respond to an emergency at the target premises. He walked out of the lounge they were in and down the stairs to the door at the rear. Using the key they had left in the lock, he carefully opened the back door and made his way around the side of the empty flat. On this side of the flat, there was a wooden gate. The gate had a bolt at the top. Once through the gate, Matt knew he would be in the alleyway that ran between the observation post and the target premises. From the briefing, he already knew there was no gate to prevent him gaining access to the rear of the target premises. He checked that the bolt on the gate could be operated quickly, then made his way back inside the observation post, out of the rain.

He walked back upstairs and said, 'It's all good outside, mate.'

Phil nodded. 'Don't let your coffee go cold. It's going to be at least three hours before Vickery arrives in his lovely new flat.'

83

6.00am, 9 March 1988
Rectory Road, Cotgrave, Nottinghamshire

At the same time as Phil Baxter and Matt Jarvis were setting up the observation post in Kirkby in Ashfield, the process was being repeated by DC Simon Paine and PC Tom Naylor on Rectory Road at Cotgrave.

The convicted sex offender Jason Mellors was being released to a first-floor flat at 22 Rectory Road. The observation post being used was at number 25. It was an empty first-floor flat that was virtually opposite the target premises.

The two men had set up their equipment and carried out a radio check. The Rectory Road flat was far more comfortable than the Warwick close one. It had only just been vacated, so there was none of the ingrained damp. The floors were all carpeted, and there was a working toilet. Unlike the Warwick Close flat, there were no curtains at these windows, so all the equipment had to be set up well back from the windows. It had been decided that putting their own net curtains up now might look odd after the windows had been bare for so long. It wasn't ideal, and great care would be needed by the officers not to give their presence away.

PC Tom Naylor checked the response route. Although there were no obstructions, it would take a little longer to respond to any threat from this observation post, as they were at least fifty yards away from the target premises.

Tom settled down in his foldaway chair and looked through the binoculars at the target premises. 'If the killer comes after our man, it will be through the rear windows.'

Simon nodded. 'You're right. It's way too open to try to break in through these front windows, especially as they would have to climb to get in.'

'The good news is the only access to the rear is through that locked wrought-iron gate at the side of the property. If they want to go in through the back windows, they'll have to go through that gate first.'

Simon chuckled. 'Well, we're not going to miss that, are we?'

Tom leaned back in the chair, away from the binoculars, and glanced at the photograph on the wall. He said, 'Hope not. How much longer before Mellors gets here?'

'He's being released from Whatton at nine o'clock. He should be here between nine thirty and ten o'clock.'

'Time for a brew, then.'

84

10.00am, 13 March 1988
MCIU Offices, Mansfield Police Station

Danny was sitting with Rob and Graham Turner. It had been four days since the planned observations had started at Cotgrave and Kirkby. It was time to iron out any minor problems.

He said, 'Let's start with Cotgrave. Any issues there?'

Graham said, 'My lads aren't happy about the uncovered windows. I think it's worth the risk of putting our own net curtains up. Nobody is paying that much attention to the flat. I think the benefits would outweigh the risks. While ever the windows are uncovered, there's a good chance of someone seeing the activity in the flat. The situation is much worse at night. Apparently, the streetlight directly outside the property illuminates the room they're using. I've been informed that one shift was forced to spend the night lying on the floor so they wouldn't be seen. That's no good, boss.'

'Okay. I'll bow to your experience. Put the net curtains up tonight. Any problems with the handovers so far?'

Rob said, 'None that have been reported. It's all going pretty smoothly.'

'Have the crews got all the equipment they need?'

'Yes, they have. That goes for the Kirkby address as well. There are no issues with equipment at all, and radio signals are spot on in both locations.'

'Let's stick with Cotgrave. Has there been any suspicious activity around the target premises?'

Graham said, 'Nothing at all.'

'What about Mellors? Does he go out much?'

'He went out yesterday to the local shop. That's it. The obs teams have reported seeing the television playing nearly all night. I think he's trying to adjust to life on the outside. He's still finding his feet. You've raised an interesting point, though, boss. Are we going to start following these men when they leave the target premises?'

'Unfortunately, I haven't got the manpower to do that successfully. As and when that becomes an issue, I'll have to have another look at it. Right now, I've barely got enough staff to maintain observations on the two target premises.'

'Has he had any visitors?'

'None since the first day when his probation officer dropped him off.'

There was a pause before Danny continued, 'So no real issues or developments at the Cotgrave address. The net curtains are to be erected tonight. Let's move onto Warwick Close. Rob, what can you tell me?'

'No issues at all with the observation point. As the target premises are a ground-floor flat, the fact that the observation post is in a first-floor flat means the teams have got a cracking elevated view of all three sides. There's no way anybody can approach the target premises without being seen.'

'That's good news. What about Andrew Vickery? Has he left the flat much?'

'He's walked from the flat to the corner shop twice. The shop is only fifty yards away, so he could be seen from the observation post all the way there and back.'

'Has he had any visitors?'

'A woman we identified as his probation officer visited yesterday afternoon.'

'Any suspicious activity around the target premises?'

'Last night, the obs team reported seeing a tall figure, dressed entirely in dark clothing, walking around the area. Apparently, this person made two circuits and eyeballed Vickery's ground-floor flat on both occasions.'

'What time was this?'

'Just after three o'clock this morning.'

'Did the obs team ask uniform to intercept?'

'They did after the second circuit. Unfortunately, uniform couldn't find any trace when they searched the area.'

'That's interesting. Who's in the obs point tonight?'

Rob flicked through the rota. 'Two of ours tonight: Glen Lorimar and Fran Jefferies.'

'Why no SOU?'

Graham said, 'Our section has a duty commitment at a Category A football match this evening. Forest are playing Liverpool, so it's impossible to provide anyone for the obs tonight. We'll need all our staff to control the football hooligans.'

'So we won't have a pair acting as backup at Kirkby for tonight?'

Rob said, 'I said there would be occasions when it wouldn't be possible to deploy four on nights. Thanks to the bloody football match, this is one of those occasions.'

'Is it the same at Cotgrave tonight? Just a single pair in the obs point?'

Rob nodded.

Danny looked troubled. 'Instruct Glen and Fran to make sure that the local uniform staff are on their game tonight. If this figure in black shows up again, I want whoever it is locating and checking.'

'Will do, boss.'

'Graham, can you let me know if there are any issues after the curtains have been put up at Cotgrave?'

'Will do. It should be okay.'

'That's it for now, then. Let's keep up the good work.'

Danny followed the two men out of his office, intending to get himself a coffee. He saw Andy and Rachel in the main office and said, 'Have you spoken to the other sister yet?'

Andy said, 'Not yet. We've been round to the house several times, but there's never any reply to knocking.'

'That's not good enough. I want you to get back out there now and sit outside the house until you see the sister. I don't care how long it takes; don't come back in until you've spoken to her. Understood?'

'Okay, boss.'

85

6.00pm, 7 March 1988
16 Milford Crescent, Ladybrook, Mansfield, Nottinghamshire

Andy and Rachel had been parked outside the semi-detached property for almost four hours. The windows were now starting to steam up as the night closed in, and the air temperature outside dropped like a stone.

The streetlights had come on as twilight slipped into night.

Rachel shivered and said, 'How much longer?'

Andy switched on the car ignition to demist the windows and let the heater warm the car through. He answered Rachel's question, saying, 'You heard the boss. As long as it takes.'

After five minutes of the engine running, the windscreen

was clear and the temperature inside the car had warmed a little, so he turned the engine off.

Once again, the silence inside the car was deafening.

That silence was suddenly shattered by loud and repeated banging on the passenger window. Rachel wound the window down and was immediately confronted by a middle-aged man with a very angry expression on his face. Before she had the chance to speak, the man said, 'Are you two going to tell me why the hell you're hanging around outside my house? Or have I got to call the cops?'

Rachel reached inside her coat pocket and took out her identification. 'I'm DC Moore from the CID. We are the cops.'

The angry expression on the man's face disappeared instantly. He said, in a much more contrite way, 'Why are you waiting outside my house?'

Rachel said, 'Do you live at number 16?'

'No. I live at number 14.'

'We're waiting here because we urgently need to speak with your neighbour, Mrs Harper. Do you know when she'll be home?'

'You're waiting in the wrong place, love. Maggie's very ill with cancer. She's in King's Mill Hospital. From what my wife was saying this morning, if you want to talk to her, you'd better get to the hospital sharpish. I don't think she's got long left.'

'Okay, thanks.'

Rachel wound the window up and said, 'You heard all that. She's in King's Mill Hospital. Let's get down there before it's too late.'

86

6.45pm, 7 March 1988
King's Mill Hospital, Mansfield, Nottinghamshire

It had taken the two detectives five minutes to drive from Ladybrook to the hospital. It had then taken another ten minutes for the receptionist on duty at the casualty department to locate Maggie Harper.

She was currently in a side room on the Sherwood Ward. The receptionist gave the detectives directions to the specialist respiratory ward and shouted after them as they disappeared towards the corridor, 'You can go up there, but I don't think you'll be able to see her! Not at this time of night.'

After what seemed an endless trek along the straight corridor that bisected the hospital buildings, they finally came to the Sherwood Ward.

They walked onto the main ward and approached the staff nurse at the desk. Andy took out his identification card. 'I'm Detective Sergeant Wills, and this is Detective Constable

Moore. I understand that Maggie Harper is one of your patients. It's imperative that we speak to her this evening.'

The nurse inspected the identification cards and said, 'What's so important? Mrs Harper is gravely ill.'

Rachel said, 'I'm not saying this lightly, or for dramatic effect, but it could be a matter of life and death. We will only need to see her for ten to fifteen minutes, if that's at all possible.'

'Wait here. I'll go and see how she's feeling this evening.'

The staff nurse walked back down the ward until she reached a door to a side room. After a few moments, she returned and said, 'You've got fifteen minutes. Maggie's in the final stages of terminal pancreatic cancer. She gets tired very quickly and is extremely poorly, but she's lucid and willing to talk to you. I mean what I say: You've got fifteen minutes to talk to her before I come in and fetch you out.'

Rachel said, 'Okay, thanks. We won't take liberties.'

The two detectives walked into the dimly lit side room. It was obvious the woman in bed was indeed seriously ill. There was nothing to her. Her wasted body barely caused a bump beneath the bedclothes. Her face was gaunt, and her eyes were deep set and surrounded by dark shadow. Her breathing was shallow and rasping. There was a tube in each nostril, helping to supply oxygen to her struggling lungs.

Rachel said gently, 'Maggie, we're from the police. We want to talk to you about the complaints you and your sister Theresa made to the police about your stepfather.'

A laconic grin formed on the woman's face. 'You're a little late, sweetheart. My sister's dead, and I'm not far behind her. What did you want to know?'

'I know this might be difficult to talk about now, but can you tell me what happened back then?'

There was a pause as Maggie tried to breathe a little deeper. After a few unsuccessful attempts at taking a deep breath, she said, 'It started as soon as our mum died. He started on Joanna first, as she was fifteen and the eldest. She had to put up with the old man's unwanted attentions for a year, but then left to join the army as soon as she was sixteen.'

'This is your sister Joanna Preston?'

'Yeah. She's a Preston because she changed her surname back to our real dad's name as soon as she joined the army.'

'What happened after she left?'

There was a long pause, and Maggie turned her head away.

Rachel said gently, 'I'm very sorry to have to ask you, Maggie, but it's important we know what happened, if you can find the strength to tell us.'

Maggie turned to face Rachel. 'Then it was me,' she hissed. 'I endured it on my own for a year before he started up with Theresa as well. After that, he made us take turns to do it.'

'What did he make you do?'

'What do you think? He would come home drunk and then get into bed with one of us. He would force himself upon us. At first, we used to fight and scream, but then we just let him do what he wanted so it was over quicker.'

Rachel lowered her voice to barely a whisper. 'Did he rape you?'

'Over and over again. The worst thing was that nobody believed us when we tried to talk about it.'

'Who did you tell?'

'We both told our teachers, and they contacted the police. Detectives arrested and spoke to the old man, but that was all. Nothing happened; they said they didn't have any proof and just let him out to come home. He left us alone for three months after that. Then one night he came home drunk, and it started again.'

'When did it stop?'

'When we were both old enough to leave home.'

'How did it affect you?'

'It was awful. I've never had a steady boyfriend. Every time I was dating and my boyfriend wanted to take things that step further to get intimate, I would freeze. No relationship could ever last. It affected my sister Theresa even worse. She couldn't live with the shame of what had happened. She suffered from depression and anxiety all her life. I'm convinced that's why she did what she did.'

'You mean the overdose?'

'Yes. I'm sure she only killed herself because she could see no other way out.'

'Did you ever talk to Joanna about what had happened to you and Theresa?'

'Because she was away with the army, I never saw much of her. She came to see us once just after she had left the army. By that time, we were both living in our own place, and the old man was becoming very ill in the old house. We never spoke about the old man. It was like an unwritten rule: We tried to make him non-existent, so we never talked about him or what he'd done.'

'When was the last time you spoke to Joanna?'

'I last spoke to her at Theresa's funeral. I told her that Theresa had killed herself, and why I thought she had done it.'

'How did Joanna react to that news?'

'By that time, she already knew that I was terminally ill with this bloody cancer. I told her everything that happened to me and Theresa that day.

'She reacted badly; she broke down totally. I've never seen my older sister so upset. She kept repeating that she shouldn't have left us. She blamed herself for leaving home and joining the army.'

'How old were you when Joanna left?'

'I was fourteen. Theresa was only twelve.'

'Do you still see Joanna?'

'I haven't seen her since my sister's funeral. It was weird because the last thing she said to me at the graveside was that she was going to visit the old man at the care home.'

'Why was that weird?'

'I just thought it odd that she wanted to go and see that piece of shit straight after the funeral. I knew for a fact that she'd never visited him at the home before.'

'Did anybody ever visit him?'

'I only went once in a blue moon, just to make sure he was still poorly. I never stayed long. Theresa never went, and I didn't blame her.'

Rachel paused for a second or two, then said, 'I've got a bit of a strange question for you, Maggie.'

'Go on.'

'As we're talking about what happened between you, your sisters and your stepfather, does a Mars chocolate bar have any significance to you?'

A single tear rolled down Maggie's yellow, waxy cheek. She blinked hard a few times.

Rachel said gently, 'I can see it means something. What does it mean to you, Maggie?'

'It means pain. It means suffering. It means shame. It was the old man's way of reconciling his actions. The pattern was always the same. He would come home late at night in drink, then sexually assault one of us. The next morning at the breakfast table, the dirty bastard would give either me or my sister a bloody Mars bar, like it was some special kind of fucking treat. He knew what he was doing to us was wrong, and this was his pathetic way of saying sorry. He must have had some feelings of guilt over his actions, but it never stopped the old bastard from doing it again. Why did you ask about the Mars bar?'

Before Rachel could answer, the staff nurse appeared at the door and said, 'That's all, Detectives. Mrs Harper needs to rest now.'

Maggie said, 'Do you believe me, Detective?'

Rachel gently squeezed the dying woman's hand and said softly, 'Yes, I believe you, Maggie. Get some rest, and thank you for talking to me.'

87

9.00pm, 13 March 1988
Mansfield, Nottinghamshire

Danny had just walked in after another long, gruelling day. He was exhausted, and after taking his jacket off, he sat on the bottom stair.

Sue, walking down the stairs, said, 'Is it that bad?'

'I'm shattered. After doing twelve hours of obs two days ago, and then another long day today, it's starting to catch up with me. To make things worse, I'm down for another twelve hours obs at Cotgrave tomorrow night.'

'Have you eaten anything?'

'I had a sandwich at lunchtime.'

'That's not enough, sweetheart. You're going to make yourself ill at this rate.'

'I'll be fine. How was Hayley today?'

'She's doing fine. I'm almost certain that we'll be able to bring her home soon. Every doctor I've spoken to says she's almost there. They just want her to put on a little more weight.'

'Did you manage to have a conversation with the child minder about our situation?'

'I did, and everything's okay. Vanessa's as good as gold.'

'That's good. Hopefully, we'll be able to at least get some sort of routine going once these planned observations are finished.'

'I don't think we'll ever manage a routine, but we'll make it work somehow. Now let me get you something to eat. What do you fancy?'

'Something quick. Beans on toast, with a couple of fried eggs on top would be great.'

Sue kissed him on the cheek as she walked past and said, 'Coming up.'

Danny walked into the lounge and sat down heavily in the armchair. No sooner had he sat down than the telephone started to ring. He grabbed it and said, 'Danny Flint.'

Andy Wills was on the other end of the line. He said, 'Sorry to call you at home, but I thought you needed to hear this straight away.'

'No problem, Andy. Hear what exactly?'

'We've just been speaking with Maggie Harper. She's in King's Mill Hospital. She's terminally ill with pancreatic cancer.'

'What did she say that's so urgent?'

'She told us that her stepfather, Fred Harper, sexually abused all three sisters. Maggie told Joanna, on the day of Theresa's funeral, that her youngest sister had killed herself because she couldn't stand the shame of the abuse she had suffered. Maggie said Joanna had been both angry and upset. She blamed herself for what had happened and went to visit the old man straight after the funeral.'

'And then the old man was found dead a few hours later.'

'Exactly, but there's more.'

'Go on.'

'Rachel asked Maggie whether a Mars bar had any significance to her.'

'And?'

'Maggie told us that every morning after he had abused them the night before, Harper would make a big thing about giving whichever of the sisters he had abused a Mars bar. She thought it was his sick way of trying to reconcile what he was doing.'

'That's the personal angle that Professor Whittle was on about.'

'What?'

'I'll explain fully later, but briefly I spoke to the professor about the Mars bar being left on the bodies. She thought it would be something extremely personal to the killer and nothing to do with the victims. Has anybody been to Joanna Preston's home address yet?'

'We drove over to Bingham straight from the hospital. The house is in darkness, and there was no car on the drive. I phoned the prison, and she's not due into work until the sixteenth. According to their records, she's on leave somewhere in the Yorkshire Dales.'

'That's great work. I want you to start preparing an operational order for her arrest tomorrow. The evidence is starting to mount up; I think we've got enough to fetch her in and question her about the deaths of the three men and possibly the death of her stepfather.'

'I'm on it, boss.'

The phone went dead. Sue shouted from the kitchen, 'Your supper's ready.'

Any appetite Danny might have felt had now vanished. He could feel the adrenalin coursing through his veins as he finally started to see the answers to so many questions.

88

3.00am, 14 March 1988
Warwick Close, Kirkby in Ashfield, Nottinghamshire

For the first time in two days, it had stopped raining. Fran Jefferies was relieved, as it meant the view through the net curtains of the observation post was now much clearer. Together with the dismal street lighting, the rain on the windows had made it difficult to maintain a clear view on the target premises.

There was a full moon tonight, so conditions were almost perfect.

The movement in the alleyway below her position immediately caught Fran's attention. She whispered to Glen Lorimar, 'It's the same person. That's the second time they've walked along the alley.'

Glen stood and walked over to the window. 'Are you sure it's the same person?'

'Positive. It's the same black hoody.'

'I'll get on the radio to the local cops and tell them to start moving towards the Coxmoor estate.'

Suddenly, the hooded figure moved out of the shadows and into full moonlight. Whoever it was, they were now making their way to the rear of the target premises.

Fran said, 'Glen, we're on. He's just gone behind number sixteen. We need to get down there.'

Having alerted the local cops to the situation, Glen shoved the radio tuned to their frequency back into his pocket. The two detectives moved quickly down the stairs and out through the back door. Glen slid the bolt on the gate back as quietly as he could, and seconds later the two detectives were at the rear of the target premises. The figure they had seen had by now forced one of the ground-floor windows and was in the process of squeezing through the narrow gap into the flat.

Glen raced forward and grabbed the legs of the intruder, pulling them out of the open window. The detective and the black-clad figure fell backwards on to the ground. It was the would-be intruder who recovered quickest, breaking free from the detective's grip. As Glen floundered on the ground, Fran stepped forward and grabbed a handful of the hood on the person's jacket.

Immediately, the burglar spun around, loosening the grip of the detective.

In that instant, the detective saw the hammer. She had no time to react as the hammer was swung viciously towards her head. With a resounding crack, the metal head of the tool connected with the side of her head. The force of the blow was enough to knock her unconscious.

As his colleague fell like a stone to the ground, Glen made a desperate lunge for her attacker. He missed by inches, and the offender ran back out into the alleyway. Glen was quickly on his feet, chasing Fran's attacker down the alleyway.

Although he could hear footsteps ahead, he could no longer see the offender. He kept running and turned several corners, into more dimly lit alleyways, each time hoping to get a glimpse of his quarry.

After two minutes of futile pursuit, he stopped and grabbed the radio from his pocket. 'This is DC Lorimar. I need urgent assistance on the Coxmoor estate. We stopped an offender trying to break into the target building on Warwick Close. They knocked my partner unconscious and escaped through the alleys. I last saw them heading in the direction of Lowmoor Road. Slim build, medium height, dressed in dark clothing with a hoody top. Armed with a hammer. I have no visual on them, so I'm returning to my partner. Over.'

As Glen raced back through the unlit alleyways, he could hear uniformed officers flooding the area, responding to his assistance call.

Fran was still where she had fallen. She was unconscious, but her breathing was normal and her pulse steady. Glen placed her in the recovery position and spoke into the radio: 'DC Lorimar to control. I need an ambulance to number sixteen Warwick Close, Coxmoor. My colleague's unconscious, having sustained a serious head injury. She's losing a lot of blood. You need to hurry!'

'Control to DC Lorimar, an ambulance has been despatched and is travelling to your position. Is your colleague breathing?'

'DC Lorimar to control. Her pulse is even, and she's breathing okay. I've placed her in the recovery position. Over.'

'From control. Ambulance will be with you in the next couple of minutes, stay with your colleague, and if there's any change in her condition, update us immediately.'

'From DC Lorimar. Understood. Over.'

Glen knelt at the side of Fran and said, 'Hang in there, Fran. The ambulance is on its way.'

Fran didn't move. Glen checked her pulse and breathing again. He felt a real sense of relief when he found they were the same as before.

Blue lights suddenly splashed on the walls of the buildings as the ambulance turned into Warwick Close. Glen stood and ran into the road, waving his arms. He was relieved when he heard the engine revs increase as the driver of the ambulance finally saw him and accelerated to his position.

As the first crew member jumped out of the ambulance, Glen shouted, 'She's down here, mate, in the back garden.'

As the ambulance man began tending to the stricken officer, the back door of the flat opened, and Andrew Vickery stepped outside. He said, 'What the fuck's going on? I'm trying to get some sleep in here.'

Barely able to contain his anger, Glen growled, 'Get back inside and close the door before I do something we both regret.'

The sex offender muttered something under his breath and stepped back inside his flat, slamming the door.

Glen turned to the ambulance man and said, 'Is she going to be alright?'

'Hard to say. That's a hell of a whack she's taken. She's got a very nasty cut to her head. We need to get her to the hospital, now.'

89

3.10am, 14 March 1988
Coxmoor Estate, Kirkby in Ashfield, Nottinghamshire

PC Stefan Druich and PC Ray Collins had been on general patrol not far from Lowmoor Road when they first heard the assistance call. Both men were experienced officers who had worked in the area for over five years. They both knew the Coxmoor estate like the backs of their hands.

They knew that if the intruder was heading towards Lowmoor Road, via the multitude of alleyways that ran through the estate, there was a very good chance he would emerge near the industrial estate that bordered that road.

Most of the alleyways filtered across that way.

Stefan Druich had reversed the police patrol vehicle into a deep shadow, which faced the entrance of the main alleyway.

The two officers then got out of the vehicle and listened.

After two minutes of waiting, Ray Collins whispered, 'Someone's moving fast.'

Stefan could now hear the footsteps of somebody running fast through the alleyways. There was a single white streetlight at the very entrance to the alleyway that gave off a dim white glow.

Suddenly, a figure emerged at the entrance. Dressed entirely in black, the figure stopped and placed both hands on their hips, as though drawing in deep breaths, getting their breath back.

Stefan whispered, 'Looks like our boy.'

Using the dark shadows to their advantage, the two cops made their way towards the hooded figure. When they were less than five yards away, they both sprinted forward. The figure was caught totally unawares and remained stock-still.

Ray grabbed the figure first, swiftly backed up by Stefan.

Ray removed the hood from the suspect's head, and for the first time the two officers realised the suspect was a woman.

In the ethereal white light of the streetlamp, Ray could see flecks of what he thought was blood on her face. The dark blood spatters contrasted starkly against the woman's alabaster skin.

The silence was shattered by a deafening clatter as a claw hammer fell from below the hooded top, landing heavily on the pavement. Stefan saw there was fresh blood on the head of the hammer. He said, 'I'm arresting you for assault.'

Ray started to carry out a very basic search of the woman's clothing. In one of the pockets of the hooded jacket, he found a pair of latex gloves and a Mars bar.

As he bent down to place the items on the ground, next to the claw hammer, the woman suddenly made a bid for freedom. She wrenched her arm from Stefan's grip and sprinted down the road. Both officers immediately gave chase. Ray was the faster of the two and quickly gained on the fleeing woman.

Without any hesitation, he hurled himself at the woman, bringing her crashing to the ground with a classic rugby tackle.

Stefan followed up, immediately placing the woman in handcuffs.

He said, 'As I just said, you're under arrest on suspicion of assault.'

He cautioned the woman, who said nothing.

90

3.40am, 14 March 1988
Mansfield, Nottinghamshire

As soon as the telephone at the side of his bed began to ring, Danny was wide awake. He snatched up the receiver and said, 'Danny Flint.'

It was Rob Buxton on the other end of the line. 'Boss, a woman has been arrested trying to break into the flat occupied by Andrew Vickery.'

'Is it Preston?'

'I don't know. Apparently, she's refusing to give any personal details to the custody staff, and she has no ID on her.'

'Do we know the circumstances of the arrest?'

'All they could tell me was that a woman has been arrested by two uniform patrol officers after Glen Lorimar put out an assistance call.'

'An assistance call? Is he alright?'

'The details they have are sketchy, but it seems that Fran Jefferies has been badly injured as she tried to detain the suspect.'

Danny gritted his teeth and swore under his breath. 'Where's Fran now?'

'She's being taken to the Queen's Medical Centre at Nottingham. She needs an emergency assessment on a possible fractured skull, plus a damaged ankle.'

'Bloody hell. And where is this suspect being held?'

'She's being booked in as we speak at Mansfield cell block.'

'Okay. I'll see you at the office in twenty minutes. Call everybody in, Rob. If it is Joanna Preston, Andy or Rachel will be able to identify her.'

'Will do.'

The line went dead, and Danny started to get dressed.

Sue started to stir in the bed. Danny bent down beside her and whispered, 'I've got to go into work. There's been an arrest, and one of my officers has been injured. It's still early; go back to sleep, sweetheart. I'll call you later. Love you.'

Sue mumbled a reply and turned over.

Danny finished getting dressed, walked into the bathroom and quickly cleaned his teeth. He tiptoed downstairs and put on the jacket and tie he'd worn the day before.

Grabbing his coat and car keys, he stepped outside into the cold night air. There was a hard frost on the ground, and he quickly scraped his car windscreen.

Within a couple of minutes, he was driving through the deserted streets. His mind was racing. How badly injured was Fran? Was it Joanna Preston who had been detained?

A cat darting across the road in front of his car caused him to brake hard and swerve. It was enough of a scare to shatter his thoughts and make him concentrate on his driving. He knew the answers would come soon enough, when he arrived at the MCIU offices.

91

4.10am, 14 March 1988
MCIU Offices, Mansfield Police Station

Danny rubbed the palm of his hand across his chin and cheeks. He could feel the stubble on his unshaved face. He poured hot water into a mug, then put a heaped teaspoonful of instant coffee in before stirring vigorously.

As he didn't live too far from the police station, Danny had been one of the first to arrive at the office. He took a sip of the scalding hot coffee and then grabbed the telephone in his office. He dialled the number for the cell block.

'It's Chief Inspector Flint. Has the woman detained at Kirkby in Ashfield been booked in yet?'

The custody sergeant said, 'Yes, sir. She's been arrested for assault and has been informed of her rights while she's in custody. We still haven't been able to positively identify her, as she's refusing to speak to anyone. I'm considering taking her fingerprints by force, to try to identify her.'

'Delay doing that. I've staff travelling into work now who may be able to identify her. Are the arresting officers still there?'

'Yes, sir. PC Druich and PC Collins haven't resumed patrol yet.'

'Good. Ask them both to come and see me in the MCIU offices.'

Just as Danny spoke, he saw Rachel Moore walk into the main office. He said to the custody sergeant, 'One of those officers has just walked in. I'll send her straight down to you. Was anything seized from this woman at the time of her arrest?'

'Yes, sir. The hammer she used to assault the detective, a pair of latex gloves and a bar of chocolate. We've also found a car key during the search as she was booked in.'

'I'll send DC Moore down to see you now. She'll hopefully be able to identify the suspect.'

'Thank you, sir. Any news on the injured detective?'

'Not yet.'

Danny put the phone down and banged on the window of his office to get Rachel's attention. He beckoned her into his office and said, 'Get downstairs to the cells and have a look at the woman who's been detained. She's refusing to give any personal details. I think it's going to be the welfare officer from the prison.'

'Joanna Preston?'

'Go and have a look. The sooner we can get her positively identified, the sooner we can organise searches and interviews.'

Rachel said, 'On my way.'

Rachel almost bumped into Rob Buxton, Tina Cartwright and Andy Wills as she walked out. She said something to

Andy, and he immediately started to walk with her towards the cell block.

Danny walked out of his office. 'Tina, Rob, grab a coffee and come in here, please.'

After the two inspectors had got a hot drink, Danny said, 'I've asked the arresting officers to come and see us, to debrief the arrest. Tina, can you get onto the Queen's Medical Centre? I want an update on Fran's condition as soon as possible, please.'

'Will do.'

Tina walked back to her desk to make the call.

Danny turned to Rob and said, 'Have you spoken to Glen yet? What the hell happened out there?'

'I've arranged for DC Blake to go straight to Warwick Close so Glen can get back here and debrief the attempted arrest and the assault.'

'That's good. Any idea when Glen will be getting here?'

'He shouldn't be long. After I called you, Sam was my first call.'

The telephone on Danny's desk began to ring. He snatched it up.

Rachel was on the line. She said, 'It's Joanna Preston, alright. Now she's been identified, she's complying and supplying the custody sergeant with her full details.'

Danny breathed a sigh of relief. 'That's great. I want you to seize all the clothes she's wearing. Then bring all her property and the items found on her when she was arrested back to the office, ready to prep for interview.'

'There won't be any interviews for a while, boss.'

'What?'

'The custody sergeant has informed me that he can't allow any interviews before nine o'clock this morning. The guidelines say she must be allowed a period of rest before interview.'

Danny growled, 'Bloody Police and Criminal Evidence Act. It's like trying to swim against the tide, with one arm tied behind your back.'

'He's not budging on it, boss.'

Danny quickly calmed down and said, 'No problem. As always, we'll work around it. There's plenty to do in the meantime. Come back up to the office as soon as you can.'

'Will do.'

Danny put the phone down and saw two uniform officers walk into the office, followed by an ashen-faced Glen Lorimar.

Danny and Rob walked into the main office. Danny said, 'PC Druich and PC Collins?'

'I'm Ray Collins. This is Stef Druich.'

Danny said, 'Good work tonight. Can you take us through what happened, please?'

'We were on patrol at the bottom of the Coxmoor estate when we heard the assistance call and the brief description of the suspect come over the radio. As soon as we heard which way the suspect was heading, we had a good idea where they might emerge from the estate. Stef parked the car at that entrance, and we got out and waited.'

'Then what?'

'We'd only been waiting a minute or so when we heard somebody running fast towards us.'

'Could you see them at that point?'

'No, we didn't see the person until they emerged out of the alleyway. The person stopped to get their breath back, and we moved in. It was only after we'd grabbed her and I pulled the hood of her jacket back that we realised it was a woman. The lighting is rubbish there, but I could see what looked like flecks of fresh blood on her face.'

'Did she resist in any way?'

'Not at first. She was very compliant until I found the things in her pockets.'

'What things?'

'As I searched her, the hammer fell from beneath her jacket. I could see what looked like fresh blood on the head and handle. Then I found gloves and the chocolate bar in her pocket.'

'Chocolate bar?'

'A Mars bar.'

'Did she resist straight away?'

'No, sir. She was crafty. She waited until I bent down to put the things I'd found in her pockets on the ground next to the hammer. She suddenly twisted out of Stef's grip and sprinted down the road. Luckily, we caught her up quickly and arrested her.'

'For assault?'

Stefan Druich said, 'Yes, sir. At that time, we didn't know exactly what had happened at Warwick Close. I knew there had been an assault of some kind, and we had the blood-stained hammer, as well as blood flecks on the woman's face. I told the custody sergeant about the blood on her face, and he took swabs, so we've got that evidence.'

'That's great work.'

Danny turned to Glen and said, 'What happened at Vickery's flat?'

'We'd seen the same person walk by the observation post twice. The figure was dressed in a black hoody. Whoever it was, they were clocking points and just looked dodgy. Anyway, this person suddenly darted behind the building, so me and Fran went down to investigate. By the time we got to the rear, the person we had seen was already halfway through one of the windows. I grabbed the suspect's legs and pulled them back out of the window. We both fell backwards onto the damp grass, and I slipped as I tried to get up.'

Danny could see that Glen was getting upset. He said, 'Take your time, Glen. Then what happened?'

'Fran grabbed hold of the suspect's jacket, and that's when she got whacked. This maniac just lashed out with something hard and smashed her on the side of the head. She was out cold before she hit the ground. It made the most horrendous crack I've ever heard.'

'I know it's hard, Glen. But we need to know what happened.'

'I tried to grab the suspect, but missed. Before I could do anything, they were running away down the alleyway. I gave chase and put out the assistance call. After I lost sight of the suspect in the alleyways, I decided to go back and see to Fran.'

'How was she?'

'In a bad way. She was spark out. There was a lot of blood coming from the wound on her head. I checked her breathing and searched for a pulse, and they were okay. I requested an ambulance to be despatched to us straight away. Do we know how she is yet?'

'Not yet. Hopefully, we'll have an update shortly.'

'I'm sorry, boss.'

'You've got nothing to be sorry about. You both acted with exemplary courage. It could just as easily have been you travelling to the hospital now. You did exactly the right thing. You put out the call that led to the suspect's arrest, and then you cared for your injured colleague. You did a good job, Glen.'

'It doesn't feel that way, boss.'

Andy and Rachel walked in carrying all the property seized from Joanna Preston. Rachel said, 'I've seized all her clothing and footwear. She's in a paper suit, getting some sleep in the cell. The car key that was found during the search, as she was booked in, looks like a Ford Sierra key to me. There's also a Yale and a Mortice key with the car key that are obviously for her house. I'm pretty sure she'll have parked the car somewhere not too far from the Coxmoor estate.'

'Great. Get onto the control room, and task officers to search the Coxmoor estate and surrounding areas. I want that car found. Once it is, I want a full lift arranged. It needs to be taken to the forensic bay at headquarters for a full examination.'

'Will do, sir.'

'Rob, get the house keys and organise a search of Preston's home address. Andy, I want you to get on to HMP Whatton and organise a search of her office there.'

Danny then turned to PC Druich and PC Collins. 'Stef, Ray, I want you to complete your arrest statements straight away while the events are still fresh in your mind. Don't forget to exhibit the items you found on her at the time of arrest.'

Ray said, 'Will do, sir.'

'It was brilliant work tonight. I'll be letting your divisional commander and the chief constable know what I think of your actions. Well done, both of you.'

The two officers smiled and nodded.

Danny turned to Glen. 'Same goes for you, Glen. Good work tonight. Get yourself a hot drink, take your time and write your statement.'

'Can't I go to the hospital? I need to know how Fran is.'

'I need that statement, Glen. Don't worry, I'll keep everyone updated how she's doing. Try not to worry. I'm sure she's going to be fine.'

A crestfallen Glen nodded and walked across the room to get a coffee.

Tina said, 'The hospital's loath to give too many details out over the phone.'

Danny was feeling the same anxiety as Glen. He needed

to know how Fran was doing. Ever since he heard she'd been badly injured, he'd reproached himself over his decision to allow her to take up a more operational role.

He said, 'Right, grab some car keys. We're going to the QMC. I need to know what's happening. Everything's in hand here. The searches are organised, and we can't interview until later this morning. Let's go.'

92

5.15am, 14 March 1988
Queen's Medical Centre, Nottingham

Danny and Tina had waited patiently in the corridor outside the operating theatres. They were waiting for news on their stricken colleague, who was being prepped for emergency surgery.

The door at the end of the corridor opened with a bang, and the detectives saw a man walking towards them. He was in his late fifties, had a full head of greying hair and was dressed in bottle green scrubs. His confident smile and bright blue eyes did little to disguise the look of concern lying just below the surface. As he approached the detectives, he said, 'Are you colleagues of Fran Jefferies?'

Danny said, 'I'm DCI Flint. Is there any news?'

'My name's Warburton. I'm the on-call consultant orthopaedic surgeon at the hospital this morning. It's not great news, but it's not terrible news either.'

'Go on.'

'We've now completed all the tests we needed to run on your colleague. We're prepping her for emergency surgery. The scans and X-rays we've taken have shown that the head injury she sustained, although nasty, was not serious. It appears that whatever object was used to strike her only made a glancing blow. It caused a flap of skin to be separated from her scalp, and that's why the resulting wound bled so badly. That flap will need to be stitched back in place, but there is no fracture to the skull and no intercranial bleed.'

He paused and then said, 'That's the good news. The bad news is that when she fell, your colleague suffered a dislocated and badly fractured right ankle. The fracture is quite complicated. That's why I'm prepping her for surgery right now, to try to repair the damage. Her condition is serious, but she's stable. Her injuries are not life-threatening, and she should make a good recovery. Obviously, I'll know more, and be able to give you a far more detailed prognosis, after the surgery.'

'How long will surgery take?'

'The operation will only take three or four hours, but we have to prep first. I'll come and find you after the operation, with an update, at around ten o'clock. I suggest you wait in the hospital canteen rather than in this draughty corridor. As soon as I'm out of theatre, I'll come and find you.'

Danny said, 'Thank you. I appreciate that.'

Danny watched as the man with the clear blue eyes turned and walked back along the corridor. He said a silent prayer for Fran, then said to Tina, 'Wait in the canteen for news. I need to get back to Mansfield, to prepare for the interviews with Preston. Call the office as soon as you have an update.'

'Will do, boss. Fingers crossed, eh?'

'I don't know about you; I've got everything crossed.'

93

7.00am, 14 March 1988
12 Abbey Road, Bingham, Nottinghamshire

Abbey Road was lined with ash and sycamore trees. It had a mixture of detached and semi-detached properties dotted along both sides of the street.

Number 12 Abbey Road was a smart semi, with cared-for gardens and a block paved driveway. There were oil stains on the pavers where a car was usually parked.

Rob had used the Yale key found in possession of Joanna Preston when she was arrested to access the property. The search of the house was being carried out by Sergeant Turner and officers of the Special Operations Unit.

Rob stayed out of their way in the hallway. He knew he could rely on them to do a thoroughly professional search. He saw Graham Turner coming down the stairs and said, 'How's it going, Graham?'

'Couple more bedrooms to search and we'll be done.'

'Have you found anything of interest?'

'In the wardrobe of the main bedroom, we've recovered a large box of Mars bars and a box of medium-sized latex gloves identical to the ones found on Preston when she was arrested. We've also seized a lot of clothing and all the footwear we can find.'

'Anything else?'

'In one of the drawers in the kitchen, we've recovered street maps that cover Sherwood and Carrington in Nottingham, Newark town centre, and the Carlton in Lindrick area. There are markings on all the maps, but we haven't had time to examine them fully, so we don't yet know the significance of those markings.'

'Good work. How much longer do you think you're going to need?'

'Another half an hour max. The lads are writing the exhibit labels and bagging up all the exhibits as they go, so it shouldn't take much longer.'

'As soon as you've finished, we need to get back to Mansfield. I'll need to go through everything that's been seized, in preparation for the interviews.'

'You can't rush a thorough search, sir.'

'I appreciate that. Just give me a shout when you're ready to call it as completed.'

'Will do, sir.'

94

7.00am, 14 March 1988
HMP Whatton, Nottinghamshire

Andy and Rachel were met at the gates of HMP Whatton by the governor, Wilson Redmayne.
As soon as the detectives got out of their car, a very flustered Redmayne approached them and said, 'I'm sorry, but I'm still finding this whole situation very hard to believe.'

Rachel said, 'Believe it, Governor. One of my colleagues is in hospital after your welfare officer struck her on the head with a hammer. Not to mention that three men, all of whom were in her care, have been murdered with a similar weapon.'

'Yes, yes. I understand all that. I'm not doubting what you've told me, Detective. What I meant to say was, I can't believe Joanna could do something like this.'

Rachel tutted and looked away, biting her lip.

Andy said quickly, 'What's important now is that we get

inside and search her office, Governor. Obviously, we'd like you to be there while we carry out that search.'

Still rattled by the whole situation and the early morning call, a shaking Governor Redmayne said, 'Of course. Follow me, please.'

Ten minutes later the two detectives were systematically searching the office of Joanna Preston.

Andy tried to open the bottom drawer of her desk, but it was locked.

He turned to Wilson Redmayne and said, 'Governor, I need to look inside this drawer. Do you have a duplicate key?'

'No, I don't. Feel free to break it open, Detective. Do whatever you have to do.'

Using a steel letter opener he found on the top of the desk, Andy quickly forced the lock and opened the drawer.

From inside, he recovered files relating to Manfred Bauer, Stewart Tighe, Wilf Kelham and Andrew Vickery.

Andy turned to the governor and said, 'Is there any reason why these four files should be kept in her drawer and not in the filing cabinets with the rest?'

'None that I can think of.'

Andy opened the file on Kelham and started flicking through the pages. At the very back, he found a loose sheet of A4 paper with a list of dates and times. The dates ran consecutively and started the day after Kelham's release. Beside each date was a start time, followed by a duration of time, measuring something. The first date shown was the eighteenth of February. The time listed was 6.20 am. The duration recorded was one hour and forty-three minutes.

All the other times and durations were similar.

Andy held up the piece of paper to Rachel and said, 'What do you make of this?'

Rachel read the list and thought for a few moments. Then she said, 'We know that Kelham liked his early morning walk along the riverbank. This could be a list of the times he left the hostel, and how long the walk took him each day. It looks to me like Preston stalked him before she smashed his skull in.'

Each of the files in the drawer had similar incriminating handwritten notes, setting out the movements of the men and details of the properties they were in.

After thirty minutes of a painstaking search, Andy said, 'That's it, Governor Redmayne. Thanks for your co-operation and assistance.'

Wilson Redmayne said, 'What happens now?'

'We'll interview Joanna Preston and see what she has to say about things. Then we'll take it from there.'

'I see. Are you taking those files with you? There's a lot of very confidential information inside those folders.'

'There's also a lot of incriminating evidence. Yes, I'm taking the files with me. I'll need you to secure this office and not allow anybody access until we tell you it's okay to do so. We may need to revisit and search again after we've spoken to Joanna Preston. Will that cause you a problem?'

'No. The release program is on temporary hold until I see how things develop.'

'Thanks, Governor. Could you show us the way out, please?'

'Yes, of course. It's this way.'

95

10.30am, 14 March 1988
MCIU Offices, Mansfield Police Station

Danny and Rob were sifting through all the evidence gathered against Joanna Preston as they prepared to interview the prison welfare officer. Worryingly, there was still no word from Tina at the Queen's Medical Centre.

He desperately wanted to hear some positive news about the emergency surgery being performed on Fran Jefferies before he started the interview with Joanna Preston.

Rob dragged him from his thoughts, saying, 'The documentary evidence found by Andy and Rachel at the prison is gold dust. I don't see how Preston can talk her way out of those notes.'

'It's good evidence, but it's still all very circumstantial. We need her to talk to us about the actual offences. Who's her brief?'

'She's got the duty solicitor, a woman called Sally Masterson, from Baker and Pickard Legal Services. I've never met her before. The custody sergeant introduced us just after I'd formally arrested Preston on suspicion of the murders of Bauer, Tighe and Kelham.'

'Did Preston make any reply after being arrested?'

'Not a word.'

'So this solicitor, Sally Masterson. What's she like?'

'She seems okay. She was very thorough when I gave her disclosure half an hour ago. She asked all the right questions, without being too anti. If you know what I mean.'

'Do you think it will be a "no comment" interview, then?'

Rob shrugged. 'From Preston's point of view, it certainly should be. Her solicitor will know that her client's got everything to lose and nothing to gain by talking to us. But you never know.'

Danny was thoughtful. Then he said, 'I think we should start the interview by talking to her about the sexual abuse suffered by her and her two sisters. I don't think she'll be expecting that, and it just might spark a response and start her talking. She may want to tell us about what her stepfather did to them all. If that does happen and she starts talking, I think it will then be difficult for her brief to stop her.'

'It's definitely worth a try.'

'Is the custody sergeant going to let us know when Ms Masterson has finished her client consultation?'

'Yes, boss. Are you going to lead the interview, or do you want me to?'

'I'll lead.'

The telephone started to ring, and Danny snatched up the handset. 'DCI Flint.'

Tina was on the line. She said, 'It's good news, boss. Fran has come through her operation. The surgeon has just told me the operation was a success. He has managed to pin the damaged ankle in place and relocate the joint. It will take time for the injuries to heal, and there could be significant impact on her future mobility.'

'How much of an impact?'

'He was very non-committal at this stage. He said she could make a full and complete recovery, or she could end up walking with a pronounced limp for the rest of her life. They need to wait and see how well the fractures heal, and what mobility she retains in the ankle joint.'

'That's not the best news I've heard today. How soon before you can see her?'

'The doctor said it will be at least another three or four hours until she comes round enough for us to talk to her.'

'Do you mind staying at the hospital? I'd like Fran to see a friendly face as soon as she's able to.'

'I don't mind at all. How are things going that end?'

'We'll be going into interview with Preston shortly. The searches yielded some very interesting evidence.'

'Has the car been found?'

'Yes. Her Ford Sierra Sapphire was located on the industrial estate, not far from where she was arrested. It's been lifted into the forensic bay at headquarters. Scenes of Crime are examining it as we speak.'

'Do you remember that farm labourer at Carlton in Lindrick? He was adamant that the car he'd seen parked up in the lay-by, near Redgate Farm, was a Sierra. Good luck with the interview.'

'It's been noted. Thanks, and call again as soon as you've spoken to Fran.'

'Will do.'

Danny put the phone down. Immediately, it started to ring again.

He spoke to the caller briefly, then replaced the phone. He turned to Rob and said, 'Preston's solicitor is ready for interview.'

96

10.30am, 14 March 1988
Custody Suite, Mansfield Police Station

The shrill alarm on the tape recorder finally stopped. Rob asked everybody in the interview room to introduce themselves; then he stated the time and date and reminded Joanna Preston that she was still under caution.

The two detectives were shocked as Preston's solicitor, Sally Masterson, said, 'I have advised my client not to answer any of your questions. However, at this time she has declined that advice and will answer your questions. I will intervene if I find your questioning inappropriate or in any way oppressive.'

Danny had recognised the sense of frustration in the solicitor's voice. Her statement had taken him by surprise as well. He had fully expected Joanna Preston to remain silent and not answer any of their questions.

He composed himself and said, 'You introduced yourself for the tape recording as Joanna Preston. Do you mind if I call you Joanna while we talk?'

Joanna's voice was croaky when she replied with two words, 'That's fine.'

Danny said, 'Tell me what life was like for you and your sisters after your mother died.'

Joanna had been staring down at the table in front of her. Now she looked up and glared at Danny. He could see the pain behind her eyes, so he said, 'What changed, Joanna?'

'Everything.'

'In what way?'

'My stepfather sold the house we had grown up in, and we moved to Mansfield Woodhouse. We had to start a new school. We left all our friends behind.'

'Why did your stepfather sell the house?'

Joanna shrugged. 'I don't know. Maybe he wanted a fresh start.'

'What was your stepfather like?'

Again, she fixed him with a cold stare. 'I think you already know what he was like. The only reason I want to talk to you today is to explain why I've done these things. The main reason is him.'

'So tell me about your stepfather, then.'

'After we moved house, he changed.'

'How?'

There was a long pause; then she said, 'He was no longer my stepfather. He became my abuser.'

'What happened?'

'The first time it happened was just after my fifteenth birthday. My two younger sisters had gone to bed, and I was still up watching the television. He had come home from the pub, roaring drunk. He was angry and ordered me to go to bed. I didn't argue; I just switched the television off and walked upstairs. My sisters were already both asleep, so I went to my room, got undressed and got into bed. I had just dozed off when I felt movement in my bed. He had got into bed beside me and had started touching me. I tried to stop him, but I couldn't. He was too strong. I couldn't cry out, because I didn't want to frighten my sisters.'

'You said "touching". Was that all he did?'

'No. My stepfather raped me, Detective. When he'd finished, he just got out of my bed and staggered into his bedroom.'

'You said "the first time". How often did this happen?'

'At least once a month, sometimes twice. Every time he went out for a drink, I knew what was coming. I always made sure my sisters were out of the way before he came home so they didn't have to see anything.'

'Did you talk to anybody about what was happening at home?'

'Who could I tell?'

'The police, a teacher, relatives?'

'I have no family. I didn't know any of my teachers, I was at a new school, and I was too scared to talk to the police.'

'When did this abuse stop?'

'It stopped when I left home and joined the army. I had never thought about joining the army, but it was the only way I could get a job and leave home.'

'My colleagues have spoken to your sister Maggie. She informed us about the abuse she and Theresa suffered after you had left home to join the army.'

A single tear rolled down Preston's cheek. She said, 'I know. That was all my fault. If I hadn't been such a coward and run away, he wouldn't have touched them.'

'When did you find out what had been happening to your sisters?'

'At my youngest sister's funeral. After I joined the army, I never contacted my sisters. I tried to forget what had happened to me, so I just turned my back on everything I'd left behind. To my eternal shame, that included my two sisters.'

'So after you had left home and joined the army, you had no contact with your sisters? When was the next occasion you saw your sisters?'

'When I left the army, I returned to Mansfield Woodhouse. Five years had passed, and by that time the family home was empty. I found out from neighbours that my sisters had left and moved to Mansfield, where they were living together.'

'What about your stepfather?'

'The neighbour said he had been put into a home. I didn't ask any questions, as I couldn't give a shit about him.'

'Did you find your sisters?'

'I did. I didn't stay in Mansfield long though. I just wanted to get away.'

'Did you discuss what had happened after you left for the army?'

'If you mean did they tell me about the abuse they had suffered, the answer's no. We never spoke about that pervert.'

'Did you stay in touch after that visit?'

'No. I just got on with my own life. I was used to a solitary existence by then.'

'When did you next talk to your sisters?'

'Six months ago, my sister Maggie wrote to me. She told me that she'd been diagnosed with terminal cancer. I went to visit her at her new house in Mansfield. I was shocked at how ill she looked, and how thin she was. I never saw Theresa when I visited. She had moved on and got her own place. I went round a couple of times, but she was never at home. Maggie told me that Theresa suffered badly from anxiety and depression, and that she may have been at home, but didn't want to answer the door.'

There was a long pause, and Danny remained silent. He knew there was more to come from Preston.

After a full minute, she said, 'The next time I spoke to Maggie, she told me that Theresa had committed suicide at home. It was at the funeral that Maggie explained to me exactly why my sister had taken her own life.'

'What did Maggie tell you?'

'She explained to me how, as soon as I'd left home, the old man had turned his attentions on her. Then, after another six months, he had started to abuse them both. Theresa was still so young when he started on her. He would force them to take it in turns to endure his unwanted attentions.'

'Was it the same as with you?'

Preston nodded and said, 'Yes. He always raped me, and he raped them, too. Maggie told me that she and Theresa had both told their teachers what was happening, and they had informed the police. She told me that the police did nothing about it, and Theresa struggled to come to terms with that. The depression and anxiety she suffered all her life stemmed from that. The fact that they hadn't been believed was almost as bad as the abuse itself.'

'And Maggie told you all this at the funeral?'

'Yes.'

'How did you feel when she told you?'

'I was devastated. I knew if I had stayed at home, my sisters wouldn't have been touched. I was angry at myself and raging about the old man.'

'I know you visited the care home to see your stepfather, Fred Harper, on the day of the funeral. Why did you go there?'

'I had to make him understand that what he had done to us wasn't right.'

'How did you do that, Joanna?'

'I suffocated him. I put my hand over his mouth and nose so he couldn't breathe. I watched him take his last breath. I only had to hold my hand there gently, as he was so weak. He could hardly breathe anyway. I made it look like he'd just stopped breathing. I had to make him pay for what he'd done to us.'

Danny said, 'Joanna Harper, I'm arresting you for the murder of Frederick Harper.'

He cautioned Joanna and said, 'When you went to the care home, was it your intention to kill Fred Harper?'

She said flatly, 'Yes. I wanted him dead.'

'With all this abuse in your past, why did you want to work with sex offenders?'

'I never wanted to work with sex offenders. Redmayne badgered me every day to work on his early release scheme. I kept turning him down, but still he kept asking.'

'So what changed?'

'After I'd killed the old man, I started to think that more of these evil bastards should pay. My sisters had both served a life sentence. Why shouldn't they have a death sentence?'

'Did you take the job running the early release scheme so you could get to these men and exact revenge?'

'Exactly that. And yes, if you hadn't stopped me, I would have carried on killing as many of these monsters as I could. They need to pay properly for what they've done, not be let out early to do it again. That's just wrong.'

'Your sister told us about the Mars bars. How your stepfather made a big thing about giving you or your sisters the chocolate on the morning after he had sexually assaulted you. Didn't you worry that by leaving the chocolate bar at the crime scenes, you would eventually be found out?'

'No. It was only my sisters and me who knew the significance. I needed to see that Mars bar on the dead men, to remind myself that what I was doing was justified. Every time I placed the chocolate bar on their smashed heads, I felt at peace.'

'Tell me about Manfred Bauer. Why did you choose him?'

'His crimes were horrendous. I read all the paperwork that the governor had prepared for his early release. I was staggered how the parole board could be duped so easily and consider him a suitable candidate for early release. He constantly feigned contrition and guilt.'

'Did you use the file prepared by Governor Redmayne to plan your attack?'

'Yes, I did. The premises he was in weren't ideal, but I knew I could get to him.'

'How did you get to him?'

'I climbed a drainpipe to the first floor, went in through the bathroom window and found him asleep in his bedroom.'

'How did you kill him?'

'I hit him with a claw hammer.'

'Where?'

'On the side of his head, three times. I knew he was dead.'

'Then what did you do?'

'I carefully placed the Mars bar on his smashed head and left the flat the same way as I got in.'

'Was it your intention to kill Manfred Bauer?'

'Yes. He should never have been released.'

'Why did you choose Stewart Tighe?'

'I hope you all realise what a big favour I've done you?'

'What do you mean?'

'Stewart Tighe was a monster. He would have gone on to abuse other children. Ask any prison officer who worked with him what he was like. I guarantee they would all say the same. The parole board aren't interested in what the people who see these monsters every day have to say. They only ever listen to the clever-arse doctors, who say they are no longer a danger to the public. What a load of shit! Tighe would have done the same thing as he did before if I hadn't been there to stop him.'

'What did you do?'

'I watched him at the farm. I saw him getting pissed every night. I silenced the dogs so they wouldn't bark, then I went inside and killed him on the sofa while he slept.'

'How?'

'The same as Bauer. Three cracks with the hammer on his head.'

'But no chocolate this time?'

There was a note of anger in her voice as she said, 'Why would you say that? I carefully placed the Mars bar right on the top of his smashed head. Did somebody move it?'

The answers from Preston were being delivered in such a flat, unemotional way that Danny had wanted to test that she was listening to what he was asking her. He needed to check that she wasn't just saying whatever she thought he wanted her to say.

Her belligerent response had shown she was listening alright.

'When you attacked Tighe, did you intend to kill him?'

'Yes.'

'How did you travel to commit these crimes?'

'I always drove to the locations. I would park up quite a way from where they lived and finish the journey on foot. I was never seen. It was easy.'

'The first two men were killed in their homes. Why was Wilf Kelham different?'

'I had always marked Kelham down to die. What he did to those two schoolgirls was identical to what my stepfather did to me and my sisters. I knew he was ill and an old man, but he still had to pay. The only accommodation I could get for him was the halfway hostel at Newark. Nobody wanted to house the old man. It made things difficult, so I watched his movements every day. My solicitor told me you have found the list of timings from Kelham's file. I watched him every day, so I knew I could get to him on his early morning walk.'

'Wasn't that risky?'

'Yes, but I had no choice. I waited until he was alone, then hit him three times with the hammer and left the chocolate near his head. I couldn't place it carefully this time, because I heard a jogger coming.'

'Did you intend to kill Wilf Kelham?'

'Yes.'

'You were arrested earlier this morning trying to break into a flat on Warwick Close at Kirkby. Why were you doing that?'

'I had housed another monster in that flat. I was going to kill him.'

'Why didn't you?'

'I had forced the window but was stopped by two people as I was climbing in, a man and a woman. I'm assuming they were plainclothes police.'

'Yes, they were. What happened after they intervened?'

'The man pulled me out of the window, and we both fell. I got up first, but then the woman grabbed me. I lashed out at her with the hammer, and she went down. I just ran off. I could hear the man chasing me at first, but I soon gave him the slip. I kept running as fast as I could, back towards my car. When I was nearly at my car, two uniformed police officers stopped me. I could have lashed out at them too, but I didn't.'

'Do you mean with the hammer?'

'Yes.'

'Why didn't you?'

'Because I wasn't panicking by then.'

'You did try to run, though?'

'Yes, I desperately wanted to get away.'

'Is there anything else you want to tell me, Joanna?'

'No. I'm glad I've talked to you. I'll tell you now that I intend to plead "not guilty" at court. I want the whole world to know what my stepfather did to me and my sisters. I also want the public to know how the parole board are constantly releasing these dangerous predators back onto our streets to harm our children.'

There was a pause, and then she continued, 'There's one other thing I want to say. I'm sorry I hit that policewoman. I didn't mean to hurt her. I just panicked. Will she be alright?'

'We don't know yet.'

Danny said the time and the date and switched off the tape recorder.

97

5.00pm, 14 March 1988
MCIU Offices, Mansfield Police Station

It had been a long day.
Danny was sitting alone in his office, reflecting on the day so far. The interview with Joanna Preston had been surprising. He understood her need to make the reasons for her killings public. The full glare of publicity surrounding her Crown Court trial would certainly achieve that.

He scribbled down a note to call Professor Sharon Whittle and update her on developments. Once again, her assessment of the murders had been almost entirely correct.

A knock on his office door disturbed his thoughts. He looked up just as Chief Superintendent Potter walked in.

Danny stood up and said, 'Come in, sir. I was just about to call you with an update.'

'I was over this way, so I thought I'd call in. I heard that an arrest had been made in the early hours, and that one of your staff had been injured. How is the officer?'

'DC Fran Jefferies has undergone emergency surgery this morning to repair a badly dislocated and fractured ankle. She fell awkwardly after she had been knocked unconscious by a blow to the head with a claw hammer.'

'My God! I had no idea the officer's condition was so serious. The only report I got was that a detective had been injured making the arrest.'

'Fran tried to arrest Joanna Preston, but Preston struck her on the head, and Fran was knocked unconscious. Preston was arrested a few minutes later by two uniform officers who were responding to DC Lorimar's assistance call.'

'Why didn't Lorimar arrest this maniac?'

'He gave chase, but lost her in the warren of alleyways that crisscross the Coxmoor estate. He had the presence of mind to immediately make the assistance call over the local police radio that was ultimately responsible for Preston's arrest. In my opinion, Glen Lorimar did exactly the right thing, to go back and look after his injured colleague. I won't hear a word of criticism about his actions. Both my detectives showed great courage and presence of mind to get this offender arrested.'

Potter sighed. 'Don't be so defensive, Danny. I totally agree; it was good police work all round. How's DC Jefferies now?'

'Sorry, sir. It's just that DC Lorimar is already feeling bad because it was his colleague who got injured and not him. The truth is, either one of them could have ended up in the hospital.'

'I understand. I could see why he would feel that way.' He paused, then repeated, 'How is his injured colleague?'

'I had an update from DI Cartwright at the hospital just

before I interviewed Preston. The surgeon said that the surgery on her injured ankle had been a success.'

'Any further updates since then?'

'Tina Cartwright called again, just over half an hour ago, to let me know that Fran had regained consciousness and was now sitting up in bed on D Ward at the QMC.'

'That's good news.'

'I'm going to see her this evening. Do you have any message for her, sir?'

'Yes. Wish her a speedy recovery and tell her that the chief constable will be made aware of her bravery.'

'Will do, sir.'

'How did the interview with this Preston woman go?'

'Surprisingly, she answered all questions and made full and frank admissions to all the murders and the serious assault on DC Jefferies this morning.'

There was a look of shock on Potter's face. 'Didn't she have any legal representation?'

'Yes, sir. She had good legal advice present with her during the interviews. She made the conscious decision to tell the world what her stepfather had done to her and her sisters. She intends to plead not guilty and go to trial, despite the confessions, because she wants the public to be made aware of the parole board's current penchant for releasing serious sex offenders early. It's all very complicated, sir.'

'Do you have any physical evidence to support her confessions?'

'Yes, we do. I've charged her with four murders and a Section 18 wounding charge just before you got here.'

'Four murders?'

'During the interview, Joanna Preston admitted suffocating her stepfather, Fred Harper, in December of last year.'

'So it was the observations carried out on the two flats that enabled you to catch her?'

'Yes, sir. It's a good job you authorised them, or we may never have caught her.'

'I take it you've stood that operation down now?'

'Yes, sir. It's served its purpose. There's no need to incur costs when we don't have to.'

'Good. Please pass on my congratulations to everyone on your team. It's another job well done. I must admit, I didn't think you were ever going to solve these murders.'

As Potter stood up to leave, Danny thought to himself, *Neither did I, sir. Neither did I.*

Potter turned at the door and asked, 'How's your daughter progressing?'

'She's doing very well, thanks. We're hoping to have her home in a day or so.'

'That's great news, Danny. Talk to you soon.'

He waited until Potter had left the main office, then picked up the telephone.

The voice on the line answered, 'Professor Whittle.'

Danny said, 'Is now a good time?'

'Hello, Danny. Now's a great time. I've just finished lecturing for the day. Do you have any news?'

'We've arrested our Mars bar killer.'

'That's great news. Who was it?'

'A woman who was sexually abused by her stepfather. He also abused both her younger sisters after she left home.'

'So she had a real grudge against sex offenders. What was the significance of the chocolate bars?'

'It was personal, just as you told me it would be. The stepfather would always give a Mars bar to the daughter he had sexually abused the night before, at breakfast the following morning.'

'Did she have any connection to the victims, or were they picked at random?'

'Not random at all. Joanna Preston oversaw the rehousing

and resettlement of prolific sex offenders after they had been released on an early release scheme being run from HMP Whatton. Through her job, she had access to all the information she needed to stalk and kill her chosen victims.'

'How did you catch her?'

'I decided to place the men being released from the prison under that scheme on daily, round-the-clock surveillance. I had no idea how many people at the prison, or other agencies, had access to the information needed by the killer.'

'Thinking outside the box again, Danny.'

'As I didn't know who the killer was, but I knew who the future victims were likely to be, it just seemed logical to watch the potential victims.'

'Very true. Good thinking.'

'Thanks for all the advice, Sharon.'

'No problem. You can always call me, anytime.'

'Thanks.'

Danny put the telephone down and grabbed his jacket. If he left now, he might get to the Queen's Medical Centre before six o'clock. He wanted to see Fran and talk to her. He needed to know for his own peace of mind that she was going to be okay.

98

10.30am, 17 March 1988
King's Mill Hospital, Mansfield, Nottinghamshire

Danny and Sue were waiting anxiously for the consultant paediatrician to return to his office. Sue held a restless Hayley in her arms and gently rocked her back and forth, knowing that the baby could start crying at any second.

Danny sat hunched forward, his hands gripped tightly together, so tight that they were starting to ache. The tests to determine whether Hayley had been left with permanent hearing damage from her illness had taken almost an hour.

Danny glanced at his watch again. *What is taking the doctor so bloody long?*

Sue looked across at her anxious husband and said, 'Try not to worry, sweetheart. Everything will be fine.'

Danny shook his head. 'If everything's fine, what's taking him so long?'

Sue knew there was nothing she could say to ease the anxiety felt by her husband, so she concentrated on settling Hayley.

The door opened, and the consultant, Tariq Majer, walked in clutching a brown folder. 'I'm so sorry to keep you waiting. I was paged to an emergency at the casualty department.'

Danny spoke with a hard edge to his voice: 'Is my daughter okay?'

Sue said in a gentler way, 'Were the tests conclusive, Mr Majer?'

The consultant sat down and addressed the worried parents. 'The tests were conclusive. They show that Hayley has a five percent deficit in her left ear. Apart from that, her hearing is perfect.'

Danny said, 'What does that mean, a five percent deficit?'

'It means that her left ear is only working to ninety-five percent of what it should do.'

'How will that affect her?'

'It will make no discernible difference to her at all. She can hear perfectly well.'

Danny breathed a sigh of relief. Then he said, 'Thank you. How is she recovering generally?'

'Hayley is doing fantastically well. Most infants who survive this dreadful illness bounce back well. They are far more resilient than we think.'

Sue said, 'When can we take her home?'

'I don't see any reason why you can't take your beautiful daughter home with you today. I would like to monitor her progress for the next twelve months at least. We will need to check that she has resumed feeding properly. Her weight is still slightly down for what we would expect of an infant at this age.'

'She's feeding fine now. She's able to breast feed again properly, and I've just started her with some solids.'

'That's good. Does she stay on the breast for as long as she did before the illness?'

'At first, she seemed to get tired quickly and stop, but the last couple of days, she's been back to normal and wants more.'

'That's good. She has a little catching up to do, that's all. Have you noticed any change in her nappies?'

'They changed when she went back on to breast feeding, but I was expecting that to happen after all the antibiotics in her system.'

'I'm sorry, Mrs Flint. I forgot you're a physician as well. Yes. We would expect to see a major change in the bowel movements as those antibiotics work through her system. Does she have plenty of energy?'

'I hate to use the word, but she does seem back to normal. It's as though the illness never happened.'

Danny said, 'But it did happen. What I want to know is, could it reoccur?'

Tariq Majer shook his head, 'A reoccurrence is extremely unlikely. It's not something we see in infants under two years of age. Hayley should make a full recovery. I do want to see her again in two months' time, early May.'

He scribbled out an appointment slip and said, 'Take this to the desk at reception. They will book Hayley into my clinic. Both of you need to try to stop worrying. Your beautiful daughter is going to be fine.'

Danny took the slip of paper from Tariq and said, 'Thank you. I don't know about the "stop worrying" bit. I have a daughter; I think I'll be worrying for the rest of my life.'

Tariq smiled and said, 'I know exactly what you mean, Mr Flint. I have three girls. They're all teenagers now, and I still worry every day for them.'

Danny shook the doctor's hand and said, 'Thanks for everything.'

'It's no problem.'

Tariq walked around his desk and said to Sue, 'Dr Flint, your daughter's wonderful recovery is mainly due to your quick and accurate diagnosis of the illness. That early appraisal made all the difference to the outcome. Well done. I'm sure our paths will cross again soon when you resume working here.'

Sue coloured up a little and said, 'Thanks for everything, Mr Majer. See you in May.'

Tariq Majer smiled and held the door open for the young family as they left his office.

99

10.00am, 21 March 1988
MCIU Offices, Mansfield Police Station

Lynn Harris knocked on the door of Danny's office, opened it and said, 'Have you got a minute, boss?'

'Of course, grab a seat. What's up?'

'I just wondered, what do you want me to do with all the intelligence me and Jag have gathered on Stealthsafe Securities Limited? We still have an awful lot of unsolved serious assaults on sex offenders on the various divisions. Should we just keep it all on file here?'

'Submit all the intelligence to each of the divisional CID offices. If the staff of this firm are as unsavoury as you think they are, I'm sure the local CID will find your gathered intelligence useful. I'm sure some of those members of staff will come to the notice of the police again soon.'

'And what about all the Guardians of Innocence intelligence? It's all irrelevant now that Brannigan's shut it all down, isn't it?'

'I don't think so. Personally, I don't think Brannigan would change his mind that quickly. He seems like an individual who, once he's made his mind up about something, will keep going until he achieves it. He's like a terrier with a bone.'

'So what do I do with it?'

'Prepare a full report on everything we know about the organisation that was the Guardians of Innocence. Keep one copy in our files, send one copy to Special Branch, and one to Chief Superintendent Potter.'

'Will do, boss.'

EPILOGUE

11.00am, 20 October 1989
HMP Drake Hall, Eccleshall, Staffordshire

The two visitors to the prison had occupied the small table furthest away from the prison officers supervising the visit. When Joanna Preston walked into the visitors room, the man stood and waved her over.

Joanna didn't recognise either the man or the blonde woman with him. She was intrigued to know who they were, so she walked over and sat down opposite the couple.

She said, 'Who are you? Why have you come to visit me?'

In hushed tones, the man said, 'My name's Davy Johnson. I was extremely sorry to hear of the passing of your sister, and it saddened me deeply to see the long sentence you received for doing the public of this country such a great service.'

Joanna started to stand, saying, 'I haven't got time for this shit. Is that all you've come here to say?'

The man said urgently, 'Please don't go. I have an important message for you, from the man I work for.'

Curiosity once again got the better of her, so she sat back down.

She folded her arms across her chest and said, 'I'm listening.'

'The organisation I represent were extremely appreciative of your efforts. They would very much like to continue where you left off. If you have any information that could help us in our quest to rid our country of these monsters, we'll be forever in your debt.'

Joanna was thoughtful for a moment. Then she said, 'How do I know you haven't been sent here by the police?'

'There's nothing I can say to you that will prove I'm genuine. You need to know that our organisation has already been responsible for numerous attacks on paedophiles across the country. We all have our own personal reasons for wanting rid of this scum. We're no different.'

'What do you mean?'

'I was repeatedly raped in a children's home when I was an eleven-year-old boy, and my wife was groomed and then gang-raped by a group of three paedophiles when she was thirteen. My wife and I hate these monsters with a passion.'

There was a brief period of silence, and then Johnson said, 'The man who runs our organisation is a man of great wealth and power. He would be able to make life extremely comfortable for you in prison if you're willing to help us.'

'I don't need your help; prison holds no fears for me.'

'I'm sorry you feel like that.'

There was a brief pause, and then Joanna said, 'As for your request, I'm willing to help you.'

Davy leaned forward and grinned. 'That's wonderful.'

Joanna looked around, to ensure nobody was listening to their private conversation, then said, 'You need to visit my old house in Bingham. In the back garden of the property, there's a large horse chestnut tree. Almost ten feet up from the base of that tree, there's a partially hidden hole in the trunk. For safekeeping, I placed duplicate copies of all my future targets in a waterproof bag inside that hole. I didn't want to keep files that should have remained at the prison inside my home, so I hid them in the tree.'

'What's in those files?'

'There's a list of twenty-five serious sex offenders all due for early release over the next three years. The files contain the men's names, photographs, planned release dates, and details of their previous convictions. Most importantly, there are details of the addresses they're going to be released to. These men are due to be released to different towns and cities all over the UK. Be my guest; get the files and continue the work I started.'

WE HOPE YOU ENJOYED THIS BOOK

If you could spend a moment to write an honest review on Amazon, no matter how short, we would be extremely grateful. They really do help readers discover new authors.

ALSO BY TREVOR NEGUS

EVIL IN MIND

(Book 1 in the DCI Flint series)

DEAD AND GONE

(Book 2 in the DCI Flint series)

A COLD GRAVE

(Book 3 in the DCI Flint series)

TAKEN TO DIE

(Book 4 in the DCI Flint series)

KILL FOR YOU

(Book 5 in the DCI Flint series)

ONE DEADLY LIE

(Book 6 in the DCI Flint series)

A SWEET REVENGE

(Book 7 in the DCI Flint series)

THE DEVIL'S BREATH

(Book 8 in the DCI Flint series)

Printed in Great Britain
by Amazon